THE WILD

A Dark Thriller Romance

KRISTIN BUONI

Copyright © 2025 by Kristin Buoni

All rights reserved.

No part of this book may be reproduced in any form or by any electronic or mechanical means, including information storage and retrieval systems, without written permission from the author, except for the use of brief quotations in a book review.

Cover by Marika Veil

IMPORTANT NOTE

This book is recommended for 18+ readers. It contains very dark topics, heavy psychological traumas, and situations that some readers may find disturbing. A full list of trigger warnings is available on the next page.

CONTENT WARNING/TRIGGERS:

Reader discretion is advised as this book contains:

- Plane crash
- Sexually explicit scenes
- Primal chasing
- Breath play/'hand necklace'
- Knife play
- Stalking
- Gaslighting
- Captivity
- Drug usage
- Blood/gore
- Murder
- Car accident
- Parental loss (backstory)
- Mention of torture (occurs off-page)
- Patricide (backstory)
- Mention of cannibalism
- Kidnapping

PROLOGUE
ARIA

4 YEARS AGO

I'D ALWAYS HEARD THAT GRIEF WAS SUPPOSED TO BLIND YOU, but I could see him watching me anyway.

Landon Ashford.

My old neighbor and nemesis. A bully who delighted in my suffering and always knew exactly where to hit to make it hurt the most. Today of all days, I didn't want to deal with him—something he was surely aware of—but for some reason he'd decided to show up at the cemetery anyway.

The sky above my mother's funeral procession was filled with ominous gray clouds, and rain drizzled softly, blurring the sea of black umbrellas surrounding the casket. Somewhere behind me, cameras clicked, reporters keeping a respectful distance but still documenting every miserable second of my family's mourning.

I swallowed the hard lump in my throat and wrapped my arms around myself, fingers pressing into the stiff fabric of my black coat. I should've kept my focus on the casket, or paid more attention to the priest's droning words about peace, but I could still feel Landon's cold gaze digging into me, and suddenly it was all I could think about.

He was standing directly across from me, on the other side of the casket, just beyond the priest. Tall and poised, with a face so striking that it was almost impossible to look away from. Dark brows, piercing blue-green eyes that never wavered, and a mouth set in something that wasn't quite a smirk but wasn't exactly sympathy either. He wore his tailored suit with the kind of effortless control that only guys like him could pull off—those born to immense privilege and power.

He wasn't supposed to be at my mother's funeral. In fact, none of his family should've been here today. Not if they had any decency. But his mother, Senator Celeste Ashford, stood right beside him anyway, solemn-faced and unreadable, and his aunt and uncle—who were also political bigwigs—flanked the two of them.

Celeste and my father were bitter rivals in the upcoming presidential election, so she usually spent a good portion of her time tearing apart his policy ideas in debates or attacking him in public speeches. But today, she'd obviously been advised to play a different role, utilizing my family's tragedy to soften her media image and show the world that she wasn't just a cold, calculating politician.

In other words, she was here to be the 'bigger person'. The one who was willing to reach across the aisle and lend a comforting hand in her opponent's terrible time of need.

I didn't care about any of that bullshit political posturing. I just wanted her gone while my family grieved.

Still, I couldn't stop looking at her son. And he didn't stop looking at me either.

Usually, I'd be creeped out by some guy staring at me, unblinking and unmoving. Especially at a time like this. But, weirdly enough, it was actually helping me somewhat. I needed a distraction from my heart-shattering loss, because it was so painful I could barely even breathe, and having Landon stare at me was certainly distracting.

So I stared back.

His expression didn't change when I lifted my chin and directly met his gaze. He tilted his head very slightly and mouthed something to me, slow and deliberate.

I'm sorry.

For a few seconds, I actually believed him. His eyes were so intense, so knowing, and I recalled with a flash of sympathy that he'd lost his father three years ago. Of course he was sorry. He knew exactly what I was going through right now. Knew the gut-wrenching pain I felt.

I dipped my chin in the slightest nod. A silent, grateful acknowledgment of his sympathy.

I thought that would be the end of our exchange, but his eyes narrowed slightly, and he mouthed the words again. Something was... off.

I frowned, watching his mouth slowly shape the words yet again, but this time I was really paying attention. If he was saying '*I'm sorry*', his lips would press together at the start to form the 'M' sound, but that didn't happen. That meant he was saying something else entirely.

I squinted, leaning forward just a fraction, watching as he mouthed the words one more time.

Not '*I'm sorry*'. Something else. Something that looked a hell of a lot like: '*I saw you*'.

My stomach plummeted, and the air around me turned thick and suffocating. *No.* It wasn't possible. Landon couldn't have seen me that day... could he?

But even as I thought that, I realized it wasn't true. Of course he could've been there. Of course he could've seen everything that happened that day. Every single thing I did in those harrowing moments. It would be a major coincidence, but given his frequent proximity to the location in question, it was definitely in the realm of possibility.

Oh, no.

Oh, God...

Nausea washed over me, making my stomach churn, and my knees turned weak, threatening to buckle. I worried I was going to collapse and fall right into the deep hole my mother's casket would soon be lowered into, but somehow, I managed to remain stiffly upright, inhaling deeply through my nose as I kept my face carefully blank.

I couldn't react. Not here. Not now.

I slowly averted my eyes from Landon's face and shifted my focus back to the casket, trying to pretend he wasn't even here. But I could feel his eyes on me anyway, making my mind flood with questions as my heart pounded painfully hard.

How much did he see that day?

What exactly did he know?

And worse... what was he going to do about it?

I
ARIA

SEPTEMBER 2ND, 2024

APPLAUSE ECHOED THROUGH THE GRAND BALLROOM, A POLITE, measured sound that filled the space without feeling too enthusiastic. I stood at the podium, my fingers curled around the edges as I took a steady breath, forcing my most practiced smile to remain in place.

A sea of designer gowns and tailored tuxedos stretched out before me, their wearers adorned with the kind of effortless elegance that came with power, wealth, and political influence.

This was my world.

Over the last four years, I'd learned exactly how to navigate it, how to say the right thing at the right time, and how to charm a room without revealing anything too serious about myself. I was doing well today too, hitting all my carefully prepared talking points.

"Of course, my father never does anything halfway," I said lightly, scanning the audience with an easy smile. "Which is why when he told me I had to give a speech at this event tonight, I assumed he also had a five-point plan drafted for exactly *how* I should do it." I paused for a beat and adopted a more casual tone, still smiling. "But it turned out that I had to write it myself, so I'm praying it's at least halfway decent—oh, and there's that halfway word again. Sorry, Dad! Anyway, if I sound a little anxious up here... well, now you know why."

Laughter rippled through the crowd. Not loud, but warm. Approving. Encouraging.

I smiled wider, glad my lighthearted comments had landed well. I'd intended for them to lighten the stiff mood and humanize me at the same time; make me seem more relatable to the crowd with the admission of my nervousness. Judging by the pleasant response, I was sure it had worked, but the second I glanced toward my father, my stomach twisted.

President Jonathan Hagan sat at the head table, his expression unreadable to anyone who didn't know him. But I knew him, and I could see the tension in his jaw, the slight narrowing of his eyes, and the tight way he pressed his lips together.

Everyone else in the room had found my comments harmless. But to my father, it clearly wasn't some relatable joke. It was a misstep. A crack in the perfect image I was supposed to uphold.

I swallowed hard and quickly smoothed my features, moving on before the silence between my words could stretch too long.

That was when I saw *him*.

Landon Ashford.

He stood near the back of the room, tall and composed, a glass of whiskey dangling lazily in one hand as he watched me. I faltered for half a second, my carefully measured words nearly catching in my throat.

Of all the people in the world, why was *he* here?

His mother was running against my father for a second time in the upcoming election, so it made no sense for him to be at an event like this—an event meant to celebrate my father's administration and rally support for his re-election campaign. And yet, here he was anyway. Watching me.

What the hell?

I forced my gaze away from him and finished my speech, heart thudding in my chest. As soon as I stepped off the stage, the political pleasantries began.

A swarm of guests closed in; senators, donors, lobbyists, and other polished power players eager to shake my hand and compliment my speech. I smiled, thanked them, and nodded in all the right places, slipping seamlessly into the role I'd been raised to play. The good daughter. The poised political princess.

Through it all, my father's disapproving stare burned in the back of my mind.

My Secret Service detail hovered just out of reach, their presence a quiet but constant weight. I spotted Agent Foster—the longest-serving member of my security team—watching me with his usual unreadable expression. He was in his fifties, built like a tank, and had the kind of 'dad energy' that made it impossible for me to rebel properly. Not that I ever had the chance to anyway.

I felt a tug on my wrist and turned to see my best friend, Sabrina Carlisle, grinning at me. My shoulders sagged with relief, and I returned her grin and hugged her, grateful to be with someone I actually knew. Not only that, but someone who had direct experience with the trials and tribulations of the DC politico circuit.

As the daughter of the House Speaker, Sabrina had been navigating these high-stakes events for a long time, and her ability to effortlessly blend in and keep her composure was nothing short of impressive. We'd only known each other for a couple of years now, after meeting at college in our first freshman semester, but in that short period, we'd become fast friends. She understood the game, the masks we wore, and the constant pressure.

"How was I up there?" I asked, voice tinged with anxiety.

"Perfect! Everyone loved it," she replied, looping her arm

through mine as we moved toward a raised table at the edge of the ballroom. "Also, I loved how you made yourself seem so real. It was so much better than that boring speech from Megan Ainscough. That woman talks like she's got a stick rammed directly up her ass."

I sighed. "The 'realness' is actually what I'm worried about," I admitted. "My dad looked like he wanted to send me to a labor camp."

Sabrina smirked. "He always looks like that to me," she said, snatching up a champagne flute from a passing waiter's tray. "But yeah, trust me, your speech was fine. It's not like you got up there and said you work at Nocturne or something. *That* would be a real scandal, albeit a hilarious one."

I frowned. "What's Nocturne?"

She arched a brow. "You've never heard of that place?"

"I don't think so."

Sabrina leaned in conspiratorially. "It's a BDSM club in Penn Quarter. Right on F Street, if you can believe it," she whispered, lips spreading in a wicked grin. "Very exclusive. I've heard lots of DC power players are members."

"Oh, right."

"Sorry, I keep forgetting how innocent you are," she went on, waving a casual hand. "It's definitely not your kind of thing."

Heat flared in my cheeks, and I forced a laugh. "Yeah."

If only she knew.

I wasn't interested in clubs like the one she'd mentioned... but it wasn't for the reason she thought.

I would never judge anyone who went to those places—after all, everyone had their own tastes and needs, and I wasn't the sort of person to yuk another person's yum. But for me personally, those places had never held much appeal.

I just found them slightly too controlled for my tastes. At most of those clubs, there were rules, safe words, strict hierarchies. A sense of rehearsed order disguised as wicked, libidinous freedom. The illusion of danger, but not quite the real thing.

For me, that all seemed a little too sanitized. Too manufactured. Not wild enough. Not dirty enough. Not *scary* enough. There was no true risk. No genuine loss of control. No sense of real, heart-stopping danger... and that was what my fantasies were made up of. Fantasies I'd probably never get to explore, given the constant security presence around me.

But I couldn't admit any of that stuff. Not even to Sabrina. I had to be very, *very* careful about what I shared with people, even my closest friends, because in my world, secrets were currency, and the wrong one in the wrong hands could destroy everything.

I sipped at a pink-hued flavored water—because the president's twenty-year-old daughter couldn't be spotted underage drinking, of course—as Sabrina started telling me about the project she'd been working on over the last few months. Like me, she was a sophomore at Belgrave University, and she was studying computer science.

Truth be told, she didn't even need to study it. She was a total coding genius. She'd been doing it since she was ten years old, all self-taught, and she'd written multiple programs that had been used in real-world applications, one even making its way into a major tech company. She was only getting the degree to please her parents, who insisted she needed university qualifications to 'prove herself'.

During a lull in the conversation, I gestured toward my purse and the small blue folder containing my speech. "Would you mind watching my stuff for a minute?" I asked. "I just need to duck to the ladies' quickly."

Sabrina nodded. "Sure. I'll guard it with my life," she said with a mischievous wink, placing a hand over her heart. "Agent Carlise, reporting for duty."

"I thought we were friends," I said, affecting a crestfallen look as I played along. Doing these dramatic 'bits' based on old movies was her second-favorite thing after coding. "But you were a secret agent all along?"

"Yup, sorry. Can't trust anyone in DC. You should know that by now." She grinned and waved a hand. "But seriously, don't worry. I'll make sure no one jacks your purse or slips anything into your drink. I promise."

I slipped away from the crowded ballroom, the low hum of chatter fading behind me as I headed down the hall, followed closely by my Secret Service agents. I exhaled deeply and pushed open the restroom door, relishing the moment of solitude as I stepped inside and pressed my hands against the cool marble sink.

It would probably sound sad or plain ridiculous to some people, but these short trips to the restroom were one of the only times I could feel truly relaxed in this crazy world. The only time I could really breathe and decompress.

That was why I never brought my purse or phone in with me —so I could be truly disconnected from my usual reality, if only for a few minutes. Just me, the silence, and the small sense of control over my own space that felt impossible to find anywhere else.

I took a deep breath, briefly shutting my eyes. Then I felt a strange shift in the air. A presence. I wasn't alone after all.

My eyes snapped open, and before I could turn, a strong hand clamped around my wrist, yanking me back. My spine hit the cold tile wall, a gasp catching in my throat.

Landon.

His tall, powerful frame blocked out the light, his fingers tightening just enough to make my pulse trip. His eyes were locked onto mine with an intensity that sent a shiver down my spine. "Hi, princess," he said with a smirk.

"What the hell?" I tried to wrench my wrist out of his grip, but his hold tightened, the sharp pressure of his fingers reminding me just how much strength he had hidden beneath his polished exterior. "How did you get past my agents?"

His arrogant smirk widened. "There's another door over on that wall," he said, dipping his chin toward the far side of the bathroom. "It's connected to a storage space for cleaning equipment, which has another entry on the other side. Always locked and only accessible by staff... or those with enough influence."

"Could you influence your hand to let go of my arm?" I snapped, struggling against his iron grip again. The silver ring he always wore on his right hand was digging into my skin.

"Not until you hear what I have to say," he said.

"What is it?" I asked in an acid tone.

"You need to make your father drop out of the race." Landon's voice was quiet, but there was no mistaking the command in it.

I blinked. "Wow. This is, um... certainly an interesting new tactic from your mother's campaign team."

His jaw flexed, his grip tightening ever so slightly before he released me. A glimpse of ink on his wrist caught my eye—part of a small tattoo peeking from beneath the crisp cuff of his suit. "This isn't about my mother," he said, eyes narrowing. "It's about your father."

I scoffed. "Right. So, what, you just suddenly developed a deep moral objection to his brand of politics?" I asked, brows rising.

"Just do it, Aria," he said. "Find a way. Announce a pregnancy before marriage, create a drug scandal... whatever it takes. Just make sure he's forced to drop out."

I let out a short, bitter laugh. "You're actually serious?"

"Deadly."

"Okay, well, I'm not doing any of that," I said. "You might've been able to push me around when I was a kid, but I'm not a kid anymore, in case you haven't noticed."

"Oh, I've noticed," he said, gaze slipping downward to skim my body. He inhaled sharply through his nose, his fingers flexing at his sides like he was holding something back.

I swallowed thickly, hoping he couldn't see right through the brave front I was putting on. "Great. So you'll leave me alone, then?"

"Sure, princess. I'll leave you alone," he said, brows rising. "As soon as you do exactly what I told you to do."

"I told you, that's not happening," I said, inwardly cursing myself as I heard the slight crack in my voice.

"Aria... you'll live to regret it if you don't listen to me." Landon's voice was lower now, edged with something dangerous. "Or maybe you won't live at all."

I lifted my chin. "Oh, so we've moved on to threats now? That was fast."

He moved even closer, until there was barely half an inch between us. His scent—expensive cologne and a hint of whiskey—wrapped around me, making my stomach tighten. "It's not a threat."

"Then what is it?" I asked, hating the way my breath hitched at his proximity.

Landon's throat bobbed, and he opened his mouth slightly. But instead of answering my question, he leaned in, his lips so close to my ear I could feel the heat of his breath. It unleashed a swarm of butterflies in my stomach, and the skin on my arms and chest instantly prickled with goosebumps.

"Just do as I tell you," he muttered. "Don't make me do something we'll *both* regret."

Then he was gone.

I stood there for a moment, my pulse pounding as my body betrayed me in ways I didn't want to acknowledge. I should've been furious. In fact, I *was* furious. But beneath the anger, something dark and illicit curled low in my belly.

I took a shaky breath, pressing my palm against my chest to steady myself.

No. I couldn't let myself go there. Not with him. Not with anyone.

Shoving the unwelcome thoughts from my mind, I stepped

THE WILD

into a cubicle to relieve myself. Then I furiously scrubbed my hands, straightened my dress, squared my shoulders, and forced myself to walk back out of the bathroom like nothing had happened. Like I wasn't still burning from Landon's touch.

I left the bathroom with my heart still pounding, the cool rush of air outside doing little to calm my nerves. My shoes clicked against the polished floor as I made my way back to Sabrina, who was standing by the table where my purse sat. She was casually leaning against it, watching the crowd with a relaxed air, but when she saw me, she smiled and returned her full attention to the table.

I glanced down at my purse and froze. There was a small white card sitting right on top of it.

I frowned and picked it up, turning it over in my hand. On the front, it said 'Defend and Conserve' in printed black lettering. When I flipped it over, a strange symbol greeted me: a tangled circular design, like vines weaving in and out of one another, curving around a faint outline of the U.S. Capitol. Beneath it, the letters *'DC'* were stamped in bold, authoritative print.

"Did you put this on my purse?" I asked, holding the card up to Sabrina.

She blinked, clearly confused. "No, why?"

"It wasn't there before,'" I said. "Did you see anyone come over to the table while I was gone?"

She shook her head, brows furrowed. "No, I didn't see anyone, but..." She trailed off, tone turning hesitant. "I wasn't looking at your purse the entire time, so I guess I could've missed it if someone just sidled up and slipped it onto the table really quickly."

I looked back down at the card, unsettled by the symbol and the nagging feeling it left in my guts. Something about it felt off, though I had no idea why. It didn't seem like a threat, but still... it was definitely odd.

Sabrina's frown deepened as she registered my discomfort.

"You should show it to Agent Foster. He'll know if it's something we need to worry about, right?"

I nodded and turned to wave at Foster. He approached, forehead wrinkling with concern. "Everything okay?"

"I'm not sure." I held out the card. "Someone put this on my purse while I was in the bathroom. Do you think it's some sort of threat?"

He frowned, turning the card over in his hand the same way I did a minute ago. Then he looked up, eyes flickering between me and Sabrina. "You didn't see anything?" he asked Sabrina.

"No, but I turned around a few times to say hi to people who were passing by. Only for a couple of seconds each time, but still..." She trailed off, cheeks flushing slightly.

She was clearly embarrassed that she hadn't paid as close attention as she'd promised she would, but I didn't blame her. I wasn't expecting her to stare directly at my stuff the entire time, unblinking, like some sort of robot.

"Could the card have already been on the table when you two arrived at it, and you just put your purse on it without noticing?" Foster asked, turning his attention back to me. "And then it got stuck to it and wound up on top when you moved the purse?"

"Um... I guess that's possible, but I don't think so. I don't remember seeing anything on the table when we arrived."

"Me neither," Sabrina added. "And I don't think either of us moved the purse, either."

"Well, to ease your minds, this doesn't seem like any sort of threat to me," Foster said, giving me a faint, reassuring smile. "This looks like a stock card for that climate change activism group that's been everywhere lately. The DC Guardians."

Sabrina's brows shot up. "Oh! Of course. That must be what the 'Defend and Conserve' slogan means," she said. "It's all about environmental conservation and protection. It's probably also why the symbol has all those vines, right?"

Foster nodded. "I think so. They're a pacifist group, so they

THE WILD

don't pose any threat. At least none that we currently know about," he said. "But rest assured, we'll look into it anyway."

"Even if they're pacifists, it feels a bit weird that they're sliding their calling cards right on top of people's bags. Especially seeing as one of those people is the president's daughter," Sabrina said, brows dipping in another frown.

"It's odd, yes, but it's not a cause for alarm," Foster replied. "I think they probably just happen to have a couple of people on the waitstaff here, and they've asked them to leave these cards lying around the room while they carry out drinks and canapés tonight. I'd say they're hoping to attract attention from senators and congresspeople. But no threat has been made, and seeing as Aria wasn't here when they left the card, I doubt they even knew they were putting it on a purse that belongs to her."

I nodded, but the words didn't do much to ease the discomfort still churning in my stomach. Despite the reassurance of having an agent whose job was to make sure nothing serious slipped past, something still didn't sit right. I couldn't put my finger on what it was, though.

"I can hold onto the card, if it bothers you," Foster went on, brows rising slightly as he turned his focus back to my face. "And of course, we'll look into all the waitstaff who work here and see if they have any connection to the Guardians, just in case. We can never be too careful."

"Oh, actually, can I keep the card?" I asked. "Just as a reminder. I want to look up the organization later, because a friend of mine told me she wants to get into some environmental activism stuff. So maybe it's an option for her."

Foster nodded and handed the card back to me. I slipped it back into my purse, and he gave me a curt nod and returned to his spot over by the wall, where he could keep an eye on me and my surroundings while still giving me enough privacy to chat with Sabrina.

I looked around the ballroom, scanning it for Landon. He was nowhere to be seen now, but somehow, I felt his eyes on me anyway. The hairs on the back of my neck were prickling, and an uncomfortable awareness was crawling under my skin. It wasn't just the usual feeling of being watched by my father's staff or security. No, this was different—like someone was studying me with intent, waiting for the right moment to strike.

I turned back to Sabrina, who was looking at me with her brows raised. After a beat, she leaned in. "Are you okay?" she asked, tone tinged with anxiety. "I'm sorry I didn't watch your stuff properly. I really thought it—"

I lifted a hand and cut her off, not wanting her to feel bad. "No, no, it's fine. It's not about the purse," I said hurriedly. "I'm just feeling a little shaken because of... something else."

"What is it? Are you still worried about your speech?"

I sighed. "I ran into Landon Ashford in the bathroom," I muttered, bitterness creeping into my tone.

"In the bathroom?" Sabrina's eyes widened, and she whipped her head around, scanning the ballroom. "What the hell is he even doing here? How did he get in?"

I shrugged. "No idea."

She looked back at me. "What did he say to you?"

"He demanded that I get my father to drop out of the race."

She rolled her eyes and let out a derisive snort. "Seriously? That's a new low from Senator Ashford. Sending her son to bully her opponent's daughter."

"He claimed he was here of his own accord. But who knows?" I shrugged, trying to pretend I didn't care as much as I did. "He's always been a total fucking prick, so I guess it wouldn't surprise me if he actually did this just to get at me."

Sabrina tilted her head, eyes flickering with curiosity. "You can totally tell me to mind my own business if you want, but I've always wondered—why exactly do you hate him so much?" she asked. "I mean, I know his mother has been your dad's biggest rival for years, but the way you've talked about him before... you *really* despise the guy, don't you?"

"Um... yeah." I swallowed hard, briefly lowering my eyes to the table. I couldn't tell her the real reason behind my attitude toward Landon. Couldn't tell her that it wasn't exactly hate.

In truth, I was terrified of him. I always tried to pretend I wasn't, because it was the only thing that kept me from totally losing my mind whenever he was around, but he knew how to get under my skin like nobody else. Every time he looked at me, it felt like he was unraveling me one thread at a time. One day, all those threads would be gone, and he'd expose me to the world.

My life would be over then.

I lifted my gaze back to Sabrina, mind whirling. I had to tell her *something* to answer her question, or else her curiosity would only grow. She just had that sort of mind; the kind that wouldn't let things go unexplored. It was what made her such a great coder.

I decided to go with something that was technically true—it just wasn't the real reason I had such a major problem with Landon.

"Remember how my family used to live in the same area as the Ashfords?" I said.

"Oh, yeah. Your property backed onto theirs, right?"

"Yup. So we weren't on the same street, but we were technically neighbors."

"God, yeah, I remember it all now. The media made such a big deal out of it during the last election," Sabrina said, rolling her eyes. "I mean, it's a pretty big coincidence that the two main candidates lived next to each other, but who really gives a shit? Sometimes a coincidence is actually just a coincidence. And that part of DC has a ton of politicians living in it. You can't throw a rock there without hitting a congressman."

"Exactly." I pursed my lips, recalling all the crackpot conspiracy theories that certain online pundits had put forth at the time.

That my father and Celeste Ashford were colluding despite being on opposite sides of the aisle. That a secret affair was going on. That Russia and Saudi Arabia were somehow involved.

None of the ludicrous theories gained much traction, because they didn't make any sense. After all, if my father and Celeste were truly hiding some sort of secret involvement with each other, wouldn't they live as far apart as possible to avoid suspicion? Still, it annoyed me every time I thought about it. People would really say anything, come up with *any* wild theory, just for attention and clicks on their content.

"Anyway," I went on. "When I was a kid, my mom was good friends with Celeste Ashford. This was before my dad and Celeste turned into major rivals, obviously."

Sabrina nodded. "Uh-huh."

"There were no other kids my age living on the same street as us, so Mom would always insist I go over and play with Landon whenever she and Celeste met up. She'd invite him over to our house all the time too," I said. "I guess she thought it would be nice for me to have a friend nearby who was close to the same age as me. Close-ish, anyway."

Sabrina lifted a hand to signal that she had a question. "He's a year older than us, right?"

"Two years older," I said.

"Oh, right." She tilted her head, brows rising. "Anyway, I'm guessing he wasn't a good playmate?"

"Nope. He was really cruel. Practically tortured me some days."

"Seriously?"

I nodded. "He always wanted to play some sort of spy game with me, where I was the 'good spy' being hunted by the 'bad spy'. And he was *rough*. He'd chase me until I was about to vomit, throw me to the ground, pin me against stuff and refuse to let me move, make crazy physical threats. Stuff like that," I said. "A few times, he even held my head underwater when we were playing in the pool. And he told me he'd do worse things if I ever tried to tell one of the adults. He was an angel around them, of course."

"Ah, so he was a full-on child psychopath." Sabrina's nose wrinkled. "I get why you don't like him now. That sort of stuff can mentally scar you."

"Yeah. People always say stuff like 'Oh, that's just how kids behave!', as if it's all a big joke. But I was seriously scared of him back then. I honestly thought he might kill me some days," I said. "Once I got older, I guess that fear morphed into anger instead."

"That's fair. And at least you're not scared of him anymore."

I nodded. "Right."

Of course, I *was* still scared of Landon, but I could never admit why.

I could also never admit that while our rough games terrified me as a child, I'd started to fantasize about them as I grew older. Even now, all these years later, I'd lie in bed at night and close my eyes, imagining I was pinned on the ground beneath Landon, wrists trapped above my head.

Every time, my body would flood with that familiar adrenaline-soaked feeling of helplessness, along with a rush of molten heat that went straight between my legs. In those moments, I could almost feel Landon's breath close to my ear as he whispered violent threats; things that should've terrified me but instead had me responding in ways that drove me wild.

It made me feel like I was sick in the head. After all, I was fantasizing about things that had happened when I was just a child. Granted, Landon and I were both fully-grown adults in all of my fantasies, but still, it felt weirdly humiliating for me.

On top of that, Landon and I absolutely hated each other. Hate-fucking wasn't a rare fantasy for a person to have, but it still bothered the hell out of me, because this wasn't just some random enemies-to-lovers trope playing out in my head.

It was real. It was *him*. The cruel, ruthless asshole who'd spent years holding a terrible secret over my head, letting me live every day trapped between fear and sick anticipation, never knowing when the hammer would finally drop.

I hated myself for it. Hated the way my body reacted whenever I thought about him. Because no matter how much I despised him, no matter how many times I told myself he was a monster... some treacherous part of me still wanted to play with him.

A hand suddenly clamped around my elbow, firm but not rough. My head snapped to the side, and I found Foster standing there, his expression unreadable.

"We need to leave. *Now*."

The hairs on the back of my neck lifted. "Why?"

"There's been a security breach."

I inwardly breathed a sigh of relief. *Thank God.* The Secret Service agents circulating the ballroom must've finally noticed Landon lurking at the event. Or maybe he'd tried to sneak into the ladies' room again in another attempt to get me alone, and this time they'd caught him in the act.

I could've reported his presence myself earlier, of course, along with his threatening behavior in the bathroom, but I'd decided against it. After all, if he knew I ratted him out, that could be the catalyst for him finally deciding to reveal my secret to the world, so it wasn't a risk I was willing to take.

Landon was dangerous, but I knew he was also calculated, a trait shaped by his family's long-standing involvement in politics. As long as I didn't push him too far and give him a reason to tip the scales, I could keep walking this tightrope, pretending he didn't unnerve me. Pretending I wasn't constantly waiting for the day he finally decided to let my world burn.

"What sort of security breach?" I asked, hoping Foster would confirm my suspicions.

He flicked a glance toward Sabrina. She picked up on the silent message immediately and stepped back. "I'll go," she said, squeezing my arm lightly. "Text me later, okay?"

I nodded, but my focus was locked on Foster. The tension rolling off him was like a live wire, sharp and urgent.

"What happened?" I asked again. I was starting to suspect it involved something more than Landon's mere presence at the event. "What kind of breach was it?"

Foster's lips pressed into a thin line. "You know I'm not supposed to share this kind of information with you."

"Please, Foster." My voice dropped, my pulse spiking. "Please tell me. You know I won't tell anyone it was you."

He exhaled heavily, scanning the room before leaning in. His voice was barely above a murmur. "There was a bomb under your car."

2

ARIA

SHOCK SLAMMED INTO ME LIKE A PHYSICAL FORCE. I STARED AT Foster, my heart pounding so hard it felt like my ribs might crack under the pressure.

"A bomb?" My voice was ragged, barely more than a whisper.

He gave me a curt nod. His expression remained impassive, but his jaw was tight, his usual professional mask strained at the edges. "It's an unfortunate reality of being related to the president. There are always extremists who want to send a message to him via his family members."

I swallowed hard as my mind spun. "I understand that," I said softly. "But it doesn't make it any easier to hear that someone is trying to kill me."

Foster lay a comforting hand on my shoulder. "I know. But if it's any consolation, the person who did this wasn't trying to kill you."

I frowned. "I thought the bomb was in my car."

"Yes, but it was a small device," he said. "Rigged to detonate fifteen minutes after you left the venue. Seeing as the driver was supposed to take you right back to Belgrave afterwards, the car would've been on Rock Creek Parkway. The explosion wouldn't have been enough to kill you outright, but it would've been enough to make the driver lose control, swerve, and crash into one of the embankments."

I inhaled sharply. "So I would've been injured. Maybe even badly. But not dead."

"Exactly. This wasn't an assassination attempt. It was a warning."

"A warning," I repeated, brows knitting together. "So they're saying they chose to let me live this time, but next time, they might not be so merciful?"

Foster dipped his chin in another curt nod. "Yes, I'd say that was the exact message they intended to send."

A cold chill crept down my spine. I wasn't naïve. I knew being the president's daughter made me a major target, so threats of bodily harm weren't exactly rare in my world. But this was different. This time, something had actually happened.

"Do you think it could be those activists we were talking about earlier?" I asked. "The ones who left the card on my table?"

"Our team is still examining the evidence, so we can't say anything for certain yet, but that group has been moved to priority one on our suspect list," he said. "It would be highly unusual for a pacifist group to suddenly veer so far into violent extremism. But it's not completely unheard of."

"I guess I won't be telling my wannabe activist friend about them, then," I muttered.

"No, I wouldn't recommend that at this stage," Foster said, already guiding me toward the back exit of the ballroom. I barely registered the movement, my thoughts still tangled in the implications of what had just happened. "You'll be traveling with your father now. I'll be right behind you with the others."

I nodded listlessly. My father and I were originally supposed to leave this event in separate cars, because I'd planned to go back to campus while he returned to the White House. Obviously, that was no longer an option, given the need to rush us both out of this place, along with the fact we were down one armored car.

As we stepped into the cool night air, my gaze instinctively swept the alley. The security detail was already in motion, their sharp eyes scanning for threats. My focus caught on one figure standing just beyond the line of black Cadillacs.

Landon. *Again.*

I muttered a curse word under my breath as I stared at him. Why did no one else seem to care that he was around? Did his status as Celeste Ashford's son really grant him this much sway in the world? Enough that even a presidential Secret Service detail was willing to let his presence slide wherever and whenever he felt like it?

Surely not. And yet, here he was.

His posture was relaxed, and he appeared to be on the phone to someone, but his eyes were focused right on me. There was something in his stare that made my skin prickle.

My breath hitched, and for a fleeting second, a dark thought crossed my mind. Was he responsible for this bomb scare?

No. That didn't make sense. He might've threatened me in the bathroom earlier, but he was calculated, not reckless. He wouldn't be stupid enough to make a threat and then immediately stick a bomb under my car.

If he wanted to hurt me, he'd do it in a way that left no trail back to him. Also, there was no way the agents would be letting him hang out in the alley like this if he was even remotely under suspicion.

Even so, I couldn't shake the feeling that he was involved somehow. That in some twisted way, he already knew exactly who was behind what happened tonight.

Foster nudged me forward. "Let's go."

I tore my gaze from Landon and ducked into the black Cadillac ahead of me, my heart still hammering in my chest.

THE WILD

"Jewel secured," Foster muttered into his radio, referring to me by my codename.

I exhaled slowly as the door shut, sealing me inside the armored state car. Across from me, my father sat flanked by two of his advisors. The overhead light cast sharp angles over his face, his expression unreadable.

"Are you all right, darling?" he asked, leaning forward slightly.

I nodded, even though my pulse was still pounding in my ears. "I guess so," I murmured. "I know I'm not supposed to know all the details, but I heard they found a bomb under my car."

He let out a quiet sigh, pinching the bridge of his nose. "I know it's frightening, but try not to worry too much," he said. "Our security teams are trained for this. They'll always catch problems before anything bad happens."

Will they, though? I wondered. They hadn't noticed Landon sneaking into the women's bathroom to intercept me earlier. That seemed like a major hole in what was supposed to be one of the world's most impenetrable security protocols.

One of the advisors gave me a sympathetic half-smile. "At least the event was going well until this happened," she said. "A lot of the attendees liked your speech. Especially the women."

"Yes," my father said, nodding slowly. "It went over quite well."

Despite his positive comment, I could tell he was still irritated about my off-script comments onstage earlier. The set of his jaw and the way his fingers drummed against his right leg gave it away. But he didn't bring it up. Probably figured a bomb in my vehicle was punishment enough.

I sighed inwardly and looked down at my lap.

My father had never called me a disappointment right to my face, but I could still see it in his expression and hear it in his tone whenever he felt that way about me. It was obvious in his actions, too—the way he so frequently had to correct me, coach me, mold me into something more palatable. The way he never looked quite proud. More like... resigned.

I knew exactly why.

He'd always been on the fence about having children, but my mother wanted at least one, and she'd eventually managed to get on him board by pointing out that it would help his political career. After all, voters loved a family man, and the vast majority also tended to be suspicious of politicians who actively chose not to have kids.

Dad realized she was right, and thus, I was conceived three years after their marriage. So for him, it was never really about wanting a child. It was all about strategy. Optics.

As my mom had noted, the image of a devoted family man was a crucial piece in the puzzle of his burgeoning career, and he'd always had his sights set on the presidency. For that, he needed the perfect background, the perfect wife, and the perfect child.

But I wasn't perfect. At least not in his eyes.

See, once he was finally on board with the idea of having a child, he'd really hoped for a son. A future heir to his political dynasty; a boy who would carry his name forward and follow in his footsteps without question. Instead, the baby turned out to be me.

My mother had pointed out to him many times that things were different these days. I didn't *have* to take another man's surname when I got married—if I even got married—and I'd expressed an interest in the world of politics from a young age, so I could still carry on his legacy along with his name, seeing as that was so important to him. Unfortunately, he was quite hard-headed in his ideas, and nothing could ever change the fact that deep down, he wanted a son to carry on his name.

My parents had tried for another baby in the hopes of getting that much-desired boy, but they encountered some fertility issues, and eventually, it became clear that it simply wasn't going to happen. I was *it* for them. The only child. The only heir to a throne my father never intended for a girl.

I couldn't complain too much, though. He'd provided me with a great life filled with incredible opportunities, and I knew he still loved me despite it all.

I just wished he could be proud of me as well.

The other advisor in the car leaned forward, clearing his throat. "The Secret Service will increase security measures at your campus, but given the nature of the device on the car, this appears to have been a warning rather than a serious attempt on your life."

I nodded. "Yes, I heard."

"It's very important that you don't panic."

Right. Because someone getting close enough to plant a bomb under one of the presidential cars wasn't a valid reason to panic.

My thoughts must've been etched on my face, because the advisor hurriedly added, "What I mean is, once the media gets hold of the story, we all need to present a strong, brave front to the world. Show them we can't be intimidated. Especially you in this case, given that you were the target."

I nodded. "Got it."

I leaned back in my seat, crossing my arms over my stomach as I glanced out the tinted window. I couldn't see much beyond the passing streetlights and the reflection of my own face, but I still couldn't shake the weird feeling that someone—somewhere—was watching me.

The rest of the drive back to campus was silent. My father had turned his attention to his phone, typing out messages to whoever had the misfortune of being on the receiving end of his clipped late-night directives. His two advisors spoke in hushed voices across from me, occasionally glancing in my direction, as if I wasn't fully capable of hearing them discuss my safety.

I kept my gaze fixed on the window, watching as the city blurred past. By the time we reached Belgrave University, the streets were quiet, the towering gothic buildings casting long, eerie shadows beneath the streetlights.

The wrought-iron gates to the east side of campus stood open, and the stone pathways leading toward the dorms were empty, the usual late-night stragglers either inside or tucked away in whatever hidden corners they gathered in.

"Remember what I said before," Dad said as the car rolled to a stop outside my dorm. "Security caught it this time, and they'll catch it next time. There's really no need to be afraid."

"I'll try my best." I nodded once, reaching for the door handle. "Night, Dad."

"Goodnight, darling. I hope you can get some sleep."

I stepped out into the cool night air, and the door shut behind me with a solid *thunk*. A black SUV was idling behind the car, its headlights cutting across the stone pathway. The Secret Service, including Agent Foster.

As much as the constant presence of a security detail irritated me sometimes, I had to admit that I was grateful they were here tonight. The bomb had rattled me, and knowing the agents would be with me until I was safely inside offered at least a sliver of comfort.

Foster and his partner exited the SUV and fell into step behind me. The old stone dorm building loomed ahead of us, its arched windows glowing faintly with light. It was grand in the way everything at Belgrave was—prestigious, historical, built for the elite.

I climbed the steps and swiped my key card at the entrance, and the door clicked open with a soft beep. The lobby was quiet and empty, save for the night guard behind the desk and the three agents who'd gone ahead earlier to sweep the building for any new security threats.

Foster stayed close as I entered the elevator, pressing the button for the second floor while his partner stood slightly in front of me, scanning the surroundings with that sharp, ever-watchful gaze that every agent had.

Once the doors slid open, they walked me down the hall, their presence a silent but heavy weight at my back. When I reached my dorm room and swiped my key card again, they finally stopped, waiting until I stepped inside before Foster gave me a slight nod.

"We'll be stationed outside for the rest of the night," he said. "Call if you need anything."

I nodded. "Thanks. Goodnight."

The door shut with a quiet click. I dropped my purse, let out a heavy sigh, and headed over to my desk. I knew I wouldn't be able to get much sleep tonight, because my body was still flooded with adrenaline, so I figured I could channel all that wired energy into something productive and dive into my foreign policy paper.

The fall semester had only begun a week ago, but I was already overloaded with assignments, because Belgrave professors loved challenging their students. The paper in question was due in a week, so if I got most of it done tonight, I could then turn my focus to another assignment from my international relations class, which was much longer and more research-intensive.

I managed to write four pages of my policy paper before a sound broke through the silence in my room. A faint rustling.

I froze, my hands stilling on the keyboard. It wasn't the heater that sat on the far-left side of the dorm. It wasn't the wind outside, either, or some whirring component in my laptop. It was something else. Something deliberate and decidedly human.

Slowly, I turned my head toward my balcony door. My stomach plummeted at the sight that greeted me.

There, standing in the shadows, was a tall man dressed in black, his face obscured by a gas mask.

3

ARIA

A SCREAM TORE FROM MY THROAT BEFORE I EVEN REGISTERED what I was doing. The man on my balcony didn't move. He just stood there, shrouded in black, the glossy surface of his gas mask reflecting the light from my desk lamp.

I lurched backward, my chair screeching against the hardwood floor as I shoved away from my desk. My heart was pounding painfully hard, breath coming in sharp, panicked bursts as icy jolts of adrenaline burst through my veins. I wanted to move, to run like hell, but I was frozen, trapped in the nightmarish moment as the masked man's head tilted slightly, like he was studying me.

Then, with only a flicker of movement, he was gone.

The door burst open behind me. "Aria!"

Foster and his partner rushed inside, guns drawn. I lifted a shaky arm, pointing to the narrow balcony door.

Foster moved toward me, his free hand raised in a calming gesture, while Agent Sanchez moved toward the balcony door. I was still shaking, barely able to speak.

"There was—" My voice cracked. I swallowed hard and tried again. "There was someone out there. A man. Dressed in black. He was wearing a gas mask."

Foster stiffened, then spun to Sanchez. "Check the perimeter."

Sanchez was already moving, flinging open the balcony door and stepping outside, weapon ready. His head whipped from side to side before he disappeared from view, presumably heading toward the fire escape.

Foster muttered something into his radio, presumably contacting the other agents on duty. Then he turned back to me, eyes scanning my face with cool precision. "Are you all right?"

"Not really," I managed to say in a ragged whisper. My chest was still heaving, pulse still pounding dangerously fast.

He gestured toward the beige sofa on the right side of the space. "Sit down," he said. "Do you remember the breathing exercises I showed you a while ago?"

I nodded, inhaling deeply and holding the breath for eight seconds before exhaling slowly. Then I repeated the process.

Foster had taught me the calming technique after noticing my nerves on my father's inauguration night. I'd been anxious as hell all evening, knowing I had to step out onto the stage for the world to see, and I almost wound up having a panic attack. Thankfully, the breathing exercise worked really well for me, and I'd managed to celebrate my dad's victory onstage without totally freaking out in front of everyone.

"That's good. Keep breathing," Foster said, his tone slightly gentler now. "When you feel up to it, can you tell me exactly what happened?"

I took a few more deep breaths before I finally spoke up. "I was sitting at my computer, and I heard a noise," I said, my voice still weak and tremulous. "I turned around and saw a guy standing out there on the balcony. At least I assume it was a guy."

"Based on build?"

"Yes. The person looked very tall, and their body shape was very masculine too."

Foster's radio emitted a tiny beeping sound, and he tilted his head and frowned, presumably listening to something coming through his earbud.

"Did they find him?" I asked.

He didn't answer for a beat. Then he shook his head. "Not yet. My partner just confirmed that he saw nothing on the balcony or fire escape, and the agents stationed outside didn't see anything either."

"How is that possible? A person can't just vanish into thin air."

Foster hesitated again. "Are you absolutely sure you saw someone out there?" he asked in a delicate tone.

I gaped at him. "Of course I'm sure! I saw him standing right there." I pointed again, my hand trembling. "You believe me, right?"

"I always believe you, Aria, but..." He trailed off and glanced at the glass door. "There's no way someone would've been able to get up to that balcony. The building is constantly monitored for your safety."

I let out a breathless, humorless laugh. "Then how did the guy get up here?"

"That's what we're trying to work out. You're one of the most well-guarded girls on the planet, so no one should've been able to get this close to your dorm."

I swallowed hard, choosing my next words carefully. "I'm not trying to insult the integrity of the Secret Service or anything, but... is it possible that the agents outside just missed him climbing up?" I asked. "I've seen them out there before, and they're almost always facing outward. They hardly ever look toward my dorm."

Foster nodded. "That's intentional, because they're constantly monitoring the surrounding area. If anyone approaches their vicinity, they'll keep a close eye on them to ensure they don't go anywhere near the fire escape below your dorm," he explained. "But they both confirmed there was no one else in the area at all."

"Oh." I looked down at the floor, mind spinning. Then I

glanced up at Foster again. "What about neighboring dorms? Someone could've quietly climbed across from another balcony, or even dropped down from the one above. And those agents outside might not have noticed, because like you said, they're usually facing away to monitor movement beyond the dorm."

The expression on Foster's face told me that he thought my theory was absurd, but he was too polite to say it. "There are mechanisms to prevent that from happening, but we'll look into every possibility. All of your neighbors will be interviewed."

"Okay."

"For now, let's close this," he said, turning on his heel to march toward the balcony. He closed the door and twisted the lock before jiggling the handle to make sure it had locked properly. Then he pulled the emerald-green curtain across the glass and turned back around with a reassuring smile. "There. Now no one can look in."

"Thanks," I said in a small voice.

His brows suddenly dipped in a frown, and he took a slow step forward, eyes focused on my laptop. "Aria... do you think it's possible that you nodded off at your desk and had a nightmare based on the content you were watching?"

"Huh?" I blinked, surprised by the question. "What do you mean?"

He pointed to the laptop. "You were watching a show on Netflix," he said. "It's paused right on a scene with a man wearing a gas mask."

My jaw dropped, and I leapt to my feet, hurrying toward my desk.

Just as Foster had stated, there was a paused episode of Pretty Little Liars on the screen, featuring a scene from the third season with the stalker who was wreaking havoc on the main characters' lives. He was standing in a basement, wearing dark clothing and an old-fashioned gas mask, and the camera was zoomed quite closely on him.

"What the hell?" I fervently shook my head, eyes wide. "I wasn't watching this. I was writing an assignment. I swear!"

Foster gave me a skeptical look. "Are you absolutely certain about that?"

"Yes! It was my foreign policy paper."

"Aria..." A flash of pity appeared in his gaze. "You've had a very long, very stressful day."

"I know," I muttered through gritted teeth.

"You spent the entire afternoon feeling horribly anxious about giving that speech. I know because you always chew on your nails when you're worried," Foster went on, gesturing to my hands. "Then things got fifty times more frightening for you when the bomb scare happened. I've trained and worked for the agency for thirty years, so for me, it's just another day. But for you? An incident like that is a serious trauma."

"I know, but it doesn't mean I've totally lost my mind and started hallucinating crazy stalkers at my window," I said indignantly, cheeks flushing hot.

He lifted a palm. "I'm not implying that at all. You know I would never say something like that about you," he replied, eyes filling with sympathy again. "What I'm trying to say is—you had a truly horrible day today, and as the president's daughter, you're also under constant stress. So it wouldn't be the strangest thing in the world for you to have an awful nightmare. One so vivid and realistic that you honestly believed it happened. In fact, I'd be surprised if someone in your position *wasn't* having the occasional nightmare."

"But..." I trailed off, shaking my head. "I remember it all so clearly. I was definitely writing my policy paper before I heard the noise at the window. I don't remember putting on an episode of that show, and I don't remember feeling sleepy either. In fact, the whole reason I was working on my assignment so late was because I *couldn't* sleep."

"Sometimes we feel like we're not tired at all, but then we

suddenly crash out at the most unexpected time," Foster said. "The human body is odd like that."

"I guess so," I murmured, mind still spinning.

What if Foster was right? What if the masked man on the balcony *wasn't* real? What if I'd really fallen asleep and dreamed the whole thing?

My stomach churned as I looked toward the curtains again.

No. I knew what I saw. There had definitely been a man on my balcony a few minutes ago, and I was wide awake the entire time, wired from the adrenaline that had flooded my body after the car bomb incident.

Also, I hadn't watched an episode of Pretty Little Liars since I was fourteen. There was no reason for me to suddenly decide to put on an episode from halfway through the series when I had much more important things to do on my laptop.

But then I turned my gaze back to the screen to see the gas mask staring back at me, and it became harder to hold onto that certainty.

How else would that episode get on my screen unless I opened Netflix and played it? No one had touched my laptop tonight except me. Even Agent Foster hadn't touched it after he noticed what was on the screen. He'd simply pointed at it to draw my attention.

"Aria, I want you to hear something before I go," he said, still looking at me with that sympathetic expression on his face. "As you know, my job is to do everything in my power to protect you. So even if this *was* a terrible dream, we're still going to investigate every possible aspect of it. We won't leave a single stone unturned. I'll make damn sure of it."

"Thank you," I said softly. A lump was forming in my throat.

"You should try to get some sleep." Foster's voice was steady, reassuring. "I'll be right outside if you need anything."

I nodded numbly, though the idea of sleeping felt impossible. Every time I blinked, I saw that masked man.

Foster gave me one last searching look before heading toward the door. "Goodnight, Aria."

"Goodnight."

The moment he stepped out, I locked the door behind him. Then I turned back to my laptop, still paused on that frozen frame with the gas mask staring straight at me. I hovered my finger over the trackpad, ready to close it, but then I hesitated.

A moment ago, I was sure the only explanation was that I'd opened the show myself and somehow forgotten due to sheer exhaustion. But now, a far more unsettling possibility had occurred to me.

What if someone had hacked into my laptop and played that episode on purpose, just to make me think I was losing my mind when their accomplice showed up at my window? Sabrina was always saying how easy it was for elite hackers to get into computers, even ones guarded by government-level firewalls.

Then again... who the hell would do that to me? And why?

Somewhere outside, a faint sound echoed. A slow, deliberate tap, like fingers rapping against glass. I flinched, heart hammering again, and stared at the closed curtains with wide eyes.

After taking a deep breath, I picked up my phone, opened the camera app on video mode, and spun toward the balcony, pulse hammering in my throat. Then I sucked in another deep breath and wrenched open the curtains, determined to catch the masked intruder on film to prove to Foster and the others that I wasn't just dreaming earlier.

My shoulders sagged when I saw Agent Sanchez standing out on the balcony, fiddling with the lock on the door. When he saw me, his expression turned contrite. "Sorry, Aria. Just double-checking that no one's done anything to damage this lock," he called through the glass. "I didn't mean to scare you."

I waved at him to signal it was okay. He gave the lock one last firm press before nodding with satisfaction. Then he went back down the fire escape, presumably to enter the building through the front and join Foster in the hall outside my door.

I closed the curtains again and backed away, my breath shuddering out in uneven bursts. Then I turned back to my laptop, closed the Netflix tab, and slammed the lid down.

As I climbed into bed and curled up under the blankets, my mind replayed the gas mask incident over and over, until it started to feel like a nebulous trick of the mind. Like when you repeated the same word so many times that it lost all meaning, warping into a weird sound rather than something real.

Suddenly I was no longer a hundred percent certain that it really happened. How could it? Like Foster said, I was one of the most heavily-guarded girls on the planet, with multiple agents working day and night to ensure no one got close to me without permission.

But still... I couldn't stop seeing that black mask in my mind's eye. The way it reflected the light, and the eerie tilt of the head, like the wearer was studying me. The way he disappeared in the blink of an eye, as if he'd never been there at all. It shouldn't have been possible, and yet somehow it was.

God, maybe I really *was* losing my mind.

But as I closed my eyes and tried my best to push the thoughts away, one in particular refused to budge.

If it was really just a nightmare earlier...

Why did I still feel like someone was watching me?

4

ARIA

I took a steadying breath before knocking on my poli-sci professor's office door.

"Come in," came his deep voice.

I pushed inside, taking in the space as I stepped forward. Dark wooden bookshelves lined the walls, overflowing with academic texts and framed newspaper clippings. A heavy mahogany desk sat in the center, neatly arranged with a computer on the right. The room smelled of leather and old paper, a nice contrast to Belgrave's sterile lecture halls.

I had all of two seconds to absorb it before the toe of my shoe caught on the edge of the rug.

A startled yelp escaped my lips as I tripped, my purse slipping from my shoulder and spilling open on the floor as I fell. Lip gloss, crumpled receipts, a pack of gum, and a box of tampons scattered across the floor.

Heat instantly flooded my face. I wanted to make a good impression, because I had no idea why Professor Cosgrove had asked me to meet with him, but I hadn't even sat down yet, and I already looked like a damn circus clown.

"Oh, my!" He rushed out from behind his desk, one hand

outstretched. "Are you all right, Aria? I think I have some plasters in my drawer if you've grazed something."

I gave him a sheepish smile. "I'm fine," I said, dusting off my pants. "Just a bruised ego, I think."

"It's all right. We all take an embarrassing tumble from time to time," he said, eyes twinkling. "At least it happened here in the privacy of my office, rather than at one of your father's rallies."

"That's true."

He dropped to a crouch. "I'll help," he said, gesturing to the scattered contents of my purse. "We'll get this cleared up in no time."

"Thank you, sir." I reached forward to grab my lip gloss. At the same time, Professor Cosgrove reached for a small card that had spilled out with the rest of my stuff.

The jovial twinkle in his eye faded, and his brows dipped in a slight frown of confusion. "Aria," he said, holding up the card. "Where did you get this?"

I craned my neck forward to get a proper look. "Oh, that," I replied, waving a casual hand. "Someone left it on my table at an event the other night. It's from that climate activism group. The DC Guardians. I forgot I even had it in there."

He shook his head. "This isn't from the Guardians."

"It's not?"

"No. But I can see where the confusion stems from," he said, rising to his feet. "It *does* look very similar to the DC Guardians logo upon first glance, and the motto could easily be mistaken for a message about environmental conversation. But it's something else entirely." He paused and beckoned to me with his left hand. "Come and have a look. This is actually rather exciting."

With raised brows, I followed him over to his desk. He went behind it and rapidly typed something on his keyboard before turning his screen so that we could both see it.

"This is the DC Guardians logo," he said, pointing to a tangled circular design with vines weaving in and out of one another. "It's almost identical to the one on that card, but as you can see, the circle of vines is surrounding a picture of the Washington Monument. On yours, it's the Capitol."

"Oh, right."

"Also, if you look closely at the circle on yours, it isn't just vines and leaves," he said, pushing his glasses up his nose. "The vines are wrapped around a snake eating its own tail. An Ouroboros."

I squinted at the underlying design. "Oh, wow. I didn't notice that before. Does it mean something?"

"It certainly does. The Ouroboros has been used throughout history to represent cycles of power, secrecy, and the elite preserving their control. Also, in general, snakes are often used as symbols of knowledge and political cunning."

"Oh, I see."

"On top of all that, take a look at this," Professor Cosgrove went on, drawing my attention back to his computer screen. "On all the posters, cards, and other paraphernalia that the DC Guardians distribute, it says their full name. DC Guardians. Not just the letters DC."

I looked at my card again. "Ah."

He followed my gaze to the 'DC' emblazoned beneath the design on the card. "You'd naturally assume that *that* particular DC also stands for District of Columbia, given our location. But it doesn't," he said. "What you have in your hand is the old calling card of the Dominion Club." He paused briefly, frowning again before he added, "But I'm assuming it's some sort of joke."

"What's the Dominion Club?" I asked, brows furrowing. "And why would it be a joke?"

"It was a secret society that used to operate right here at Belgrave," he said. "But it's been defunct for years. Decades, in fact."

"Oh, wow." My mind instantly filled with images of golden-masked people in black robes, stone altars in a forest, and bizarre rituals. "What did they do?"

The animated expression returned to Professor Cosgrave's face. "There's all sorts of stories about them," he said. "They were shrouded in mystery for the most part, for obvious reasons. But what we know for certain is that they recruited and operated out of Belgrave, and they traded in secrets. That was their currency."

My forehead wrinkled. "Secrets as currency?"

"Yes. Membership spanned an entire lifetime, and their members often wound up with high-ranking government positions, or other careers that granted them privileged access to sensitive information. Also, the members were trained to essentially function as spies."

"Oh, wow."

"They used surveillance and strategic infiltration to gather as much intelligence as possible, along with secrets. Secrets that could be used to destroy other high-ranking government officials if they were seen to violate the ethos of the Dominion Club," Professor Cosgrove went on. He cocked his head. "Do you recall the motto on the other side of that card?"

I nodded. "Defend and Conserve."

"That's it—their ethos. And it wasn't about the environment. It was about defending and conserving a particular set of ideals in American government," he said. "If they believed a senator, congressman, or even someone higher up was acting in a way that could harm America and its citizens, they would use the secrets they had on that person to force them out. Blackmail, essentially. They were known to have ousted at least three major candidates for certain positions, and it was also widely suspected that they could influence elections."

"I see." I tilted my head. "So what happened to them?"

"Well, back in the 80s, President Breeland decided he'd had enough of their existence. After all, these men and women seemingly had more power and control over the government than him.

So he orchestrated an operation to unmask the members and put them away. On trumped-up charges, of course. After that, the society ceased to exist," he said. He dipped his chin toward the card again. "So, I'd say whoever left that card on your table wasn't a climate activist. Rather a prankster with a detailed knowledge of obscure historical facts."

"Ah, right."

He smiled. "Anyway, my apologies for the excitement. Seeing that logo was a bit of a blast from the past," he said. "Back in the day, the Dominion Club held quite the level of intrigue amongst budding politicos such as myself."

I returned his smile. "I get it. Secret societies are pretty interesting."

"They certainly are." Professor Cosgrove gestured to the seat beside me. "Anyway, take a seat. We should get to our actual topic of discussion before the day is over, shouldn't we?"

I swallowed hard, heart thudding faster. "Yes, sir," I said, hoping I didn't sound too nervous.

Professor Cosgrove was a fantastic educator, but he was also known to be a total hard-ass. Ever since I received the email from him requesting this afternoon meeting, I'd been on the edge of my seat, fretting and wondering if I'd accidentally done something wrong. Had I dozed off in a lecture last week? Forgotten about a small assignment?

"So." He leaned forward, steepling his hands on his desk. "I wanted to discuss something related to your performance in my freshman-level classes last year."

"Oh. I thought I did quite well," I said in a tremulous voice.

He smiled. "Aria, there's no need for modesty. You were my top student last year. Aced absolutely everything. And your other professors have reported similar results after having you in their classes," he said. He paused for a moment to let the compliment wash over me. "Have you ever heard of the Veritas Forum?"

"Yes," I said, nodding. Every political science student had heard of the Veritas Forum.

It was an exclusive event that took place in a different city each year, bringing together the brightest young American minds in politics, law, and international relations from every major university in the country. They'd gather for a week of debates, keynote speeches, and high-stakes discussions of national and global issues. Invitations were scarce, reserved only for the top students at each college.

"This year, the Forum is taking place in Anchorage. It's happening in five weeks, from October 11th to the 18th," Professor Cosgrove said. "Usually, we only pick high-achieving students from our junior and senior classes to attend, but occasionally, we have such an outstanding student in a lower class that we decide to include them too. You're one such case, Aria. So I'd like to offer you a place at the Forum. You'd be one of ten from Belgrave."

My eyes widened. Attending the Veritas Forum would be an undeniable boost to my résumé. Practically a golden ticket into the world of politics.

"Wow," I said, cheeks flushing with delighted warmth. "Sir, that's such an honor. Thank you so much!"

"You're very welcome, Aria. You've earned it," Professor Cosgrove said with a warm smile. He paused for a beat and lifted a palm. "Anyway, I wanted to discuss this with you privately first, because I'm aware that due to your father's job, your schedule is very likely planned out months in advance. I'm sure it's also very busy, especially with the election happening in three months. Not to mention all the security arrangements that would be necessary to organize, should you choose to accept the invitation. So, I thought it would be best for you to find out if attendance is even a possibility before we lock you in. Just in case."

My shoulders sagged slightly. "I didn't even think of that," I said softly. "But you're right. My dad will probably veto it if I bring it up. There's just so much to do with the election getting closer and closer."

"I may be able to offer a suggestion on swaying him," he said, leaning forward with a conspiratorial gleam in his eye. "Did you know he was invited to the Forum in his junior year here at Belgrave?"

I nodded. "Yes, he's talked about it before."

"I was actually here when he was chosen, if you can believe it. I was just a TA at the time, but I remember him very well. He was a brilliant student, and he was utterly thrilled when he was chosen as an attendee," Professor Cosgrove said. "I have a feeling that he'd be just as thrilled to have his child following in his footsteps. And of course... it doesn't hurt that your attendance could be a net positive for his re-election campaign."

I raised a brow. "You think so?"

He nodded. "If you attend, I'm willing to bet that several media outlets will do nice little puff pieces on it. Then voters will read all about it, and I bet a lot of them will think, 'Golly, not only is Jonathan Hagan an effective president, but he's also taken the time and effort to raise a smart, wonderfully-accomplished daughter. I should definitely vote for a man like that'. In short— it'll make him look good."

I smiled faintly. "Or they might just think I'm a nepo baby."

He waved a hand. "The Veritas Forum is known for being genuinely exclusive. No nepotism."

"Well, I'll definitely ask my dad if it's a possibility."

"I'm very glad to hear it." Professor Cosgrove smiled. "I'll give you until the end of the week to get back to me. Is that all right?"

"Yes. I'll let you know as soon as I have an answer," I said. "And thank you again, sir. This is such an amazing opportunity."

I left the office feeling like I was walking on air. I knew I'd done well in my first two semesters at Belgrave, but I didn't realize I'd outperformed everyone else in my classes. I'd never expected an early invitation to the Veritas Forum, either. I'd never even heard of a sophomore being invited.

I stepped out into the chilly afternoon, pulling my blazer tighter around myself as a sharp gust of wind sent a shiver down my spine. The sky overhead was a dull, overcast gray, and the air carried the scent of damp pavement and something faintly metallic, like a storm was brewing in the distance.

As I descended the stone steps of the political science building, a strange prickle crawled up the back of my neck, like ghostly fingertips skimming over my skin. Someone was watching me. I could feel it.

My gaze flicked to the quad, scanning the sparse clusters of students huddled against the wind, their heads bent as they hurried to their destinations. No one seemed out of place, and no lingering eyes were tracking my movements.

I exhaled deeply, shaking my head at myself. It was just the eyes of today's Secret Service detail that I felt on me. Two agents were always shadowing me, hovering at a slight distance. I was just feeling paranoid because of the incident with the gas mask guy the other night.

Now that a couple of days had passed, I was no longer sure any of it had even happened. The images of the incident were fading in my mind's eye, slipping away, eroded by time and uncertainty. My other memories of the evening felt looser too, more malleable, shaped more by the doubts of others than by my own thoughts about what I'd experienced.

I was now leaning toward Foster's theory being correct—I was just so exhausted and stressed that night that I fell asleep at my desk and had a vivid nightmare. Maybe even some sort of sleep paralysis.

Also, I could no longer be sure that I hadn't been mindlessly watching Pretty Little Liars when it happened, because most of the night was hazy now, like I'd been walking through the motions of a dream.

The only thing that *wasn't* hazy was the fear; that sheer, visceral terror that gripped me that night. That part hadn't faded, and I could still feel the suffocating weight of it pressing down on my chest.

And yet...

Shame curled hot and tight in my gut. Because fear wasn't really the only thing I remembered clearly.

The other feeling was harder to name. It was darker, more insidious... but something deep inside me had *liked* what I thought I saw that night. The way the masked man stood there, silent and still, watching me. The way his presence made my skin prickle, made my breath catch, made my pulse flutter like the wings of a trapped bird.

My breath quickened at the memory, and my fingers clenched around the strap of my bag as if I could strangle the thought before it fully formed.

It was messed up. Sick, even. So why the hell had I spent the last two nights lying awake, replaying that moment in my mind and twisting it into something more than a bad dream?

Something worse. Something I wanted anyway.

I'd told myself it was only because I'd been scared half to death that night. That the rush of adrenaline had done something weird to my brain, tangled my instincts into knots. But deep down, I knew that wasn't true.

I squeezed my eyes shut for a second, exhaling sharply through my nose. *Stop it.*

I opened my eyes, squared my shoulders, and pushed forward, mind switching its focus back to the amazing opportunity my professor had just handed to me.

Once I was back at my dorm, I settled on my bed and dialed my father's number. The call was automatically directed to his secretary's desk, and she answered with a pleasant greeting. "Hello, Aria! Lovely to hear from you! How can I help?"

"Hi, Mrs. Langridge. I was wondering if you could get a

message to my father," I said. "I know he's really busy, but if and when he's got a spare minute, would he be able to call me back? I have something important I want to discuss with him as soon as possible."

"You're in luck, my dear. He had a call scheduled with the Japanese Prime Minister, but it's just been canceled. Apparently the PM has come down with a flu. Not so lucky for him, of course," she said. "Anyway, I can transfer you to your father right now."

"Oh. Thank you!"

There was a beep as Mrs. Langridge redirected the call to the Oval Office. My father's voice came on the line a moment later. "Aria, is everything okay?" he asked, voice tinged with a mixture of concern and irritation. "Ellen said you had something very important to tell me."

"Don't worry, it's good news," I said. I quickly recapped what Professor Cosgrove had told me earlier, including the dates and location of the Veritas Forum. "It's such an amazing opportunity for me. And it would look great on my résumé, wouldn't it?"

"Yes, the Veritas Forum is a fantastic opportunity," he replied. His words were positive, but his tone was hesitant.

"So... can I go?" I asked, pulse racing with anticipation.

Dad was quiet for a moment. Then I heard him let out a heavy sigh. I could picture him in my mind's eye, forehead leaning against one hand as he slumped behind the Resolute Desk.

"I don't know," he finally said. "Alaska is so far away, and you have a lot of commitments here."

"But we have a Secret Service field office in Anchorage, right? So my usual team here could coordinate with them to set up a protection detail over there?"

"The distance isn't the only issue," he replied. "The election is only eleven weeks away, so you have a lot of campaign events scheduled, and they're all important."

"It's only for a week in October. Can't we move some of the

stuff around?" I asked. Then I hurriedly added, "Also, Professor Cosgrove said this could actually *help* with your re-election campaign, because the media would hear about me attending the Forum, and then they'd probably write positive things about me following in your footsteps. Things like that can help with public perception, because people love family-oriented politicians."

"I have to admit, the man has a good point," Dad said slowly.

My heart skipped a beat. "So you'll consider it?"

"Well... there'd be a lot of logistics to sort out because of the short notice. But we could make it happen. And we'd definitely have to set up some media coverage on it. It would look good for the campaign, like your professor pointed out," he said. "Also, as you said before, it's a wonderful opportunity for you."

I inwardly rolled my eyes at the order he'd put his response in. Of course he was considering his campaign first and leaving my future career as an afterthought. I wasn't going to argue with him about it, though. Not when it sounded like he was leaning toward a 'yes'.

"Should I tell Professor Cosgrove it's a maybe, then?" I asked in a tentative tone, not wanting to get too excited just yet.

"No, no, don't tell him that," Dad replied. My heart sank, but then he went on. "You can tell him it's a yes."

My brows shot up. "Really?"

"Yes." His tone was slightly more upbeat now. "I needed a minute to let it all sink in, but now that it has, I can see that you're right. This could be good for both of us. A few people might get annoyed at us for rescheduling other commitments, but... well, I have it on good authority that your old dad is quite an important man. So they'll just have to deal with it, won't they?"

"Yeah, I guess you *are* kind of important, Dad," I said with a playful laugh.

He chuckled. "I'll have Ellen contact the head agent on your detail to begin making the arrangements. All right?"

"Okay. Thanks so much!"

"You're welcome, darling. Anyway, duty calls, so I have to go now. We'll have a proper discussion about all the details later."

Once I'd ended the call, I pumped my fist in the air and whooped so loudly that one of the agents posted outside my door rushed in, concerned that I was shrieking with terror. After I'd reassured her that I was just giddy with excitement, I Facetimed Sabrina.

"Hey!" I said, waving at the camera when she answered. "Are you free to hang out tonight? I just got some really good news, and I want to celebrate."

"Oh my god, you must be psychic. I was literally *just* about to text you!" she replied. "Some of the girls decided to throw a last minute party tonight, because Kayla finally dumped that asshole Dean. So I was going to ask you if you think your security detail would let you come."

The girls she was referring to were her sorority sisters at Theta Lambda Chi. She'd rushed last year because her mother was a legacy member who insisted she follow in her footsteps.

My mother was also a Theta back in the day, but I wasn't able to rush alongside Sabrina, because the head agent on my Secret Service team decided that it was too much of a security risk to have me living in a sorority house. Apparently, the dorms were easier to secure.

"They should be fine with me coming," I said, nodding slowly. "But would the girls mind me being there as a non-member?"

Sabrina's eyes widened. "Of course they won't mind! The party will be open to everyone, not just Greek life. Everyone except Dean Haverford, that is. And also, the girls *love* it when you visit the house!" she said. "Although... some of them are still a bit salty at your Secret Service peeps for not letting you join. It would've looked amazing for us to have a First Daughter as a member."

"Oh, well. You know what the Secret Service can be like."

She rolled her eyes. "Yeah. So annoying," she said. "Anyway, do you want to come tonight? Please say yes!"

I grinned. "Yes. I'll definitely come."

"Awesome! I can't wait!" She let out a little squeal of excitement before continuing. "We're telling everyone to arrive around nine, but I was thinking you could come a bit earlier so we can get dressed and do our makeup together? If that's okay with you."

"Sure." I glanced at the clock on my desk. "How about I meet you there at eight-thirty?"

"Great. See you then!"

"Oh... Sabrina?" I said hurriedly before she hung up.

"Yeah?"

I hesitated. I was going to ask her about the laptop issue from the other night—if it was possible that someone could've remotely accessed it without anyone from the IT side of my security detail noticing the breach. Then I shook my head, feeling silly. "Never mind," I said. "It's no big deal."

"Wait. I'm totally the worst," she replied, eyes wide and voice laced with guilt. "You said you have good news, and I didn't even ask what it is! Sorry!"

"It's okay." I smiled and waved a hand. "I'll tell you while we get ready later."

I arrived at the Theta house at half past eight on the dot, thanks to the promptness of my security detail. The house was an architectural mix of old-money charm and modern excess—white columns framing the grand entrance, ivy creeping up the red brick walls, and a sweeping porch lined with rocking chairs that no one ever actually used. Inside, it smelled like vanilla candles and expensive hairspray.

An hour later, Sabrina and I were finally primped and ready. Downstairs, the party was already in full swing.

We descended into a sea of glossy-haired girls in designer heels and frat guys in their uniform of pastel polos and boat shoes. Music pulsed through the house, shaking the floorboards with a bass-heavy pop song that people were half-singing, half-screaming along to, and the glittering chandelier above the staircase trembled slightly from the sheer number of bodies crammed into the space.

A group of girls squealed in greeting near the open kitchen, where an oversized punch bowl sat on the counter, its purple contents likely strong enough to knock out a small horse.

Sabrina grinned and led me closer, one arm linked through mine. She briefly ducked into the kitchen before returning with a glass of punch for herself and a can of raspberry lemonade for me.

"One *non-alcoholic* lemonade for my bestie," she said loudly for the Secret Service's benefit as she handed the can to me. Then she leaned closer, brows raised as she whispered, "This lemonade is actually no longer a virgin. I deflowered it myself, so you know it's safe."

I giggled softly. "That's a very dramatic way of saying you spiked it with vodka," I whispered back, clinking the can against her glass. "Or is it gin?"

"Vodka. And hey, you *love* my drama queen-ness," she said, eyes sparkling. She tilted her head, nose wrinkling. "Queen-ness. Is that even a word?"

"I don't think so."

She shrugged. "I guess I won't be trying for an English lit degree anytime soon."

"Yeah, maybe stick to coding for now," I said, playfully nudging her. "Then you can hack into Belgrave's system and award yourself a free lit degree, if you really feel like it."

She laughed and took a sip of her punch. Then her face fell. "Ugh. Look who's here," she muttered, dipping her chin to the right.

I followed her gaze, my stomach doing an entirely unnecessary flip when I spotted Landon Ashford across the room.

Dressed casually in a fitted black T-shirt and dark blue jeans, he somehow managed to look both effortless and impossibly put-together at the same time. The soft cotton of his shirt clung to his torso, highlighting his broad shoulders and tanned, muscular arms, and his confident posture only added to the aura of quiet strength he exuded. A few strands of his dark hair had fallen over his forehead, and he pushed them back with a careless swipe of his fingers, his gaze scanning the room with a mix of boredom and sharp awareness, like he was taking in every detail while pretending not to care.

Unsurprisingly, a lot of girls were watching him. Whispering, giggling, throwing lingering glances in his direction as if he might suddenly decide to sweep one of them off her feet and disappear into the night.

"It's *so* annoying that he's so hot, isn't it?" Sabrina said, rolling her eyes. "It's always the sexiest ones that are the biggest assholes."

She was right. Landon was a cruel manipulator, an infuriating asshole, and an arrogant bastard, but above all that, he was hot as hell. It annoyed the crap out of me. Why couldn't his face and body match his twisted personality? It would make it much easier for me to ignore him then.

"Yeah," I muttered, dragging my gaze away from him.

"Don't shoot me for saying this, but I can totally picture you two together," Sabrina went on. "If he wasn't such an asshole, I mean."

My brows shot up. "Me and *Landon?*"

"Yeah. I mean, it's just so Romeo-and-Juliet-coded, isn't it?" she said, eyes glimmering with amusement. "Two rival families. Their sexy young offspring falling in love and sneaking around together. It would be so illicit. So *hot.*"

I laughed and shook my head. "Never gonna happen."

She looked at Landon again. "Hey, never say never. Maybe he'll turn over a new leaf and stop being such a prick to you. Then I can live vicariously through your scandalous relationship."

I followed her gaze back over to Landon. "I doubt that'll ever happen," I said. "And I'm not interested in him anyway."

I kept my tone light, pretending like I was completely indifferent, but I wasn't. Not even a little. Because, as much as I despised Landon, part of me *was* interested. A hormone-soaked, lizard-brained part of me, but still... it was there, simmering beneath my skin, impossible to ignore.

I tried to tear my eyes away from him again, but like most girls in the room, I had a bit of trouble with that, so my eyes remained locked in place, acutely aware of every move he made. Like how he shifted his weight, the way his fingers drummed idly against the side of his cup, the slight smirk that played at his lips whenever someone spoke to him.

Just as I finally summoned the strength to look away, his eyes flicked directly to me, pinning me in place like a predator catching sight of its prey. His expression remained unreadable, but his gaze darkened, sharpening with a quiet intensity that sent a shiver down my spine.

It wasn't just a look. It was more like a warning. A silent acknowledgment that he'd seen me and marked me with some invisible brand. That no matter how quickly I tried to disappear into the crowd, it was already too late.

I finally forced myself to look away, shoving Landon's piercing gaze to the back of my mind. I wasn't going to let his presence spoil my good night.

Sabrina and I finished our drinks and melted into the crowd. We danced, twirling under the lights and laughing as we bumped into other girls who were just as tipsy and carefree as we were.

After we'd exhausted ourselves dancing, we moved closer to the edge of the main room and mingled, chatting with sorority sisters and friends-of-friends. It was easy to get lost in the fun, to let the warmth of the party and the buzz of the alcohol drown out the feeling of being watched.

Close to midnight, on my way to grab some food from a table stacked with mini cupcakes, the heel of my left shoe slipped on the polished floor. My stomach lurched as I tipped forward, but thankfully, a tattooed arm shot out beside me, gripping my arm and yanking me upright.

I looked up to see who'd saved me, and my breath hitched as my eyes met Landon's intense gaze. His grip was firm, holding me just long enough to ensure I wouldn't fall again.

"You need to be careful, Aria," he said, his voice low.

I swallowed hard and forced out a murmured, "Thanks."

He dropped my arm, and I dropped my eyes from his frustratingly handsome face. Then I continued on my way across the room, trying to ignore the way my wrist still burned where he'd touched me.

Sabrina reappeared at my side a moment later. "Hey, are you okay? You almost went ass over teakettle," she said, eyes flashing with concern.

"I'm fine, but it's the second time I've tripped over my own feet today," I said, cringing slightly. "How embarrassing."

She shrugged. "It's fine. Hardly anyone saw, and everyone here is mega-drunk anyway, so they don't give a shit."

"That's true."

Sabrina arched a brow. A gleam had appeared in her eyes, replacing the concern. "By the way, was I just seeing things, or did Landon rescue you?"

"Um. Yeah. I guess he just happened to be standing there."

"Hmm." Both brows were raised now, and she pressed her lips together in a thin line, like she was stopping herself from saying something. "Anyway... let's grab some food."

I nodded and followed her, pretending my heart wasn't still racing. Pretending I couldn't feel Landon's eyes on me as I walked away.

At midnight, a shift change happened with my security detail, replacing agents Parker and Wilson with Foster and Sanchez. Foster caught my attention a while later and tapped his watch, silently telling me it was time to leave the party.

I said goodbye to Sabrina and the other girls around us, and then I headed outside with the agents, wobbling slightly on my heels as I pulled my coat tighter.

I briefly turned my head over my shoulder to wave to someone, but my attention was quickly drawn upward, to something strange in a second-story window.

The light in the room was off, but I could make out a shadowy figure standing motionless in the dim space, staring down at me. Or at least that was what it looked like. Their face was obscured by a twisted black-and-red mask, making it impossible to tell exactly where their gaze was directed.

A chill ran down my spine, and I blinked, questioning whether I was just seeing things through the fog of alcohol. When I looked back, the window was empty.

Yup. Definitely imagining it.

"Are you all right to walk?" Foster asked, presumably noticing the wobble in my step as I turned and walked toward the car. Sanchez was lingering a few yards behind us, taking up the rear of my escort.

"I'm fine," I said with a soft giggle, concentrating as hard as I could on keeping my balance. If I tripped *again* today, I'd never let myself live it down.

Foster raised his brows. "Were you drinking tonight?"

"Um... maybe a couple of vodkas," I said, voice tinged with guilt. "But no one took any photos or videos of me. And the drinks looked like cans of lemonades."

He smiled faintly. "It's all right. I won't mention it in the debrief later."

"Thanks, Foster." I grinned at him. "You're the best. Have I ever told you you're my favorite agent?"

"You have now." His faint smile widened slightly. "By the way, I heard about the Veritas Forum. Congratulations."

"Thank you. It's so exciting."

"It certainly is," he said, dipping his chin in a nod. "For me too, because I'll be accompanying you to Anchorage with Agents Parker, Bradford, and Sanchez."

"Oh, that's awesome!"

He hesitated. "Forgive me if this is an overstep, but I'm proud of you, Aria," he said. "And I think you should be proud of yourself too. You've really accomplished something great."

"Thanks." I beamed at him, glowing from the compliment.

My smile suddenly dropped when I realized my father hadn't told me he was proud of me during our conversation earlier. Sabrina had said it at least twenty times over the course of the night, and now Agent Foster had kindly said it too... but nothing from my own dad.

I sighed and looked down at the ground.

"Are you all right?" Foster asked, registering the sudden shift in my mood.

"Just a bit of a headache," I said, rubbing my forehead. I didn't want to tell him what I was thinking about, because it seemed so small and petty compared to the problems other people had going on in their lives.

"Drink plenty of water when you get back to your dorm," he said. "Take some aspirin too, if you have any. You'll wake up feeling fresh as a daisy."

I took his advice and chugged three whole glasses of water along with an aspirin once I was back in my room. Then I collapsed onto my bed and closed my eyes.

I drifted off quickly, still giddy and fuzzy from the drinks, but when I woke up again an hour later, it was like a switch had been flipped. My head was totally clear.

I stared at the faint red glow of the digits on my clock, confused about what had yanked me out of my slumber. Then it hit me. That strange image from the Dominion Club card—the one that was half-hidden by twisted vines. A snake devouring its own tail.

I'd seen that symbol before... tattooed on Landon's wrist.

5
ARIA

THE FOURTH FLOOR OF BELGRAVE LIBRARY WAS NEARLY deserted, just the way I liked it.

A quiet hush had settled over the towering shelves, broken only by the occasional rustle of a turned page or the distant clack of a keyboard. I ran my fingers along the spines of the books as I scanned the titles, my pulse steady and my thoughts anything but.

I was looking for something specific. A few specific somethings, in fact.

Earlier today, after I finished work on an assignment that was due soon, I'd logged onto the library database and noted down every single book in their collection that could possibly contain information on Washington-based secret societies.

More specifically, I was searching for information on the Dominion Club.

I exhaled through my nose, shaking my head slightly at the ridiculousness of the situation. This was what my life had come to; digging through dusty books in search of information on an organization that most people seemed to believe was nothing more than an old legend. But I was sure I knew better.

I was sure the society had been restored, and I was also sure that Landon was a member.

The ouroboros tattoo on his wrist was almost proof enough. A serpent eating its own tail—the exact same symbol hidden within the Dominion Club's insignia. But it wasn't just that.

There was also the insane request he'd made of me in the restroom at the gala last week. That told me he was very likely involved in the sort of organization Professor Cosgrove had described to me the other day—a group hellbent on silent political domination through the manipulation of secrets and power.

Or... maybe Landon was just an asshole. That was always an option.

But then there was also the matter of the Dominion Club card. Someone had left it on my purse at the gala. Was that just an accident, or had it been placed there deliberately by Landon or someone else? And if it *was* deliberate, what did it mean?

I pulled another book from the shelf, flipping through the pages. No matter how much I read, my mind kept circling back to the same set of questions.

Did the Dominion Club want something from me? If so, what did they want?

Was it—as I already suspected—the reason why Landon had confronted me in that restroom, demanding I convince my father to drop out of the presidential race? Or were they after me for something else?

Or was Professor Cosgrove right after all? Was the card nothing more than an elaborate prank, and Landon simply nothing more than an asshole who wanted to seize power via his mother's potential presidency?

In addition to that... did the Dominion Club even *want* to contact me? The card had been left at the table when Sabrina was the only one standing there. So maybe it was actually *her* they were trying to contact. If the whole thing wasn't just a stupid prank, that is.

I chewed on my lip, staring at the open book in my hands. The text on the page claimed that the Dominion Club never really existed—that it was just a conspiracy theory many people believed in back in the day, with no evidence to suggest any of it was real.

I was turning the corner, eyes still on the book in my hands, when movement in my peripheral vision made me freeze.

A man dressed in black stood at the end of the next row. Tall. Motionless. Staring right at me.

But it wasn't his presence that made my stomach drop. It was the skull mask he wore. White bone against black voids where his eyes should be.

A strangled squeak escaped my mouth as the book slipped from my hands and hit the floor with a dull thud. Then my legs buckled, sending me crashing to my ass.

Heart pounding, I scrambled backward until my spine pressed against the cold wood of the bookshelf.

Not again.

I squeezed my eyes shut, my breath coming fast and sharp. It had to be another waking nightmare, just like that time with the gas mask guy I thought I saw on my balcony. A trick of my stressed, overworked, paranoid brain.

I forced myself to count to three.

One... My fingers curled against the marble tiles beneath me.

Two... A tremor ran through my spine.

Three... I opened my eyes.

The aisle was empty.

I sucked in a shaky breath, my pulse still hammering against my ribs. *Holy shit.* I really was losing my mind.

I braced my hands against the floor, my limbs trembling as I pushed myself upright. My breaths were still coming fast and uneven, but I forced myself to inhale deeply and hold it as long as I could, just like Foster taught me all those years ago.

One. Two. Three. It wasn't real. It wasn't real.

I ran a shaky hand through my hair, exhaling slowly. Just stress. Lack of sleep. Too many unanswered questions swirling in my brain. That had to be it.

I turned... and nearly jumped out of my skin.

Landon stood a few feet away, hands in his pockets, a smirk tugging at the corner of his mouth. He was dressed in black jeans and a slate-gray Henley that emphasized his muscular physique.

The simple outfit wouldn't have looked like anything special on any other guy, but it made Landon look even more effortlessly attractive. I could feel a treacherous heat creeping up my neck as my eyes involuntarily roamed over him. *Dammit.*

I hated how handsome he was. How his presence seemed to command attention without trying. How I always found myself noticing the sharp cut of his jaw and the way the fabric of his shirt clung to his chest, making it all too easy to imagine what he looked like without it.

"Did I scare you?" he asked, voice dripping with cruel amusement.

I lifted my chin, schooling my face into something indifferent. "No."

His smirk deepened, like he could see straight through me. "You shouldn't be here."

"Excuse me?" I replied, eyes narrowing.

He stepped closer, black shoes echoing on the marble floor. "You shouldn't be walking around alone," he said. "It's not safe. Especially for a girl like you."

"I'm not alone. My security detail is here."

Landon raised one brow and took another step closer. "Oh, yeah? Where?"

"Not far. They give me enough privacy to do what I want. But if something happens, all I have to do is scream, and they'll be here in ten seconds."

His smirk widened. "What if you don't have ten seconds?"

I bristled. "What's that supposed to mean?"

THE WILD

His expression didn't change, but something flickered in his eyes—amusement laced with something darker. He stepped even closer, slow and deliberate, the spicy scent of his cologne wrapping around me like a noose.

"I think you know what it means, but I'll spell it out for you," he said, voice low.

As he spoke, he closed the gap between us. I swallowed hard, instinctively stepping back, only to feel the cool press of the bookshelf against my spine. Landon didn't stop moving until there was barely an inch between us, his body caging me in, one hand lifting to rest against the shelf beside my head. The air felt charged, electric, my pulse hammering so loud I was sure he could hear it.

"What if you don't get a chance to scream?" he murmured, his breath warm against my cheek. His gaze dropped to my lips for the briefest second before meeting my eyes with his taunting gaze again. "What if someone grabs you and clamps a hand over that pretty little mouth of yours before you can make a single sound?"

"Is that a threat?" I asked, trying to pretend that my heart wasn't about to explode right out of my ribcage.

He drew back and laughed. "I'm just pointing out the holes in your security detail."

"Thanks. I'll pass your feedback on to the Secret Service," I muttered sarcastically. "I'm sure they'll be thrilled to bump the security risk at Belgrave Library to DEFCON 1."

The vague amusement in Landon's eyes faded, replaced by a hard stare. "Have you done what I told you yet?" he asked.

"What are you talking about?" I asked indignantly, as if I didn't know exactly what he meant.

His eyes narrowed slightly. "Did you figure out a way to make your father drop out of the race?"

"No." I lifted my chin, daring to challenge him. "I don't take orders from you."

That same old cruel smirk reappeared on his frustratingly handsome face. "You will soon enough."

His eyes were filled with an intensity that made me feel naked, exposed. Aroused despite the fear coursing through me.

I'd never, ever admit any of this to Landon, but beneath all my indignation and defiance, there was a traitorous part of me that *wanted* to be controlled, because I was incredibly turned on by the idea of being told what to do.

The idea of surrendering, of being stripped of choices and resistance, of being his to command... it should've repulsed me. But instead, it left me breathless. Just the thought of obeying without question, of being molded by his will, sent a dark shiver down my spine. Like I was a doll; an object with no purpose beyond pleasing him.

I liked the fear it stirred in me, too. The sharp, breathless thrill of it. The way it curled through my veins like a forbidden drug, leaving me jittery and alive in a way nothing else ever could.

None of it made sense. I should hate the fear. I should hate *him*. And yet, despite my better judgment, I couldn't deny the way my pulse quickened at his commands, or the way my body responded to the threatening tone in his voice.

I swallowed hard and tried my best to look and sound unaffected. "I won't. Not ever," I said. "And I don't take orders from your mother either, if that's who put you up to this. In fact... I'm actually *helping* Dad's campaign. Definitely not sabotaging it."

Landon let out a low scoff. "You really think those little speeches you give at donor events make a difference?" he said, voice dripping with scorn. "Newsflash: those people were already planning to vote for him anyway."

"I'm not talking about that," I said, keeping my head held high. "I was invited to participate in the Veritas Forum, and that'll help his campaign by making voters see that I'm actually invested in the future of this country. Just like him. And that'll give his reputation a nice boost, because it'll make people realize that he raised a daughter who works hard and cares about the same issues they do. Not just some spoiled brat who wants everything handed to her."

Landon frowned, looking slightly taken aback by my diatribe. "I thought only juniors and seniors get invited to the Forum."

"Apparently, there are rare exceptions, and I'm one of them," I said, glad I'd caught him off guard for once.

His eyes narrowed. "So your father's okay with you flying to Anchorage for a week in the middle of one of the most critical parts of his campaign? Even though ninety percent of Alaskans wouldn't vote for him if they were paid to?"

"He's fine with it, because like I said, it'll—" I frowned, cutting myself off. "Hang on, how do you know where it is?"

A wicked smile curved up Landon's lips. "I attended the Forum last year, and I was invited back this year."

My stomach dropped. "You can't be serious."

"I am. If you ever paid attention, you'd know I'm studying poli-sci and economics before I go to law school next year."

I wanted to snap back and tell him I wouldn't pay attention to his life even if my own life depended on it, but, as always, I knew I couldn't push him too far. I was scared of what he might say if I did. Of what he might do.

"Right," I ended up muttering instead. "Congratulations on the invite, I guess."

His wicked grin widened. "Think we'll be sitting together on the plane?" he asked, cocking his head slightly. "Actually, it's two planes to get to Anchorage from here, isn't it?"

"Yes," I said sullenly. "We have to go to Seattle first. But we won't be sitting together."

"You never know," he mused, rubbing his jaw. "Two flights, two chances to sit next to you. Maybe they'll even make us share a hotel room."

I rolled my eyes. "Why would that happen?"

"Anchorage isn't very big, and there'll be a ton of people there for the Forum. So who knows? Maybe we'll wind up in a one bed, two people situation. Like in all those cute romance books you like to read."

My eyes narrowed. How the hell did he know what I liked to read?

"You wish," I muttered.

Landon laughed. "See you around, Aria."

With that, he turned on his heel and stepped away.

I blinked, heart racing, and summoned up a final burst of courage. "Wait," I called out.

Landon turned back, brows furrowing. "Yeah?"

"I was just thinking... seeing as you're apparently such a genius that you got invited to the Veritas Forum twice in a row, you probably know a lot about political history, right?"

"Sure. Why?"

"I was wondering if you've ever heard of a secret society that supposedly operates here in Washington," I said lightly. "My friend's roommate told me about them. They're called the Dominion Club."

I waited for the flash of recognition in Landon's eyes that would confirm his knowledge of the society. Maybe even a flash of anger or concern that his secret side hustle with them had possibly been exposed.

Instead, his expression remained neutral, and he shook his head. "I don't think I've heard of that before."

"Are you sure?" I asked, eyes wide with practiced innocence. I didn't want to give away the fact that I'd noticed the connection between his tattoo and the Dominion Club's logo. It was better to let him think I was merely asking questions based on something a friend of a friend told me. Let him think he had the upper hand.

He nodded. "Sounds like a conspiracy theory or urban legend. Most stories about secret societies turn out to be one of the two," he said. "But you could try the history section. Lots of stuff about myths in there."

"Oh, it's no big deal. I was just wondering because it sounded cool," I said, casually shrugging a shoulder. "But it's probably just an urban legend, like you said."

"Right." Something was flashing in Landon's eyes now, but it wasn't anger or concern. More like curiosity. "By the way, have you checked your emails recently?"

"Um... no," I said, confused by the change of subject. "Not for a few hours. Why?"

"Professor Cosgrove just sent out an email about the Veritas Forum. If you were invited, you should have it too," he said, brows rising slightly. "He wants the ten attending Belgrave students to meet up on Thursday to discuss the game plan for the speech. Four-thirty in Winthrop Hall."

I was aware that the ten of us had to collaborate on a speech about ethics in international relations that one of us—yet to be determined—would present at the Forum, but I hadn't seen Professor Cosgrove's request to meet in person yet.

"Well, I guess I'll see you there," I murmured, wondering how likely it was for a bolt of lightning to strike Landon down between now and Thursday afternoon. Presumably not high, but the weather *had* been pretty nasty lately, and hey... a girl could dream, right?

Landon nodded curtly. "Yeah. See you there."

With that, he turned and strode away, and I resumed my search in the stacks. The next book on my research list had a different code to the last two, which meant it was in the next aisle over.

I turned the corner, my pulse still unsettled from the encounter with Landon. That was when I spotted it: a black hoodie, crumpled on the floor. Next to it, a skull mask, its hollow eye sockets staring up at me.

A fresh wave of unease rippled through me. My mind screamed at me to walk away, to leave it alone, but my body refused to listen. Heart hammering, I took a hesitant step closer, then another, until I was crouching beside the discarded clothing.

I swallowed hard, my fingers hovering over the hoodie before I finally picked it up. It was warm, like it had been worn recently, and beneath the faint traces of fabric softener, there was some other scent. Something familiar.

I brought the hoodie closer to my face, inhaling cautiously. Then I dropped it, heart pounding as I finally placed the scent. It was Landon's cologne.

The realization hit me like a freight train.

I wasn't losing my mind after all. Wasn't hallucinating shadowy figures in masks. It had been Landon all along. Stalking me. Playing these mind games with me. Trying to scare the shit out of me.

And for what? To scare me into submission? To make me look and feel crazy, so that my father could eventually be forced to drop out of the race to focus on my mental health issues?

That motherfucker.

I had absolutely no idea how he'd managed to pull off the incident outside my dorm last week, but at this point, I wouldn't put anything past him. Especially if I was correct about his involvement in the Dominion Club.

I clenched the hoodie tighter in my fist, skin prickling with fury. If Landon thought he could play these games with me— taunt me, stalk me, make me question my own sanity—he was wrong. I wasn't going to run. I wasn't going to cower.

In fact... I was going to stalk him right back.

After all, if he was really part of the Dominion Club, he had to meet up with his fellow members eventually. And when that happened...

I intended to be there.

6

ARIA

OPERATION 'STALK LANDON BACK' WAS AFOOT.

It turned out to be easier than I thought to track the arrogant bastard, thanks to my brilliant bestie. After I filled Sabrina in on the plan, she told me exactly what I needed to do and wrote a special program for it. Then it was *on*.

At the meeting Professor Cosgrove arranged for the Veritas Forum invitees from Belgrave, I'd floated the idea of a shared cloud-based document where all ten of us could casually discuss the event and add our suggestions—keynote speakers we couldn't miss, questions we wanted to ask, or cool spots to visit or eat at in Anchorage whenever we had a bit of downtime from the event, which only ran during the daytime.

Everyone was grateful that I'd taken the initiative to set it up, and all attending students, including Landon, clicked on the link to the document in the email I sent out later.

Of course, it wasn't just a link to a shared document—it was also a phishing link created by Sabrina, designed to give us GPS data from anyone who clicked it. Once they did, backdoor access to their device was granted to the hacker, and all traces of the

67

phishing attempt were erased, ensuring there was no risk of anyone catching on.

Just like that, I had access to Landon's GPS data, as he'd clicked the email link from his phone rather than a laptop, just as Sabrina and I had hoped.

Over the last six days, the two of us had monitored his behavior, but he hadn't gone anywhere strange or suspicious. Mostly lecture halls on campus, his mother's place a couple of times, a house in Dupont Circle which we discovered belonged to his mother's campaign advisor, and a few bars and restaurants.

Now, the map was finally showing something strange.

It was nearly eleven o'clock at night, and Landon was slowly crossing the old graveyard at Belgrave. It was a heritage-listed area on the north side of campus, containing the final resting places of some of the university's earliest founders and a scattering of long-forgotten students, along with one of the oldest churches in the city.

The church was no longer in use—too risky due to its age and deteriorating structure—but it was always listed in Belgrave brochures as an important landmark for visitors to look at because of its striking Gothic architecture.

However, hardly anyone ever did. People were much more likely to visit the historic library, the renowned philosophy hall, or the grand botanical gardens rather than some forgotten chapel nestled amongst the bones of centuries-old university chancellors and fallen scholars.

It was even less likely that someone like Landon would choose to visit it at eleven PM on a Friday night, when most guys his age were out on Tinder dates or drinking themselves stupid at bars.

And yet... he was heading straight for it.

It felt like the perfect place for a secret society's clandestine meeting; a place shrouded in history and undisturbed silence. I absolutely *had* to find a way to be there.

Unfortunately, there was the matter of my security detail.

"Okay, get ready for these fine-ass acting skills," Sabrina said in a playful tone over the phone. "Let me know when you're ready."

"We can do it now," I said, heart racing. The longer it took for me to slip my detail, the more likely it was that I'd miss the Dominion Club meeting. "I'm heading to the door."

"Got it. I'll start crying in three seconds."

I put the phone on loudspeaker, opened my door, and waved at Foster and Sanchez, who were stationed out in the hall for the evening. Foster moved closer, brows furrowing with confusion.

"Please, please, *please* say you'll help me," Sabrina howled down the phone. "I really don't know what else to do. I can't believe I forgot this shit! I'm usually so good at remembering!"

Foster mouthed her name to me with a questioning look in his eyes. I nodded and whispered the words 'possible emergency' back to him, before shrugging like I was just as confused as him.

"Wait a minute," I said to Sabrina. "Why are you even in that class?"

"Because of the stupid new STEM rules!" she said in a tearful tone. She sniffed and went on. "All STEM students, including computer science students, have to do at least two liberal arts classes over the course of their degree. It's meant to broaden our perspective. I picked political history because I thought it would be easy, but I forgot about this essay, and I totally suck at writing them! If I'd remembered sooner, I could've managed it, but there's no way I can get all this done tonight! Not without help."

"Take a deep breath," I said soothingly. "When exactly is it due?"

"Eight o'clock tomorrow."

"That's not so bad. You can wake up early and spend the whole day working on it."

"Eight in the morning, Aria!" Sabrina shrieked. "I'm totally fucked!"

"Oh. Shit."

"None of the other girls here know anything about politics. Plus, most of them are out tonight. Or they already went out and came home wasted," she said. "I know it's really late, but can you please, *please* come over and pull an all-nighter with me? You're so good at this stuff, and I really need you now. *Please*, Aria!"

"I'll try. Just give me a second." I lowered the phone for a moment and looked up at Foster. "Can I go and help her? I know it's late, but she sounds hysterical."

Foster's lips pressed into a thin line. Then he glanced at Sanchez and nodded. "We'll sort it out. Just give us a few minutes to contact the rest of the team."

Fifteen minutes later, I arrived at the sorority house. I felt bad for lying to my agents, but I knew there was no way they'd allow me to sneak off to the old graveyard to stalk the son of my father's biggest rival, so I had no choice but to sneak around behind their backs.

Sabrina greeted me at the door, face arranged in a harried expression. She'd even splashed some eye drops down her face to make it look like she'd been crying. "Thanks so much for coming," she said, throwing her arms around me. After the brief hug, she peered around me, toward Foster. "Are you coming in too?"

He shook his head. "We'll be stationed outside," he said. "Good luck with the paper."

Sabrina gave him a watery smile and thanked him before ushering me in and closing the door. Then her crestfallen expression switched to a bright smile. "I bet you *really* love my dramatic streak now, huh?"

"Always have," I said, grinning.

"I honestly feel like I'm in a movie right now," she went on, rubbing her hands together. "I mean, I just helped the president's daughter slip her security detail. It's so cool."

I laughed. "I'm not out of the woods yet, so to speak."

"True." She nodded toward the stairway. "This way."

She led me down to the basement of the sorority house, her

grip firm around my wrist as she yanked open the door and pulled me inside. The air was thick with the scent of old wood and dust, the dim overhead light flickering slightly.

"Here," she whispered, shoving a bundle of dark clothes into my hands. "Change into these. You'll stand out too much in that."

I peeled off my white sweater and pale blue jeans, trading them for the black hoodie and leggings she'd given me. As I pulled the hoodie over my head, Sabrina dug into her pocket.

"One more thing," she said, holding out her hand, which now contained a crumpled black N95 mask. "You should wear this. It won't cover your eyes, but it's better than nothing, right?"

"Yeah, good idea," I said, hooking the mask straps over my ears.

"Oh, also, you'll need to give me your phone before you go," Sabrina added, still holding her hand out.

I hesitated. "How come? I was going to use it to take photos or videos of the meeting."

"That's a nice idea, but if your Secret Service babysitters are tracking you through it, you could be busted before you even make it two blocks away," she said, raising a brow. "So it's definitely better that you go phoneless."

She had a point. With a sigh, I pulled my phone out and dropped it into her palm. She stuffed it into her back pocket, then nodded toward the far wall.

"The window's over there. It's small, but it opens all the way. You should be able to fit."

I turned and spotted it—a narrow, rectangular window, set high on the basement wall.

"Are you sure the agents won't notice it?"

She nodded. "It's covered in ivy on the outside, so it's almost impossible to notice."

She padded over to it and pried it open, the hinges creaking slightly. Cool night air rushed in, bringing with it the faint scent of damp grass and the campus beyond.

"Come on," she whispered, crouching down. "I'll give you a boost."

I placed my hands on the window ledge and lifted one knee, and she braced her hands against my hips, pushing me up. The rough brick scraped against me as I wriggled through, twisting onto my belly to pull myself out. I clawed at the dirt and ivy on the other side, dragging myself free until I landed in a crouch.

I glanced around. This side of the property was quiet and empty. No movement. No agents lurking in the dark. They were all stationed around the other sides of the house, where there were noticeable entry points.

I turned back to the small window. Sabrina flashed me a worried look. "Be careful, okay?" she whispered.

I nodded, tugging my hood over my head. Then, without another word, I turned and disappeared into the night.

The graveyard would usually be a twenty-minute walk from the sorority house, but I sprinted, so I made it there in ten. Once I'd passed through the arched wrought iron entrance, I headed to the far-right side and moved silently between the rows of tombs and crooked gravestones.

Ahead, the old church loomed. Ivy curled up its stone walls like skeletal fingers, and its arched stained-glass windows were dark except for a faint flicker of golden light glowing from within.

I pressed myself behind a broad, crumbling headstone as movement caught my eye. Shadows shifted between the graves—figures slipping beneath the moonlight, all heading toward the church.

My heart pounded. *I knew it.*

This wasn't just some late-night curiosity like mine. These people knew exactly where they were going and what they were doing.

I flattened myself lower, fingers digging into the cold stone as I watched the last of the figures disappear through the church doors. A hush settled over the graveyard once more, but the flickering candlelight inside promised that whatever was happening in there was just beginning.

I crept up to one of the church windows and peered through it, pulse thrumming in my ears. Two more people entered the church and turned left, their movements practiced and smooth. No hesitation. No uncertainty. They'd done this before.

I watched as they approached a rack on the left-hand side of the church, each grabbing a black hooded robe from the railing. Once they'd slipped into the robes, they headed to a table beside it and grabbed two different masks to put on. Then they headed farther into the church before disappearing behind the altar like dark specters.

My heart soared as I watched. This was my way into the Dominion Club meeting. All I had to do was grab a robe and mask, and I could pretend to be a member.

Part of me worried it was almost *too* easy, but then I considered it from the club's point of view. If they had security guards stationed at the graveyard and church, that could attract suspicion from outsiders passing by on late-night walks. They'd undoubtedly wonder why an old graveyard needed such a serious security presence, and then they'd be more likely to grow curious and explore.

So it made sense for the Dominion Club to simply rely on secrecy and discretion rather than overt security. The isolation of the church on the edge of campus, the eerie reputation of the graveyard—those were deterrents enough. After all, who in their right mind would wander into a decaying relic of the past in the dead of night?

No one... unless they already knew exactly what they were looking for.

My heartbeat sped up as I crept toward the church entrance, keeping my head low. Inside, the air was tinged with the acrid scent of candle smoke.

I moved swiftly to the rack, grabbing one of the robes and

throwing it over my clothes. It was heavier than I expected, the fabric thick and slightly rough. The mask I chose was a simple, faceless design—smooth silver with slits for the eyes. It felt cold against my skin as I slipped it on before pulling the hood lower over my head.

Three more people entered the church just as I finished getting ready. I was afraid they'd try to talk to me, so I ducked down and lowered my gaze, pretending to be deeply interested in tying my shoelace.

Out of the corner of my eye, I watched the newcomers. They didn't pay any attention to me. They simply dressed in robes and masks like the others before them, and then they headed deeper into the church, slipping behind the altar.

I trailed behind them at a careful distance as they moved toward an unremarkable wooden door. To any random outsider, it would probably seem like nothing more than a storage closet. Plain and unassuming, easily overlooked. But the way the masked people moved toward it with purpose, the way none of them hesitated before stepping inside, told me otherwise.

I waited until they'd all slipped through it, and then I slowly approached, heart pounding. As I suspected, it wasn't a normal door. It led to a narrow, spiraling stone staircase that twisted downward into the dark.

The air grew colder as I descended, my footsteps muffled by the ancient stone beneath me. At the bottom of the steps, the passage opened into a dim tunnel. There were no flaming torches as I'd initially pictured in my head—only small iron sconces holding tiny flickering candles that cast shifting shadows along the length of the passage.

At the very end of the tunnel stood two enormous wooden doors, slightly ajar. Beyond them, a low murmur of voices drifted through.

I moved closer, careful to keep my steps silent, and peered inside.

The room beyond was vast and circular, like an underground amphitheater. Tiered rows of stone seating surrounded a central floor, and more robed figures stood along the edges, their faces hidden behind their masks.

I was definitely in the right place. But if I got caught here... *No.* I couldn't think about that.

I took a deep breath and forced myself to step further inside, blending into the crowd as best as I could. People were gathering in small clusters, their hushed conversations echoing off the stone walls. I had no way of knowing which one of them was Landon, but I knew he was here somewhere.

My gaze drifted to the center of the chamber, and everything inside me went cold.

An unmasked man sat strapped to a heavy wooden chair, thick metal cuffs locking his wrists and ankles in place. Despite the dim lighting, I recognized him instantly.

Special Agent Marcus Randall. He was on my father's security detail.

I stared at him, heart hammering. What the hell was he doing here? What were these people planning on doing to him?

My eyes skated over to a table a few feet away from him. Resting on top of it was a glass enclosure. An aquarium. A large snake coiled lazily inside, its smooth, scaled body shifting as it slithered against the glass.

I swallowed hard, a sickening realization creeping in. Something terrible was going to happen here tonight. Something I couldn't do anything to stop without blowing my cover.

I took another deep breath and pressed myself against the back wall, trying not to look at anyone in particular.

"Val?"

A society member approached me, but I kept my head down, pretending I hadn't heard him call out to me. He was tall with a black and red mask that made him look a bit like Darth Maul from Star Wars, minus the facial spikes.

"Val, is that you?" he said, stepping right up to me.

Shit. I had to respond, or else he'd get suspicious.

I turned my head directly toward him, as if I'd only just noticed him. Then I nodded, lifting one hand in a casual wave.

"I thought it was you. Not many other five-foot-nothing members, are there?" he said in a cheerful tone. He cocked his head and went on. "Where were you last week? I didn't see you anywhere."

I motioned to my throat. "Flu," I rasped, hoping that would effectively disguise the fact that my voice didn't actually belong to the woman he knew as Val.

"Oh, damn. You still sound pretty bad," he said, voice tinged with sympathy.

"I feel better, but my voice isn't fully back."

"Ah. I hate it when that happens," he said. He reached out to pat me on the shoulder. "I'm glad you're better, though."

"Thanks."

"Speaking of the flu..." Darth stepped a little closer and ruffled the collar of his robe. "Every time I wear this thing, I feel feverish. It's so damn hot. I'm sweating like a pig under here."

I nodded. "Me too."

"But this is the worst part, isn't it?" he went on, tapping the top of his mask. "These things are always so itchy."

"Yeah. I can't even remember why they make us wear the damn things all the time," I rasped, hoping he'd reply with something useful. For all I knew, the different masks could mean something important to the members. If that was the case, I hoped to God I hadn't picked the wrong one.

"No shit. We all know each other," Darth replied in a sour tone. "But I guess they're right. If an outsider happens to stumble in here one night, they won't be able to identify any of us before we scatter."

"True." I nodded slowly, shoulders sagging slightly with relief. From what Darth had just told me, the masks didn't seem to mean much beyond protecting the members' identities from outsiders, so it was unlikely that I was going to be caught out by anyone for wearing the 'wrong' one.

Another member sidled up to us. This one was wearing a golden mask with a small, curved beak.

"Do either of you have the time?" she asked.

"No, sorry," Darth replied. "I always leave my phone in the car before these things. But it was eleven-thirty when I arrived, and I've been here for around fifteen minutes, so it's probably about a quarter to twelve." He paused and looked at me. "Val, you have a watch, right?"

Gold Beak turned her attention to me, her head tilted in a questioning stance.

I shook my head. "No, sorry," I rasped, rubbing my throat again.

"God, you sound *terrible*," Gold Beak said. "What happened?"

"She had the flu last week," Darth said. "That damn thing's really been making the rounds. Half my office was out from it last week."

Gold Beak was still staring at me. "I'm sorry, Val, but you really can't be here. Not if you're sick."

"I'm fine now," I muttered.

"Yeah, she's past the contagious stage," Darth added. "But her voice isn't back yet."

Gold Beak shook her hooded head. "I hate to sound like such a stickler for protocol, but if there's even the *slightest* chance that you're still sick enough to infect any of us, then you have to go. If it starts spreading around, and we all get sick... well, the work is too important to risk that happening. You know that, Val."

Shit. I couldn't argue. If I did, I might end up getting unmasked... and I didn't even want to know what would happen if these people discovered that 'Val' was actually little old me.

"Okay." I lifted a conciliatory hand. "You're right."

"Don't worry," Gold Beak said. "We'll catch up on Monday. I'll tell you what you missed then."

"Thanks."

"Feel better soon."

Darth and Gold Beak waved at me as I turned away, heading for the doors. I forced myself to walk at a steady pace, as if I truly belonged here, and the moment I stepped into the tunnel beyond, I exhaled deeply, grateful I hadn't been caught out.

I didn't leave immediately. Instead, I crouched near the edge of the passage, pretending to tie my shoelace again as my ears strained for anything useful.

A few more members trickled into the tunnel. None of them paid me much attention—just a few fleeting glances—until one very tall guy stopped in front of me.

"Are you going in?" he asked. "It's almost midnight, so the doors are locking soon."

"Yeah, just a second," I replied in a low mutter. "This stupid shoe..."

He nodded and continued inside. Three minutes later, a deep, resonant gong sounded through the underground space, and the enormous wooden doors creaked shut.

I exhaled slowly, then crept to the right-hand door, pressing my ear against the cold surface.

A deep masculine voice boomed from within. "Hello, everyone," he said. "Thank you for joining us tonight. As you can see, we have a very special guest with us. But before we begin with him, does anyone have anything they'd like to say?"

There was a rustling sound, followed by the murmur of voices.

"You first," the man commanded.

There was a brief scuffing noise—someone standing. Then a woman spoke. "I looked into the logistics again, and Landon was right," she said. "That car bomb wasn't enough to kill Aria Hagan. It needed to be much bigger for that kind of... effectiveness."

My blood ran cold as her words sank in.

The Dominion Club had tried to kill me.

Not scare me. Not warn me. Not force me into obedience. *Kill.* And Landon knew.

The woman continued, her voice as casual as if she were simply discussing a class project. "So, I think we should—"

Someone cut her off. "Hold on. Sorry for the interruption, but... Val? Is that you?" they said. It was Gold Beak.

"Yes, it's me," the woman replied. "Why?"

"Didn't we just kick you out of here a few minutes ago?"

"Excuse me?" Val replied. "You don't have the authority to kick me out. What the hell are you—"

"Sorry, I didn't mean it like *that*," Gold Beak cut in again. "I just meant... you sounded terribly ill. We told you to leave and get some rest."

"I have no idea what you're talking about," Val said. "I'm fine. I haven't been sick in years."

"Well, the woman we spoke to identified herself as Val," another voice said; one I recognized as Darth. "I'm sure of it."

"She was the right height too," Gold Beak added. "I really thought it was you."

"Well, it wasn't!" Val said indignantly. "I didn't talk to either of you before the meeting started."

"If it wasn't you, then who was it?" Darth said. "You're the only person named Val here."

Another voice piped up. "I saw someone outside a few minutes before the doors closed. They were dressed like one of us, so I didn't think much of it at the time, but maybe it was someone trying to sneak in?"

Oh, shit.

It was time for me to get the hell out of here before it was too late. These people had already tried to kill me once. Sticking around any longer would be like handing myself over on a silver platter, gift-wrapped for execution.

I bolted down the tunnel, heart pounding as adrenaline

flooded my veins. The heavy robe tangled around my legs, slowing me down, so I yanked it over my head mid-sprint and tossed it aside. My hoodie and leggings were dark enough to keep me hidden in the shadows for now, but that wouldn't matter if I didn't get out of here fast enough.

Once I reached the spiral stairs, I took them two at a time and hurried back through the church. I burst outside, my breath ragged, my heart slamming against my ribs. The flickering candlelight from inside cast eerie shadows over the graveyard, stretching the stones out like twisted fingers in the dark.

I ran blindly, not knowing where I was going. I only knew that I had to put distance between myself and the people who were undoubtedly heading up the tunnel right now, in search of the intruder.

Suddenly it hit me. There was nowhere to go. No way to outrun them all. I'd counted at least a hundred members down in that place, and that meant they'd be able to spread out every which way in the graveyard and its surroundings.

Panic clawed up my throat, but I forced it down, scanning the graveyard for something—anything—that could save me. My pulse roared in my ears, drowning out the sound of footsteps pounding through the church behind me, and then—

Up.

I hadn't climbed a tree since I was a kid, running from Landon during one of our childhood spy games, but my body still remembered how.

I sprinted toward the nearest oak, its thick, gnarled branches sprawling out like arms reaching for the sky. I caught hold of the lowest branch and scrambled upward, my fingers scraping against rough bark as I pulled myself higher and higher. My muscles burned, but I didn't stop. Not until I was at least ten feet up, perched against a thick bough, my body curled tight against the trunk.

Just in time.

Below, dark figures poured out of the church, their masks glinting under the moonlight as they fanned out across the graveyard. My breaths turned shallow as I pressed my forehead against the bark, heart hammering so hard I was sure they could hear it.

"You go that way!" a voice called out. "And you three—look over there!"

I clenched my hands into fists, nails digging into my palms. I couldn't move. Couldn't make a sound.

I wasn't sure how long I clung to the tree, but it felt like an eternity. I kept worrying that someone would shine a light upward and catch me, but thankfully, it never happened.

"We already told you, she left several minutes before the doors closed," I eventually heard Darth say to someone as a group of six masked members passed by my tree. "She probably had a car nearby, so I bet she's halfway across the city by now."

"Exactly. She's long-gone. Why are we even looking?" Gold Beak grumbled.

"Because someone tried to infiltrate us, and they damn near got away with it," another person snapped. "If they're still around, we need to find them and find out what they know."

"You must've been followed tonight, Val," Gold Beak said, turning to look at the shorter woman.

Val stopped in her tracks, hands on her hips. "Are you serious? I wasn't followed! Do you think I'm stupid?"

"None of us think that, but the intruder was using your name," Darth said, halting along with the others. "So it stands to reason that you were the one being targeted by them."

"Did she *actually* use my name? Or did you just call her by my name, assuming it was me because of her height, and then she went along with it?" Val snapped back.

"I, uhh... well, shit." Darth's tone turned uncertain. "I'm not sure. I can't remember the exact wording of our conversation."

Another member snapped a finger before speaking up. "Listen. I don't know how, but *someone* in our ranks has obviously been compromised," he said. "Have any of you ever said anything to an outsider about this place?"

"No. Like I said, I'm not fucking stupid," Val said. "I would never break my vows."

"No one necessarily broke their vows," another member piped up. "Someone could've been suspected as a member and then targeted by a phishing scam to have their location data tracked. That's how the New Jersey Nightstalker followed his victims around, remember?"

"That's true," Darth said. "Have any of you clicked any weird links lately?"

"No," Val said. "But we should definitely ask everyone else."

"Agreed. Let's get back down there."

The group turned and headed for the church, their voices fading away.

I stayed frozen in the tree, my pulse still hammering against my ribs. I counted the seconds, then minutes, waiting until I was absolutely sure no one remained in the graveyard.

Finally, I uncurled my stiff fingers from the branch and began my descent. My legs trembled as I dropped onto the damp grass, but I didn't waste a second. I took off, slipping through the shadows of the graveyard, past the crumbling tombstones, and back across the darkened campus toward Sorority Row.

By the time I reached the Theta house, my hoodie was damp with sweat, and my lungs felt like they were on fire. I crept along the side of the house toward the basement window, heart pounding as I crouched in front of it.

I'd just gripped the edge of the window frame when a cold, masculine voice cut through the cool air.

"Hello, Aria."

7

ARIA

A CHILL SKATED DOWN MY SPINE AS I WHIRLED AROUND. AGENT Foster stood just a few feet away, arms crossed. Judging by the expression on his face, he wasn't in the mood for bullshit.

"Enjoy your little field trip?" he asked.

My stomach twisted. "I... I was just..."

"Take that mask off, please."

My hands shot to my face. I'd forgotten I was still wearing the silver mask I'd stolen from the old church, along with the black N95 Sabrina gave me earlier. I pulled them both off and let them fall to the ground beside me.

"Do you really think we don't notice when the person we're assigned to protect suddenly disappears?" Foster asked, taking a slow step forward. "Or did you just hope we were all too incompetent to keep up?"

I swallowed hard. "I'm sorry. I was just—"

"Don't even *try* to tell me you just went out to get some fresh air," he cut in, lifting a palm. "Once we realized you'd sneaked out, Sabrina told us everything."

Shit.

"She did?" I asked in a small voice.

"Yes." He arched a brow, unimpressed. "She said you desperately wanted to go dancing at an underground nightclub on Marlow Street, so you two hatched a scheme together so you could sneak out for a few hours."

A wave of relief washed over me. *Thank you, Sabrina.*

I didn't want Foster, or any of my other assigned agents, to know where I'd really gone tonight, because if they found out what I'd seen and heard, they wouldn't let it go. Instead they'd investigate, confront the Dominion Club, and try to handle it the way they were trained to.

And that would very likely get them killed.

I'd learned tonight that not only was the Dominion Club still active, they also had more power and influence than anyone realized. They had no problem taking down federal agents—they'd already captured Marcus Randall tonight—and I also knew they had no problem with killing, given their remarks about me and the car bomb.

Foster didn't deserve to die just because I decided to snoop around the headquarters of a deadly secret society.

"I'm sorry," I muttered. "I just never get the chance to go out and do normal stuff."

"If you wanted to let loose so badly, we could've arranged something." Foster's usually composed expression was tight, his eyes flashing with irritation. "We're a lot more flexible than you think. You should hear some of the things we had to arrange during the last administration. The vice president did things that make your nightclub excursion seem like a visit to a daycare center."

"I'm sorry," I murmured. "If it helps, I was masked the whole time. No one knew it was me. And I didn't drink anything."

"No, that actually doesn't help much," he said coolly, shaking his head. "Do you have any idea what could've happened to you tonight? Do you know what sort of people are out there, just waiting for a chance to get their hands on someone like you?"

"I'm sorry. I really wasn't thinking straight."

"I don't mean to sound like your father. I know that's not my job," Foster went on, lifting a palm again. "But it *is* my job to protect you."

"I know," I said softly. "I messed up."

He exhaled deeply. "I care about you, Aria. Everyone on your detail cares about you. But when you pull a stunt like this, it makes our job a hundred times more difficult. We had no idea where you were. No way to track you. Anything could've happened to you out there. *Anything.* And we would've been powerless to stop it."

Guilt clawed up my throat, and I swallowed hard, wrapping my arms around myself as if that could shield me from the weight of Foster's disappointment.

I'd put him in a terrible position tonight, and I hadn't even considered that until now. If something had happened while I was out earlier—if I'd been taken, hurt, or worse—his job would be on the line. He could've lost everything because of me.

"You're right," I said in a tremulous voice. "I was really selfish tonight. I didn't even consider what might happen to you and the other agents. You could've lost your jobs. I'm really, really sorry."

Foster exhaled sharply, running a hand down his face. When he spoke again, his voice was softer. "Aria, this isn't about my job. That's not why I'm upset," he said. "I just worry about you. We all do. So please... don't do anything like this again."

The knot in my chest tightened, and I dropped my gaze, shame burning through me. "I won't. I swear. It'll never, ever happen again."

"Just let us know next time you want to do something, all right?" he said. "I was your age once. I remember what it was like. All those urges to go out and experience everything the world has to offer," he said. "But I had freedom. I can't even imagine how stifling it must be for you, being followed around all the time, and always having to worry about protecting your father's image."

"Thanks for being so understanding," I replied in a small voice. I still felt terrible, guilt churning in my stomach as if I'd swallowed a bucket of acid.

"I'm serious, Aria. If you want to go out and do something that you think is on the 'forbidden' list, like visiting a bar or nightclub, just let us know. We can sort something out." He paused for a beat, lips curving in a faint smile. "But maybe wait until *after* the election before you think about hitting the clubs, eh?"

I knew that final sentence was meant as a lighthearted remark, and I knew I was supposed to smile back.

Instead, I burst into tears.

Everything I'd seen and heard earlier was finally hitting me, slamming into my chest like a wrecking ball.

The Dominion Club wanted me dead. Not just threatened, not just injured. *Dead*. Their car bomb had failed, but something else was surely in the works, so now it was a matter of waiting for that hammer to drop. Would it be a bomb next time, or would they send someone to finish the job up close? Would my agents be killed alongside me?

There was also the issue of Agent Randall, who was probably suffering right now in that ritual chamber beneath the graveyard.

A sob wrenched from my throat, and I pressed a trembling hand to my mouth. It did nothing to stop the flood of tears, my entire body shaking as fear and guilt tangled inside me.

Foster's expression shifted instantly, all frustration melting away into something else. Something gentler. "Hey," he said, stepping closer. "Aria, it's all right. I didn't mean to make you cry."

"No, *I'm* sorry," I choked out, head shaking. "This isn't... you didn't make me cry. And I'm not trying to manipulate you with tears, I swear. I just..."

Foster hesitated for a second before placing a firm hand on my shoulder. "You're shaking," he said, concern thick in his voice. "Breathe, okay? Just breathe."

I tried, but it felt impossible. My whole world had cracked

open, and the darkness underneath was threatening to swallow me whole.

"What's going on, Aria?" Foster asked, eyes searching my face. "What's gotten you into this state?"

I wanted so badly to tell him, but I couldn't.

"I just... I feel like such a selfish bitch," I murmured, electing to tell the truth but not the whole truth. "I wasn't lying last week when I said you're my favorite agent. You really are. I would never, *ever* want you to get in trouble, but I was so awful tonight. So selfish. I didn't even consider you. And if something happened to you, it would be my fault. All my fault."

"Hey, c'mon." He patted my shoulder again. "You made a mistake, and you apologized. That's good enough for me. You really don't need to beat yourself up."

I swallowed the hard lump in my throat. Guilt was still coursing through my system like toxic sludge. I had to say *something* about Marcus Randall, even if I couldn't tell the truth about where I'd seen him.

I took a deep breath and swiped a hand across my face to remove the tears. "Foster... something happened tonight," I said in a low voice.

He stiffened, eyes widening slightly. "Did a man try—"

"No, no. Nothing like that." I waved a hand. "I'm fine. But you know Special Agent Randall? From my dad's detail?"

"Yes." Confusion flickered in his eyes. "Why?"

"I think I saw him getting attacked."

"Attacked?" Foster's brows shot up. "Where? And by whom?"

"I'm not sure about the exact location, and I didn't have my phone, so I can't check the route I took. But I saw a man beating someone up in an alley, and the one getting attacked looked exactly like Agent Randall. I feel horrible for not doing anything to help. I was scared, so I just... I ran. I left him there."

My voice cracked with emotion on that last part, because it was true.

I *did* leave Agent Randall behind tonight, trapped in that creepy ritual chamber with the entire Dominion Club. If they didn't intend to kill him, they at least intended to torture him, and I'd done nothing to help. Hadn't even tried. Instead, I'd chosen to save myself.

"Oh, Aria." Foster exhaled slowly. "It's very sweet of you to be worried, but I doubt that was Agent Randall. It was probably just someone who looked like him."

I sniffed back another flood of tears. "No, I really think it was him."

"I trained with him back in the day, so I know for a fact that that man can handle himself. So, wherever he is, I'm sure he's fine," Foster said. "And even if it *was* him getting mugged in that alley, you shouldn't blame yourself for running away. You're a small young woman. You can't take on a full-grown man in a fight, let alone someone violent enough to jump a federal agent. Running was the smartest thing you could've done."

I swallowed hard, guilt and fear still twisting in my gut. "But what if he isn't okay? What if he really needed help?"

Foster sighed, rubbing a hand down his face. "Listen, Aria, I get it. You saw something awful, and it shook you up. But if Randall really got in trouble tonight, I'd know about it. Hell, the whole Secret Service would know. No way something like that would stay quiet."

"Maybe no one knows yet," I said. "It could've been his night off. So maybe no one's even realized he's missing yet."

"If it makes you feel better, I'll put in a call soon," Foster replied. "Just to check."

I nodded quickly, relief washing over me. "Thank you. I know I sound kind of nuts. I'm just... I'm really worried."

He studied me for a long moment, his expression softening again. "Can I tell you something? I think it might help."

"Okay," I replied in a ragged murmur. "What is it?"

He smiled faintly. "Do you remember when we got your family together to come up with your code names?"

I did. It was four and a half years ago, right after my father secured his place as a major-party nominee. My mother was still alive then, so all three of us had been assigned a Secret Service detail.

When I nodded, Foster continued. "Do you remember what we told you about how the names are picked?"

"You said most families either pick a meaningful theme or go with words that start with the same letter."

"That's right. Your family went with a royal theme," he said. "Not because you saw yourselves as American royalty, but because of your favorite childhood movie."

"The Princess Bride," I murmured.

"Yes. Your parents said you used to watch it on repeat, and you'd always make them watch it with you when they were free," Foster said, eyes twinkling. "For a while, it was the only time the three of you would actually get to sit down and spend time together, given your father's very busy schedule."

I nodded slowly. "Yeah, that's right."

"We settled on Baron for your father's code, because his favorite part of the movie was the swordfight filmed in the Baron's Hall of Penshurst Place. Your mother was Wish, because she loved the '*As you wish*' line Westley always made to Buttercup. And you were Jewel. Do you remember why we suggested that for you?"

"Because I couldn't pick a word. There were just so many options I liked," I said softly. "You suggested Jewel to me because I loved the necklace Buttercup wore, and 'jewel' sounds way nicer than 'necklace' for a codename."

"That's just what we told you at the time," Foster said, smiling faintly again. "But the truth is, we picked it because from the moment we met you, we could all see that you were the heart of the family. The crown jewel that would always shine the brightest."

My throat tightened, and I looked down, blinking hard. "I don't know about that," I murmured. "I've never thought of myself that way."

"I do. We all do," he replied. "Of course, we aren't meant to pick favorites, but we're only human." He hesitated before lowering his voice. "And your father doesn't exactly make it easy to be anyone's favorite, does he?"

I huffed out a quiet laugh. "I guess he can be kind of abrasive sometimes."

Foster arched a brow. "That's one way to put it. But I never said that, in case anyone asks."

A ghost of a smile tugged at my lips.

"What I *can* say is that you aren't just a job to me, or to the other agents on your detail. We genuinely care about you, and we've always been able to see how kind and resilient you are. It shines through even when you don't believe in yourself."

"Thank you," I murmured. "That really means a lot to me."

"I'm glad to hear it," he said. He straightened his stance and cleared his throat. "Now, let's talk about your sleeping arrangements for tonight. Seeing as your whole detail has already been moved here, and it's very late, we think it's best that you sleep here. The bedroom next to Sabrina's room is free, because one of the girls recently moved out, so you'll be in there. Is that all right?"

"Yes. Thanks for sorting it out."

Foster gave me a nod, his eyes still carrying a layer of concern, before he motioned for me to follow him inside the sorority house. My head was still spinning. The threats from the Dominion Club, the horrifying realization of how close I'd come to danger, and the overwhelming guilt that refused to release its claws... it all felt wildly suffocating.

I made my way to the bedroom he'd mentioned and said good-

THE WILD

night to him and Sanchez, who would be joining him in guarding the hall. The room was spacious and comfortable, and the faint scent of lavender in the air calmed me slightly, helping with the chaos still churning inside.

I shed my clothes and sat on the edge of the bed, letting out a deep breath. Someone—presumably Sabrina—had left my phone and purse on the small white bedside table, next to the lamp.

I switched off the lamp and lay back, staring at the ceiling as I replayed every moment from tonight in my mind. I wasn't sure how long I lay there, trapped in my thoughts, but eventually, sleep claimed me, though it was fitful at best.

I was woken just after two in the morning by my phone pinging with a message notification. I yawned and rolled over, blinking the sleep out of my eyes as I reached for the table to grab my phone. The message was from an unsaved number.

Did you have fun stalking me tonight?

I sat up straight, heart pounding. It had to be Landon, surely. Who else would send a message like that?

I switched to my email folder and opened the list of Veritas Forum attendees that Professor Cosgrove had sent out last week, which included every participant's email address and number.

Yup. It was definitely Landon.

I tapped out a reply, deciding to play dumb. *What are you talking about? Who is this?*

You know who it is, and you know exactly what I'm talking about, he shot back.

I really don't, I said. *But I'm assuming this is Landon, given the nasty tone. Please lose my number.*

His next reply took a little longer.

Play innocent if you want, but I know it was you, princess. You were at the DC meeting tonight. I have to admit, I'm actually impressed you got so far. You might be one of the first people to manage that in decades.

Me: *I have no idea what meeting you're talking about. I've been in my* dorm all night.

 Landon: **No, you haven't.**

 Me: *How could you possibly know that? Are you creeping around on my balcony in a gas mask again? PS. I know that was you, so don't even try to deny it.*

 Landon: **I know you aren't in your dorm, because I'm standing in it.**

 My blood ran cold. Heart in my mouth, I tapped out another message.

 Me: *Get the hell out of there. Right now.*

 Landon: **Relax. I'm not actually in your dorm. But now I know you lied to me about being in there. So where are you, princess? Still hiding in an old tomb, or wherever else you managed to sneak off to earlier?**

 Me: *I'm at the Theta house, because I was studying with the girls all night. I didn't tell you because it's none of your business. And stop calling me princess.*

 Landon: **Ah. You're with Sabrina. I'm guessing she helped you with that phishing link you sent me.**

 Me: *I really have no idea what you're talking about. Please stop harassing me.*

 Landon: **You always were a little brat when we were kids. I see nothing's changed. Maybe some punishment would fix your attitude.**

 My fingers hovered over the screen, my breath catching in my throat. I hated how Landon's words sent a shiver down my spine; how they stirred something deep within me that I'd tried so hard to bury.

 Why did he have to be like this? How did he know exactly how to get under my skin?

 I clenched my jaw, determined not to give him the satisfaction of a response. But then my phone buzzed again.

 Landon: **Still there, little brat? Or did I scare you off?**

 Little brat. The words sent a slow, unwelcome heat curling through my stomach, tangling with my frustration. God, he was infuriating. Always had been. Always knowing exactly how to press my buttons until I was burning with need.

The smart thing would be to ignore him. Let him think I wasn't affected. Instead, I typed before I could stop myself.

Me: *I'm not scared. I just didn't reply because I think it's weird as hell that you're thinking about me as a kid. Now leave me alone.*

Landon: **Oh, please. You know exactly what I meant. I was talking about you right now, as an adult woman. A very bratty woman in serious need of a hard lesson.**

My cheeks flushed, and I dropped my phone and squeezed my eyes shut, trying to ignore the heat pooling in my stomach. This was ridiculous. I shouldn't be feeling this way. Not about *him*. Not after everything.

But my traitorous body didn't seem to care about 'shouldn't'.

Against my better judgment, my right hand slowly edged its way down to my underwear. I inhaled deeply and slid my fingertips inside, grazing my clit. I was already wet, and a tingle was starting to move down my spine.

Images from earlier in the night began to play out in my head like a movie, but this time, it all turned out differently in the end.

This time, Landon spotted me in the ritual chamber, eyes pinning me through the dark holes of a skull mask. I tried to flee, terrified for my life, but he caught me and roughly dragged me to the center of the room. Then he stripped me and tied me to the chair in a bent-over position before savagely claiming me in front of all the other masked people, leaving bruises on my hips from his iron grip and red, stinging skin from the blows he rained down on my ass.

I begged for mercy, begged for him to spare my life when it was over, but he ignored my pleas. He grunted and groaned as he fucked me harder, somehow knowing that I truly did want him despite my claim otherwise. He took my pussy first, leaving me aching with a twisted need for more, and then he switched to my ass, only using spit as lube so that the pleasure unfurling within me would be laced with pain.

"You love taking it in the ass, don't you, princess?" he muttered in my ear as his cock slammed inside me again. "You love being a filthy little slut for me."

One hand went around my throat as he spoke, squeezing it until my air was almost cut off. He was ten times stronger than me, body rippling with muscle, so if he wanted to, he could seriously hurt me. Knowing that and feeling his hand around my throat made me feel utterly helpless and yet so unbelievably alive at the same time.

He was right. I loved it.

"Y-yes," I choked out.

"Look at you now, baby. The precious, innocent daughter of the president with the cock of his worst enemy's son in her tight little ass," he growled, thrusting into me again. "What would people say if they knew, Aria? What would they do?"

My orgasm hit me then, body trembling in the bed as stars exploded across my vision. I pressed my lips tightly together to stop myself from moaning, and after one last jolt, I rolled over, panting.

My phone buzzed a moment later. Landon again.

Still struggling to catch my breath, I unlocked my phone and read the message.

Stay away from the Dominion Club, or you'll regret it.

I tapped out a response, trying to steady my trembling hands.
I'm not scared of you, Landon.

The words felt hollow as they left my fingertips. I was trying to sound confident, like I was totally in control, but my heart was hammering in my chest, and a cold sweat was dripping down my back. I wasn't fooling anyone, especially not Landon.

I *was* scared of him. Terrified, in fact. No amount of defiance could erase that, but I wasn't going to let him see it.

Not now. Not ever.

8

ARIA

I BOARDED THE PLANE, SLIPPING PAST THE FIRST-CLASS SECTION without a second glance. My father had offered, of course, but I knew what he really thought. *Flying first class on taxpayer money isn't a good look.* I agreed. Besides, I didn't need luxury. I just needed to get to Alaska.

Usually, the children of presidents were able to fly on private government planes to avoid all the public scrutiny that came with flying commercial, but I wouldn't have felt right taking one of those planes for the same reason I didn't feel comfortable traveling in first class. It just felt so indulgent and snobbish to fly privately when all the other Veritas attendees were flying commercially, and I wanted to fit in. Not act like I considered myself to be above them in some way.

The aircraft I'd just boarded was slightly smaller than the first jet I'd taken from DC to Seattle, with only two seats in the side rows instead of three. My agents were strategically placed—two ahead of me, two behind—as we headed down to the back of the plane. I'd specifically requested a seat there, because I knew most of my fellow Veritas attendees were sitting in the back too, and I wanted to be close to them.

Someone ahead of us was taking a while to load their carry-on into the overhead compartment, so the queue came to a standstill. While we waited, Agent Foster turned his head over his shoulder to look at me, one brow slightly raised. "Getting excited yet?"

I grinned and nodded. "I've been excited for the last four weeks."

"Understandable," he said, eyes twinkling. "I've been looking into this event. Did you know every single president we've had over the last eighty years was a Veritas attendee in their college days?"

"Yup."

"Maybe I'll see another President Hagan in my lifetime, then," he said, raising a brow again.

I laughed softly. "Maybe. But let's not get too far ahead of ourselves."

The line finally started moving again. Foster briskly turned back to face ahead, leading me farther down the aisle.

He'd done as I asked four weeks ago and enquired about Agent Randall's wellbeing, and I was relieved to learn that the man was still alive. However, the Dominion Club had definitely gotten to him the night I spotted him in their ritual chamber.

Later that same night, he'd been dropped off at a hospital emergency department by an anonymous person who claimed to have found him lying on the ground while out on a late-night stroll. He was unconscious with three snake bites on his body and a boatload of venom coursing through his system.

When he finally woke up, he informed his medical team that he'd been walking his dog by a creek near his house, and a snake had slithered out from the nearby reeds and bitten him, presumably spooked by the dog's barking.

THE WILD

I knew that wasn't true, but I understood why he'd chosen to lie. The Dominion Club must've threatened him with repercussions if he told the truth about the torture he'd undergone that night. Repercussions so terrible that he was still afraid for his wellbeing despite being surrounded by fellow Secret Service colleagues day in, day out.

I'd gone to visit him in hospital a couple of times—under the pretense of delivering flowers and passing along well wishes from my father—hoping for a chance to speak with him privately about what had happened. Unfortunately, he was asleep both times I visited, and I couldn't return after that.

After all, repeatedly visiting his hospital room was bound to attract suspicion from certain eagle-eyed observers, and the last thing my father's campaign needed was whispers of a scandal, with rumors flying about his daughter having an affair with a member of his security team.

So, after everything that had happened, I still had no idea what the Dominion Club was really after, or what they wanted from me... apart from my death, of course. That much was clear. What I couldn't understand was *why* they were so determined to see me dead.

The only conclusion I could draw was that it was a power play set up by Celeste Ashford—a way to destroy my father and tip the election in her favor. But that seemed utterly psychopathic. Even though she was my father's long-standing rival, I just couldn't see her doing something that awful.

Her son, on the other hand...

Foster turned back to me. "Almost there. 57A for you, right?"

I nodded. The aisle seat beside my window seat was vacant when we made the booking, but as I glanced up, I noticed a black case crammed into the overhead compartment above row 57. Someone must've claimed the seat after we'd secured mine.

I hoped it was Shaye Setton. She was one of my fellow Veritas attendees, and she was absolutely lovely. Also, after spending the entire flight to Seattle alone, I wouldn't mind having some company.

I craned my neck to look past my agents, and my face instantly fell when I saw the person who'd taken 57B.

It was Landon.

"You've got to be kidding," I muttered.

He smirked when he saw me approaching. "What a coincidence," he said, rising to his feet and stepping into the aisle so I could get to my window seat. "We're sitting together after all."

"I have a feeling this isn't a coincidence at all," I said stonily.

He held out one hand, gesturing for me to give him my carry-on bag. "Please, allow me. It's hard for you to reach."

I ignored his attempt at niceties and stood on my tiptoes to shove the bag in the overhead compartment myself. Then I slid into my window seat, trying to ignore the furious heat flooding my cheeks.

Landon settled back in his seat and looked over at me, lips still quirked in that irritating smirk of his. "Looking forward to flying together?" he asked.

"I'm looking forward to opening the emergency exit and throwing you out at 30,000 feet," I muttered.

His wicked grin widened like that was the exact response he wanted.

Before I could come up with something sharper, the pilot's voice crackled over the intercom.

"Ladies and gentlemen, due to the storm system moving in from the Pacific, we'll need to alter our flight path. Normally, we'd head directly northwest over the Gulf of Alaska, but for safety reasons, we'll be flying due north first, right into Canada, before cutting west to Anchorage. Unfortunately, this will add approximately two and a half hours to our total flight time. We deeply apologize for the inconvenience, but your safety is our top priority. On the bright side, you'll get a fantastic view of the Canadian

Rockies as we pass over them. Once again, my apologies for the inconvenience, and I hope you enjoy the flight."

A groan slipped out before I could stop it.

An extra two and a half hours next to Landon. *Great.*

The plane taxied down the runway, and my fingers tightened around the armrest as the aircraft lifted off, tilting upward into the sky.

Landon shifted beside me, stretching his long legs into the limited space between the seats. "Not a nervous flyer, are you?" he asked, voice dripping with dark amusement.

No.

It wasn't that I was afraid of flying. I was afraid of the guy I was stuck sitting next to for the next six hours. I wouldn't give him the satisfaction of letting him know that, though.

Ignoring him, I closed my eyes and let my head rest against the window. I needed to get some sleep. Not just to avoid Landon, but because I wanted to be well-rested for my arrival in Anchorage.

I slowed my breathing, letting the low murmur of voices and the steady drone of the engines lull me into a light slumber.

When I woke up, the cabin was dim, the overhead lights turned down to a soft glow. A glance at my watch told me I'd been out for three hours. Landon was watching a movie beside me, headphones in, while most of the other passengers were asleep, heads tilted against seats and bodies wrapped in blankets. Even my agents, always hyper-aware, seemed at ease.

Despite that, something seemed strangely off. I felt it deep down, an unease thrumming inside me, quiet but insistent.

I sat up straight, senses sharpening as I took in my surroundings.

The flight attendants were moving quickly up and down the aisles, their usual polished efficiency replaced with something more urgent. Their faces were composed, but their movements betrayed them—too brisk and harried. On top of that, their calm demeanors seemed forced, like actors trying to hide their nerves onstage.

One whispered something to another near the galley, then hurried away. I sat up even straighter, my pulse ticking up a notch as the subtle tension in the air began to weave its way into my skin. Something was definitely wrong. I just didn't know what.

As another attendant hurried back down the aisle, I lifted my hand to attract her attention. "Excuse me."

She stopped and leaned in slightly, giving me a polite smile. "What can I do for you, ma'am?"

"I was just wondering... is everything all right with the flight?"

"Yes, ma'am, everything is totally fine," she said. She sounded calm, but her smile looked tight, and it didn't quite reach her eyes. "Can I bring you anything?" she added. "A drink? Hot towel?"

"No thanks, I'm okay," I replied. "Sorry to bother you."

"It's no bother. Let me know if you need anything."

With that, the attendant continued on her way to the back of the plane. I watched her go, stomach still twisting with uncertainty.

Landon pulled his headphones out and followed my gaze, brows furrowing. "Is something wrong?" he asked, turning back to look at me.

I slowly shook my head. "She said everything's fine," I replied. I let out a heavy sigh and pinched the bridge of my nose before going on. "I just... I don't know. The attendants are all rushing around, and I'm picking up a really weird vibe. But I guess it's nothing."

I wasn't sure why I'd told Landon any of that. He wasn't my friend. Quite the opposite, in fact.

He briefly glanced toward the aisle again. "They're probably just getting the food service ready," he said. "There's a lot of passengers to feed, and they have to do it fast to make sure everyone eats at the same time. Pretty stressful work."

I exhaled slowly, shaking off the unease creeping up my spine. "Yeah, you're right," I murmured. "It's probably just that."

Forcing my muscles to relax, I leaned my head back against the window and closed my eyes again. Sleep didn't come as easily this time, but I focused on steadying my breath, pushing away the nagging sense of wrongness. Eventually, the quiet hum of the cabin and the gentle vibration of the plane lulled me into a doze.

A sudden, earsplitting bang from somewhere at the back of the plane jolted me awake again.

"What the hell was that?" a man shouted amidst the panicked shrieks filling the cabin.

A split-second later, the plane lurched violently to the left.

More screams filled the air as overhead compartments snapped open, luggage tumbling into the aisle. Flight attendants were thrown off their feet, slamming against seats and armrests, and one of them shouted for everyone to put on their seatbelts, her voice filled with panic.

The lights flickered, then went dim as the plane tilted sharply to the right to regain its usual position. The sudden shift made my stomach lurch.

"What the fuck just happened?" someone shouted. "What was that noise?"

"Fasten your seatbelts, please!" one of the flight attendants shouted, her voice strained as she tried to push herself up off the ground, clearly disoriented.

I gripped my armrests, knuckles turning white, as my heart pounded in my chest like it wanted to leap right out.

For several painstakingly-long minutes, the plane remained steady. The commotion finally began to die down, though the uneasy murmurs of concerned passengers still swirled around us. No one was screaming anymore, which should've been a good thing, but the quiet was suffocating, as if we were all waiting for the next shoe to drop.

"Are you all right, Aria?" Foster asked from the seat behind mine.

I leaned over in my seat, peering through the small gap between us. His face was tight, his eyes scanning the cabin with the same nervous energy I felt bubbling inside me.

"I feel like I just had a heart attack," I said, my voice shaky. "But apart from that, I'm fine. Are you okay?"

He nodded, his jaw clenched. "That was a rough few minutes," he muttered. "But they seem to be getting it under control. I think we'll be okay now."

As if on cue, the plane began to settle back into its usual rhythm. The tension in the air didn't lift, but at least the ride wasn't as bumpy.

Ten minutes passed, but every second felt like an eternity. The flight attendants slowly regained their composure, standing up with varying degrees of effort. Some went to check on the passengers, others hurried to the back or front of the plane, their faces drawn but composed. They dodged questions with rehearsed calm, offering little more than, *'Please don't worry, we're checking on everything now.'*

That response didn't exactly ease my nerves. We'd all just been through something terrifying, and now we were supposed to trust that everything was fine because they said so?

At the same time, I had to admit that the attendants likely knew just as little as the rest of us. The tilt we'd experienced, and the unnatural noise, had clearly been more than a simple turbulence shift. Something had clearly gone wrong with the tail, forcing the plane into a sudden, uncontrolled tilt, and it was only thanks to the pilots' quick thinking and skill that we hadn't dropped from the sky.

I turned to look at Foster again, my voice barely above a whisper. "Do you have any idea what could've caused that bang?"

He set his jaw, his eyes narrowing as he processed the question. After a moment, he shook his head slowly. "Bird strike, maybe? But honestly, I don't know. Whatever it was, it seems like the pilots have it under control now."

"It was scary as hell," I said, my voice trembling despite my best efforts to steady it. "I honestly thought we were going to crash."

"We're okay." He gave me a faint smile, though it didn't reach his eyes. "But I've got a feeling we might all decide to sail back to DC when the Veritas Forum is over."

I returned his small, weak smile. "A cruise would be nice right about now."

Another half hour passed without incident, and I finally began to breathe easy again. I couldn't possibly sleep after everything that had happened—I'd probably be awake for the next three days, replaying the terrifying moments in my mind—but at least the plane wasn't hurtling toward the side of a mountain, or any of the other worst-case scenarios my brain had concocted in the aftermath of that bang.

Then, without warning, an alarm blared through the cabin; a shrill, ear-piercing sound that made my heart skip a beat. A red light blinked urgently at the front of the plane, and panicked shouts erupted from all around us.

"What the hell is happening now?" someone yelled, standing up in the middle row.

"Are we going to make it to Anchorage or not?" another passenger shouted, their voice sharp with fear. "Why aren't you telling us anything?"

The flight attendants sprang into action, racing up and down the aisles, their faces drained of color. Despite the panic spreading, they were doing their best to maintain calm, offering only vague assurances. "Please stay seated and fasten your seatbelts," one of them called out, but it was clear from their expression that they were just as in the dark as the rest of us.

I clawed at my seatbelt with trembling hands, making sure it was still locked in place. Then I turned toward the window beside me, opened the shade, and looked out, heart pounding.

The jagged peaks of the Canadian Rockies stretched below, without any hint of civilization in sight. Thick evergreens covered the mountainsides, their dark green canopies interrupted only by the occasional rocky outcrop or glimmering ribbon of a winding river.

It was all far too close, and it was getting even closer by the second.

"Oh my god," I said in a ragged whisper to no one in particular. "I think we're going down."

Landon leaned over my lap so he could see what I was seeing. "Holy fuck," he said, eyes widening. His voice was low, almost detached, but the panic in his expression was unmistakable. "You're right."

"What the fuck is happening?" a woman screeched from somewhere ahead of me.

"We're crashing!" a man shouted back. "We're fucking *crashing*!"

The cabin filled with screams and cries again, rising to a fever pitch. Landon's voice cut through the chaos again, and I whipped my head around to look at him.

"I never thought they'd take it this far," he said woodenly, staring directly ahead. His eyes were filled with a mixture of shock and grim resignation. "Not in a million years."

"*What?*" I said, confusion gnawing at my already-churning stomach. "What the hell are you talking about?"

His mouth moved, but I couldn't hear his response over the sudden deafening roar that filled the cabin.

The plane dropped, plummeting fast and hard.

Oxygen masks dropped from the overhead panels with sharp metallic clicks, swinging wildly as we continued our terrifying descent. A choked gasp caught in my throat as I grabbed mine with trembling fingers and fumbled to pull it over my face.

In my panic, I couldn't get it to go on properly, but Landon helped me, his hands steady as he guided the elastic over my head and pressed the mask firmly against my nose. "Breathe," he shouted. "You'll be okay."

My breath came in frantic, shallow bursts, fogging up the plastic as the sharp, artificial scent of oxygen filled my nostrils. *This isn't happening,* I tried to tell myself. *It's just a bad dream.*

I knew that wasn't true, though. I also knew that Landon was wrong. I wasn't going to be okay. None of us were.

The alarm kept blaring, high-pitched and relentless, a terrifying counterpoint to the screams echoing throughout the cabin. My stomach flipped as the plane shuddered violently, sending another spike of icy panic through my veins.

This was it. We were all going to die in the next few minutes. Possibly even seconds.

Landon's hand suddenly found mine, gripping it so tightly it almost hurt. I turned to him, my eyes wide with terror.

He yanked his oxygen mask off, leaning in so close I could feel the heat of his breath against my skin. His voice was sharp, fighting to rise above the deafening chaos. "I need to tell you something, Aria," he said, his eyes flickering with something I couldn't quite place. Something raw, vulnerable, and entirely unlike him. "I've always wa—"

Another violent lurch sent people flying against their restraints, and there were more piercing screams, drowning out Landon's voice yet again. Those sounds were followed by a deafening crack from somewhere outside.

The plane shuddered again, metal groaning under the strain, and my breath caught in my throat as I snapped my head back to the window, registering just how close we were to the treetops.

The forest was now rushing toward us at an impossible speed. Sunlight glinted off a river snaking through a nearby valley, the beauty of the untouched wilderness at sharp odds with the horror clawing through my chest.

I couldn't scream. Couldn't even speak or breathe. All I could do was stare in silence, utterly paralyzed with fear, as the forest rushed up to meet us.

The last thing I saw was a blur of dark green, and then... *impact.*

Agony exploded through my body as I was slammed forward.

The world tilted, twisted, shattered—

And then everything went black.

9

ARIA

A LOW, ACHING THROB PULSED THROUGH EVERY INCH OF MY body, dragging me up from the depths of unconsciousness. My head felt too heavy for my neck, and my limbs felt stiff and bruised. The taste of metal coated my tongue, and a deep cold had seeped into my bones.

I blinked sluggishly, my vision swimming as I tried to make sense of where I was. Above me, the sky stretched out, a blue so brilliant it looked like something off a postcard. A jagged tree line framed the horizon, the dark green canopy standing stark against the bright daylight.

I was lying on something soft, but I had no idea what it was. I weakly tapped one hand beside myself to find the plush fabric of a blanket. Someone must've moved me. But why? What happened? I couldn't think straight. Couldn't remember anything.

Think harder, I told myself. *You need to remember.*

A distant murmur of voices filtered in, growing sharper as I forced myself to focus. People were moving around the small clearing surrounding me, their figures shifting through the periphery of my blurred vision. Some were limping, while others crouched over what appeared to be motionless bodies.

Oh, god...

Something terrible had happened. Bits and pieces were coming to me in short flashes now, but I couldn't tell if they were real or simply from a dream. My mind was still too muddled, the images too hazy.

My fingers curled against the blanket, numb and slow, as if my body wasn't fully my own anymore. Footsteps approached. A shadow fell over me.

"Aria."

I turned my head, wincing as pain flared at the base of my skull. Landon was crouched beside me, his expression unreadable, jaw tight with something that looked almost like relief.

I swallowed hard, my throat raw and dry. "I had a horrible dream," I choked out.

"That wasn't a dream," he said. "It happened. We survived."

I stared at him, my pulse hammering in my ears.

No.

This *had* to be a dream. A horrible nightmare.

"I..." My voice broke. I swallowed again, forcing the words out. "The plane—"

"It crashed," Landon said. No mocking smirk, no sarcasm. Just grim bluntness. "But you're okay. You took a rough hit, but you're in one piece."

I blinked, struggling to grasp if this was truly happening or just a crazy hallucination. Landon certainly seemed real, and the pain in my body was undeniable, but somehow, it still felt like a dream, distant and surreal.

"My head hurts," I murmured.

"I think you hit your forehead on the screen in front of your seat," he said, eyes skating upward. "It's bruised. Badly. But that seems like the extent of the damage to your head."

I groaned and tried to sit up. As I did so, a searing pain shot through my ankle, and I winced, sucking my lips against my teeth.

"Yeah, don't do that," Landon said, shifting closer. "Your left ankle's badly swollen. You need to stay off it for a while."

"Is it broken?" I rasped.

He shook his head. "I think it's just a sprain," he said. "You're very lucky. Nothing else is broken, either."

I blinked, mind still swimming with a mix of confusion and dread. "Maybe there's something under my clothes. Everything hurts."

"I checked earlier, and you're fine. Just some minor cuts and bruises," he said. He shifted even closer. "I know how you feel. Like you just got hit by a truck. I feel it too. But you got lucky. You're gonna be fine."

Under normal circumstances, the thought of Landon Ashford lifting my clothes to examine me while I was unconscious would've mortified me. But right now, all I felt was relief that I was still alive. Relief that I was okay aside from a few bumps and scratches.

I exhaled shakily, pressing a hand to my temple. "The plane," I whispered. "How... how many..."

Landon glanced away for a second, as if debating how much to tell me. Then his gaze met mine again, and I saw the answer before he even spoke. "The front took the worst of it," he said. "Most of them didn't make it. Over a hundred. And the ones from the front that *did* make it... I don't think they'll last much longer."

A hollow ringing filled my ears, my heartbeat pounding against my ribs.

"Other survivors?" I rasped.

"So far, about twenty," he said. "But we're still pulling people out. There's definitely more."

My stomach twisted, and I turned my head, eyes scanning the small clearing around us. "Where's Foster?" I asked, heart hammering in my chest. My eyes shot back to Landon. "He's okay, right? And the others? Are they pulling people out like you said?"

Landon shook his head. "Sorry, Aria," he said gruffly. "Your agents didn't make it."

I blinked, the words barely registering. "They did. They had to."

His mouth pressed into a thin line, and he shook his head again. "I'm sorry. All four of them are gone."

"No. *No*. That... that can't be right," I said, voice hitching. "They were practically right next to us. If we survived, they should have too."

Landon let out a heavy sigh. "I really wish that was how it worked."

A sharp, keening pressure built in my chest, something hot and unbearable pressing against my ribs.

My agents. They'd been there, right beside me. Always. And now... now they were just *gone*. It didn't seem possible.

"Can you check again?" I asked, words coming out thick and husky. "Maybe they're just unconscious like I was?"

Landon exhaled deeply, rubbing his forehead. "Trust me, Aria. They didn't make it."

The world blurred as devastation roared through me. I was alive, and the agents weren't. It wasn't fair.

And they were dead because of me.

The awful thought lodged itself deep, a jagged icicle twisting in my guts. I knew it wasn't my fault that the plane crashed, but it *was* my fault that all four agents were on it with me. If I hadn't insisted on doing things differently, we would've taken a private government jet. One that wouldn't have gone down in a freak accident like this one had. We'd all be in Anchorage right now, safe and warm. Alive.

I swallowed hard and squeezed my eyes shut, pressing my trembling fingers against my forehead. *My fault, my fault, my fault.*

"I can tell what you're thinking, and it's not your fault this happened," Landon said in a brusque tone that didn't quite match the compassionate nature of his words. "Seriously, Aria. It's not your fault they died."

I couldn't reply. Emotions were rising too thickly in my throat, choking off any words before they could form.

"If it's any consolation, it happened instantly for them," Landon went on. "Judging by what I saw."

"Are you sure?" I managed to choke out, eyes fluttering open again.

He nodded. "They didn't suffer. I'm certain of it."

I didn't ask exactly what he'd seen to make him so certain. I couldn't bear to think of it. I just wanted to remember the agents as they were before this horrible tragedy. Not by the way they looked now.

I slowly managed to push myself upward, resting my weight on one elbow. Bile rose in my throat as I took in the sight of the wreckage ahead of me.

It stretched out in jagged, broken pieces across the forest floor. The plane's wings were completely gone, and the fuselage lay in massive, dented sections, some parts crushed beyond recognition while others remained eerily intact.

The middle and rear sections were still largely in one piece, though warped and split in places, the metal crumpled and peeling away like torn paper. The rows of seats inside were twisted and displaced, some hanging at unnatural angles while others were missing entirely. Overhead compartments had burst open, spilling luggage and debris everywhere.

The front of the plane... I couldn't look for long. Most of it was unrecognizable. A mangled heap of steel and shattered windows, crushed against the trees like a discarded toy. No wonder hardly anyone made it out of there.

Beyond the wreckage, the towering evergreens stood like silent sentinels, their thick trunks scorched and stripped where the plane had torn through. Broken branches littered the ground, mingling with scraps of fabric, metal shards, and the personal belongings of passengers.

Smoke still curled up from where the wreck had gouged into the earth, but there were no flames. No raging inferno consuming everything in its wake. Just the cold, awful reality of all the destruction.

"I can't believe it really happened," I said in a hollow voice.

"Me neither." Landon slowly shook his head. "And I can't believe so many of us survived. At least ten percent of the passengers. Maybe even more."

"What are the chances of that?" I asked. "Do you have any idea?"

He shook his head. Then he leaned down to pick up a bottle of water and pressed it into my hands. "You should drink this," he said, his voice steady despite everything. "It'll help."

I hesitated, my fingers barely working as I fumbled with the cap. He helped me twist it off, watching closely as I took a sip.

It felt weird, being around Landon like this. Back in our usual world, we were enemies, but right now, we were united by the shock and devastation of the crash, and all the issues I had with him and his cronies in the Dominion Club suddenly seemed to be a million miles away.

In a moment like this, it was easy to look past his shocking personality and acknowledge what every other straight woman saw when they caught sight of him: he was stupidly, infuriatingly gorgeous. The kind of attractive that made heads turn in every room he walked into, with those piercing eyes that could strip a person bare with a single look.

Even now, disheveled from the crash with dirt smudged along his temple and a cut trailing down the side of one cheek, he radiated something magnetic. Something impossible to ignore.

I hated that I noticed it. Hated even more that, for what was definitely *not* the first time, I wasn't sure I wanted to look away.

"You said I'm not injured, apart from the sprained ankle," I said after I swallowed the water. "But what about you? Anything broken?"

He shook his head. "I'm pretty sore, but apart from that, I'm fine. We both got really lucky."

As he spoke, a small, hesitant figure appeared at his side. She was tiny. Couldn't be more than eight years old, with tangled brown hair and wide blue eyes. She was a little dirty, but I couldn't see a single cut or bruise on her, let alone any obviously-broken bones.

"Could I please have some water?" she asked in a timid voice, eyeing the bottle in my hand.

I handed it straight to her. "Of course you can," I said, gaze quickly skating over her again to check for any injuries that I might've missed the first time. "Are you okay?"

She nodded. "I'm just thirsty."

"Where did you come from?" Landon asked, crouching to meet her gaze. "I didn't see you earlier."

After the girl had taken a sip of water, she pointed to the wreckage. "I was sitting at the front."

Landon and I exchanged a stunned glance. No one had survived from that section. At least not in one piece. But here was this little girl with barely a scratch on her. It was a miracle.

I sat up straighter, ignoring the sharp protest of my muscles. "What's your name, sweetheart?"

"Hannah," she said, rubbing at her tear-streaked face.

"Were you flying with your parents, Hannah?"

She shook her head. "No, I was by myself."

Landon frowned. "You were *alone?*" he said sharply.

"Yes. I live with Mommy in Seattle, but Daddy lives in Anchorage. I was going to visit him, and one of the ladies from the plane was looking after me. But..." Hannah blinked, eyes brimming with tears. "She... she's not okay now. She was lying on top of me and I had to crawl out."

I winced at the thought of her crawling out from under the

flight attendant's corpse, only to find herself surrounded by hundreds of other broken, bloodied bodies. The poor kid. She must've been terrified.

Landon patted her shoulder. "You're a very brave kid, Hannah," he said. "We're gonna take care of you until you can get back to your mommy or daddy, okay?"

She nodded quickly, sniffling.

"We won't be stuck here for long," I added, reaching for her hand. "The rescue team will get our signal and come for us as soon as they can."

She blinked up at me, her tiny fingers curling into my own. "Do you promise?"

"I promise. It might take them a while to fly here, but they're definitely coming," I said, forcing my lips into a small, encouraging smile. "Planes have emergency beacons that get activated when they crash. So all we have to do is wait."

Landon stood, scanning the clearing around us. More survivors had gathered—around thirty now. Some sat on the ground, staring blankly ahead, while others sobbed quietly for lost loved ones.

A few were very badly hurt. One man lay a few yards away, his leg twisted unnaturally beneath him, the bone pushing grotesquely through his skin. Someone was in the middle of tying a jacket around it in an attempt to stop the bleeding, and the man moaned weakly, his face gray and twisted with pain.

Someone suddenly gasped, and I turned my head just in time to see a man staggering toward us from the wreckage, his body listing heavily to one side. Blood streaked the side of his face, thick and dark, trailing from a deep gash above his temple. His uniform was torn, and the left sleeve was soaked with blood.

Landon rushed forward to help him. "You're one of the pilots, aren't you?" he said as he caught the man's arm, trying to steady him. "I checked what was left of the cockpit, and I thought—"

"That we were both dead?" the man cut in. His voice was

THE WILD

hoarse. "Honestly, for a minute, I thought I *was*. I thought I was in hell."

His knees buckled, and Landon slowly lowered him to sit on a large log. He blinked up at the sky, eyes glassy with shock. "Captain Reed didn't make it. I don't even know how I did," he muttered. "I... I should've been crushed."

Another survivor crouched beside the log. "I'm sorry about what happened to your colleague, but you're going to be okay," she said firmly. "The rescue teams will get the signal from the beacon, and they'll come for us later today."

The pilot lifted his head, and his haunted gaze locked onto hers. His face was pale beneath the smears of blood. "That's not going to happen."

The woman raised her brows. "Because we're so far out in the middle of nowhere?" she asked, tilting her head. "You think it might take more than a day for them to get a team out here?"

Another survivor cut in. "I think we should be prepared for at least a two-day wait," he said. "Some parts of the Canadian Rockies can be pretty hard to reach."

The pilot shook his head. "No, you don't understand," he said, his voice hollow. "The rescue teams aren't going to find us."

"I think you're in shock," the woman said, squeezing his shoulder in a sympathetic gesture. "That's totally understandable, given what just happened to you. To all of us. But it's 2025. They can't just lose a plane. Especially not one that crashed on land."

"I'm not in shock," the pilot replied sharply. He dragged a hand through his blood-matted hair, inhaling deeply before exhaling in a slow, measured breath. "There were complications during the flight, the crash, and in the aftermath. It's a long story. But the bottom line is: they won't be able to find us."

"That can't possibly be true."

"Believe me, I wish it wasn't. But it is," the pilot said grimly. "No one is coming for us."

10

ARIA

"What the fuck are you talking about?" a tall, bulky man shouted, moving closer to the log the pilot was sitting on. "How can no one be coming for us?"

Others in the clearing were walking—or dragging themselves—closer as well. I did the same, rising to my feet and limping over on my good leg with Hannah by my side.

I noticed four tall, familiar figures pushing through the crowd to surround Landon. Their broad frames towered over the others as they stepped toward him, and I narrowed my eyes, wondering where I'd seen them before.

A jolt of recognition suddenly shot through me. I'd seen all four of them hanging out with Landon on campus before. But they weren't Veritas attendees. So why were they on our flight to Anchorage? Had Landon decided to bring an entire posse with him for moral support? Or did he just want friends to hang out with during our downtime from the event?

Weird.

One of the guys reached up, rubbing the back of his neck. When his hand dropped, my eyes caught on something inked onto his skin. A small, unmistakable tattoo.

The Dominion Club's symbol.

I blinked, certain my mind was playing tricks on me. After all, I'd smacked my head pretty hard during the crash, so it was possible I was starting to see things. But when I looked again, the tattoo was still there.

What the hell?

The sight sent my thoughts spiraling. My heart began to pound, and for a few seconds, the shock and confusion roaring through my veins drowned out every ounce of pain in my body.

Were all four of those guys members of the Dominion Club alongside Landon? Had they simply been on that flight to support Landon, like I initially wondered? Or had they boarded the plane on a society mission—sent to Anchorage to finish what they started against me in DC?

"Hello?" a woman said to the pilot, snapping her fingers. "Are you ever going to answer us?"

"Sorry," he muttered, rubbing the side of his neck. "I don't know where to start. I'm trying to figure it out."

The man who'd shouted at him earlier narrowed his eyes. "How about you start by telling us what the fuck happened up there?" he said, jabbing his thumb toward the sky.

"What *didn't* happen is a better question," the pilot replied, rubbing his temples. "About ninety minutes into the flight, our computer system malfunctioned, and we lost all communication signals. Usually, it—"

Someone lifted a palm and cut in. "Hold on, are you saying we lost contact with the outside world?"

"Yes. First, our radios went dead, cutting us off from air traffic control. That alone isn't unheard of, but then our transponder failed too. After that, our satcom system—the backup that should've still worked—went offline as well. We tried rebooting everything, but nothing responded."

"Holy shit."

"Believe it or not, even with all the technology we have these days... sometimes these blackouts just happen," the pilot said, lifting his shoulder in a weary shrug. "But they usually don't last long."

"Well, how long did *this* outage last?" someone asked.

"Our communication capabilities never returned once the blackout happened. But we still had full navigational capability and the right amount of fuel to get us to Anchorage. So we actually weren't too concerned at first."

Another person chimed in, their voice tight. "So we were completely cut off from the world for most of the flight?"

"Yes. But like I said before, these incidents aren't unheard of," the pilot replied. "The comms malfunction was honestly more of an annoyance to us at first. Strange, but not the end of the world. We still thought we'd make it."

I pressed my lips into a thin line as his words sank in. I hadn't been imagining things earlier, when the flight attendants started rushing around, their faces tight with barely concealed panic. The plane had lost all contact with the outside world for a long period of time, and they had no idea why.

But they *had* known we could still reach Anchorage safely. That was why they'd kept it quiet; why they hadn't told me anything when I asked if everything was okay. Because once fear took hold, it spread like wildfire, and the last thing they'd needed at thirty-thousand feet was a cabin full of people losing their minds.

"And then?" someone asked, raising a brow. "What was that horrible noise we all heard?"

"That was the tail," the pilot said grimly. "There was a fire, and half of it blew off. That's why we suddenly tipped to the left. We lost stability."

"What the hell happened to make the tail catch on fire? Was it a bomb?"

At the word 'bomb', I turned my attention back toward Landon and his friends. I knew the Dominion Club liked to work

with bombs, given their failed attempt on my life five weeks ago...
but surely they wouldn't have planted one on *this* flight. Not when
several of their own members were onboard.

No, of course not. That made no sense. I shoved the thought
aside and turned my attention back to the pilot.

He was silent for another moment, seemingly lost in thought.
"I really don't think it was a bomb," he finally said, shaking his
head. "Planes are thoroughly checked for devices like that before
takeoff. If there *had* been one, it would've been found."

"But what the hell else could make the tail suddenly catch on
fire and explode?"

"You'd be surprised by how many things are capable of causing
sudden fires," he replied, forehead wrinkling. "I can't be sure what
happened. Not until a proper investigation is carried out. But I
have a couple of theories. The first is a bird strike."

"What's that?"

"It's exactly what it sounds like. Collision between birds and
aircraft," the pilot said. "If a bird strike ingests multiple large
birds into an engine, it can cause a fire. Then, if the fire spreads
and damages hydraulic lines, electrical systems, or fuel lines, it can
cause a secondary fire in the fuselage or tail section. That could
cause part of the tail to blow up."

"So a bunch of fucking *birds* took the plane down?" someone
said, voice dripping with incredulity.

"It's possible, but it's not the theory I'm leaning toward,
because it's so rare for birds to be flying at such high altitudes,"
the pilot said. "Of course, it *can* happen, so I wouldn't rule it out
entirely. I'm leaning toward APU damage, though."

"APU?"

"Auxiliary Power Unit. It's located in the tail. If any of the
components are damaged, debris ingestion or fuel leaks can ignite
a fire, and that fire could easily blow part of the tail off."

"Why do you think that's more likely than the bird thing?"

"Because of the complete communications blackout we experienced." The pilot paused for a beat, sighing heavily. "I don't want to sound like a conspiracy theorist, but... I think we could've been hacked."

The woman who'd first approached the pilot took a step back, eyes widening. "*Hacked?*"

The pilot lifted a palm. "As I said, it's just a theory. But it was very, *very* odd that our entire communications system went down, and we couldn't get it back up despite multiple reboot attempts. So I think it's possible that someone on the ground could've used a cyberattack to get into our system, and then they could've manipulated the avionics and overloaded the power distribution network. That could've caused things to overheat in the APU, and then... well, you know the rest."

"So you think the plane was intentionally brought down," the woman said. Her face had turned slightly gray.

"I said it's possible, and it's the theory I'm currently leaning toward," the pilot said. "But I can't say anything for sure."

His eyes landed on me as he spoke, and it hit me why he was so focused on that idea. He knew I was on the flight—everyone on board did—so he probably thought an extremist group had figured it out too. From there, they could've targeted the plane, hacking into the system to bring it down as part of an assassination attempt.

The thought sent a chill through me, and the guilt I'd been trying to push down resurfaced in full force.

My fault.

I should've just taken one of the private government planes. They were unhackable, at least as far as I knew, so if I'd done that, none of this would've happened. Over two hundred people would still be alive, including Foster and the other agents, and this tragedy might never have occurred. That is, if it was indeed an assassination attempt.

"But didn't you say it could be any number of things?" another woman piped up.

"Yes." The pilot nodded, gaze drifting away from me. "We won't know the truth until the wreckage is analyzed."

I swallowed hard, trying to suppress the gnawing guilt. There was no way to know exactly what caused the plane to crash. As the pilot had pointed out earlier, it could've just been a freak accident, like a flock of birds in the wrong place at the wrong time. Blaming myself wouldn't change anything.

Landon stepped closer, brows drawn in a frown. "You seemed to have things under control after the tail blew off," he said. "We didn't crash for forty-five minutes after that. So what happened?"

The pilot pinched the bridge of his nose and sighed. "After we realized half of the tail was gone, we knew we were going to have to make an emergency landing as soon as possible. We changed course to head directly east, because we knew there was a very large valley in that direction, with what we hoped was enough flat terrain to make the landing. We started dumping fuel on the way, and—"

"What?" someone shouted, cutting him off. "You were *dumping fuel*? Fuel that we needed?"

"Please listen to me," the pilot said curtly. "When you make a rough emergency landing like the one we were planning, there's an enormous explosion risk. So, you dump as much fuel as possible to avoid that happening."

"Oh." The person who'd shouted looked mollified now. "Sorry."

The pilot took a deep breath and went on. "Unfortunately, we ran out just before we made it to the valley. Once we recognized that we weren't going to make it there, we located a close stretch of forest that appeared to be relatively flat and free of large obstacles. Then we prepared for a forced landing there. It was our only remaining option."

"What are the survival odds of that?" Landon asked, brows furrowing.

"Honestly?" the pilot said. "Extremely low. But as I said, it was our only remaining option. It was either that or simply crash without any control. And no one would've survived the latter."

"I see."

"As we went down, we skimmed the treetops, and that slowed our descent a bit. Then we hit the ground at a shallow angle and slid right into the forest," the pilot went on. "The wings sheared off when they collided with the trees, but that was actually a good thing. See, the fuel tanks are housed in the wings, so any remaining drops of fuel in there could've caused the rest of the plane to explode upon impact."

"That's why so many of us survived?" Landon asked.

The pilot nodded. "That, and the fact that we did everything we could to control the descent, even with so much already out of our hands by then," he replied. "We tried our hardest, but we knew there would still be many casualties, and given our position at the front... we assumed we'd be in those numbers. I still don't know how I walked out of that cockpit."

The pilot's voice cracked at the last sentence, and he looked away, his eyes unfocused as if he were seeing the crash again in his mind's eye. His hands trembled slightly where they rested on his lap.

"I—I really shouldn't be here," he went on, almost to himself. "I don't know why I survived when so many others didn't make it."

I could see the torment in his expression. Every memory of those harrowing moments before the crash, every scream of every person he couldn't save despite his best efforts, was haunting him, consuming him from the inside out. Despite the stoic face he'd put on for most of the conversation, it was clear his miraculous survival had left a mental scar he might never heal from.

The woman beside him patted his shoulder. "It sounds like you did the best you could, and by my count, you saved thirty-four people," she said softly. "That's... what? Twenty percent of the passengers?"

"Closer to fifteen," someone else said. "Still, that's much better than the 0.1% that usually survives something like this," he said, turning his attention back to the pilot. "You and your colleague were heroes, man."

The rest of the group murmured their acknowledgement.

"I appreciate the sentiments, but I'm not done," the pilot said. "I haven't explained what happened to cut off our tracking capabilities."

"Did something happen to the black box?" someone asked.

"No. I checked it before I came out here, and it's fine. They're designed to withstand almost anything."

"So then *we're* fine," the woman next to him said, face brightening again. "Those things have tracking beacons, right?"

"No, that's a myth," the pilot said, shaking his head. "Black boxes are just flight recorders. They exist so investigators can determine what happened in the event of a crash, and most don't have beacons on them. Instead, most planes have something called an ELT. Emergency locator transmitter."

"Oh. So how do they work?"

"They're designed to activate and emit emergency signals on impact, especially with water, since many crashes happen over the ocean. They'll also trigger in a hard land crash." The pilot exhaled slowly before continuing. "But you see, our crash was slow and relatively controlled compared to most, because we were trying our best to land in order to save as many people as possible. So there weren't enough impact forces to make the ELT automatically switch on."

The woman's half-smile faltered. "Surely you can manually switch it on?"

"Yes, but—"

"What the fuck are you waiting for?" a red-faced man shouted from the edge of the group. "Go and turn it on right now!"

The pilot glared at him. "I can't. That's what I was trying to tell you before you interrupted me," he said. "I looked at it before I came out. The main cable to the antenna has been cut."

"Was it damaged in the crash?" someone else asked, eyes wide with concern.

"No." The pilot's throat bobbed as he swallowed hard. "It was cut by a person."

Silence hit the group like a wave. Someone had deliberately cut the cable. And that meant someone wanted us stranded out here.

"Surely it could've been torn apart by the impact," a woman finally said in a tentative voice.

"No. It's a very clean cut. It looks like someone got a pair of scissors and—" The pilot paused, miming a snipping action. "If you don't believe me, go see for yourself. But either way, that ELT isn't transmitting any signal, and it can't be fixed."

"Holy shit," someone muttered.

"What kind of sick fuck would do something like that?" someone else said, voice at a fever pitch. "Why would they cut off our only lifeline?"

"Wait." The woman beside the pilot lifted her hands, signaling for everyone to calm down. "It's okay. They know our flight path, so they can still find us. Right?"

Landon gave her an incredulous look. "Didn't you listen to him at all?" he asked, jerking a thumb toward the pilot. "He said we flew off course for almost an hour, trying to get to that valley for the emergency landing. And we lost all communication signals long before that, so no one back home has any way of knowing that we went off course, or where we went."

"Exactly," the pilot said. "They'll certainly come looking for us, but they won't be in the right place. We're hundreds of miles away from anywhere we were supposed to be."

"But still, they *have* to find us at some point, right?" the woman said, eyes saucer-wide.

"Given the remoteness and vastness of this part of the world,

THE WILD

it could be weeks before anyone even comes close to finding us, and that's if we're being optimistic," the pilot said. "It'll very likely be months. Possibly even forever, in the absolute worst-case scenario."

"*Forever?*" someone screeched. "Are you fucking serious?" Another person chimed in. "That's not possible!" he said, vehemently shaking his head. "They have to find us! A whole plane can't go missing forever!"

"Listen, I'm not trying to scare you," the pilot said in a clipped voice. "I'm trying to prepare you all for the worst, just in case. It's rare, but sometimes planes really *do* go missing forever, and unfortunately for us, we have all the correct conditions in place for that to happen."

Another heavy silence fell over the clearing, thick with dread.

The woman beside the pilot finally shook her head, her hands trembling at her sides. "No," she said. "That really can't be right."

The pilot exhaled, his face lined with exhaustion. "I know it's hard to hear, but it's the truth. Like I said, we're deep in one of the most remote regions on Earth with no way to send a distress signal. No one knows where to start looking."

Murmurs of disbelief rippled through the group. Someone let out a choked sob. Another person dropped their head into their hands.

I barely registered the rising panic around me. My mind was stuck on one terrifying train of thought as my eyes locked on Landon and his Dominion Club friends—the same men who'd already tried to kill me once.

Had Landon cut the ELT cable after he woke up and realized that I'd survived too? Had he seen the crash aftermath as an opportunity to kill me before rescuers could track us down? An easy way to finish the job the Dominion Club had ordered him and his cronies to do in Anchorage?

It seemed likely. Very likely. Because why else would someone do something so reckless, so monstrous, as cutting the ELT cable?

Why would anyone deliberately ensure we wouldn't be found for months... unless they had a reason to keep us stranded?

Out here, away from civilization, witnesses, and my Secret Service protection, there were a hundred ways for Landon—or one of his friends—to potentially get rid of me. He could push me off a cliff. Hold me underwater in a river. Smash my head with a rock and claim that I tripped. And no one would ever know it wasn't an accident.

Oh god, oh god, oh god.

My throat went dry as I stared right at Landon, my pulse hammering in my ears.

No one was coming to save us. That fact was already gut-wrenchingly scary enough. But on top of that, I was stuck out here with *him,* knowing he wanted me dead... and that terrified me more than anything.

11

ARIA

Chaos erupted around me as panic set into the group. People shouted over each other, their terror rising in the clearing like a tidal wave. Some argued, others cried, and a few just stood there, frozen in shock. As I watched, my pulse pounded in my ears, my breath coming too fast.

Landon's voice cut through the noise, sharp and commanding. "Enough!"

The group quieted, all eyes snapping to him. His usual arrogance was gone, replaced by something steadier. "Panicking isn't going to help. I know we're in a fucked-up situation, but we need to try our best to stay calm right now," he said. He motioned toward the pilot. "Like he said, we could be stuck out here for months, so we need to prepare for that. We *can* survive out here, as long as we have a plan and work together. Got it?"

A few people nodded and murmured their agreement.

"Here's what we're going to do for now," Landon went on. "Anyone who's able-bodied, start gathering whatever you can from the plane. Food, water, medical supplies, warm clothes, blankets... anything that might help us. Bring it all to this clearing and leave it right there."

He paused for a beat, pointing to a spot a few yards away from my feet.

"Anyone who's too injured to walk or carry anything, stay out here," he went on, sweeping his gaze around the survivors again. "Also, if there's anyone with any sort of medical training or knowledge, it'd be helpful if you stayed out here to help those who are injured. Everyone got it?"

No one argued. Maybe it was the shock, or maybe it was the way he said it, like there was no room for debate. One by one, people started moving toward the wreckage to scour it for supplies, while those who were injured sat down on blankets or logs.

Landon's attention snapped to me. "Aria, you can't walk too much on that ankle, so you can keep an eye on Hannah, and the two of you can categorize the supplies in separate piles as the rest of us dump them here. Food, medical gear, et cetera. You might have to hobble around a bit, but you can handle that, right?"

I exhaled, my fingers clenching into fists to stop them from shaking. Then I nodded, not meeting Landon's eyes. "Yup. I can do that."

Without another word, he strode toward the wreckage.

A surprising amount of stuff had survived the crash, and our supply piles built up quickly. Hannah was very helpful, sorting through items with quick efficiency. Meanwhile, I did my best to keep up, shifting supplies into neat piles despite the persistent ache in my ankle.

Every so often, I caught glimpses of Landon in the wreckage, barking orders, lifting heavy debris like it weighed nothing, his presence as commanding as ever. It was strange seeing him like this. Focused, determined, dependable.

But that didn't change who he was. Or what he was capable of.

I shoved those thoughts aside and focused on the task at hand. Survival came first. Everything else—our history, my hatred for him, the secrets swirling beneath the surface—would have to wait.

My gaze flickered to the man with the compound fracture. He was lying on a blanket, his face pale and slick with sweat, while a slim brunette woman crouched beside him. Judging by the efficient way she worked, she clearly had some kind of medical background. She'd managed to maneuver his twisted leg back into its usual position, and the jagged edge of bone was no longer visible.

I was relieved the man was getting help, but deep down, I didn't like his chances. If infection set in, he wouldn't last long.

"Aria?"

My attention snapped back to Hannah. "Yeah, sweetie?"

"Which pile does this go in?" she asked, holding up a can opener.

"Cookware," I said, dipping my chin to the left. "Thanks for all the help, by the way. You're doing a really great job."

She smiled shyly. "Thank you."

Before she could turn away, I put a gentle hand on her shoulder. "Hannah... I'm sorry I made that promise to you earlier. The one I couldn't keep," I said. "I really thought we'd get rescued today."

"I know. It's okay," she said. "I still think someone will find us soon."

I smiled at her optimism. "I hope you're right."

Someone dumped a fresh pile of stuff they'd pulled out of someone's case—two bottles of medication, toothpaste, a flashlight, a roll of gauze, and a small sewing kit. My gaze landed on one of the medications, and my brows lifted.

"Hannah, let's take a break for a minute," I said, waving her over. "I think this medicine could help that man."

We crossed the clearing to where the injured man lay, and I held the bottle out to the brunette woman once we were close enough to speak.

"Hey, I think these might be antibiotics," I said. "Can you use them?"

The woman rose to her feet and took the bottle, turning it over to check the label. Then her face lit up with relief. "Yes! This is a great find. Thanks."

"We've got some other medical stuff that might help too. I'll bring it over soon, so you can take a look," I said. "There's also plenty of bottled water, so I'll grab you some of that too."

The injured man forced a smile, despite the awful pain he was likely feeling. "I guess I'll live to see another day, huh?" he said. "I'm Clint, by the way."

"And I'm Carrie," the woman added.

"I'm Ar—"

"Aria Hagan," Clint finished for me. "We all know who you are. Never thought I'd have the president's daughter fetching me meds and drinks, but hey, stranger things have happened, eh?"

I returned his small, weak smile. "That's true."

Carrie looked at Hannah. "And who's this cutie-pie?"

She stepped forward, smiling shyly. "I'm Hannah."

"She was traveling alone, so I'm going to look after her until help arrives," I explained.

Carrie nodded slowly. "I can help with that too. I was also flying alone, so it'll be nice to make a new friend," she said, smiling at Hannah again. She turned her gaze back to me. "I'm guessing you weren't traveling alone, given who you are."

"No, I was with some students from my college and my Secret Service detail," I said softly, feeling a pang of grief and guilt again. "We were heading to an event in Anchorage."

"How many made it?" Clint asked, eyes filling with sympathy.

I turned and pointed to a short redheaded girl and a lanky guy with black curly hair, both of whom were on their way to the supply pile with more salvaged items. "Those two were part of the group," I said. "And Landon, too. He's the guy who told us what to do earlier."

"Ah. He seems like a natural leader," Clint said. "Calmed everyone down pretty well."

I swallowed thickly. "Yeah, he's really something," I murmured. "Anyway, I'll go grab that water for you."

"Great. Thanks," Carrie replied. "And thanks again for the antibiotics! They're a godsend."

A few more hours passed. Eventually, the wreckage had been stripped, and the supplies had been packed into bags, boxes, or emptied-out passenger cases for transport to wherever we ended up settling.

Landon clapped his hands together to draw everyone's attention, his sharp gaze sweeping over the group. "All right. I think we've pulled out everything useful from the wreckage, so it's time to figure out our next move," he said. "In a few minutes, I'm going to take a small team to scout out the surrounding area. Hopefully we can find a decent spot to set up camp for the night."

"Why can't we just stay here?" someone asked. "There's lots of logs. I was thinking we could use them to build some sort of shelter."

Landon gave the guy a hard look. "We can't stay too close to the plane. The bodies might attract predators, and then there's also the matter of the smell," he said. "There's no water supply here either, so we need to find a river or lake to settle near, because the bottled water is going to run out pretty fast."

"Oh. Right."

Another voice cut in. "Before you go scouting, I think we should go around and introduce ourselves. Maybe mention any skills that could help the group."

Landon gave a curt nod. "Good idea. You can start."

The man squared his shoulders. "Mark Grimes. I'm an accountant now, but I used to be an EMT fifteen years ago," he said. "Might be rusty, but I still remember plenty."

"That's good," Landon said. He cocked his head slightly to one side. "On that note, who else here has medical training?"

Carrie stuck her hand up. "I'm a dentist, but we have to go through medical school to get qualified, so technically, I'm a doctor," she said. "Oh, and my name is Carrie Leavitt."

A petite middle-aged woman raised her hand. "I'm Glynnis, and I'm an ER nurse."

Mark grinned. "This is great. We've got a solid medical team," he said. His gaze drifted to Hannah, who stood between me and Carrie, her small hands clasped in front of her. "What about you, kid? What's your name?"

"Hannah," she said in a small voice.

"Have your parents ever taught you any wilderness survival skills, Hannah? Or anything else that might help us out here?"

She shrank back a bit, clutching my hand. "Um... I don't think so."

"Great," Mark muttered, shaking his head slightly.

"She's only eight," I said, my voice clipped. "Did you expect her to have a degree in environmental science or something?"

"She was very helpful today," Carrie added, shooting Mark a pointed look.

I nodded. "Yeah, she was. She helped organize the supplies, and let me tell you... it would've taken twice as long without her working her butt off."

"She's also totally uninjured, so she can run around and fetch stuff, which a lot of other people can't do at the moment," Clint chimed in from the blanket he was sitting on. "People like me."

Mark raised his hands in mock surrender. "All right, all right. Point taken." His gaze shifted to me, an assessing glint in his eyes. "And what about you, Ms. Hagan? When you're not swanning around the White House with Daddy, what do you do?"

"You can call me Aria," I said, ignoring the bite in his tone. "I'm studying political science, which I realize isn't too useful out here in the wilderness, but I did Girl Scouts for years when I was a kid, so I know some helpful stuff. Like how to identify which berries and nuts are safe to eat. How to treat water so its drinkable. Things like that."

Five other survivors raised their hands and identified themselves. All of them had done some variation of Scouts, Guides, or wilderness survival training as well.

When they were finished, Landon lifted his hand. "I'm not an ex-Scout, but I used to go hunting with my father, so I know my way around that whole scene," he said. "We have some weapons from the Secret Service agents who were on board, so we'll be able to hunt deer."

The group murmured their collective agreement with that notion. Then Landon's four friends, who were flanking him, raised their hands and identified themselves one by one. Sebastian, Knox, Theo, and Cole. Apparently, they were all seasoned hunters too.

My stomach churned as the realization set in. I was already frightened enough of Landon and the rest of those guys, but to learn that all five of them were expert hunters... that made my blood turn to ice in my veins.

"Hold on." Mark lifted a hand. "Do you guys know each other? I noticed you've all got the same tattoo in various places."

Landon nodded curtly. "We're in the same organization."

"And what organization would that be?"

Landon shrugged. "Just a college thing."

I barely stopped myself from rolling my eyes at that. I'd hardly describe a deadly secret society as 'just a college thing' but hey, it wasn't like Landon or his friends would ever admit the truth, right? Besides, if I tried to tell the rest of the group what I knew about the society, I'd either cause mass panic or make myself look insane. Neither would help the situation.

Mark studied Landon for a beat, then exhaled sharply. "What are the odds that all five of you survived that crash?" he asked. "It's a bit strange, isn't it?"

I thought Mark was a bit of an asshole, but I had to admit, he had a point. How was it that all five Dominion Club members had survived relatively unscathed while so many other people had died?

Landon met his gaze. "We all booked seats at the back of the plane," he said coolly. "Statistically, it has the highest survival rate in the event of a crash."

"I can confirm that," the pilot chimed in. He'd identified himself earlier as Tony. "The chances of survival are *much* higher at the back. Hence my total and utter shock that *I* survived."

Mark nodded slowly. "Huh. Didn't know that. But if I ever get on a plane again... well, I guess I'll be insisting on a seat at the back, won't I?"

Silence settled for a moment before Clint raised a hand. "Hi, everyone. I'm Clint. When my leg isn't broken, I'm an excellent fisherman. So, if we find a river or lake like Landon suggested earlier, I can teach a few of you some techniques."

"Great." Mark pointed at a petite blonde woman. "You haven't said anything yet. Who are you?"

"I'm Leigh, and I'm a doctoral candidate," she replied softly, eyes nervously flitting around. "I'm sorry, but I don't have any wilderness survival skills. I've been camping a few times for my studies, but it's not really the same—"

"Wait." Mark cut her off, brows furrowing. "Did you just say you're a doctor?"

"No." Leigh cleared her throat and raised her voice. "Doctoral candidate. I'm not in the medical field."

"Ah, I see. What's your field of study? It could still be useful to us in some way."

"Sociology and anthropology. I was flying to Anchorage to meet with some researchers for my thesis."

Mark snorted. "Well, we can scratch what I said about your usefulness, then."

"Hey!" I clicked my fingers to draw his attention back to me. "It's not like anyone here *knew* we were going to crash and wind up stranded out here for months, so we couldn't exactly plan ahead and take survival courses. So maybe lay off a bit, okay?"

Landon nodded. "Even if some of us don't have wilderness knowledge or other relevant skills, that doesn't mean they're useless," he added, his tone surprisingly level and calm. "We can teach them things, and there's always work to be done. Cooking, gathering firewood, helping to build shelters. Things like that."

I blinked at him, momentarily caught off guard. There it was again—rational, reasonable Landon, sounding almost... kind? It was jarring. The same man who could be ruthless enough to plant a bomb in my car was capable of *this*. Of being the sort of guy who cared about sticking up for others.

Just for a second, it was almost enough to make me forget who he really was. But then, just as quickly, the chilling reminder of what he'd done—and was probably still planning on doing— slammed me back to reality.

Mark's lips pressed into a thin line. "I suppose so," he finally muttered. Then he straightened. "Anyway, who hasn't introduced themselves yet?"

A few more people spoke up, listing their names and backgrounds. Once the last person had spoken, Landon clapped his hands together. "All right. Now that we've got introductions out of the way, we need to find somewhere safe to camp. I'll take a few people and scout the area. See if we can find somewhere with decent cover and a good water source. Anyone with experience tracking or navigating, come with me."

Several people stepped forward, including Sebastian and Knox, and they set off into the woods. The rest of us stayed behind, shifting uncomfortably as we tried to ignore the scattered bodies near the wreckage.

Time dragged. I had no idea how long the scouting group was gone, but by the time they returned, the sun was beginning to dip below the trees, and the air was turning frigid.

"We found a good spot, and it's only thirty minutes away,"

Landon told us. "There's a lake with a natural shelter beside it, beneath an outcrop. It's not a cave, but there's an overhanging rock big enough to fit at least ten to fifteen people under it. We can also make it into a bigger, more closed-off shelter by leaning logs against it, and that way we'll be able to fit everyone in there. That'll be a job for tomorrow, though. For now, we should just get moving before it gets too dark."

A murmur of agreement swept through the group, and people started gathering up the bags and cases of supplies we'd salvaged.

As I pushed myself up, pain flared in my ankle, making me wince. Hannah noticed and slipped a hand into mine. "Are you okay, Aria?"

"Yeah. Thanks for asking." I forced a breath through my teeth. "Let's get out of here."

With that, we left the wreckage behind and started the long walk to what would be our new home for now. Hopefully not for too long, though.

My ankle throbbed with every step I took, but I gritted my teeth and forced myself to keep going. The air was crisp, carrying the scent of pine and damp earth, and when we finally broke through the trees, the sight before us made my breath catch.

A lake stretched wide and dark beneath the twilight sky, reflecting the last streaks of orange and purple. An outcrop jutted over the sandy shoreline from the nearby cliffside, creating a natural overhang large enough for shelter, just like Landon said. It wasn't perfect, but it was safe.

"Let's get a fire going," Landon said, snapping his fingers. "It'll keep us warm and give us light while we figure everything out."

Theo and Cole took charge of the fire, gathering dry branches and kindling while one of the others pulled out a lighter from the salvaged supplies. Within minutes, flames flickered to life, crackling and casting shifting shadows against the rock face.

"We'll need to boil water from the lake," I said, glancing out at the water. "That way we know it's safe to drink."

"Good idea." Carrie nodded, hugging her arms to her chest. "The plane had a few pots and pans in the galley, right?"

"Yup. We can use them."

"Great," she said. "On that note, I think we should keep the fire going at all times. The smoke could help rescuers find us."

Leigh—the anthropology student—nodded and leaned forward. "There might also be hunters and trappers somewhere out here. They could see the smoke and come to check it out."

"That would be great, because they might have a radio or satellite phone," I replied. "They could call for help."

"Or they could assume it's just another hunter's campfire and totally ignore it," Theo said brusquely, scratching his jaw.

A tense silence followed, but eventually, Landon nodded. "It's still a good idea. We'll keep the fire burning."

The conversation turned to tomorrow's plan. Landon divided everyone into groups—some would search for logs and branches to build a more secure shelter, while the injured would stay behind to rest and recover. A few, including Landon himself, would scout the area again, checking for any signs of other people.

"Everyone good with that?" he asked, scanning the tired faces around the fire.

There were a few muttered agreements, and some reluctant nods. No one really had the energy to argue.

With that settled, we set up for the night. Some people curled up beneath the overhang, using salvaged blankets and coats for warmth. Others stayed near the fire, stretching out on the dirt with whatever padding they could find.

Hannah and I huddled close together at the back of the shelter. "Goodnight, Aria," she murmured, her voice barely audible.

"Night, sweetie."

I closed my eyes. Sleep came in fits and starts, restless and full of half-formed nightmares, but at some point, exhaustion won out, dragging me into darkness.

When I woke up again, light was creeping into the shelter. I blinked the sleep out of my eyes, one hand reaching for Hannah to make sure she was still beside me. She was, snoring gently.

I breathed a sigh of relief and stretched my arms out, enjoying the cool morning air against my skin. My body still ached from the impact of the crash, but my ankle was no longer throbbing. The long rest had done it a world of good.

A sudden scream shattered the morning silence.

I bolted upright, heart hammering against my ribs. Around me, people were scrambling to their feet, eyes wide and breath sharp.

Another scream. This time, I recognized the voice.

It was Carrie.

12

ARIA

At first, I thought it might be a scream of excitement. Maybe Carrie had spotted a rescue team in a hydroplane cutting across the lake, or even just a helicopter in the distance.

"What's happening?" Hannah asked sleepily, rubbing her eyes.

"I'll go and see. Stay here for now," I said, patting her shoulder. "Just in case."

She nodded, wide-eyed, and I bolted from the shelter. My feet pounded against the damp sand as I ran along the lakeshore, hope and anticipation buzzing through my veins.

Shouts rang out behind me, and more footsteps pounded the ground. The others seemingly had the same thought I did—that help had finally come.

As we drew closer to Carrie, I felt a chill creep along my spine.

Mark was sprawled on the sand, his face turned slightly toward the water. Carrie was standing over him, frozen in place, her eyes wide and haunted. "He's dead," she said, voice hollow. "I just came out and found him like this."

"He must've been injured in the crash, and we didn't notice," Tony said, craning his neck to look past the person in front of him. "Internal bleeding, maybe?"

"No. Just look," Carrie murmured. Her voice was distant, hollow. "This is definitely... external."

She stepped away from Mark's body, and I finally saw it—one of the sharp cooking knives we'd salvaged from the plane galley. It jutted from the side of Mark's neck, dark with dried blood.

My pulse pounded at my temples, and I slapped a hand over my mouth as nausea rolled through me. This wasn't a natural death, caused by latent injury. Someone did this. Someone among us.

A small hand found mine. My head snapped around, and dread gripped my chest.

Hannah.

She was standing beside me, eyes on Mark's body. Her face was ashen.

I crouched down, grabbing her shoulders and spinning her around so she couldn't see him anymore. "Hannah, I asked you to stay in the shelter."

"I'm sorry. I thought it would be okay," she said, staring at me with wide eyes. "Everyone sounded happy, and I heard someone say we might be getting rescued."

"I get it, but you really shouldn't see this," I replied, my voice cracking slightly. The poor girl had already seen enough death and destruction in the last twenty-four hours.

"It's okay. I already saw it," she said in a small voice.

"Well, it's not good for you to keep looking at it," I said, squeezing her hand. "So let's focus on something else, okay?"

She nodded, morose eyes landing on the sand at her feet.

Behind us, the murmurs of the others swelled into frantic questions.

"What the hell happened to him?" Leigh asked. "Did anyone see?"

"How long has he been there?" someone else asked.

Carrie sighed. "I can't give you an exact figure, but I'd say he's been dead for a few hours, at least," she said. "I have no idea what happened, other than the glaringly obvious. I didn't see anything until I got out here."

"What were you doing out here?" Knox asked in a sharp tone.

"I woke up earlier than the rest of you, so I decided to go for a walk to stretch my legs. Then..." Carrie trailed off for a few seconds, motioning to the sand. "At first, I thought the same as the rest of you. That Mark must've been suffering from some sort of internal injury that we weren't aware of. But then I saw the knife."

For a long moment, no one replied. The only sounds were the gentle lap of the lake against the shore and the occasional rustle of wind through the trees. I knew exactly what everyone was thinking.

If someone killed Mark... who was next?

Tony's voice finally sliced through the heavy silence. "Did anyone else see anything? Or hear anything?"

Heads shook all around, and a murmur rippled through the group. No one had seen or heard anything that could help us figure out who attacked Mark. At least no one who was willing to admit anything.

Suddenly, something clicked in my brain. A single sentence from a small, trembling voice.

I looked down at Hannah, my heart thudding painfully against my ribs.

"Sweetie..." I crouched to her level, hands gripping her arms gently. "When you said you already saw Mark lying here ... did you mean now? Or did you see something before?"

She hesitated, hands twisting into the hem of her rumpled sweater. Her lips were pressed together tightly, like she was unsure if she should speak.

Finally, she whispered, "I saw what happened to him. Last night."

A collective inhale swept through the group.

"Oh, sweetheart." I wrapped Hannah in a tight hug. "Why didn't you say anything before?"

"I thought... maybe it was just a bad dream. I have them sometimes."

"I understand," I said softly, rubbing her back. "But it wasn't a dream, and we need to find out what happened, so it's really important that you tell us what you saw. Okay?"

"Okay," she murmured.

My throat was tight and dry, but I forced my voice to stay calm. "Can you tell us what you remember?"

Hannah swallowed hard, then nodded. "I woke up last night," she said timidly. "I needed to pee."

I nodded encouragingly, even as my stomach twisted.

"I didn't want to wake you up, so I went by myself. I walked down the beach a little bit, because I thought I could go behind one of the big trees." She gestured vaguely toward the dense line of trees just beyond the sand. "But then... I saw two men up ahead."

"Two men?" Leigh echoed. "What did they look like?"

Hannah shook her head. "I don't know. They were completely black, so I couldn't see their faces."

"You mean silhouettes?" I asked gently. "Like when there's light behind something, so all you can see is a dark shape?"

"Yes."

Someone swore under their breath.

"What happened next?" Carrie asked.

Hannah shifted on her feet. "I think they were just talking at first. Then they started arguing. I couldn't hear what they were saying, but one of them sounded really mad." She paused, taking a shaky breath. "And then... the angry one lifted his hand up and hit the other one in the neck. He fell down and stayed there."

There was a collective intake of breath, and a few people muttered in shock.

Hannah's voice wobbled as she went on. "I hid behind the tree. I was scared the angry man would hurt me if he saw me."

A fresh wave of nausea rolled through me, and I squeezed her little hand, my own fingers ice cold.

"Did you see where the angry man went?" Carrie asked.

Hannah nodded again. "I peeked out a little bit, and I saw him walking back to the shelter," she said. "So then I waited a while, so he would go to sleep. Then I went back too."

"So the killer is definitely one of us," Tony muttered. His bruised face was pale, his jaw tight.

"No shit, man," Cole said tersely. "Who the hell else would it be? Have you seen anyone else out here?"

I squeezed Hannah's hand. "You poor thing," I murmured. "You should've woken me up and told me."

"I was going to. But then I thought maybe it was just a dream," she said, her voice barely audible. "And I didn't want anyone to be mad at me for waking them up."

She let out a small, broken sob, and I pulled her into my arms again. She clung to me, shaking, her tears soaking into my sweater. "No one's mad at you," I said soothingly, stroking her back. "You can always wake me up."

"Okay," she said, voice muffled by my sweater.

"Hannah," Carrie said gently, taking a couple of steps closer. "I know you didn't see the angry man's face, but do you think you can remember anything else that could help us figure out who he was? Maybe something like his height or weight? Or how his voice sounded?"

Hannah pulled back slightly and sniffed, considering the question for a moment. Then she nodded. "He was really tall. Like my daddy."

Carrie nodded slowly. "If we line everyone up, could you point out anyone who's tall enough to match the man you saw?"

"What the hell is this? Law and Order: Wilderness Edition?"

Landon said, eyes flashing with disdain. "She's just a kid! Every grown man is going to seem tall to her."

"No shit," Cole said. "Do you have any idea how unreliable a child's testimony can be? Especially one who thought the whole thing was a dream until five minutes ago."

"Hannah is the only one who saw what happened," Carrie said frostily. "And in case you haven't realized, having a murderer in our group is pretty damn bad for our survival odds, so we need to figure out who it is."

Cole waved a hand. "Go on, then," he muttered. "Keep interrogating the poor kid."

"It's not an interrogation. We're just trying to figure out what happened," Carrie said. She clicked her fingers and raised her voice. "All right, everyone. Please line up."

The survivors shuffled into a loose line, the air thick with unease. Even those who weren't suspects—like Leigh, a relatively short woman—complied just in case, faces drawn with apprehension. Only the severely injured, like Clint, remained back at the shelter, and they were automatically ruled out of the suspect pool anyway.

Hannah clung to my hand as I guided her forward. Her small fingers trembled in mine, but she kept her chin up, her gaze flitting between the people standing in front of her.

"Take your time, honey," Carrie said, her voice softer now. "Just look at them and see if anyone is as tall as the man you saw."

Hannah hesitated, biting her lip. I could practically feel the tension crackling in the air like static electricity.

Landon, standing near the center of the line, exhaled sharply. "This is fucking ridiculous," he muttered.

Hannah's wide eyes darted up to me. I gave her a small, encouraging nod.

Finally, she lifted her arm and pointed. Hesitation. Then another. And another. By the time she was finished, she'd singled out seven men, all of whom were ordered to step forward.

A murmur passed through the group, and I forced myself to breathe evenly as I looked at the ones she'd chosen.

Landon. His four friends, Sebastian, Cole, Theo, and Knox. Two other men, both in their late thirties.

One of them, Matthew, shook his head. "This is insane. I was asleep all night."

The other, Owen, was leaning against a tall, thick stick he'd found in the clearing yesterday. He'd been using it as a makeshift crutch ever since the crash. "It couldn't possibly have been me," he said. "I can't walk without limping because my left leg is so banged up. You've all seen that."

"You could be faking it so that no one would ever suspect you," someone shot back.

Owen snorted. "Are you kidding me?" he said. "You think I immediately started faking an injury after the crash just so I could sneak out later and murder a guy I didn't even know?"

Carrie cut in, lifting a hand. "I saw Owen's leg yesterday, and it's not in good condition," she said. "So he's not lying—he can't walk without the stick right now."

Landon let out a dark chuckle. "I guess you're free to go, Owen."

"What about me?" Matthew said sharply. "Like I said, I was sleeping all night. And I was right next to Clara and Leigh in the shelter, so they would've woken up if I tried to leave at any point."

"We can't know that for sure," Tony cut in, fixing him with a hard stare. "They could be heavy sleepers."

"Hannah," I said, focusing on her again. "Are you absolutely sure all of these men are about the right height?"

She nodded. "Yes. But I can't tell which one it was. I'm sorry."

"It's all right, honey. There's no need to apologize," Carrie said. "You did your best."

Cole scoffed. "So what's the plan now?" he asked, folding his arms over his chest. "Six of us are apparently suspects, but only *one* of us actually did it. So what are the rest of you gonna do? Keep all six of us tied up for three months until we're rescued?"

The reality of what Cole said hung in the air like a storm cloud. No one wanted to say it out loud, but we all knew the truth: we might not be rescued in three months. It could be longer. It could be forever.

"We obviously can't keep you tied up for months on end," Carrie said. "But we also can't ignore the fact that one of you killed Mark, and we have no way of knowing who it is. Unless one of you would like to save us all the trouble and make a confession?"

Silence reigned for a moment.

"Didn't think so," Carrie muttered.

"Well, like you said, you can't tie us up, so what's the next step here? You let us go, and we all live together knowing one of us is a secret killer?" Landon said, his tone dripping with mockery. "Or will the six of us wind up with our throats slit in the middle of the night, just to ensure the killer is eliminated?"

Murmurs rippled through the crowd. No one wanted to say it, but everyone was obviously thinking the same thing. The only way to guarantee safety for the non-suspects was to get rid of all six suspects. But not in the violent way Landon had just mentioned.

Something else.

Exile.

It was Tony who finally voiced it. "I think the six of you should leave. Make a new camp somewhere else, far away from the rest of us."

"You can't be fucking serious," Theo said, tone dripping with contempt.

"I know it's harsh, but we don't have a choice. One of you is a murderer, and they might decide to kill again. If we let you stay, how do we sleep at night knowing that?"

"You think kicking six people out into the wilderness is any better?" Matthew snapped. "When five of them are innocent?"

"There are twenty-seven others we *know* are innocent," Carrie pointed out. "I'm sorry, but Tony is right."

"It's not an easy choice, but it's the safest one for the greatest number of people," Tony added. "Surely you can see that."

More arguments erupted, voices rising and overlapping. Some agreed, others protested.

I kept my gaze on Hannah as the debate raged on. Her little face was tight with unease, her small hand still gripping mine. She'd just wanted to help by telling the truth, and now it had turned into *this*. A full-on kangaroo court.

"You really expect us to go off and die out there?" Matthew spat. "Even though most of us did nothing wrong? Apart from the awful crime of being six-two, of course."

"No one is saying you have to die," Carrie said, arms crossed. "It's just like Tony said. You can make another camp somewhere else. Far away from the rest of us."

Knox laughed bitterly. "You mean take our chances in the forest while a killer sleeps beside us?"

Silence stretched, thick and suffocating. No one spoke. No one even dared to look at each other.

I wanted to raise a hand and say, *Don't worry, Knox. You and your DC buddies have no problem with murder and torture, right? So if Matthew turns out to be the one who killed Mark and decides to come for the five of you next, I'm sure you'll all handle it just fine.*

But, of course, I wasn't about to open that can of worms.

Landon exhaled sharply, dragging a hand down his face before throwing up his palms. "You know what? It's fine. We'll do it," he said, glancing at his friends. "It only took us a few hours to find this spot yesterday, so I'm sure we can find another place to camp by the end of the day. But we're taking a share of the supplies. One-fifth of everything."

"No fucking way," someone snapped from the back of the group.

"We helped gather that stuff, and we also carried most of it here," Knox said in an acid tone. "You want us to leave? Then we're taking our fair share. One-fifth of it should cover it, like Landon said."

"That's—"

"Actually fair," Tony interrupted.

Several people turned to look at him.

His bruised jaw flexed. "There's six of them and twenty-seven of us," he said. "Around one-fifth of the supplies should be theirs."

Leigh nodded slowly. "Yeah, you're right. It's not fair for us to send them away with nothing. Especially when most of them are innocent."

Landon's eyes narrowed. "We're also taking one of the guns."

Immediately, there was a surge of protests.

"The hell you are," Carrie snarled.

Landon lifted a palm. "There are six of us and only *one* murderer. You're forcing the five innocent ones to sleep next to him," he said. "So some of us might need to defend ourselves at some point."

A muscle ticked in Carrie's jaw. She didn't like it. None of us did. But it was a point we couldn't argue.

"We also need to be able to hunt once the food from the plane runs out," Landon added. "A diet of wild berries isn't gonna cut it for six big guys."

"Fair enough," Carrie finally said. "One gun. But that's it."

Landon turned his attention to me. Something sharp and unreadable lurked in his expression. "You're coming with us, Aria."

The words landed like a punch to the gut. Why the hell would he say that?

"No way." I tightened my grip on Hannah's small shoulder,

tucking her closer. "I'm staying with her. And there's no way in hell anyone is ever going to let her go with your group."

Carrie and Leigh muttered their agreement, stepping up to stand beside me and Hannah.

Landon held my stare for a long moment, his jaw clenched and his eyes burning with something I couldn't quite place. Challenge. Frustration. A flicker of something deeper.

Then, finally, he gave me a slow, deliberate nod. "Fine."

Without another word, he turned on his heel, leading the other five men toward the shelter to gather their share of the supplies.

I watched them go, shock and confusion still roiling in my stomach. Why the hell would Landon demand I leave with him?

The question looped in my mind, gnawing at the edges of my thoughts like a parasite. It wasn't just the demand itself... it was the way he said it. The weight in his voice, like he expected me to instantly obey him.

But why would he *ever* think I'd do that? Did he seriously think I was stupid enough to follow him into the woods, knowing that he and his Dominion Club friends were more than likely planning to kill me?

"Why did he want you to go with them?" Tony asked me, like he'd read my mind.

"They're friends back in the real world," Carrie said before I could respond.

I bit my bottom lip and nodded. "Not exactly friends, per se, but we're in the same social circles, and we used to be neighbors," I added.

"Ah, I see," Tony replied, his tone easing. Whatever suspicion had been flickering in his eyes a moment ago faded, replaced by something more neutral.

Four people stayed on the beach to deal with Mark's body. The rest of us headed back to the shelter to watch over the six suspects as they gathered up their supplies. Once we were satisfied that they'd only taken a fifth of the food and water, we quietly watched them head toward the tree line.

Landon was the last to go.

Before he disappeared into the woods, he threw one last dark look over his shoulder, his gaze finding mine with an intensity that sent a shiver through me.

It wasn't just a passing glance. It lingered, heavy and intense, his sharp eyes locking right onto mine. The expression in them didn't seem like one of anger. It was something colder. More calculating. Like he was committing this moment to memory, filing it away for later.

Not just a warning.

A promise.

13

ARIA

FOUR WEEKS HAD PASSED SINCE THE CRASH.

Disaster movies always focused on the desperate struggle to survive the initial catastrophe, the gruesome injuries, and the frantic search for food and water. But what they didn't show was what came after that. The long, grinding monotony. The endless cycle of doing the same tasks over and over, just to stay alive.

The perishable food from the plane had only lasted five days before it turned bad. There was a lot of it, enough for over two hundred passengers, so we'd utterly gorged ourselves those first few days, figuring it was smart for us to gain some weight while we still could. When it ran out, we rationed the non-perishables —crackers, chips, granola bars—using them sparingly to supplement what we managed to hunt and gather.

As boring as it was, the daily routines we'd developed kept us from spiraling. Some worked at boiling water, refilling bottles so we had enough to drink. Others fished after receiving instructions from Clint on how to build makeshift nets and lines. A few went hunting with the guns, but so far they'd only brought down two deer. The rest of us, myself included, went off in pairs each day to scavenge whatever we could find in the forest. Berries, nuts, roots, mushrooms, the occasional wild fruit.

It wasn't glamorous, but we were surviving. For now. The problem was what came next.

Winter.

The unspoken fear of its imminent arrival was constantly hanging over us. The nights were already getting colder, and eventually the animals would move on and the trees would stop bearing fruit. Even the fish might disappear, the lake freezing over or running too low to support them.

We didn't talk about it very often, but the worry of potential starvation was always there, lurking behind every conversation. We'd even discussed using the alcohol from the plane as a last resort; an emergency source of calories if things got truly desperate. But when we went looking for it, we realized it was all gone.

It hadn't taken us long to figure out why.

Apparently, when the six exiled men packed their things a month ago, Landon's friend Cole had walked off with the case we'd stashed the alcohol in like it was his own suitcase. No one had questioned it at the time, assuming it *was* in fact his personal belongings.

It was only later, when we realized all the bottles were missing, that someone recalled the description of the case he'd carried. That was when we put it together. He'd made off with six bottles of wine, three bottles of scotch, a bottle of vodka, and several smaller bottles of beer and flavored liqueurs.

Asshole.

It was no wonder that Landon was friends with him. Birds of a feather and all.

And speaking of Landon... I hadn't seen him since the day he and the others left, but I knew he was still alive and thriving out there.

I knew it because I was certain he'd been watching me.

Obviously, I had no official proof of this. No glimpses or whispers through the trees, no strange footprints in the dirt. It was just a phantom presence, really. A prickle on the back of my neck when I was alone in the woods. That overpowering feeling of being seen, even if I never saw anyone in return.

Somehow, I just *knew* it was Landon, keeping an eye on me. Waiting for the perfect time to strike, perhaps.

Or maybe I was just losing my mind. At this point, I wouldn't be surprised if that was the case, considering everything that had happened over the last month.

Aside from Landon, the exiled group of men had kept their word. They hadn't come back to take anything else from the supplies, nor had they tried to make contact. It was almost strange how well they were sticking to the terms of their banishment.

Someone had started calling them 'the Lost Boys' a couple of weeks ago. It happened when we were all sitting around the fire, trying to entertain Hannah. She'd been quiet that evening, curling up beside me with her head on my shoulder, eyes a little too vacant. To cheer her up, Clint had started telling his own offbeat version of Peter Pan, complete with exaggerated voices and dramatic gestures.

He'd gotten to the part about the Lost Boys when Tony snorted and said, "That kinda works for the other six, don't you think?"

Everyone laughed. It was a tense, exhausted kind of laugh, but it was real. And just like that, the name stuck. It was easier to say than *'the exiled guys'* or *'the ones we kicked out',* and there was something strangely fitting about it.

The Lost Boys.

Of course, in Peter Pan, the Lost Boys were a band of kids who never grew up, running wild and free in Neverland, and in our world, the six guys were fully-grown men who'd been cast out into the wilderness on suspicion of murder. Hardly the same thing. But somehow, it just worked.

"Hey, you okay?"

I glanced up to see Leigh paused mid-step, looking back at me. The two of us were out foraging together while Hannah stayed back at the shelter with Clint, who'd taken on babysitting duty during the days while the rest of us worked.

"I noticed you were wincing a little," Leigh added, brows furrowing.

"I'm okay," I said. "It's just my ankle. I get a weird twinge in it sometimes."

"But you're still okay to walk?"

I nodded, jaw set in a firm, determined line. "Yup. I'm fine."

Truthfully, I had no idea if I was actually fine. For all I knew, the crash could've done some permanent damage to my ankle. But as long as I could still walk or run unimpeded most of the time, that was good enough for me. Our survival could very well depend on it, because we needed every helping hand available. Or foot, in this case.

Leigh and I pushed deeper into the wilderness, the golden afternoon light slanting through the towering evergreens. The underbrush crackled beneath our boots, and the occasional gust of wind sent a flurry of red and yellow leaves spiraling to the ground.

If I closed my eyes, I could almost forget where we were. Almost pretend we were just two friends on a fun hike instead of two crash survivors combing the forest for anything edible to sustain the people back at camp.

A while later, Leigh spotted a hazelnut tree, its tangled branches weighed down by their small, round bounty. Relief flooded me as I hurried to her side to begin gathering them.

Our group had made do so far, with our meager rations of plane food and whatever we could hunt, but hunger was beginning to gnaw at us... and hunger could be dangerous.

"This is perfect," I murmured, reaching up to pluck a handful of the nuts. Leigh did the same, grinning.

THE WILD

Our excitement faded fast. The longer we gathered, the more we realized how little there actually was, and when we emptied our palms onto the ground to count, the truth sank in: what we'd found wouldn't even add up to three nuts per person.

Leigh sighed, tucking a stray curl behind her ear. "I guess it's better than nothing, right?" she said. "Maybe we'll find more later."

I nodded, but disappointment sat heavy in my chest. How much longer could we stretch what little nature provided? How long before hunger made people desperate?

Before we set off again, Leigh reached into her pocket, grabbed a strip of fluorescent pink fabric, and tied it tightly around a low-hanging branch. The bright color stood out starkly against the endless greens and browns of the forest.

We'd been doing this from the very beginning—cutting up brightly-colored workout clothing to use as trail markers that would lead us back to our lakeside camp once we were done for the day. So far, it had worked. In all our weeks wandering the wilderness, no one had gotten lost yet.

Leigh wiped her hands on her jeans, then glanced at me. "That's the last of them," she said. "We should cut up some more before we keep going. Did you bring the scissors, or did someone else get them today?"

I reached into my jacket pocket, pulling out the tiny pair of scissors from the plane's first aid kit. They were laughably small, the kind meant for trimming gauze, with flimsy handles barely big enough for two fingers.

Leigh held up a pink spandex shirt we'd salvaged from someone's abandoned luggage and let out an exaggerated sigh. "Seriously, what genius decided to put *these* in a first aid kit?" she grumbled as I handed her the scissors. "They're so hard to work with. It would almost be easier to tear the shirt into strips with my bare hands."

"Yeah, they're tiny. It's really annoying."

"What if someone needed to cut a big strip of bandages on a flight?" she went on. "Like, what if someone had a massive head wound from turbulence or something?"

"Tony actually mentioned that to me the other day," I replied. "There *is* a bigger pair in the kit. Or at least, there *was*."

Leigh looked up. "What do you mean?"

"They're missing," I said. The words tasted bitter in my mouth. "Whoever cut the ELT cable probably used them to do it. Then I guess they threw them away somewhere. God knows why, though."

She sighed. "I still can't believe someone cut that cable," she said, shaking her head. "We could be home right now, eating a burger and fries. Instead, we're out here playing 'survive the wilderness' like we're trapped in a B-grade thriller. It's so fucked up."

I swallowed, throat dry. "Yeah, I can't believe it either."

"Do you have any idea who it might've been?" she asked, pausing mid-snip.

My fingers tightened around my sleeves. The answer was hovering on the tip of my tongue, but I couldn't bring myself to say it. It would make me look paranoid, maybe even delusional.

Besides, even if Leigh and the rest of the group believed me, the last thing any of them needed was the added worry that a team of secret society assassins had cut the cable and trapped us all in the wilderness just so they could sneak up and toss me off a cliff one day. They already had enough problems to deal with.

I forced a shrug. "All I know is that whoever did it is a psychopathic asshole."

"No shit." Leigh snorted and went back to cutting the fabric into long strips.

Once we had enough markers to continue, we pressed on, moving deeper into the forest. As we stepped down into a sloping valley, something strange caught my eye.

"Wait," I said, grabbing Leigh's arm. "What's that?"

THE WILD

A few feet ahead, carved into the trunk of a thick tree, was an arrow, pointing to the left. A dark stain was smeared over the lines.

Blood.

It had dried to a reddish-brown, cracked and faded, but it was still unmistakable.

Leigh tilted her head, examining the strange carving. Her fingers brushed over the rough grooves, where the dark stain stood stark against the pale bark. "It must be a tracking marker left by hunters or trappers who used to live out here," she finally said.

"That's blood, though," I said, voice tinged with anxiety. "Right?"

"Yes, but it looks old. And it's really not as creepy as it seems."

"You don't think so?"

She shook her head. "Not at all," she said. "Think about it: you're a hunter in the 1800s, living off the land. You need to mark trails or leave symbols to guide your way. You want something visible, but spray paint isn't exactly an option. So what's the next best thing that's readily available to you?"

"Animal blood."

"Yup." Leigh raised her brows, offering a small, reassuring smile. "I think it's actually a good sign that we've found this."

"How come?"

"It's a sign of human occupation," she said. "I mean, it's probably very old, given how we haven't actually seen any sign of people out here so far, but it's still a good sign, because it means people have lived in this area before, and they were able to survive. And if they could do it... we can do it too."

"Good point." I studied the symbol again. "Do you think this was made by indigenous people? Or later settlers from overseas?"

"No idea. My field of study is anthropology, but I focus on modern urban sub-cultures, not historical ones. So my knowledge of this area, and the people who've lived here over the centuries, is scant at best," she said. She paused, then added, "I've heard a few things, though."

Something about her tone made my skin prickle. "What things?"

"Well, I know some English settlers tried to move into part of the Rockies at one point, and a few small towns were built to support whatever industry they were trying to build. Canneries along rivers, mining exploration, logging, and so on. They didn't last long for various reasons, but..." Leigh trailed off and shifted her weight, chewing on her bottom lip as she glanced at the carving again.

"But what?" I asked, eyes wide with anticipation.

She waved a casual hand. "It's silly, really, but there's this old story that first-year anthro students always love. One of those 'what if' things," she said. "Not just about Canada. About any vast, remote area in North America. Like the Appalachians, for instance. You'll hear similar stories if you go there."

"Leigh, you're absolutely *killing* me with the suspense," I said, throwing up my hands. "What stories?"

She laughed. "Sorry. The idea is that, a long time ago, some people just... left. Disappeared from society entirely and went to live in the wilderness."

I raised an eyebrow. "You mean like hermits?"

"Sort of," she replied. "But not just individuals. Whole families, sometimes even small groups. People who decided civilization wasn't for them. Maybe because of war, disease, or just a deep distrust of modern life. Some might've been trappers or prospectors who never returned. Others could've been settlers who inadvertently lost contact with civilization and adapted."

"And they just stayed out here? For decades?"

"Possibly even generations," Leigh said, nodding. "Think about it. There are parts of the continent that no one has ever fully explored, and the Canadian Rockies is one of them. We like to *think* we've mapped everything, but that's not true. This place

THE WILD

is incredibly vast, and the terrain is unforgiving. So it's entirely possible that some people found ways to survive out here, passing knowledge down to their kids and living off the land with no need for the outside world."

I glanced around at the towering trees, the endless expanse of wilderness. "Do you think that actually happened?" I asked. "That there are people living out here without any contact with the rest of the world?"

"I doubt it. It's more of a theoretical thing. A romanticized idea of backcountry self-sufficiency," she said with a shrug. "There's no real proof. Just rumors. So I think it's probably just a story people made up to scare or entertain others."

"Oh. Like a campfire story."

She smiled. "Exactly. It's easy to theorize about, and it sounds intriguing, but it's impossible to prove. Unless someone combs through every single part of the Rockies, which, let's be real, no one is ever going to do. The place is just too vast."

"But.. it's still possible, right?" I said, casting my eyes back to the arrow symbol on the tree.

Leigh followed my gaze. "Possible, but not probable," she replied. "Like I said before, I'm not an expert in this field. But if I had to make an educated guess, I'd say this symbol was left by a hunter who used to live out here but eventually moved on with all the others, once it became apparent that this region was never going to become highly populated."

"Hm. Okay."

We moved on, leaving the tree behind, and soon stumbled across another discovery; one that made my stomach twist with both excitement and hesitation.

An enormous shrub stood in front of us, its branches drooping under the weight of clusters of plump berries. They looked safe. Their deep blueish-purple color and waxy skin reminded me of blueberries, but I'd never seen anything quite like them before.

Leigh let out a low whistle. "These could be a game-changer," she said. "What are they called?"

"I'm not sure. I've actually never seen them before."

She stepped closer, examining one of the berries with a critical eye. "They seem to match all the safety criteria you told me about," she said, gently squeezing the berry between her thumb and forefinger. "They're soft, the right color, and growing in aggregate."

"Yeah, that's true. But it's not a foolproof method to determine safety, so I can't be totally certain that they aren't toxic," I said. I rubbed my temple and let out a heavy sigh. "As much as this sucks... we might have to leave them, just in case. We don't want to risk poisoning everyone."

Leigh hesitated, lips twisting as she stared at the bush. "I have an idea," she finally said. "If they're poisonous, one or two wouldn't kill a person, right? It'd just make them sick."

"Yeah. You'd get cramps, nausea, vomiting. Stuff like that."

"Well, how about I take one for the team?" she said. "I can eat a few right now. Then we can wait an hour or so. If I start feeling violently ill... well, there's our answer. But if I don't feel sick at all, we can assume the berries are safe, come back here, and pick them all."

"I don't know," I said, voice tinged with reluctance. "I'd hate to see you get sick."

"But there's hundreds of berries here. That's extra calories that we all need."

"True," I said, nodding slowly.

I didn't love the plan, but we *did* need the extra food. So as Leigh chewed and swallowed three mystery berries, we continued our foraging, gathering what we could while we waited for any signs of a bad reaction.

An hour passed. I glanced at Leigh, brows furrowed. "Are you still feeling okay?"

"Yeah, I feel fine," she said brightly. "No cramps. No nausea. Nothing."

My shoulders slumped with relief. "Thank god," I murmured.

We turned around to head back to the valley with the berry bush. On the way, we passed through a small clearing. Leigh paused in the center of it to do a little twirl, arms spread wide as she tilted her face up to the sky.

I giggled softly as I watched her. "What are you doing?"

"Finding the silver lining," she called out, stretching her arms wider.

"Erm, what?"

She lowered her gaze from the sky and looked over at me. "I was just thinking... as much as this situation fucking *sucks,* isn't it actually kind of cool at the same time?"

I slowly shook my head, confused. "How so?"

Leigh spun again, her sneakers kicking up a spray of fallen leaves. "Back home, I have nonstop stress about my thesis. On top of that, I'm always worrying about paying rent and bills. Worrying if I filed my taxes correctly. Stuff like that. Not to mention the daily flood of bad news from every corner of the world," she said. "And I can't even imagine how much worse it is for *you,* being the president's daughter and all. You're under constant scrutiny from the media. Always being watched and judged. Worrying about even the tiniest slipups."

"That's true."

She stopped, inhaling deeply. "Out here, it feels like none of that stuff exists anymore, because we're so disconnected from it. I mean, sure, we have to worry about feeding ourselves, and that really sucks. But at the end of the day... it honestly feels like we're freer here than we've ever been back home," she said. "And on top of that, it's just so goddamn *beautiful* out here, isn't it? Even the air smells heavenly."

I sucked in a slow breath, letting the crispness of the air fill my lungs as I took in our surroundings. The fresh, woodsy scent of pine and damp earth. The gentle rustling of trees swaying in the wind. The way the sun made the golden leaves glow.

Leigh was right. It *was* beautiful out here. And in all these weeks, it hadn't even occurred to me to notice that.

I gave her a sheepish smile. "Back home, the first thing I do every morning is check my phone for news, just to see if anything bad has been written about my father and his administration. Or even me," I admitted. "But I can't do that out here, for obvious reasons, and... you're right. It actually *does* feel kind of freeing to be so disconnected from everything."

"Exactly! It's almost like a vacation," Leigh replied. "A really shitty vacation compared to most, but still, you know what I mean."

"Yeah, I do. Although we should probably keep this conversation to ourselves," I said, raising a brow. "Otherwise people might get the wrong idea and think *we* cut the ELT cable so we could take a break from society."

She snorted out a laugh. "Oh, god, I didn't even think of that," she said. "Just to be clear, it *wasn't* me. I'm just trying to inject some positivity into this weird world we've found ourselves trapped in, because if I don't, I might lose my mind."

"I get it," I said, flashing her another smile.

Leigh glanced up at the sky again. "It's getting late. We should probably hurry up and pick all those berries before we end up walking home in the dark."

"Yeah, we should. By the way, how did they taste?"

"A bit like blueberries, but less tart," she said. "Our little camp is in for a treat."

As the sun dipped lower, streaking the sky with pink and gold, Leigh and I made our way back to camp with everything we'd gathered. The nuts, though disappointingly few, were carefully tucked away for our winter supply—a small insurance against the harsher months ahead.

The berries, on the other hand, were fair game for tonight.

They wouldn't last long, and after weeks of mostly fish and whatever roots or seeds we could scavenge, something fresh and sweet felt like a luxury.

The scent of charred wood and roasting fish greeted us as we neared the fire. Someone had managed to catch a decent haul today, and the smoky, savory aroma set my stomach rumbling.

"Nice timing," Tony called out, flashing a grin as he turned one of the fish over on a makeshift spit. "You two bring back anything good?"

"A few mushrooms, some crab-apples, and some hazelnuts," Leigh said, dropping the small collection into one of the crates we used for storage. "Not a hell of a lot, but the nuts will keep for winter."

"We've also got dessert for tonight," I added, holding out the tote bag we'd filled with berries earlier. A few people perked up at that.

"Holy shit, those are huge!" someone said. "What are they?"

"I don't know, but I haven't dropped dead from eating them yet, so I'd say we're in the clear," Leigh added, grinning as she sank down onto a log by the fire.

Dinner was a quiet affair, with the kind of silence that came from hunger and exhaustion rather than discomfort. The fish was fresh and flaky, the warmth of it seeping into my bones as I ate, but the real highlight was the berries. Bursting with sweetness, they were the closest thing to a real dessert we'd had since we finished the apple and cinnamon breakfast muffins from the plane.

"Hannah, are you not having any?" Carrie asked, looking over at the little girl. She'd ignored the pile of berries we'd given to her on a small plate.

She shook her head. "I'm still full from the fish," she said in a sleepy voice. "Can I go to bed?"

"Sure, honey. I'll take you."

Carrie took her hand and led her toward the shelter to get her tucked into her little bed at the back.

"More berries for us, I guess," Clint said, grinning as he leaned over to grab the plate.

"We should've tried fermenting them," Tony mused, popping another into his mouth. "Made some wine or something."

A few people hummed in agreement.

"I'd love a glass of wine right about now. Too bad that prick Cole took all the booze when he left," someone else muttered.

Leigh scoffed. "Yeah, because nothing says 'survival' like hoarding every last bottle of vodka."

"It *is* technically a survival tool," Tony said. "You can disinfect wounds with it."

"Uh-huh," Leigh said, rolling her eyes. "I'm sure that's exactly what they're doing with it."

A few people chuckled, but the mention of the others cast a brief shadow over the conversation. No one said it out loud, but I could tell some of them were still wondering if we'd made the right choice in kicking them out.

But then someone tossed another log onto the fire, sending a burst of embers into the night sky, and the moment passed. Leigh nudged me with her shoulder, offering a small smile.

"Not a bad night, all things considered," she murmured.

I glanced up, taking in the endless stretch of stars above us, and the scent of pine needles and burning wood mingling in the crisp night air.

"Yeah," I said, smiling faintly. "Not bad at all."

The fire crackled softly, its warm glow flickering over the circle of faces around it as a low murmur of conversation filled the air. Someone cracked a joke, and laughter rippled through the group, light and unrestrained.

I leaned back on my hands, soaking in the moment. It was the first time in weeks that the tension had eased, that we weren't just surviving but actually *existing*, and enjoying something as simple as each other's company. Maybe it was the full stomachs thanks to the huge haul of fish we'd enjoyed earlier, or maybe it was just the relief of another day gone by without disaster. Either way, everyone was in an unusually good mood tonight.

Warmth curled low in my belly, slow and creeping, like the afterglow of a drink I hadn't had. A faint buzzing sensation tingled beneath my skin, subtle enough that at first, I thought I was imagining it. But as I glanced around, I started to notice things.

People were happy. In fact, they were almost... euphoric.

Shoulders swayed with the rhythm of conversation, movements looser, laughter sharper, more infectious. Carrie was curled up beside me, humming under her breath, a lazy smile on her lips. Clint grinned at something Tony said, his expression so open, so untroubled, that it felt almost unnatural given everything we'd been through.

A wave of warmth washed over me again; a slow, syrupy heat that made my limbs feel light and my head a little too floaty.

Something was definitely off.

The fire crackled louder, sending embers swirling into the night sky, and the air buzzed with laughter and chatter, getting louder by the minute. Someone started banging on an overturned crate like a drum, and others clapped along, feet stomping against the dirt in a chaotic rhythm. Voices rose and fell in drunken song; off-key, half-forgotten lyrics blending into nonsense.

It wasn't until I saw Tony trying to climb a tree, shirtless and yelling something about becoming one with the raccoons, that my hazy mind put the pieces together.

The berries.

They weren't poisonous... but they'd gotten us high as hell.

No wonder Leigh was so cheerful earlier this afternoon, twirling in the clearing and raving about the beauty of nature and the freedom of our new reality. At the time, I thought she was just trying to find the silver lining in our shitty circumstances, and honestly, everything she'd said had made sense, so I hadn't questioned it.

But now, it seemed obvious. She was actually on a very slight high when she was saying that stuff, because she'd had a few berries—just enough to give her that dreamy, floaty optimism. Not enough to make her fully inebriated.

Not like we all were now.

I turned, eyes scanning the fire-lit lakeshore. Leigh was sprawled out on the ground, arms stretched to the sky like she was trying to absorb the moon's energy. Two men were wrestling near the water's edge, except neither of them seemed to be winning, because every time one of them landed a move, they both burst out laughing and rolled apart, only to start again. Three other people had inexplicably stripped nude, and they were making shadow puppets against the edge of the shelter, cackling hysterically at the misshapen figures they created.

And then there was me.

I could feel the intoxication everywhere now, like my brain was floating, like everything was so damn funny for no reason at all. My skin tingled, warmth flooding through me, and I couldn't stop moving. My feet barely even touched the ground as I skipped and spun across the sand, giggling, arms outstretched like I might take off into the night.

"Aria! Come dance with me!"

I wasn't sure who was calling out to me, but I ignored them, too caught up in the sensation of freedom coursing through me. The cold air felt delicious against my skin, and I couldn't remember a time I'd ever felt this wonderful in my entire life.

The world blurred into streaks of firelight as I moved, my body thrumming with something strange and electric. Laughter and song pulsed behind me as the others continued the festivities, and my focus suddenly narrowed to a single person.

A woman stood at the edge of the woods, just beyond the reach of the fire's glow.

My mother.

My breath caught in my throat. She looked exactly as I remembered. Long dark hair cascading over her shoulders, soft eyes, a warm smile.

The sight of her should've shattered me. Should've sent grief knifing through my chest like it always did. But there was no grief now. Only joy.

She was here. She'd found me. She was going to save me. Save us all.

"Mom!" I shrieked, clapping my hands together. "How did you find us?"

She turned and disappeared into the trees.

I followed.

The world became a blur of shifting shadows and silver moonlight, branches tangling above like a cathedral ceiling. The ground felt impossibly soft beneath my bare feet, like the forest itself was welcoming me, pulling me forward.

I didn't know where I was going. Didn't care.

I danced through the trees, spinning and laughing, my arms outstretched to the night. My heart pounded with something beyond exhilaration. Something almost sacred. I felt weightless, untethered from reality, like I was floating through a dream.

My mother's voice whispered to me on the wind. "Come, darling. Come with me."

I ran faster. "I'm coming, Mom!" I called out. "Don't worry!"

I wasn't sure how long I moved like that, lost in the haze, the world tilting and shifting in strange, beautiful ways. Time just didn't seem to exist anymore. There was only the warmth in my veins, the echo of my mom's voice, and the promise that if I just kept going, I'd reach her.

And then, suddenly, there was light.

I stumbled to a stop, breathless, my pulse roaring in my ears. A cabin stood in front of me. It was weathered but sturdy, and its windows glowed with warm, golden light. Through the closest one, I could see Matthew and Knox, deep in conversation.

"Oh my god," I whispered.

This was where the Lost Boys ended up. They'd found a whole damn building to live in. No wonder they hadn't come back to bother the rest of us at the lake.

I took a step forward, heart still racing. And then—

"You're not safe with him, darling."

The voice was soft, almost sorrowful. My mother's voice.

I turned, a question on my lips, and froze.

A shadow was peeling itself from the trees, impossibly tall, its form shifting, distorting. My breath hitched, and my stomach plummeted as I looked up... right into the face of a monster.

14

ARIA

A scream ripped from my throat as I stumbled backward, heart hammering.

The thing in front of me—tall, hulking, covered in a tangle of leaves and long grass—moved too fast. Before I could turn to run, it grabbed me, strong hands locking around my arms. I thrashed wildly, but the monster held firm.

"Aria, stop!"

My blood ran cold. The monster knew my name. I must have summoned it with my intoxicated forest dance; an ancient ritual performed purely by accident.

I kept squirming and struggling, breathless gasps escaping my mouth.

"Aria, for fuck's sake, *stop*. It's me."

Landon.

Relief crashed into me so fast it made me lightheaded, and my legs nearly gave out beneath me as I blinked at him, my breath coming in ragged gasps. He was wearing a weird kind of camouflage suit that covered him from head to toe, the fabric blending seamlessly with the forest around us.

Usually, I wouldn't be relieved to run into *him*, of all people, in the middle of the night. Especially not while I was alone in the deep, dark woods. In fact, I'd be downright terrified, considering what I knew about him. But between him and a real monster... he was definitely the preferable option. Better the devil you know, as they say.

He drew back and pulled off the hooded head part of the suit, revealing his face. He opened his mouth to speak, but I got in first.

"What the hell?" I wheezed, stumbling slightly backward. "Why do you look like a swamp monster?"

He grabbed my arm again, holding me steady. "It's a ghillie suit," he said. "Some animals come out more at night, and this helps me move around without being seen. I was scouting for game when I heard you crashing through the trees like a lunatic."

"Oh my god." I exhaled deeply and put a hand over my heart, feeling the racing beat. "I honestly thought you were some sort of mutant creature hellbent on eating me."

"Sorry about that," he said with a smirk that didn't match his apologetic words. "I forgot I was wearing it when I saw you."

"Well, congrats. You scared at least five years off my life," I murmured, head shaking slightly.

"Yeah, you were really freaking out there," he said, smirk widening. "So I guess it's good that I grabbed you so fast. If I didn't, I probably would've had to chase you all the way through these woods to get you."

His words sent a jolt up my spine, and I swallowed hard, averting my eyes.

Relief was still flooding through me in waves, but underneath it, something else was simmering. A strange, forbidden thrill that curled through my veins, sending a shiver down my spine.

I'd always had an inexplicable fascination with being chased. Hunted. It wasn't something I ever talked about out loud, but in the deepest, most secret corners of my mind, I imagined it all the time. The pulse-pounding fear. The helplessness. The moment when strong, dangerous hands finally caught me, overpowering me, pressing me into the earth—

I shoved the thought away, annoyed with myself. This was different. It wasn't a fantasy. It was *Landon*, for god's sake.

And yet, my heart wasn't just hammering from fear. My breath was coming too quick, my skin felt too hot, and my body was too aware of his grip on me.

It occurred to me once again that in normal circumstances, I'd be terrified of running into Landon in the middle of the woods. Not turned on, or thinking about my secret fantasies. No, I'd run away immediately, clawing through the darkness, heart pounding with the certainty that this was *it*—that he'd finally caught me, that whatever sick game the Dominion Club was playing would end with my broken body buried in the dirt.

That was how it *should* feel, knowing what I knew about him and his intentions. But right now... it didn't feel like that at all.

The fear was suddenly distant and dulled, like it was happening to someone else. Like I was floating just above my own body, watching this unfold as if it were all a dream. The kind of dream where nothing quite made sense, but it didn't matter because it wasn't real.

That's it.

The thought hit me like a thunderbolt. None of this was real.

Landon wasn't Landon right now. At least not the version of him I was frightened of. He was just a hallucination, like my mother earlier. A shadow moving through my hazy world, slipping between the trees like something conjured from the night itself. And I wasn't me, either. Not the girl who would usually be afraid. I was someone else right now, my whole body humming with a strange, reckless exhilaration.

Maybe that was why I didn't flinch when Landon grabbed me. Why, even as his grip tightened, his fingers digging into my wrists hard enough to leave bruises by morning, I only stared up at him and thought: *this feels right.*

Because he wasn't really here.

Right?

I blinked rapidly, wondering if the vision of him would suddenly disappear, but he remained directly in front of me.

"What are you doing out here?" he asked, scanning my face with a frown. "Did you get lost?"

"Um..."

Now that the initial shock of seeing him had faded and my pulse had steadied, the strange berry haze was completely engulfing my mind again, thick and intoxicating. A giggle slipped past my lips before I could stop it, then another, bubbling up uncontrollably.

Landon's frown deepened as he studied me, obviously mistaking my laughter for the kind of post-adrenaline hysteria that sometimes came with a scare.

"Aria, did you hear me?" he asked, head tilting slightly as he dropped my wrist from his grip. "Why are you here? Were you looking for us?"

"No." Another giggle rose in my throat. I coughed to tamp it down and tilted my head, trying my best to look normal. "I was just... running."

"Running from what?" His eyes flicked up, assessing our moonlit surroundings. "Was something chasing you? Someone?"

"No. I just felt like running and dancing."

His gaze snapped back to me. "*Dancing*? Are you fucking kidding me?"

I barely heard him. I was too busy giggling softly at the way the trees seemed to breathe around us, swaying in rhythm with something I couldn't quite name.

Landon crossed his arms over his chest, staring down at me. "Aria... do you have *any* idea how dangerous it is out here?" he said in a low voice. "You could've been eaten by a fucking bear."

I slid away from him and did a little twirl, face tilted toward the starry sky. "Don't worry. The bears are my friends," I said, throwing my arms out dramatically.

The whole forest seemed to shimmer around me, every leaf and shadow pulsing with some secret, beautiful rhythm.

"Everything under this sky is my friend," I went on. I swiveled back to Landon, pointing a shaky finger. "Except *you*."

"Holy shit." He groaned, rubbing a hand down his face. "You're drunk. That's why you're being so weird."

I scoffed. "I'm not *drunk*. Your asshole friend stole all the liquor, remember?"

"So what then?" he asked, forehead wrinkling. "You downed a bottle of cough syrup or something?"

"There's no cough syrup in the first aid kit," I said, rolling my eyes. "And if there ever *was*, I'm sure Cole would've taken it to guzzle down with the rest of the stuff he stole."

Landon studied me for a moment, expression skeptical. "If you're not drunk, then what the hell is going on with you?" he asked. "Because you're sure as hell *acting* drunk. Or high."

"Well, I guess I *am* high. High on life," I said, grinning beatifically. I spun again, feeling the wind rush against my skin, the world tilting and blurring around me in a way that was both dizzying and euphoric. "It's just so beautiful out here, isn't it?"

Landon snorted. "Well, shit... that didn't take long, did it?" he said, rubbing his jaw as he watched me. "Four weeks in the wild and you've already lost it."

"I haven't lost anything," I said breezily. "I've just accepted that this is my life now. At least it will be for a long, long time. So I'm embracing it. Having fun with it."

His eyes narrowed. "Aria, you're seriously acting nuts. Are you sure you didn't take something?"

"What would I take?" I said, throwing my hands up. "We're living out in the wild, remember? There's no drugs here."

"Right." Landon scrubbed a hand across his face and sighed.

"You should really go back to your camp. It's not safe for you out here."

Not safe. That was ironic, coming from *him* of all people.

"Hold on." I frowned, hazy eyes taking in his strange suit again. "I want to know something before I go. Where did you get this gill suit, or whatever it's called? And how did you find that cabin?"

"Ghillie suit. It was in the cabin," he said. "Which we found by pure luck. And it's a good thing we did, because it's an old hunting cabin, and whoever owned it never cleared it out. I guess he must've died, and his family forgot about the place."

"So... you have hunting stuff there?"

"Yup. Knives, rifles, all sorts of shit. And there's a well out the back, too, so we have fresh water," he replied. "We've actually been doing pretty well for ourselves. That's why we returned all the non-perishable food to you guys."

I blinked, still wildly uncertain if this conversation was actually happening. "What?"

Landon frowned. "You didn't see? I brought all the stuff back to your camp a couple of weeks ago," he said. "I sneaked in when you were all sleeping."

I knew it. I knew I'd sensed Landon lurking around our camp. I wasn't just paranoid or losing my mind.

"I didn't see anything," I said, shaking my head. "Where did you put it?"

"That big blue container at the back of the supply pile. I dumped it all in there," he said. "Figured you guys might need the extra food, seeing as you exiled five of the group's most qualified hunters."

"Oh." I blinked a few times, vision swimming. "We haven't used that container since we finished the supplies that were in it, so we've had no reason to open it."

"Well, it's all there." Landon crossed his arms. "You can go back and check right now."

I glanced back at the cabin, and then toward the woods. "Um... would you mind pointing me in the right direction?" I asked, cheeks flushing hot. I hated having to ask Landon for any kind of help. Absolutely *despised* it. Even when it was just a vision of him.

He snorted. "You can't be serious."

"I think I got a little turned around when—"

He cut me off, lifting a palm. "I'm obviously *taking* you there, Aria," he said. "You don't seriously think I'd let you walk back alone in the middle of the night, do you? Especially when you've been acting like a total fucking maniac ever since you appeared here."

He didn't wait for a response. He just gripped my wrist and pulled me forward.

"Wait." I planted my feet, blinking up at him. "I want to know something first."

"I already told you where I got the suit."

"Not that. Something else." I took a deep breath, trying to focus my gaze on his face, but it was hard when everything was still shimmering. "I've started remembering stuff from before the crash. *Just* before it, I mean. And I want to know what you tried to tell me."

Landon stared down at me, expressionless. "I have no idea what you're talking about."

"Just before we crashed, you said you needed to tell me something. But then you were cut off because everything was so loud. So what was it?" I asked, tilting my head. "Were you trying to admit something? Guilty conscience, maybe?"

"You must've dreamed that," he said stiffly.

"It wasn't a dream. I remember it clear as day now," I said. "You thought we were about to die, and you suddenly felt the need to get something off your chest. I want to know what it was."

"That didn't happen, Aria."

I sighed, eyes rolling upward. "Fine," I muttered. "Keep your secret."

The conversation seemed to be over, but something was still buzzing inside me, a wild, untamed impulse that refused to settle.

Maybe it was just a side effect of the berries, or maybe it was the deep, dark part of me that I'd spent years hiding. Either way, I felt a sudden need to unburden myself of that secret, as if getting it out in words would get it out of me altogether.

Besides, nothing I said right now would actually matter in the end. Reality had blurred at the edges tonight, turning everything into a strange, surreal dream where actions had no consequences and words were just whispers in the wind.

I could say anything I wanted right now—confess my ugliest thoughts, my most shameful secrets—and it wouldn't matter. Because I wasn't really here, and this wasn't really happening. I wasn't even talking to the *real* Landon. Just a figment of my imagination.

"I'll tell you *my* secret," I blurted out. "Even if you won't tell me yours."

"Oh, yeah?" Landon crossed his arms over his chest, watching me warily. "What is it?"

Another intoxicated giggle rose in my throat, and I beckoned him with one hand. "Come closer. I have to whisper it to you."

"Why?"

"You'll see."

He let out another heavy sigh and moved closer. I stood on my tiptoes and leaned in, close enough to feel the heat of his breath against my cheek. His jaw flexed, but he didn't move away. I took that as permission and moved my mouth as close as I could to his left ear.

"Do you remember the games we played when we were kids?" I whispered. "How you used to chase me around? Pin me down? Practically torture me sometimes?"

"Yeah," he said in a low voice. "I remember."

I pulled back, staring up at him. "I used to be so scared of you," I admitted, my voice almost conspiratorial. "But later, when I got older... I started thinking about it in a different way."

Landon's brow lifted. "What way?"

"A fantasy kind of way," I murmured breathlessly. "I liked thinking about it."

Silence stretched between us, charged and heavy. Then Landon's lips curled into a slow, knowing smirk. "Is that why you used to watch me through my window when I had girls over? Or when I jerked off?" he asked. "From your own bedroom window?"

My jaw dropped, and I took two faltering steps backward. "You knew about that?"

"Of course I did. You weren't exactly the best at hiding it," he said, his smirk widening. "Did you really think I never noticed?"

"Yes." I felt my face heat. "I had no idea you saw me."

Landon studied me for a long moment. "Do you still feel that way about me?" he finally asked. His voice was lower now, more deliberate, and the way the words rolled off his tongue sent a jolt straight through me. "Still have those fantasies?"

"Of course not," I said quickly. A little *too* quickly. "We're... enemies."

"*Enemies?*" he said. His tone was incredulous. "Is this the eighteenth century? Are we dueling at dawn?"

"You know what I mean," I muttered.

"No." He cocked his head. "I want you to explain it to me."

My heart thundered in my chest as Landon's gaze burned into me, daring me to admit what I'd been hiding from the world all these years. A secret far bigger and darker than a raw, primal sexual fantasy. A secret only *he* knew existed.

I swallowed hard, looking away. "You know exactly why we're not friends."

"Say it."

"No," I shot back. "You don't get to tell me what to do."

"I thought a girl like you might *like* taking orders, given what you told me a few minutes ago."

His words sank into me like hooks piercing my skin, unraveling the reckless berry-fueled haze that had clouded my mind just moments ago. It was as if a fog had suddenly been lifted, and I was finally seeing things with sharp, painful clarity.

This wasn't a damn dream. This was real. All of it.

Oh, god...

What the hell was I thinking?

I'd told him. I'd actually *told* Landon about my fantasy. The one I'd sworn I'd take to my grave rather than admit, even to myself. And now he was looking at me—really looking. Like he saw everything and wasn't about to let me bury it again.

A fresh wave of panic rolled through me, tightening around my ribs. Maybe I could take it back. Laugh it off. Make it sound like I was just exhausted and spouting pure nonsense.

No. It was far too late for any of that.

I clenched my jaw, forcing my expression into something cold, unreadable. I wouldn't let him see how much I regretted running into him tonight. How much I suddenly wanted to disappear into the trees and pretend none of this ever happened.

"You don't get to tell me what to do," I repeated, my voice harsher than before. A feeble attempt to regain control. To put space between us. "Ever."

But Landon only smirked, that knowing glint still in his eyes. "If you say so," he said. "I'll take you back to your camp now."

"No, it's fine," I said in an acid tone, trying to mask the humiliation that was still burning through my veins like poison. "I remember the way back now, so I don't need your help anymore."

He released a sharp breath, raking a hand through his hair. Then he stepped closer, his presence overwhelming my senses.

Why did he have to be so tall? And so impossibly hot? It wasn't fair. It made it so damn hard to hate him.

"Aria," he said, drawing my name out like it was somehow a

threat. "I'm taking you back to that camp, even if I have to tie you up and throw you over my damn shoulder to get it done."

"What? You can't—"

As I protested, I jerked away from him, but he was faster. In a flash, he grabbed me, spun me, and pinned me against a tree, his body so close I could feel the heat radiating off him. His grip was firm and unyielding, but not cruel. My breath caught, my words drying up in my throat.

"Still such a brat," Landon murmured, his voice laced with dark amusement. His gaze flickered over my face, lingering on my parted lips. Then he tilted his head, his breath teasing my cheek. "You wanna know something?"

I swallowed hard. "What?"

"All those times you fantasized about playing games with me... " His voice dropped lower, rougher. "I can guarantee you I thought about it ten times as much."

My stomach flipped, a shiver skating down my spine. That was the last thing I ever expected to hear come out of Landon Ashford's mouth.

"But... you stopped, right?" I said, my voice barely audible.

"No." His gaze burned into mine. "Never."

"Really?" The word came out as a tiny squeak.

"Yeah. Really." His lips curled slightly. Then his hand moved, fingers brushing lightly over the curve of my wrist, tracing higher, just enough to make my skin prickle. "And you know what else?"

I shook my head, heart hammering.

"I think you're a liar," he said smoothly. His hand ghosted over the bare skin of my arm, making me shudder. "I don't think you stopped either. That's why you always act like such a fucking brat around me."

I let out a shaky breath.

"I think you *like* being a bad girl." His voice was like dark silk now, wrapping around me, winding tight. "You like getting in trouble because you want me to chase you down and punish you."

His fingers curled around my wrist, just tight enough to keep me from bolting. "Just like you always fantasized about."

I opened my mouth, but no words came out.

"I'm right, aren't I?" he said in a taunting tone. "You're a dirty little liar, and you want me to give you exactly what you deserve, don't you?"

"I..."

That was the only word I managed to eke out before my throat closed up again.

Landon leaned in, his lips just grazing my ear. His breath was warm, teasing. "I'm going to give you what you want, Aria," he murmured, his tone edged with something dangerous. "And I'll take what I want at the same time. I've waited long enough."

A shudder tore through me. "What do you mean?" I whispered raggedly, finally able to muster up the words.

"You know exactly what I mean," he said, pulling back.

He tilted his head, eyes glittering with malicious amusement as he pulled a hunting knife from a hidden pocket in the suit. The blade caught the moonlight, flashing silver between us.

"We can do this the easy way," he went on, voice low, almost amused. He turned the knife in his hand, his smirk widening. "Or the hard way."

My pulse pounded against my skull. I took a step back. Then another. "I... I don't understand."

Landon took a slow step forward, casually twirling the knife. "Hard way it is, then," he said. "But I'm feeling generous, so I'll give you a good head start."

My stomach twisted. "*What?*"

"I'm gonna count down from ten." He took a slow step forward, knife twisting in his hand. "And then I'm coming after you, baby."

My breath caught. He wasn't serious. Was he?

"Ten..." Another step. "Nine..."

Oh, shit.

Landon *was* serious. Deadly serious.

The air between us vibrated with something electric; something dark and thrilling and terrifying all at once. I sucked in a deep breath and spun away from him, feet almost slipping on a pile of leaves.

Then I ran like hell.

15

ARIA

BRANCHES WHIPPED AT MY ARMS AS I TORE THROUGH THE woods, breath coming in short, sharp bursts. My heart was pounding so fast it barely felt like individual beats anymore. Just one long, unbroken surge of panic.

Landon's voice followed me, lazy and taunting. "Eight... seven..."

I had no idea where I was going. The trees were just dark shapes in the night, shifting and stretching as if they might close in around me at any second. The world tilted and spun slightly—whether from the berries still in my system or the sheer terror flooding my veins, I wasn't sure.

As leaves crunched underfoot, my breath came in sharp, ragged gasps, and my heart pounded against my ribs, hammering so hard it hurt. I didn't dare look back, but I could feel Landon behind me. Hunting me.

Six... five... four... three...

Was he actually still counting back there? Had I really been given a full head start? I had no way of knowing, because I couldn't hear him anymore, and time had turned to liquid, slipping through my fingers as adrenaline took over.

A sudden thrill shot through me, sharp and electric. I shouldn't have felt it—not with all this terror curling in my gut and my body screaming at me to run faster—but deep down, in some twisted, unspoken part of me, I did.

Because this wasn't just any chase. This was *him*. Landon fucking Ashford.

The boy who used to drive me crazy. The man who made me want to set fire to everything around me. The one who hated me so much he wanted me dead; who had even tried to kill me before.

And yet...

Somewhere, buried beneath all the panic, was something else. Something dark and breathless.

Excitement.

Because I'd fantasized about this. Not anything as specific as Landon chasing me through the woods with a knife after a plane crash stranded us together in the wilds of Canada, of course, but still... I'd dreamed of something similar. I'd spent countless nights touching myself under the blankets as I lay alone in bed, imagining myself being hunted. Being caught. Being pinned down. Being claimed.

My body burned with the thought, shame rising hot in my throat. *This isn't a fantasy game, Aria,* the logical part of my mind told me. *Landon isn't playing. He's really trying to kill you.*

But when his voice echoed through the trees again—low, taunting, filled with savage promise—I nearly stumbled, and I wasn't sure whether it was truly an accident or if part of me had actually willed it to happen.

"Two... one..."

He was counting down very slowly. Giving me time. Toying with me.

The realization sent a shiver through me. He wanted to draw out the terror as long as possible. Wanted me shaken, breathless, and right on the edge of breaking down.

I pushed harder, weaving through the trees, searching desperately for a place to hide. I needed to think, but my mind was a chaotic mess, torn between the terror of being hunted and the aching, undeniable thrill of it.

I spotted a massive tree up ahead, its thick trunk curling around an outcrop of moss-covered rock. It looked like a good hiding place, so I veered toward it, pressing myself into the shadows and willing my body to disappear into the night.

I clapped a hand over my mouth to quiet my gasps. The forest was thick with the scent of damp leaves and pine, and the air was so still I could hear my own heartbeat.

Then I heard him.

"Ready or not, here I come..."

Crunch. A slow, deliberate footstep. Then another.

I squeezed my eyes shut. *Please don't see me. Please don't see me.*

Silence. It seemed to stretch on for an eternity, and then—

"I see you, baby."

A chill shot straight through me. I launched from my hiding place, darting between the trees, but I barely made it five steps before I felt a sharp tug on my arm, strong fingers curling around my wrist.

I yelped as Landon yanked me back, his body colliding with mine.

"Gotcha," he murmured.

I gasped, twisting hard, but his grip was iron. He shoved me against a tree, just like before, his body pressing against mine, trapping me in place.

My breath came in frantic, desperate pants, but not all of it was due to fear. It was because Landon was everywhere. His scent—cedar laced with a hint of smoke and something undeniably male—wrapped around me, and his breath fanned against my cheek, the warmth of his body searing through my clothes.

"You picked the worst possible hiding spot," he said, voice

dripping with amusement. "Almost like you *wanted* me to catch you."

I shook my head fervently. "No."

"No?" He tilted his head, smirking. "You sure about that?"

"Y-yes," I said, internally cringing at the quaver in my voice.

"Are you scared of me, Aria?"

"No." I lifted my chin, trying my best to sound brave. "I... I'm not."

He chuckled at my cringeworthily obvious lie. "Then why are you shaking?"

I opened my mouth, but nothing came out. He wasn't wrong. I *was* shaking. Not just from terror, but from something deeper. Something hotter.

He leaned in, lips grazing the shell of my ear. "You know, for a second back there, when you were running so fast, I *almost* believed that you really didn't want me to catch you."

I swallowed hard. "I didn't. I just told you that."

A chuckle. Low, dark, knowing. "Liar."

A tremor ran through me. I *was* a liar. There was some sick, twisted part of me that wanted this. Wanted him to chase me, to catch me, to press me against this tree and take whatever he wanted from me. No permission. No boundaries. Just him using my body for his pleasure.

His fingers trailed along my arm, slow and teasing. He wasn't restraining me anymore, but I didn't move a muscle. Didn't dare.

"You should've run faster," he murmured. His hand traced lower, fingers brushing the curve of my hip. "You shouldn't have let me catch you."

I swallowed, my mouth suddenly dry. "I... I tried."

"Not hard enough."

He pulled back slightly, just enough to look me in the eyes, and the moonlight caught his face, casting sharp shadows over his cheekbones and jaw. His expression was unreadable, his gaze burning.

Then, in a slow, deliberate movement, he brought the knife up. My stomach clenched, but he didn't press it to my throat. He dragged it down my arm instead, barely grazing the skin, just enough for me to feel a slight sting. A warning.

"Next time I count down," he said in a low voice, "you better pray I don't catch you."

Then, just as suddenly as he'd caught me, he let go. I stumbled backward, breath shuddering out of me, my body burning and my mind spinning.

Landon smirked. "Run, baby," he said. He twirled the knife in his hand, eyes glinting. "*Run.*"

I turned and fled.

This time, the chase felt different. Before, I had been running for my life, but now, I wasn't entirely sure why I was running. Was it because I was actually terrified? Or because I *wanted* to be terrified?

Or was it because I knew that no matter how fast I went, no matter how hard I tried, Landon was going to catch me... and I wanted to know what would happen when he did?

The forest stretched out before me in endless shadows and tangled roots, moonlight slicing through the canopy in fractured beams. My pulse roared in my ears, and my legs felt like they were on fire from the first chase, but I forced myself forward anyway, pushing through brambles and dodging low-hanging branches.

From somewhere behind me, I heard him.

Not running. Not crashing through the underbrush like I was. Just... moving. Steadily. Patiently. Like a predator stalking his prey. An alpha hunter who knew he couldn't possibly miss his target.

A shiver ran down my spine, but I didn't dare to stop. I veered left, leaping over a fallen log, then sprinted across a narrow strip of moonlit clearing before plunging back into the thick shadows of the trees.

"Five..."

Landon's voice drifted through the trees, smooth and lazy. Mocking.

I swallowed hard, pushing forward, breath coming faster.

"Four... three... two... one..."

Landon's voice was suddenly much closer. I could hear his footsteps now too. Heavy but unrushed. Once again, he wasn't in a hurry, because he knew how easily he could catch me.

"Here I come..."

I bit down on a whimper and pushed harder, feet barely touching the ground as I vaulted over another fallen log. My bad ankle twisted slightly on impact, pain shooting up my leg, but I didn't stop. Couldn't stop.

A laugh echoed through the trees behind me, dark and knowing.

I lurched forward again, tearing through the underbrush. My heart was beating so fast it felt like it would explode right out of my ribcage, and my legs hurt like hell, but I didn't slow down.

I stumbled down a small incline, catching myself on a tree trunk just before I went flying. My breath hitched. God, where the hell was I going? There was no path out here. No sense of direction. Only the raw, primal instinct to flee.

More footsteps crunched behind me. *Shit, shit, shit.* I wasn't outpacing Landon. He was already closing in.

I veered right, nearly skidding as I spotted a narrow dip in the earth. It was a gully, half-hidden by ferns. If I could get down there, crouch low enough, maybe...

No. I wasn't going to make it. I bolted again instead, weaving between trees in desperate, frantic zigzags.

"You're making this too easy, Aria."

Landon's voice was even closer now. How was he doing this? How was he so damn fast? Obviously, he was much bigger and stronger than me, but with all the head starts, I thought I'd at least make it far enough away to have a chance at escape.

I gasped, lungs burning. I couldn't let him catch me, couldn't let him—

A rough hand snagged my wrist. I yelped, twisting violently, but Landon was already yanking me back; an unyielding force crashing into me from behind. I bucked against him, but he spun me easily, and my back slammed against a tree, his body pinning me there.

Caught.

A sharp breath tore from my lips, my chest heaving against his. My mind spun, but the haze was gone. No more dizzying warmth from the berries. No more dreamlike daze making everything feel soft and unreal. The sheer, brutal adrenaline of the chase had burned it all away in an instant.

I was stone-cold sober. And now, with terrifying clarity, I could feel and understand everything.

Landon's grip was firm and unrelenting as his fingers curled around my wrists, pinning them above my head against the rough bark. His body pressed into mine, heat searing through my clothes.

I kicked out instinctively, thrashing, but it only made him press harder, a sharp breath escaping his lips as his knee wedged between my thighs, keeping me locked in place.

A dark chuckle vibrated against my skin. "You almost made it that time," he murmured. "But we both know you were never going to make it in the end."

I whimpered and turned my face away, but he caught my chin between his fingers, tilting my gaze back to his. His eyes almost looked black in the moonlight, dark pools of malice.

"You liked it, didn't you?" he said softly.

I shook my head, the denial automatic, but I could feel my own body betraying me. My chest heaved against his, and a traitorous shiver slid down my spine.

"You did." He studied me for a long, agonizing moment. Then

he smirked. "Should I count down again? Give you another chance to run?"

My stomach twisted, but words wouldn't come. I didn't even know what I'd say if I *could* speak.

Landon leaned in, lips barely grazing the shell of my ear. "Or maybe I was right before," he muttered. "You wanted to be caught."

A sharp exhale left me. He was right, and I hated that he knew it.

Tree bark dug into my back as my chest heaved, each ragged breath scraping my throat. The chase had left my muscles burning and my heart hammering like a war drum, and suddenly I couldn't stop whimpering. It was the animal side of me, primal and relentless.

I'm prey. Like I always wanted...

I should've been thrilled to have my fantasy realized, but every ounce of the exhilaration I'd felt throughout the chase vanished the moment I saw Landon's knife again. Moonlight gleamed off the sharp edge as he turned it between his fingers, lazy and unhurried, as if he had all the time in the world.

A hollow, aching numbness spread through my limbs, turning my blood to ice. This was it. Landon was done toying with me. He was finally going to end it.

Tears burned at the back of my eyes, but I refused to let them fall. Refused to give him that satisfaction. Instead, I forced myself to meet his gaze. Then I swallowed hard, my voice barely above a whisper. "Just get it over with."

Landon stilled. For a second, he said nothing. Just watched me, the knife motionless in his grip. Then, to my shock, his lips curled into a smirk.

"Get it over with?" His voice was low, amused. "No, baby." He moved even closer, the heat of his body radiating against mine. "I plan on taking my time with you."

He reached out, trailing the blunt edge of the knife up my

arm. My skin prickled beneath the cold metal, my breath coming in shallow gasps.

He leaned in, lips grazing the shell of my ear. "Did you really think I'd let you off that easily?" he muttered. The cruel amusement in his tone made my insides clench.

I couldn't move. Couldn't breathe. Landon wasn't just going to kill me. He was going to torture me first. Really savor it.

He took a step back, his gaze dragging over my body. "Strip," he commanded.

My stomach plummeted. "W-what?"

"Strip," he repeated, voice calm but edged with warning. "Don't make me say it again, Aria."

A shudder rolled through me. I had no choice but to do as he said. Defying him would probably only worsen whatever twisted torment he planned to inflict upon me.

With stiff, halting movements, I peeled myself away from the tree and kicked off my shoes and socks. My fingers trembled as I gripped the hem of my thick sweater, dragging it over my head before slipping out of my shirt and leggings. The night air licked at my exposed skin, leaving goosebumps in its wake.

Straightening, I lifted my chin and forced myself to meet Landon's gaze. It was cold. Unrelenting. He took a slow step forward, lifting the tip of his blade between my breasts.

"That too," he murmured, eyes flicking to my bra.

I swallowed hard and reached behind me, unhooking the clasp with trembling fingers. As the lacy fabric slid from my shoulders, my nipples hardened. Not just from the cold, but from the sheer force of Landon's stare as his gaze raked over me.

The tip of the knife pressed against my sternum again, urging me backward. I moved hesitantly, step by step, until my spine met the cold bark of the tree trunk behind me.

Landon quickly closed the space between us, his body sealing me in. I shivered and squirmed beneath him. Wild, frantic, desperate. I knew he had me trapped, but my body was running

THE WILD

on instinct, seeking any angle of escape. Anything to get away and—

His free hand suddenly collared my throat. "Stop fighting," he growled.

Defiance flared in me, white-hot and desperate. I stubbornly kicked out at his leg, but he didn't even flinch. Instead, his lips curved into a wicked smirk, and he tightened his hold, cutting off my air just enough to make my vision blur at the edges.

Realizing I was totally and utterly beaten, the fight drained out of me again, and I went limp.

"Good girl," he muttered, pulling his hand away.

His fingers uncurled from my throat as he pocketed the knife, freeing both hands. Before I could process the shift, he grabbed my shoulders, yanked me forward, and spun me around. My back crashed into his chest, and his arms wrapped around me like a cage.

I barely had time to gasp before he pressed me against the tree again, this time facing it. My bare breasts met the rough bark, but instead of scraping my skin raw, the layer of moss growing on it softened the impact. A small mercy.

One of Landon's hands wrapped around my throat again, holding me in place so the back of my head rested against his shoulder. The other hand tangled in my hair, yanking hard enough to make tears prick at my eyes.

He shifted slightly, leaning in until I felt his stiff cock pressed against my lower back. My terror twisted, mutating into something hotter that coiled deep in my belly, like a tightly wound spring. The shift was instant and overwhelming, and shame crashed into me right behind it.

What the hell was wrong with me? I was staring down death at the hands of a violent predator, but my body didn't seem to care. Heat pulsed between my thighs, my skin tight and oversensitive, and my nipples were so hard they ached.

A hot tear slipped down my cheek, and a broken whimper escaped me. "Please," I said, voice barely audible. I didn't even know what I was begging for. Mercy? Freedom? Or the release my traitorous body craved?

Landon's breath ghosted over my ear. "Stay still and it won't hurt," he muttered.

But everything already hurt. Not from his grip on my scalp, or the way he had me caged against the tree. No, the real agony came from the unbearable tension winding inside me. From the raw, aching need I couldn't suppress. The heat. The want. The sick, twisted arousal that made my thighs clench even as I trembled with fear.

Landon's fingers finally slid from my hair, and for a split second, relief shuddered through me. Then my stomach flipped at the unmistakable swishing sound of the knife sliding free from his pocket.

I sucked in a sharp breath as the cold blade skimmed down my right side, an agonizingly slow descent that left a trail of goosebumps in its wake. Then, with one swift motion, he sliced through the thin cotton of my underwear.

The ruined fabric slipped down my legs, pooling around my ankles as a strangled noise lodged in my throat.

The knife disappeared again, and so did Landon's grip on my neck. He stepped back, and I heard a rustling sound behind me. I didn't dare turn my head to see what it was. Didn't dare move at all.

Before I could even begin to speculate about what he was doing, he moved back to me and gripped my right hip, slowly running his hand around to my front before finally reaching my pussy. I was so wet that I could feel the arousal slicking down my thighs... and now Landon knew it.

A groan escaped him as he gathered up my wetness with his fingers, spreading it all over my aching clit. "Fuck, baby," he murmured. "You love this, don't you?"

I let out a whimper in response. I wanted to hate absolutely everything about it. Instead, I found myself arching my back and spreading my legs as delicious heat rushed down my spine, because Landon was right. I loved this. Fucking loved every twisted, excruciating second.

Every muscle tensed with anticipation as his fingers swept down, splaying my lips before teasing my clit. Then I felt his body slide lower behind me as he slowly bent at the knee to accommodate our height difference.

With that, he angled the head of his hard cock right at my entrance, sending another burst of arousal through me. Now I knew what he'd been doing behind me before—removing his suit.

I whimpered with a mix of relief and pure desire as I felt him there, just teasing the slick edges of my entrance with the very tip of his cock. Without warning, he suddenly thrust forward, sliding into me until he bottomed out, his thick length filling me perfectly. At the same time, his hand returned to my throat, curling around the base.

"Oh, fuck," he growled. "You feel so fucking *good*."

I couldn't help the needy sounds that escaped my mouth as he withdrew his cock and slammed back into me, meeting almost no resistance because I was so damn horny. He did it over and over, punctuating each thrust with heavy breaths and filthy words.

"So. Fucking. Wet," he gritted out, slipping his free hand between our bodies to find my clit again. "You take me so fucking well, baby."

"Yes," I whimpered. "Oh, god... *yes*."

"Don't hold back now, baby," he said, voice deep and commanding. "Scream for me. Let everyone in this whole fucking wilderness hear what a filthy slut you are for me."

"Yes!" Stars began to glimmer in my vision. "Please... more!"

"Say it," he commanded. "Say how badly you want to come. Say it like a good little whore."

"I... I want to come," I panted. "Please let me come!"

He let out a primal grunt, hand tightening ever-so-slightly around my throat. "What would everyone think if they saw you like this, Aria?" he asked in a low voice. "The president's daughter getting fucked in the forest like a dirty slut. Like a fucking animal."

He was right. We were just two animals in the wild right now, taking from each other in a frenzy of primal hunger and reckless abandon.

"You were made for this," he went on. "Made to be my perfect little fucktoy."

"Yes," I whimpered as the pressure inside me built and built.

"This is what you always wanted, isn't it, baby?" Landon growled against my ear, rubbing my clit. "This is what you imagined."

"Ye—"

I suddenly lost the ability to speak as the orgasm finally hit me.

My muscles clenched around Landon's cock, my back arching even more as my nerve endings sparked blissfully hotter. Loud gasps spilled from my lips, and I was barely able to remain standing as my knees buckled.

Landon kept me upright with his powerful arms, hips snapping against mine as he fucked me through my climax. "That's it," he muttered. "Come on my cock like the dirty little slut you are."

"M-more," I managed to choke out as his hand tightened around my throat again. "Please..."

"Don't worry, baby. When I'm done using you, you'll come again," he said in a hard voice. "Won't you?"

That almost made me melt into a puddle at the base of the tree. *Yes!* I wanted to scream. But words were failing me again. Instead I just moaned, eyes rolling back with pure ecstasy.

"Fuck, Aria," Landon ground out, slamming into me again. "You know what you're doing to me, don't you?"

I tried to shake my head, but his grip around my throat made the movement barely more than a tremor.

He released me and leaned in slightly, tilting my head back to kiss me. It was rough and savage, and I tasted a bead of blood springing up on my lips as he swallowed my whimpers.

"You know I can never walk away from this now," he finally went on, pulling back. At the same time, his fingers collared my neck again. "Not when I've had this sweet, perfect pussy wrapped around my cock."

He slammed his hips into mine, fingers pressing hard on my throat. This time my air was cut off entirely, and black spots began to dance in my vision. A second later, he let go, allowing me to suck in a singular breath before he did it again.

And again.

"Please," I whimpered. "Can't... breathe."

"That's the point, baby," Landon muttered. "You'll see."

I wanted to argue. Wanted to gasp for every available bit of oxygen. But when my head started swimming, I finally realized what the lack of air was doing to me. It was heightening my arousal—something I didn't even think was possible at this stage—and when Landon's fingers squeezed my throat again, the scream I let out had nothing to do with fear.

"I'm... I'm going to come again," I whispered raggedly.

"Beg for it," he snarled, snatching his hand away from my clit.

Tears of desperation sprang to my eyes. "Please. *Please*. Let me come. Let me—"

He cut me off, hand squeezing my throat until the black spots returned to my vision, along with a smattering of stars. At the same time, his cock thrust back into me, brutal and violent, and his free hand went between my legs to rub my clit again.

My legs were shaking like crazy now, knees threatening to buckle as more stars burst across my vision. *Oh, god.* I was going to die like this, with Landon's thick fingers wrapped around my throat.

But just as everything started to feel fuzzy again, he released his hand, and another orgasm hit me like a tidal wave, so powerful it almost tore me apart. It should've hurt, but I was pretty sure I'd never come this hard before, and the overwhelming pleasure drowned out any pain.

Tomorrow, I'd be covered in bruises, and it would be painful to swallow, but right now... none of that mattered. All that mattered was this climax; the most intense pleasure I'd ever experienced.

"There you are, baby," Landon muttered as my muscles clenched wildly on his cock. "I knew you had it in you."

"Y-yes," I managed to gasp out, body jerking and shuddering with pure bliss.

He gritted out a curse word and leaned down, teeth sinking into the side of my neck as his hips collided with mine one last time. Then he grunted and stilled, finding his own release.

As I felt his cum spurt inside me, I silently thanked the White House doctor, who'd suggested I get a birth control implant in my arm when I told her that I wasn't currently sexually active, but definitely would be if I could simply find a decent guy.

Just in case you suddenly meet him and get caught up in the heat of the moment, she'd said at the time. *I remember what it was like at that age.*

And thank god she did, because I couldn't imagine getting pregnant and giving birth out here in the wilderness.

A sudden wave of exhaustion crashed over me, so heavy it nearly stole the breath from my lungs. The adrenaline that had kept me running, fighting, and surviving earlier... it had drained away in an instant, leaving my limbs heavy and useless.

I barely registered the way my body sagged, or the way the earth seemed to tilt beneath me. One second I was standing and the next I was sinking, my legs no longer able to hold me up.

Strong arms caught me before I could crumple to the forest

floor. A firm chest pressed against my back, steady and solid, anchoring me against the overwhelming pull of unconsciousness.

"I've got you," Landon muttered.

I wanted to fight him. Wanted to tell him not to touch me, not to act like he cared, not when I knew what he was underneath all the lust and fervor. But I couldn't summon the words. Couldn't summon anything. My body had given up, betraying me once again.

Landon's grip tightened, one arm banding across my stomach, the other curling around my shoulders as he lowered us both to the ground. "It's okay," he murmured, his lips close to my temple. "I've got you."

I've got you.

The words barely registered before the darkness swallowed me whole.

16

ARIA

I WOKE WITH A SLOW, HEAVY GROGGINESS THAT CLUNG TO MY limbs like wet sand. My head throbbed, and my mouth was dry and cottony, as if I'd been drinking all night.

Those goddamn berries.

I blinked up at the crude ceiling of the shelter, the logs stacked against the rocky outcrop to form makeshift walls. Golden morning light filtered through the gaps, casting thin stripes across the dirt floor.

A blanket was tucked snugly around me, and my body was curled in the exact same spot I always slept in. My clothes, the same ones I wore yesterday, were still on. They were totally intact, as if nothing had happened.

I swallowed, confusion prickling at the edges of my sluggish thoughts. Had I imagined everything that happened last night? The hunt, the cold bite of a blade against my skin, the wild sex up against the tree? Had it all been some twisted hallucination brought on by exhaustion and whatever lingering effects the berries had left in my system?

I was starting to think that was definitely the case, but then I tried to move.

A deep ache immediately radiated through my body, and I sucked in a harsh breath, my muscles protesting as if I'd been running for my life... because I *had*.

I sat up slowly, wincing, and peeled back my sweater sleeves. Bruises, dark and fresh, ringed my wrists. My stomach twisted as I tugged up the hem of my shirt. More bruises, scattered across my ribs and hips. Scratches lined my skin too, thin and stinging. And underneath my leggings...

No underwear.

A shudder ran through me, and my breath came faster, heart thudding as it all crashed back in a violent wave.

It was real. The chase through the woods. The way Landon caught me. The knife gliding against my skin. The way I'd desperately wanted it.

But the last thing I remembered was the sheer exhaustion hitting me all at once, my legs giving out, and the world tilting sideways before everything went dark.

Landon must have dressed me—minus my wrecked underwear—and carried me all the way back here. He must've sneaked into the camp while everyone else was already asleep, brought me into the shelter, and laid me down so carefully that I never even stirred.

And he knew exactly where to put me.

That meant he'd watched us before. More than once. He knew the camp, knew our routines. Knew every detail of my current existence.

I swallowed hard, my pulse still unsteady as I sat up straighter, scanning the shelter.

Beside me, Hannah snored softly, with Carrie curled up on her other side. Both of them looked fine. So did everyone else, most of whom were still asleep in their usual spots. The only evidence of last night's chaos lay at the shelter's edges, where a few people were sprawled in various states of undress, obviously too inebriated to crawl to their beds before passing out.

I exhaled quietly, relieved that Hannah had been too full to eat any of the berries. Things could've gone so much worse if she did.

Moving carefully, I slid out from under my blanket and tiptoed outside, making my way to the secondary shelter. Some people in the group had built it during the first week as a makeshift storage hut to protect our personal belongings and supplies from the elements.

I knelt beside my suitcase, rifling through an unzipped pocket until my fingers closed around my compact mirror. Flipping it open, I lifted it to my face and inhaled sharply.

My neck was covered in bruises. Not deep purple, like I'd been strangled half to death, but enough to stand out. There was a bite mark, too.

I snapped the compact shut. I'd have to wear my hair down for the next few days. Or a scarf, perhaps. The weather was getting colder each day, so at least I'd have a good excuse for that.

I shoved the compact away and grabbed some fresh clothes, shampoo, soap, and toothpaste from my case. Before heading out, I hesitated by the food supplies. Then I opened the large blue container that none of us had used since the perishables we originally stored in there ran out.

It was packed to the brim with the Lost Boys' share of the non-perishables. Granola bars, chips, mini cans of Pringles, nuts, pretzels, and bags of candy.

I almost cried with relief at the sight of it all. It wasn't the healthiest assortment of food, but it could help our group through the harsh winter when it came. It could even be the difference between life and death.

Landon actually told me the truth last night.

That stunning realization should've brought me nothing but relief. Instead, it twisted inside me like a knife. How could someone so ruthless, so utterly unfeeling in one moment, turn around and do something that might actually save us? How could the same man who wanted me dead also be the one secretly ensuring that I wouldn't starve?

It didn't make any sense.

I wanted to keep hating him. I *should* hate him. And yet, knowing he'd done this—provided for our group in his own way— made it impossible to place him neatly into the role of 'villain'.

He wasn't just cruel. He wasn't just sadistic. He wasn't just *anything*. He was a contradiction in every single way.

That scared me, because it meant I couldn't predict him. It also meant that somewhere beneath the violence and domineering control, there was something else. Something... human.

I clenched my jaw, forcing the thought away. It didn't matter why Landon did this. It didn't make up for anything. But as I shut the container, sealing away the proof of his strange mercy, I couldn't ignore the way my hands trembled.

With a sigh, I slipped out of the storage shelter, padding down the beach past the fire pit. The shore curved to the right ahead, leading to a secluded portion of the lake that was mostly hidden from the main camp. It had become our unofficial bathing spot, offering at least a semblance of privacy.

A rope hung between two trees nearby, a makeshift clothesline for drying towels and garments. I grabbed my towel from the end and set it on a rock with my clean clothes. Then I stripped down, bundling my dirty outfit in one hand while clutching my shampoo and soap in the other.

The moment I stepped into the lake, icy water licked up my calves, sending a shiver through me. But as I waded deeper, the cold dulled my aching muscles, making me groan in relief.

Once my body adjusted, I lathered up, suds trailing down my skin and into the water. My clothes bobbed nearby, soaking in the runoff. It was a poor substitute for washing detergent, but better than nothing.

When I was done, I quickly slipped out of the lake to hang my wet clothes on the line. Then I returned to the water and floated on my back, eyes closed. The cold had seeped deep into my limbs by now, numbing the lingering aches and pains, dulling the bruises and scratches.

For a moment, it was easy to pretend that none of last night had happened. That I hadn't been chased through the woods like prey, caught, pinned, and broken down by a man who was both my captor and my savior. But the phantom weight of his hands still lingered on my skin. The rasp of his voice in my ear. The rough scrape of tree bark against my back.

I exhaled slowly, forcing the memories away. The lake was peaceful, the early morning stillness only interrupted by the occasional birdcall or rustling in the trees. Here, I could just exist. No fear, no hunger, no Landon. Just water and sky.

A sudden voice shattered the quiet.

"Aria?"

I gasped, jerking upright in the water, arms wrapping around myself on instinct. My heart slammed against my ribs as I spun around, searching for the source of the voice.

Leigh stood a few feet away on the shoreline, hands raised in surrender. "Sorry," she said quickly, grinning. "I called out a few times, but I think your ears were underwater."

I pressed a hand to my chest, willing my pulse to slow. "It's okay," I said, returning her smile as I waded closer to the shore. "I didn't know anyone else was awake yet."

"Yeah, everyone else is still asleep." Leigh took a step closer to the water's edge, and her eyes widened. "Oh my god, what happened to you? Are you okay?"

My stomach dropped as I glanced down. The water had washed away most of the dirt and grime on my body, leaving the bruises and scratches stark against my pale skin.

I forced a sheepish smile. "I ran into the woods when I was high on those berries last night," I said. "I think I may have run into a few trees along the way."

I felt bad for lying, but the truth was so much worse.

If I told her what really happened—if I admitted that Landon had hunted me down, pinned me against a tree, and bruised my skin with his hands and teeth—what then? Would she actually believe me when I said I wanted it? That the terror of the chase had twisted into something else entirely by the time Landon caught me?

No. It was better to keep it to myself.

Understanding flickered across Leigh's face. "Oh god, I remember now," she said, pressing the heel of her hand into her forehead. "I saw you running toward the woods, and then you just disappeared."

I shrugged, forcing out a quiet laugh. "Honestly, I'm lucky I didn't break something. Or get completely lost."

"No shit." Leigh lowered herself to sit on the sand, rubbing her temples with a sheepish smile. "When it happened, I was so high that I had the craziest thought for a second. I genuinely believed some kind of pagan forest deity had spirited you away to another realm."

I grinned and arched a brow. "Seriously?"

"Yeah." She laughed softly, shaking her head. "I was sitting there thinking, '*The God of the Woods has taken her as payment.*' Probably because we ate too many fish from the lake or something. It seemed like such a normal thought process to have at the time."

I thought back to the number of times I'd whimpered '*Oh, god*' last night and privately thought that Leigh's intoxicated assessment actually wasn't too far off.

"We were all high as hell," I said, giving her a faint smile. "I hallucinated my mother. That's why I ran into the woods. I was trying to follow her."

Leigh rubbed her forehead. "Some crazy things happened to me too. I honestly believed I was sitting by the fire chatting to Nicole Kidman for a whole hour."

"Lucky you. She's one of my favorite actresses."

"Mine too." She smiled, but it quickly faded. She looked down and hesitated, chewing her bottom lip, before looking up at me again. "Hey, um... I need you to be real with me about something."

My stomach twisted. *Oh no.*

She knew I'd lied before. Knew exactly what I'd done last night. That I'd slept with the enemy.

"Okay," I said lightly, trying not to let my nerves creep into my voice. "What is it?"

She frowned. "Maybe you should get out of the water before we talk. Your lips are starting to turn blue."

I swallowed hard and nodded, slipping out of the water to grab my towel. After drying off, I sat beside Leigh, my heart pounding.

She turned to me, brows still furrowed. "So... be honest with me, please. Don't sugarcoat things just to make me feel better," she said. She took a deep breath and went on. "Do you think the group might vote to exile me after what happened last night?"

I blinked. "What?"

"Because of the berry thing." She dropped her gaze to the sand, fidgeting with a stray twig. "I'm worried everyone will hate my guts now. I mean... the whole thing was my fault."

"No, it wasn't," I said firmly. "Those berries seemed safe, and you even tested them first. You couldn't have known we'd all end up tripping balls for hours."

"But you warned me," she said, meeting my eyes with guilt written all over her face. "You told me we should leave them behind, and I insisted on taking them anyway."

"You were just trying to make sure we had enough food," I said. "It's not like you *meant* to drug everyone."

She exhaled shakily. "Yeah, but... what if something terrible ended up happening last night? What if Hannah ate them, wandered into the lake, and drowned while we were too high to notice? What if someone fell out of a tree and cracked their skull open? Or what if you got lost in the woods and didn't come back?"

I squeezed her shoulder. "Leigh, none of that happened. We got lucky. And no one is going to blame you for something you didn't mean to do."

She looked at me again, eyes wide with anxiety. "You're sure?"

"Yes. Positive. You're trying your best out here. We all are," I said. "And look, even if the others *did* decide to be total assholes and kick you out... I'd go with you."

"Really?"

"Yeah, really. I wouldn't let you go off alone. But like I said, that won't happen, because no one will want to exile you over this." I gave her shoulder another reassuring squeeze. "And honestly? I think most people *enjoyed* last night, even if it was a little dangerous in hindsight."

A small smile tugged at her lips. "I guess that's true. I did have a lot of fun."

"I'm a bit jealous that you got to talk to Nicole Kidman, to be honest," I said, trying to lighten the mood.

Her smile widened. "She told me she was making a movie about us, so she came out here to research everything we've been doing. And she brought snacks, too. She filled up that blue box in the storage shelter." She laughed, shaking her head. "I swear, I actually *remember* eating a candy bar. It felt so damn real."

My stomach flipped.

Leigh must have stumbled across Landon's little surprise while she was still high. But sooner or later, she and the others would realize the food was really there, and then they'd probably lose their minds trying to figure out how it got there.

I had to get ahead of it.

"That blue box *is* full of food," I said. "I noticed it this morning. The lid was half off."

Leigh's eyes widened. "Wait, what? How's that possible?"

"I think it might be..." I hesitated, scrambling for an excuse.

"I saw something in the woods last night. At first, I thought it was just a hallucination, but now... I think it might've been real."

She leaned in slightly. "What did you see?"

"A cabin. A big one, all lit up. I could see Matthew and Knox through the window. There was a well outside, and a bunch of hunting gear on the porch."

Leigh's brows dipped in a contemplative frown. "You think that's where they've been staying?"

"Yeah, it must be. And if they have resources there, maybe they felt bad about taking the plane food and decided to return it all."

She nodded slowly. "That's actually really decent of them. Especially considering we tossed them all out on their asses."

"Yeah," I murmured. "Really decent."

Leigh blew out a deep breath, shaking her head. "So... the Lost Boys aren't so lost after all," she said. "Good for them, I guess. Apart from whichever one of them killed Mark."

I forced a small smile, but inside, my stomach was twisting. I hated lying—even lying by omission—but lately, that was all I seemed to be doing.

"Hey... Leigh?"

We both turned at the sound of a hesitant voice. A dark-haired man stood a few feet away, waving awkwardly. It was Ryan—one of the guys who'd been tasked with hunting. He'd taken down both of the deer the group had managed to bring back so far.

"Sorry to interrupt," he added, rubbing the back of his neck.

"It's fine. We were just chatting," Leigh said. "What's up?"

"You work in anthropology, right?"

"Yup. How come?"

He hesitated for a few seconds and moved closer. "I didn't bring this up last night because... well, honestly, I was high as a kite," he said. "I guess we all were. But anyway, when Trent and I were scouting for deer yesterday afternoon, we took a completely different route than usual, and we found something.

Something weird. We figured you were the right person to ask about it."

Leigh's brows lifted. "What kind of weird?"

"I don't really know how to describe it, because I don't know any of the right terminology. It was definitely man-made, though. And it felt... significant. Like it meant something. We figured maybe it was some sort of cultural site or marker?" He scratched at his jaw. "I don't know, I'm not an expert. But I thought you might be able to figure it out."

Leigh exchanged a glance with me before turning back to him. "I'd love to come and check it out, if you're heading back there today."

"Awesome. You two can forage while we scout," Ryan said. "We'll help, obviously. And hopefully, we'll find another deer along the way."

I nodded, and Leigh did the same. "Sounds like a plan," she said. "Give us a few minutes to get ready, and we'll meet you back at camp."

Ryan grinned. "Perfect. See you soon."

Two hours later, we were deep in the wilderness with the two hunters. My legs ached from the constant walking, but when Ryan suddenly stopped ahead of us, my fatigue vanished in an instant.

"We're close," he said, voice laced with excitement. "This is what made us notice it in the first place. That path."

As he spoke, he pointed to the right, and for the first time, I saw it too—a well-trodden trail winding up the side of a slope.

We followed the path uphill, and it wasn't long before the trees thinned, revealing an enormous clearing.

"This is it," Trent muttered, halting.

I stepped up beside him, and my breath hitched.

Nestled in the clearing was a ring of stacked stone cairns, weathered and worn but deliberately placed. Some were only knee-high, while others rose taller than me, their jagged edges casting long, eerie shadows.

The entire site had a strange, almost ritualistic feel, especially with the symbols carved into some of the stones. They reminded me of runes, though I didn't recognize any of them. But what really caught my eye were the arrows. There were at least thirty of them, etched into the stones. Scratched into tree trunks. Arranged with sticks and bones on the ground. All pointing in the same direction.

"Wow." Leigh crouched beside one of the cairns, peering at one of the carved symbols. "This is incredible."

Ryan crossed his arms. "Any idea what it is?" he asked. "Do you think it's Native American?"

"Older sites aren't really my specialty, but if I had to make an educated guess... then I seriously doubt this site is Indigenous," Leigh said, rising to her feet. "The symbols have definite Celtic influences. That makes me think it's much more modern than it looks."

Trent cocked his head. "So who built it?"

"Historically, a lot of European migrants—especially those in the logging and trapping industries—settled in remote parts of Canada for a while. They brought their beliefs and traditions with them, and some of those traditions may have been rooted in ancient Celtic beliefs."

"Any idea what it could mean?" Ryan asked, motioning around the clearing.

Leigh's lips twisted with contemplation. "Well, if this was built by one of those groups, it could've been a boundary marker or a ritual site. Or maybe even something we don't fully understand. I really can't be sure," she said. "But this is definitely worth looking into once we're finally rescued. I know a couple of archaeologists at Berkeley who'd be utterly thrilled to see this."

A shiver crawled up my spine as I took another look at the symbols. Some of them resembled eyes. Watching us.

I swallowed. "When we were talking the other day, you

mentioned some old legends. You know, about groups living off the grid?"

Leigh turned to look at me. "Uh-huh. What about them?"

"What if it's true after all?" I said. "What if there are people still living out here, shunning modern society? Maybe they still follow old traditions, and maybe this site is part of it."

Ryan let out a low whistle. "Now, that would really be something."

"It would also mean there's a possibility of help for us," I said hurriedly. "If there's really people living off-grid, they won't have a phone or radio, for obvious reasons, but they could still help us in some way, right?"

"Yeah, they'd know exactly how to live off the land. Where to find animals. How to cultivate nuts and fruits. Stuff like that," Trent mused.

Leigh lifted her hands. "Hold on. I think we're getting a bit ahead of ourselves," she said. "The most likely explanation for this is that it's an old site from the 1800s, built by early settlers who've long since moved on. Possibly the early 1900s too, up to the 1940s or 50s at an *absolute* stretch. It's certainly not proof of current occupation."

"But it's still worth checking out, right?" Trent said. "We could just follow these arrows to see what they're pointing to. It'll probably end up being nothing, but hey... might as well give it a shot, just in case."

Ryan nodded. "Even if all we find is an abandoned township, that's still good for us. There could've been a few things left behind that we can use at our campsite. Extra tools, or scrap material we can use to build a better shelter."

"Well, I guess I can't argue with that," Leigh said, shrugging. "Let's go."

We followed the arrows out of the clearing, pushing deeper into the wilderness. The trek was grueling—another two and a half hours of winding trails, thick underbrush, and uneven terrain.

Eventually, the path sloped downward, leading to a large stretch of land that had been cleared long ago. The trees thinned, giving way to an eerie quiet.

"There," Ryan muttered, pointing.

In the enormous clearing, about two hundred yards away, was a small settlement.

At first, it was hard to tell what we were looking at. The buildings were barely more than old shacks, roofs sagging under the weight of time. Some looked barely intact, like a strong wind might be enough to send them crashing down. Others had been patched up and reinforced, evidence that someone had taken the time to keep them standing.

Behind the settlement, a towering granite cliff rose sharply, its pale, weathered face streaked with darker veins. The jagged edges caught the light, casting deep shadows in the crevices, while higher up, the cliff gave way to the dense tree line of the mountain that loomed beyond, its peak lost in a haze of fog.

"Jesus," Trent murmured. "This town looks like something straight out of the 1800s."

Leigh nodded slowly. "It probably was. A lot of trapping or mining settlements were abandoned before the twentieth century. But... look. Aria was right. Someone's living here."

I followed her gaze and felt my pulse spike. In the distance, a little boy was visible. Blond-haired, barefoot, maybe six or seven years old. He was playing alone near one of the sturdier cabins, dragging a stick through the dirt.

For a long moment, none of us spoke.

The sight of him was both relieving and deeply unsettling. On the one hand, it meant the old legends were actually true. There were really people living out here. People who might be able to help us. On the other hand... were they friendly or hostile?

"I guess the adults are out hunting and gathering," Trent said, frowning. "Or maybe some of them are inside."

I opened my mouth to reply, but then I saw something that made my stomach curdle.

A vertical log fence surrounded part of the settlement, built from thick, uneven tree trunks sharpened at the tips. Some had symbols carved into them; more of those strange markings we'd seen back at the stone site. But it wasn't the symbols that made my stomach drop.

It was the pike. Tall, positioned just to the right of what looked like an entrance gate. And on top of it...

A human skull.

"What the *fuck*," Ryan whispered. "You guys see that, right?"

Everyone else nodded, but no one spoke for several seconds. We just stood there, frozen, staring at the thing as dread thickened in the air between us.

"That's..." Trent finally said, his voice hoarse. "That's a goddamn human skull."

"Yeah. It is." Leigh's voice was tight. "But maybe it's just meant as a deterrent. It doesn't mean these people are violent or dangerous."

Ryan turned to her, incredulous. "Are you kidding?"

She gestured toward the shacks. "If they didn't want anyone here, that skull would be a good way to scare them off, right?" she said. "But it could just be the skull of a long-dead ancestor. Not necessarily someone they've murdered in cold blood, or whatever else you're thinking right now."

Ryan let out a slow breath. "Still. It's a human skull. That's creepy as hell."

"That means it really works as a deterrent, I guess," I muttered.

I squinted at the little boy again. He was still playing, utterly unbothered.

"We need help," Trent finally said, lifting a hand. "I get that these groups shun the modern world, but we're not just some outsiders trying to intrude on their way of life. We don't even *want* to be out here. We just want some help until we can get rescued. If they're human like us, then they're human enough to understand that. Right?"

Silence.

Leigh's brows furrowed. She didn't look convinced. None of us did.

"Look," Trent said, rolling his shoulders like he was shaking off his nerves. "We can just go carefully. We don't charge in there, don't do anything that could piss them off. We just... try. And if worse comes to worst... well, we have guns, remember?"

Leigh finally nodded, inhaling deeply. "Okay. We can try. But you need to keep the guns hidden. We don't want to go in there looking hostile right off the bat."

Trent nodded back at her. "Got it."

None of us moved for several beats. Then, finally, we stepped forward.

We moved carefully, each step feeling heavier than the last. The settlement remained eerily quiet except for the distant sound of the little boy's humming. No other signs of life. No adults stepping out of the shacks. No voices. Just the skeletal remains of a place time had forgotten.

As we neared the outer edge of the log fence, a rancid smell hit us.

I gagged, bringing my hand to my nose. "Oh, God."

It was the stench of rot. Something foul and lingering, carried on the damp forest air.

"What *is* that?" Ryan asked, nose wrinkling as he looked around.

We all spotted it at the same time.

To our right was a grotesque collection of animal bones and carcasses. Some looked like deer, while others were smaller—rabbits and birds. Flesh clung to some of them, blackened with decay. Skulls peeked through the mess, antlers tangled with rib cages, hollow sockets staring blankly.

"Shit," Ryan muttered as we stepped closer. "That's a hell of a lot of bones."

"Looks like their version of a garbage dump," Trent said.

Leigh nodded. "It makes sense that they don't want animal remains inside the settlement once they're done with them. It could attract rodents and other scavengers. Or bears."

"True."

We took a few more steps toward the settlement, covering our noses to mask the smell from the dumping ground as we passed by it.

Leigh suddenly sucked in a sharp breath beside me, her entire body going rigid. "Get down," she said. Her voice was a barely audible whisper, but the sheer force behind it sent adrenaline spiking through my veins. "*Now.*"

She crouched so fast that it took me a second to register what was happening. I dropped to a knee, and the others followed suit, all of us ducking low on the path.

"What's wrong?" Trent asked. "Is someone aiming a sniper rifle at us or what?"

Leigh didn't answer right away. Her face was pale, her breathing unsteady. Finally, she turned to us, her voice low and firm.

"I'm sorry, I know we came all this way, but we have to go back."

Ryan frowned. "What? We haven't even—"

"I'm serious," she hissed, eyes flicking between us. "Let's go."

"Can you at least tell us *why?*" Trent asked, peering around. "I don't see anyone."

Leigh was silent for a few seconds, clearly weighing up her words. "These people aren't going to help us," she finally said. "It's best that we leave right now."

"But we haven't even spoken to them. And we're so close. All we have—"

Leigh cut him off. "They won't help us. Trust me."

Something in her expression made my stomach turn. I wanted to ask her to elaborate, but the words stuck in my throat.

She wasn't just nervous. She was terrified.

Trent exchanged a look with Ryan. Leigh wasn't an irrational person, and she was also highly-educated. If she was this certain, there was a reason.

"Fine," Ryan muttered. "Let's go."

"We should stay low. Move as quickly and quietly as you can," Leigh said. "I'll explain everything soon."

We crept backward, careful not to snap any twigs or disturb the brush too much. It took everything in me not to break into a full sprint as we put distance between ourselves and the settlement.

As we headed uphill and ventured back into the deep woods, Leigh kept her jaw set and her eyes forward the whole way, refusing to answer any questions from me, Ryan, or Trent.

An hour passed before Ryan finally stopped in his tracks and snapped his fingers. "All right, Leigh, it's been *ages* since we left. Are you ever going to tell us why?"

She stopped, turning to face us. I noted the tension still coiled in her frame.

"I didn't want to say anything back there, because I didn't want any of you to panic and draw attention to our group, just in case there was anyone there apart from that child," she finally said. "I thought it was best that we just slip away as quietly as possible."

"I get that, but keeping us in suspense for an hour really sucks," Ryan said, eyes narrowed. "So what happened?"

"When we passed the dumping ground, I saw some bones near the edge," she said. "Human bones."

"So? They dump animal remains there. Maybe they dispose of their own dead there too."

Leigh shook her head. "I took a couple of osteology and forensic anthropology classes in my third year of undergrad, so I know what cut marks on bones look like," she said. "And every single one of the human bones I saw had cut marks. Just like the animal bones."

A chill slithered through me. "Cut marks? As in—"

"They were butchered," she said bluntly.

I clapped a hand over my mouth, suddenly feeling ill. "Are you sure?" I said in a muffled voice.

"Yes. The marks were made by sharp tools used to strip flesh from bone. In forensic anthropology, those are telltale signs of dismemberment and processing," she said. "Also, the bones didn't even look that old. Based on their condition, whoever they belonged to was probably killed within the last few years."

Silence stretched between us, thick and suffocating.

"Also, remember, this settlement contains people who build elaborate structures in areas they deem significant, like those cairns you found," she finally added. "I find it very hard to believe they'd do that and not also have some sort of funerary customs."

"Well... maybe they eat their own dead," Ryan said, uncertainty threading through his voice. "That's been a custom for some cultures over the years, right?"

Leigh gave a slow nod. "Yes. That's called endocannibalism—consuming members of your own group. When it's outsiders, it's exocannibalism," she said. "So yeah, you could be right. Maybe they only eat their own after death. Maybe it's some kind of ritual. But are any of you willing to go back there and find out exactly what kind of cannibals they are?"

"No," we all said in unison.

The rest of our walk back was spent looking over our shoulders, paranoia creeping into every step. The settlement was four and a half hours away from our camp, but was that far enough? What if they'd already seen us? What if they were watching us right now? Following us?

A branch cracked in the distance, and my heart skipped a

beat. Ryan tensed beside me, his hand hovering near the gun on his belt.

"Probably just an animal," Trent murmured, but his hand was hovering over his own gun too.

We kept moving, our pace quickening with every shadow that stretched too long, every whisper of wind that sounded too much like movement. The silence between us felt fragile, like glass stretched too thin, one wrong step away from shattering.

A week ago, I'd been scared of Landon lurking in the shadows. Of whoever killed Mark, if it was one of the other Lost Boys. Of possible starvation.

Now, I had something else to fear. Something worse. Because the wilderness might be merciless, and Landon and the Lost Boys might be dangerous...

But at least they weren't hunting us for food.

17

ARIA

THE FIRST FROST HAD COME TWO NIGHTS AGO. A THIN SHEET OF ice had crusted over the shallowest parts of the lake, and the wind carried the sharp bite of winter's approach. It made everything feel more urgent. Every handful of berries we gathered and every nut we stuffed into our bags felt like it had to last forever.

Leigh and I had been out foraging for hours, combing through the undergrowth with our fingers numb from the cold. Our extra supplies from the plane were nearly gone, and one granola bar a day wasn't really enough to cut it anyway. Hunting had been scarce. Fishing was becoming unreliable. If we didn't start stockpiling as much as possible now, we'd be in real trouble when the deeper cold set in.

Another week had passed. Another seven nights of curling up in the dark, whispering silent prayers for rescue. Maybe today. Maybe tomorrow. But no one had come.

I tried not to think about the other ones out there. The cannibals. They didn't seem to have noticed our presence yet, but I kept worrying they'd spot our smoke one day, curling up in the air. That might prompt them to come looking... and I didn't even want to imagine what might happen then.

The rest of the group were aware of their existence—apart from Hannah, who we felt was too young to handle the information—and after a brief discussion, we'd assigned new roles to two people. They now slept during the day and awoke in the late afternoon so they could stay up all night with the guns, monitoring for any sounds or signs of movement in the woods beyond our camp.

Nothing had happened yet, but how much longer could we stay invisible?

Leigh suddenly exhaled sharply and bent at the waist, one hand clutching her stomach.

"Cramps?" I asked, brows knitting with concern.

She nodded through gritted teeth. "Yeah. Feels like someone's trying to scoop out my insides with a butter knife."

"Do you want to go back?" I asked. I motioned to the berry shrub we were currently picking. "We've gathered a decent amount today, so we can always come back and get the rest tomorrow."

Leigh shook her head. "No. We need all of it." She winced and forced herself upright. "The berries are already starting to shrivel. If we don't get them now, they could be useless by tomorrow. And the hunting team brought back practically nothing this week."

She wasn't wrong. Every time we ate, it was with the gnawing knowledge that tomorrow might bring less.

I nodded slowly. "That's true. But I can finish up here by myself, if you want to head back with everything we've already gathered."

Leigh hesitated. "I'd *love* to curl up by the fire right now, but I don't like the idea of you out here alone."

"I won't be long. All I have to do is finish stripping this shrub, then that nut bush over there, and then... done," I said, throwing up my palms. "I'll be an hour at most."

She chewed her lip, torn between practicality and worry. "Are you absolutely sure it's okay?"

"Yeah, it's fine," I said, waving a casual hand. "Cramps are the

THE WILD

worst, so I totally feel your pain. And we've tied up all those markers, so I'll be able to find my way back as long as you leave them up when you go."

Finally, Leigh nodded. "Okay. I'll head back with what we already have. But if you're not back in an hour, I'm coming to find you."

I gave her a small smile. "Deal."

She adjusted her bag and turned away, pausing once to glance over her shoulder before disappearing into the trees to follow our markers back to camp.

I worked as quickly as I could, stripping the last of the berries from the tangled vines and picking through the fallen nuts. By the time I was done, my bag was full, and my shoulders were aching.

I should've left then.

But through the thinning trees to my right, I spotted a crab apple tree, its branches still heavy with fruit. It wasn't far. Maybe thirty yards away.

Just in case, I rummaged in my bag for the small pair of scissors from the first aid kit and the bright yellow Lycra crop top that Leigh and I had been using for markers today. Then I cut a strip of fabric, knotted it around the nearest branch, and started walking.

I was just reaching up to pluck one of the apples when movement caught my eye.

Through the trees, barely fifteen yards away, a figure emerged from the brush. Camouflage clothing. Matching camo face paint. A rifle raised and aimed straight at me.

Landon.

For a split second, I froze, my breath caught in my throat. Maybe it wasn't him. Maybe my mind was playing tricks on me. But then he shifted, and I saw the hard set of his jaw, the glint of his eyes beneath the paint.

It was definitely him... and he was aiming right at me.

A crack split the air.

Instinct kicked in. I dove sideways as the shot rang out, heart slamming against my ribs. Bark exploded from a tree beside me. He'd missed, but that was probably only because I moved.

Oh my god.

He was actually trying to kill me.

I turned and bolted, branches whipping against my arms, my breath coming in sharp gasps. This was the moment I'd been dreading for weeks now, ever since I realized that Landon wanted me dead. The moment he finally decided to go through with it.

It was a moment I'd started to believe would never actually come.

I'd stupidly convinced myself that he wouldn't do it, not after the night we spent together. The night he pinned me down, fucked me until I couldn't think straight, and made me fall apart under his hands. The night he carefully dressed me and carried me back to my camp like I was a fragile doll.

I thought that all meant something. That his touch, his hunger for me, proved he didn't really want me dead. I thought it meant he wanted me for more than just my blood on his hands.

Clearly, I was dead wrong.

I'd let myself get pulled into his orbit, caught up in the darkness of his allure. Let his ruthless charm lull me into a false sense of safety. Let myself be hypnotized by the way he looked at me like I was something he both craved and wanted to destroy.

I *really* thought that craving for me would outweigh the desire for my destruction.

God, I was so fucking stupid.

Landon's voice echoed through the woods a moment later.

"Don't run from me, Aria!" he called out. His warning tone made the blood in my veins turn to ice. "Get back here!"

Like hell, psycho.

I veered off the narrow path, crashing through underbrush, thorns snagging at my clothes. I had to lose Landon. The forest was dense, but he was much faster and stronger than me, so he'd catch up soon. That meant my best bet at evading him was to find a good hiding place.

There.

A rocky outcrop jutted from the earth, shadowed by a thick cluster of bushes. I threw myself beneath it, yanking broken branches over me as fast as I could. My pulse thundered in my ears, my breath coming too fast, and I pressed a hand over my mouth, forcing myself to be silent.

Leaves rustled. Footsteps crunched closer.

"I'll find you," Landon said, taking a few more slow steps. "You know I will."

He was right there. Just feet away.

I swallowed thickly and tightened my grip on the small pair of fabric scissors in my pocket. It was a pitiful weapon, but it was all I had, and it was better than nothing.

When Landon drew even closer, unknowingly walking right in front of my hiding spot, I launched out and upward, slamming the tiny blade into his abdomen with a guttural cry.

A sharp inhale was the only sound he made. His eyes widened, and he stared at me, stunned. Clearly, he never thought I'd fight back. At least not in such a violent way.

He staggered backward, one hand pressing on the wound, and his rifle slipped from his grasp. Before he could stoop to pick it up again, I snatched it up and ran.

Behind me, Landon let out a furious roar.

I sprinted toward the break in the trees ahead, where the underbrush was thinning, the sky widening. There was a clearing up ahead. *Shit.* That made things harder for me, because there was nowhere to hide on an open patch of land.

I had to use the rifle. It was my only hope now.

I'd only ever seen people using them on TV, but I could figure it out. I simply *had* to. I took a deep breath, spun around, and lifted the rifle to my shoulder, my body shaking so badly that the barrel wavered in front of me.

Landon crashed through the underbrush, cursing viciously, painted face twisted in a pained grimace. The wound had slowed him, turning his usually purposeful strides into a stilted, unsteady stagger.

I gulped and squeezed the trigger, hoping like hell it would work.

Nothing happened.

Fuck!

Panic clawed at my throat as I realized the rifle was empty. Landon must've used the last bullet when he shot at me before, and of course, any spare ammo was still on him, so I couldn't reload. I wouldn't even know *how* to reload the damn thing anyway.

I turned and ran again, bursting through the last of the underbrush and into the clearing. The ground here was flat and open, stretching out under the cloudy sky.

My pulse pounded in my ears as I whipped my head around, searching for cover, but just as I expected, there was nothing useful near me. Only brittle grass and scattered rocks.

Behind me, Landon's heavy footsteps crashed through the woods. He wasn't trying to be quiet. He didn't need to be.

My chest burned as I pushed myself harder, sprinting toward the other side of the clearing. It was so far off in the distance that I could barely even see it—just a line of thick green shrubs at the top of a slight slope. If I could reach it, I'd have a chance to lose Landon again as the shrubs gave way to larger trees.

His voice cut through the air again, sharp and furious. "Aria! Stop fucking running!"

I didn't dare look back, but I could hear his footsteps getting louder. Closer.

My lungs felt like they were on fire, my legs were screaming in protest, and my heart felt like it was about to explode. I couldn't keep this up much longer, but I had to try. I couldn't just stop and give up. Not after everything I'd already been through.

I pushed myself even harder as the ground finally sloped upward beneath my feet. My vision swam as terror clawed at my thoughts, but I forced myself to focus on the shrubs ahead. I was close to them now. A few more steps and I'd be there.

And then—

The world suddenly dropped away.

I screamed and reached out, grasping for anything, but there was nothing but empty air surrounding me.

I was falling.

18

ARIA

THE WORLD FADED IN AND OUT LIKE A BAD DREAM—FLASHES OF gray sky, jagged rock, and the unrelenting roar of water crashing nearby. Every inch of me throbbed with pain, but somehow, I was alive.

I sucked in a shaky breath, feeling grit scrape against my cheek as I tried to move.

Slowly, I forced my eyes open, squinting against the harsh light filtering through the gray clouds above. My head was pounding, and something soft was propped beneath it. Someone's jacket. I bit back a groan as I pushed myself up a little, every muscle screaming in protest.

I took in my surroundings, trying to make sense of where I was. A strip of sand and dirt stretched out on either side of me, bordered by a furious, churning river that was way too wide and fast to cross. Jagged rocks jutted from the water, white foam crashing around them, and I could feel the chill of the spray on my skin even from here. The opposite bank was a distant blur of greenery and rock.

Behind me, a cliff face loomed. The jagged walls stretched both left and right, wrapping around the narrow stretch of ground and leaving no path of escape, like a cage of stone. Thick clusters of trees crowded right up to the cliff's edge.

A sharp crackle made me whip my head around, and I froze when I saw Landon sitting a few feet away, poking at a small fire with a stick. He looked almost calm, but there was a tightness around his eyes, and his shirt was stained dark red where I'd stabbed him. I couldn't see his rifle anywhere.

My pulse pounded, and I forced myself to stay still, watching him through narrowed eyes. He didn't look injured apart from the stab wound, and his movements were still quick and purposeful as he nudged the fire to keep it going. The flames flickered weakly, fighting against the wind blowing off the river, and his gaze kept darting to me, as if waiting for me to wake up.

I swallowed hard, trying to keep my breathing steady. Why hadn't he killed me while I was unconscious? Why make a fire and put his jacket under my head?

My hands clenched in the sand, and I glanced around for any sign of a weapon. Anything I could use to defend myself when he inevitably came for me. The fabric scissors were long gone, probably lost in the fall, and I didn't see any sharp rocks within reach.

Dammit.

Landon's eyes flicked to mine, and a ghost of a smile quirked up his lips. "Finally awake, huh?"

My stomach twisted with fear, but I refused to let it show. "What happened?" I rasped, my throat dry and raw.

"You don't remember?"

"I remember I was running. And then I suddenly fell. Nothing after that."

Landon jerked his head toward the cliff. "That's where you were running. Up there. You really didn't see the edge?"

I strained to recall the frenetic chase from earlier, and my eyes drifted back to the tall trees crowded right up to the cliff's edge. Those must have been what I saw before I went over, mistaking them for shrubs in my panicked haze.

"I thought the treetops were shrubs," I muttered.

"Ah. That explains it."

I blinked and dragged myself a little closer so I could hear better. "How did I survive running right off a fifty-foot cliff?"

"You got lucky," Landon said. His eyes skated over to the same trees I'd just looked at. "I saw it happen. As you fell, you landed right on top of one of those trees, and that broke the momentum of the fall. Then you kind of bounced off it onto another shorter tree right next to it, and so on, until you landed on the ground. Each hit slowed you down just enough to keep you from splattering when you landed."

I swallowed hard, staring at the trees. "So... I basically pinballed my way down?"

He snorted. "Pretty much. You're lucky you didn't break your neck on one of those branches. Or hit the rocks at the bottom." His gaze flicked back to me, a strange intensity in his eyes. "You shouldn't have survived that fall. Most people wouldn't."

"Well, I'm glad I did," I muttered.

"You might just be the luckiest girl in the world, Aria," he said, still staring at me. "You survived a plane crash five weeks ago. Now you've survived a fall off a cliff. Maybe it's time to stop tempting fate, huh?"

"Yeah, maybe," I murmured, looking down at a deep scratch on my wrist. "I don't know how much more my body can take."

"You're surprisingly okay despite the fall," he said. "You're covered in scratches and bruises, but there's no broken bones. At least none that I can see. No head injury, either. I think you just fainted from the shock of it all."

"Oh." I sat up straighter, wincing as pain flared in my ribs. I glanced over at the unforgiving cliff again. "How did you get down here?"

Landon's lips pressed into a thin line, and he poked the fire again before replying. "I climbed down. I knew you'd need food and warmth when you woke up. So here I am."

Something stuttered in my brain. "Why would you help me?" I asked. "Don't you want me dead?"

His brows shot up. Then he barked out a sharp laugh. "You think I want you dead?"

"You were shooting at me in the woods!"

"Oh, for fuck's sake," he muttered, raking a hand through his hair. He let out a sigh, shoulders slumping, and then shook his head. "I wasn't shooting at you. I was shooting *past* you."

"Why?"

"You had a bear on your trail. She was gaining on you fast. Really fast," he said. "I'd say she was only a minute away from grabbing you. Maybe even seconds."

A chill shot through me. "Are you serious?"

"Yeah. Those things can be shockingly quiet despite their size," he said. "Anyway, I only had about five seconds to decide what to do. I decided against yelling at you to run, because that would put you at risk. So I shot past you to scare the bear off. And it worked. She went scampering off into the woods."

"I... I thought—"

"I know what you thought," he said brusquely. "From that distance, it probably looked like I was aiming right at your face. But I wasn't. I was aiming to your left, way above your shoulder. I wanted to hit that tree."

I frowned. "Why didn't you aim for the bear?"

"She was too close to you. If I missed, I would've hit you," he said. "Besides, bears that big... one bullet isn't going to kill them. It's just going to make them fucking angry. More aggressive. Then you would've been in *more* danger. But loud, sudden noises—that works. Scares them off."

"I can't believe I didn't notice a bear behind me," I said softly, rubbing my arms as goosebumps peppered my skin.

"Like I said, they can be very quiet. Helps them stalk their prey. But the one following you really didn't like the gunshot, so it lumbered away right after it happened," he said. "You would've heard *that* if you hadn't screamed and crashed through the woods in the opposite direction like a fucking maniac."

"Oh. Right."

Landon frowned and went on. "That's why I kept shouting at you to stop running away from me," he said. "I was worried you'd get yourself lost or run right into another bear."

"I didn't know you were trying to help. I honestly thought you were trying to shoot me in the head."

"Yeah, I figured that was the case when you stabbed me," he said, arching a brow. "Thanks a lot for that, by the way."

"Sorry," I mumbled.

I knew I shouldn't feel too bad for defending myself against a man like Landon, given how everything I knew about him told me he was dangerous. But the way he looked at me a second ago—like I'd betrayed him—made my stomach twist anyway.

It didn't make sense. Just because he'd helped me with the bear didn't mean he wasn't still dangerous. One good deed didn't erase everything else I knew about him.

He waved a hand. "It's no big deal. You didn't hit anything. It just hurt like a motherfucker and bled a whole lot," he said. "But I cleaned it and sealed it off, and I've been keeping pressure on it when I can. It'll be fine."

"Are you sure?" I said skeptically.

"Yup." He reached over and patted his backpack. "I always keep some plasters and first aid stuff in here when I go out, just in case. The guy who owned the hunting cabin had a ton of it lying around."

"That's good," I murmured. The inexplicable guilt was still gnawing at my guts. I looked back at the cliff. "So, um... how do we get back up there?"

Landon shrugged. "No fucking idea. When I came down here, I was only focused on making sure you were okay. I wasn't really thinking about what would happen after that," he said. "But as you can see, the way the cliff curves around on both sides of the riverbank seals us in. And we can't go into the river. The current is too strong to make it across to the other side without getting swept away."

"Well, you climbed down here. Could we climb back up?"

"Climbing down is a lot different than climbing up, unfortunately," he said. "So unless you're secretly a pro rock climber, we're stuck down here for now."

"But our camps—"

"Are up there," he said, cutting me off. "I know. We're going to have to find another way back." He paused and motioned to his left. "I spotted a cave entrance over there, so I'm hoping it leads through to the other side. That would be the best case scenario."

I nodded. "Yeah, that'd be good."

"I don't know how safe it is in there yet, but I know there's no bears lurking inside, at least," Landon went on with a ghost of a smile. "It looks way too small for that. They wouldn't even fit through the mouth. But yeah... I haven't properly checked it out yet. Didn't want to leave you alone while you were out cold."

I swallowed thickly. "Well, um... thanks for taking care of me," I murmured.

"No problem." He frowned, tilting his head. "Why was your first instinct to think I was trying to kill you?"

Indignant fury rose in my chest at his question, stomping out all the embers of guilt. "Is that a joke?" I snapped, sitting up straighter.

"No. Why the hell would I want you *dead*, Aria? Just because your group threw me and my friends out?" His tone was incredulous. "We've been doing just fine on our own. In fact, we're thriving. Hence the food we delivered to help you guys out."

"It wasn't because of that," I muttered, narrowing my eyes.

Landon nodded slowly, like pieces were finally clicking into place. "Ah. You think I'm the one who killed Mark that night."

"Well, that's not the only—"

"I did kill him," he said, bluntly cutting me off. "So your instincts were dead on."

Shock shot through me like ice water. "You killed Mark?" I said, heart suddenly pounding. "Why?"

Landon's jaw tightened. "He thought of himself as one of the group leaders, and I guess he saw me as a co-leader or something, because he asked to speak to me in private about our situation after everyone else was asleep that night," he said. "We walked down the lakeshore so we wouldn't wake anyone up."

My pulse thudded in my ears. "What did he say?"

His expression darkened. "I don't know if you remember much about him, because he was only with us for a few hours, but he really wasn't a good guy," he said. "I guess he figured I was just like him, so he confided all this shit in me. He pointed out that there were thirty-four of us and only a very slim chance of rescue within a few months. On top of that, winter was coming."

"Yeah, we all knew that."

Landon looked away, jaw clenching. "He had a very specific plan for it," he said. "He wanted us to get rid of anyone who couldn't effectively contribute. Dead weight, as he called it. Framed the whole thing as a pragmatic decision. One that *had* to be made so the rest of us could survive."

"By get rid of, you mean—"

"Kill." He nodded curtly. "At first, he didn't say it outright. Just danced around it with phrases like 'thinning the herd' and 'practical solutions.' But it was clear what he meant. I let him talk, just to see how far he'd go, and he eventually admitted it."

"What an asshole," I muttered.

"Yeah. He wanted to kill Hannah first. She was just a useless mouth to feed, in his view." Landon's mouth tightened, and he went on. "He also wanted to kill Clint, because his leg was so badly broken that he wouldn't be able to do anything. He mentioned that other woman, too. The one you always forage with."

"Leigh."

"That's right. Leigh. And he mentioned several others, too." He hesitated, then looked me dead in the eye. "Including *you*."

My heart skipped a beat. "Me? But I—"

Landon cut me off again. "You have foraging skills from your time in the Girl Scouts. He knew that. But it didn't matter to him. He still viewed you as small and weak. A liability and a waste of resources," he said, voice hardening. "He named at least fifteen people he wanted to 'cull', as he put it. Mostly women."

"Oh my god," I said, voice barely above a whisper.

Landon's jaw clenched, his knuckles turning white around the stick he was holding. "I gave him a chance to back off. Told him we didn't need to start playing God with people's lives. But he didn't listen. He kept saying it was the most pragmatic thing to do."

"And he wanted you to help him do it?"

"Yeah. Like I said, he'd somehow convinced himself that I was the right guy for it. He really thought I'd agree," he said, jaw tightening. "I knew right then and there that I had to get rid of him. If I didn't, and just refused to help, he would've carried out his plan alone. He'd start killing people when no one was looking. Maybe even start with you. So I did what needed to be done."

My heart raced as his words sank in, leaving me breathless.

I'd always thought that Landon might've been the one who killed Mark, but now I knew for sure, and I also knew why. That changed everything.

He'd done something terrible, something unthinkable, but I couldn't deny the small, sick sense of relief that bloomed deep inside me now that I knew the whole story. He'd done it for Hannah and the others, and he'd also done it for me.

So it wasn't just shock or horror I felt—there was a complicated, tangled gratitude buried under the fear, because in a twisted way, I owed Landon my life.

"You saved half the group by killing him," I said in a low voice.

"Yeah. And I don't regret it for a second," he replied, eyes drilling into mine.

"Why didn't you just explain all of this to everyone?" I asked, throwing my hands up.

He scoffed. "Would you have believed me if I did?"

I hesitated, lowering my gaze. "I... I'm not sure. But I think most of the others would have."

"I doubt that," he said, slowly shaking his head. "I think most of them would've looked at me the way you've been looking at me for the last five minutes. Like I'm a monster. A loose cannon who might snap and kill someone else at any second."

I swallowed hard. "I don't know about that."

"Well, I do," he said grimly. "I think it would've been a matter of time until one of you decided to eliminate the risk by sticking a knife in my back while I slept. So the guys and I agreed not to reveal which one of us did it. We knew you'd probably suspect us at some point, but we also knew you wouldn't come after any of us, because none of you would want to risk killing the wrong guy."

My brows rose. "Your friends all knew you killed Mark?"

"Yeah. I woke them up and told them right after it happened," he said. "The only one in the exiled group who *didn't* know was Matthew, but we told him eventually. He was pissed at first, as expected, but he understood in the end."

"Right," I muttered.

Landon cocked his head and frowned. "Why did you think I was the most likely culprit?"

"Does it matter?" I asked. "You just admitted it *was* you."

"I know. But what makes me seem like a killer?" he asked. "Mark thought the same thing, clearly. So I'm curious to know what it is about me that sets off those alarm bells in people."

I narrowed my eyes. "I have no idea why Mark assumed you were a psycho who'd have no issue killing kids and women," I said. "But *I* assumed you were a psycho because you've been trying to kill me for the last few months. Is that enough reason for you?"

Landon's brows furrowed. "What?"

"Don't deny it," I said, rolling my eyes upward. "You've been stalking me with those masks, for one. Trying to make me feel like I'm going crazy, I guess. And you're also in the Dominion Club, who want me dead for some reason, so I know you're the one who planted that bomb in my car at the donor gala. You were there. You even threatened me earlier that night, in the bathroom. And when I sneaked into the society meeting, I heard one of the members say your name along with something about the bomb not being enough to kill me." I paused to inhale before going on. "So yes, Landon, I think you're a cold-blooded killer, and right now, I'm very fucking confused, because I still can't figure out why you *helped* me after I fell off that damn cliff. Or why you stopped that bear from eating me. Nothing you've done lately makes any sense!"

Landon stared at me as the words rushed out of me, expression unreadable. Finally, he shook his head, laughing bitterly. "You're wrong about everything."

I folded my arms. "Oh, really?"

"Well, you're right about me being in the Dominion Club, obviously. But we aren't trying to kill you," he said. He rubbed a hand over his face, the laugh morphing into a humorless snort. "It's the same thing as you and that fucking bear. You thought we were trying to hurt you, but we've actually been protecting you all along."

My brows shot up. "*Protecting* me? By sticking a bomb under my car?"

"That's not what—" Landon suddenly grimaced and clutched his abdomen. "Fuck," he said through gritted teeth. "It's bleeding again. Must've twisted too fast just now."

I sighed. "Lift your shirt up and keep pressure on the wound. I'll grab another plaster from your bag. You said you had some more, right?"

"Yes." He grimaced again as his hand pressed harder on his bloodstained shirt. "Front pocket. There's antiseptic fluid too."

"Okay." I crawled over to the backpack and unzipped the front pocket. "I'll do this, and you can elaborate on your so-called protection scheme afterwards. Although knowing you, I'm assuming it's something like a mafia protection racket. So not actually protection at all."

As I rummaged through the pocket, my fingers brushed against something cold and metallic. Frowning, I pulled out a pair of scissors.

At first, I figured they must've come from the first aid kit in the hunting cabin. But then I noticed a small sticker wrapped around one of the handles. *Trans-American Airlines.*

A mix of shock and dread spiraled in my gut as the realization slammed into me.

Landon cut the ELT cable.

I wasn't even sure why I was surprised. I'd suspected it was him from the very start. Now I just knew for sure.

I also knew that he'd been lying for the last few minutes. He didn't want to protect me or save me from anything. After all, he was the one who ensured that we'd all be left out here to suffer in the wilderness.

I took a deep breath and lifted the scissors, staring him down. "It was you," I said. "You destroyed the ELT. You took away our *one* chance for immediate rescue."

Some tiny part of me was hoping he'd say no. That this was just a terrible misunderstanding. That he'd found the scissors after the real culprit ditched them in the woods and decided to keep them for their utility.

I wasn't sure why that part of me was still grasping at straws to humanize him. After everything he'd done—the stalking, the threats, the way he looked at me with those cold, calculating eyes like he was always three steps ahead—I should've known better.

But still... I couldn't shake the way he'd helped me after I fell, the way he scared off the bear to save me, and the angst on his face when he talked about killing Mark to protect me and the others. It just didn't add up.

The callous villain I'd painted him as in my mind shouldn't have cared whether I survived that fall earlier. He shouldn't have risked his life to save mine, and he definitely shouldn't have looked at me like it almost broke him to see me hurt.

I didn't want to believe he'd really doomed us to die out here. I didn't want to believe that the man who'd made sure I was safe when I was at my most vulnerable—more than once—was the same one who'd condemned us to this nightmare in the first place.

Instead, I wanted to believe there was more to him than the ruthless mask he wore. That he wasn't just a monster in human skin. I wanted to believe that maybe, despite everything, there was some twisted, messed-up version of good in him.

But that tiny flicker of hope was snuffed out the second he squared his jaw and dipped his chin in a curt nod.

"Yeah," he said, meeting my gaze without flinching. "It was me."

19

ARIA

My mind raced, thoughts crashing together in a maelstrom of fear and fury as my fingers curled around the scissors I'd yanked from Landon's bag.

He was the reason we were stuck out here.

He hadn't even tried to deny it. That was what broke me—the way he just looked at me with that calm, unrepentant stare, like this was all part of his plan.

I forced myself to stand, sucking in a ragged breath as the ground seemed to tilt beneath me. My stomach was churning wildly, and I pressed a trembling hand to my mouth, fighting the rising bile.

"You... you really did this," I whispered, my voice shaking. "You're the reason no one's coming for us."

Landon rose to his full height and stood there staring at me, face grim. "Yes."

"You've killed us," I choked out. "All of us. *Why*? Why the hell would you do that?"

I just couldn't process it. Couldn't wrap my mind around the fact that he'd made the choice to trap us out here. To cut off any chance of rescue and leave us to fend for ourselves.

"I had my reasons," he said in a low voice.

Suddenly I couldn't breathe. Couldn't think straight. Couldn't hear any more of Landon's twisted excuses and lies. It felt like his mere presence was suffocating me.

I needed to get the hell away from him.

Spinning on my heel, I bolted, my feet pounding against the uneven ground.

Landon's voice instantly cut through the frigid air, harsh and commanding. "Stop doing this, Aria!" he called out. "Stop running away!"

I didn't listen. I couldn't. I just had to get away from him. *Now.*

As I pushed myself to run faster, my gaze darted around, desperate for a place to hide. The river roared on my right, the white-capped waves crashing over jagged rocks, and on my left, the cliff walls loomed. Then I finally saw it—the tiny cave entrance Landon mentioned earlier, half-obscured by hanging ivy and loose stone.

I had no idea if it was safe inside, but right now I didn't even care. I needed somewhere to go. Anywhere away from *him*.

I darted inside, scraping my shoulder on the rough stone as I squeezed through the narrow mouth. Then I forced myself deeper into the cave, stumbling over uneven ground as I tried to put as much distance between us as possible.

A scuff of footsteps at the entrance made my stomach twist with dread. I froze, pressing myself against the cold stone wall.

"Aria," Landon called out, his voice low and firm. "You can't hide from me. You know that."

I swallowed the sob clawing up my throat and moved deeper into the cave, feeling my way through the darkness. My outstretched hand hit solid stone, and I sucked in a breath, panic seizing me. Dead end.

"No," I whispered, frantically searching for another way out.

But there was nothing. Just solid, immovable rock trapping me in place.

A shadow moved somewhere behind me, and I spun around just as Landon appeared at the entrance, his broad shoulders almost blocking out the fading light.

He stalked toward me, breathing hard, and I brandished the scissors at him, my hand trembling. "Get the hell away from me," I snarled.

"Aria," he said, his voice low and rough. "You don't understand."

"I understand perfectly," I shot back through gritted teeth, raising the scissors higher.

He didn't even flinch. Just kept moving closer, his eyes dark and intense. "You really don't," he said. "I can explain, but it's not that simple. Just give me a chance to make you understand. Just a few minutes."

With every slow step he took toward me, I felt the war inside me intensify.

One second, Landon was the enemy. The man who'd brought chaos and danger into my life. The next, he was my savior, pulling me from the edge of something terrible. Then he'd go right back to being the enemy again.

The mental whiplash was driving me insane, and what was happening in my body was even worse. It was constantly betraying me, responding to Landon with heated desire, even though that was the last thing I wanted right now.

I hated myself for it. I should be terrified of him or repulsed by him, but instead, all I could think about was how good his sinful mouth tasted, and how good it felt when his treacherous hands roughly gripped me.

Stop it, I silently scolded myself.

There was nothing Landon could say or do that could justify his decision to trap us all out here, no matter how much time I gave him. *Nothing.* And lusting over him wasn't going to make things any better or less confusing.

"No," I finally said, voice dripping with fury. "Just get the fuck away from me."

"I can't do that." His jaw flexed, and he took another step closer, towering over me. "You need to listen to me, Aria."

"I said no!" I screamed, my voice echoing off the stone walls.

I bolted to the side, desperate to find any way around Landon, but he was faster, his arm snaking out to catch my wrist and twist me back against the wall. The scissors clattered to the ground, the metallic clang swallowed up by the thunderous pounding of my heart.

I fought him, struggling against his hold and clawing at his arms, his chest, anything I could reach. But he didn't let go. Didn't budge an inch. Just caged me in with his body, his face mere inches from mine.

"You don't get to do this, Landon!" I snarled, my voice breaking. "You don't get to decide our fate like you're some kind of god! There's no excuse!"

His lips pressed into a thin line, his eyes blazing with something between fury and desperation. "You think I wanted this?" he growled, his voice low and raw. "You think I made that choice easily?"

As he spoke, he leaned closer, his breath brushing my lips, and I couldn't help the shiver that raced through me. I hated him. Hated how my body betrayed me, how even now—trapped and furious and hurt—I still wanted him. *So. Fucking. Much.*

His hands tightened on my wrists, pinning them above my head against the stone. I glared at him, refusing to let him see the way I trembled.

"You're such a stubborn little thing," he muttered. "Always so damn determined to fight me."

I sneered at him, refusing to look away. "You deserve it. You're a monster."

Something dark and unreadable flashed through his gaze, and before I could react, his mouth crashed down on mine, fierce and unrelenting. I tried to push him away, but his grip didn't waver as his lips dominated mine, angry and possessive and wild.

My mind screamed at me to fight harder, to make him pay for every lie, every betrayal, but my body had other ideas. Heat instantly surged through me, and I cursed myself for the way I melted into him, for the way my mouth opened under his, letting him deepen the kiss. I hated how good it felt. Hated how my body arched into his despite everything that had happened.

His hands released my wrists, but before I could shove him away, they were on my hips, pulling me against him.

"Tell me to stop, Aria," he muttered against my lips. "Tell me you don't want this."

I couldn't do that. I just couldn't force the words out. Instead, I grabbed the front of his shirt and yanked him closer, capturing his mouth with mine. He groaned low in his throat, his hands roaming over my body like he couldn't get enough, like he needed me as much as I hated needing him.

I clawed at his shirt, desperate to feel his skin against mine, to burn away my anger with the heat between us. He broke away just long enough to yank the fabric over his head, and I did the same with my top, sweater, and bra. Then his mouth was on my neck, kissing and biting me. Marking me.

Seconds later, his mouth found mine again, harder and fiercer, like he needed to consume me to prove I belonged to him. At the same time, his hands slid under the waistband of my pants, and I gasped as he yanked them down, his fingers brushing over my bare skin.

His hands found my thighs again, lifting me up, and I wrapped my legs around his waist instinctively. My back scraped against the rough stone, but I didn't care. I needed him closer, harder, rougher. Needed the way his touch sent sparks skittering through my veins.

God, I hated him so fucking much. But I wanted him way more than I despised him.

The frantic, angry energy between us didn't slow or soften. It only burned hotter. Landon kept kissing me, devouring every sound I made as he ground his hips against me, making me feel how hard he was through the thick fabric of his pants.

I whimpered, arching into him, and he bit down on my bottom lip before pulling back just enough to look at me. "You drive me fucking insane, Aria," he muttered, his fingers tracing the curve of my hip. "I even want you when you're trying to kill me."

I didn't want to hear his words. Didn't want to think about how they made my heart clench. I just wanted him to make me forget how broken I felt right now.

Even though I didn't say any of that out loud, he seemed to understand it anyway, because he didn't try to speak to me again. Instead, he slid me to the left so that my ass was resting on a smooth ledge on the cave wall. Then he sank to his knees, letting my legs drape over his shoulders.

When his hot breath skated over my inner thighs, I instantly turned liquid, and a needy whine bubbled up in my throat. I didn't consciously tell my hips to roll, but they did it anyway, a dance of primal instinct and pure want.

Landon's nose brushed my clit, and then he started licking me up and down, languidly but possessively, like I was prey he'd hunted and taken down to be savored. He was tasting every inch of my pussy, not for me, but for his own satisfaction.

When his slick tongue finally slid over my clit, my brain short-circuited.

Sensation overwhelmed me, and my hands gripped his hair as I bucked against his mouth, desperate for more. He growled against my pussy—a low, primal sound that sent shivers up my spine—and pressed his tongue harder, ruthlessly flicking and circling.

This was all for me now.

I couldn't hold back the moans that tore from my throat, my whole body tightening as Landon worked me over with his hot lips and tongue. He didn't let up for a second, forcing me higher and higher until I was close to shattering against him, pleasure burning through every nerve like wildfire.

"Oh, fuck... yes!" My vision blurred as my legs tightened around his neck, and my fingers raked through his hair, pulling his head even closer. "More. *More.*"

He sucked my clit into his mouth again, letting out a rough, guttural grunt through his nose. That grunt almost tipped me over the edge. It was the hottest damn sound in the world; his sheer, unbridled delight at bringing me pleasure.

Before I could fall apart completely, he pulled his head away, rose to his feet, and lifted me in the air, making me wrap my legs around him again. The thick head of his cock nudged insistently at my entrance.

"Tell me to stop," he muttered against my ear, his voice a gravelly rasp. "Last chance."

I gritted my teeth. "No," I whispered. "Never."

I didn't care about anything else right now. Not the danger, not the betrayal, not the fear. Just him. Just *us*, tangled together in this cave like we were made to tear each other apart and put each other back together. Nothing else mattered but the way he touched me; possessive and desperate, like he couldn't get enough. And I didn't want him to stop.

With that, Landon surged forward, impaling me in one brutal thrust that stole my breath.

He set a hard, fast rhythm, giving me no time to adjust as he pounded into me. The tantalizing burn of his thick length stretching my pussy had me seeing stars in the dim cave, and gasp after gasp escaped my mouth as I locked my legs behind his back, taking him even deeper.

There was no tenderness to any of this; not even for a second.

Just raw, desperate passion that tore through both of us. Landon's movements grew harder and faster, and I met him every time, giving as good as I got, desperate to feel something other than betrayal.

"This is what you want, isn't it?" he grunted in my ear, punctuating the last word with a thrust more savage than the last. "My cock splitting your tight pussy right open."

"Yes," I moaned, fingernails raking down his bare back. The wet, sinful squelch of his cock driving into me echoed obscenely through the small cave. "Fuck, yes..."

I was so close to unraveling now, my pussy clenching wildly on Landon's cock. "Please," I whimpered. "Let me come."

"Do it," he growled, picking up speed. A few more hard, punishing thrusts was all it took to send me careening over the edge, my climax crashing over me in hot, intense waves.

With a guttural groan, Landon buried himself to the hilt and went still. I felt his cock jerking in me as he found his own release.

As the waves kept hitting me, I shattered in his arms, my desperate whimpers muffled against his shoulder. He kept holding me tight, his harsh breaths mingling with mine in the heavy, heated air.

We stayed like that for a moment, tangled together and breathing hard. I didn't try to move, too overwhelmed to think straight. Landon's hands remained firm on my hips, almost possessively, and I could feel the rapid thud of his heartbeat against my chest. The weight of him, his heat, the way his lips brushed my temple like he couldn't stop himself... it all made something break apart inside me.

God, why did it feel like I needed this? Like I needed him.

A sudden hot twist of anger curled in my gut, slicing through the lingering pleasure. I couldn't let myself fall for that lie again. For *him*.

I shoved at his chest, forcing him to let me down. Now that

the pleasure had faded, guilt and regret were sinking their claws into me, chilling me to the bone.

How could I still want Landon after everything he'd done? How could I crave his touch when I should be fighting him with every ounce of strength I had left? It was sick. Beyond twisted.

I didn't look at Landon as I put on my clothes, refusing to acknowledge the ache in my chest or the way my hands trembled. His fingers brushed my arm, but I jerked away, my voice low. "Don't touch me."

I didn't want to think about what we'd just done. Didn't want to feel the way my body still hummed with the aftershocks of him. I just wanted to forget.

I pushed my way out of the cave, my pulse thrumming. The air outside was cooler, the sun already dipping behind the distant mountains beyond the river, casting long shadows over the riverbank. I forced myself to take a steadying breath, ignoring the ache between my legs and the way my hands still shook.

"I wasn't lying earlier, Aria."

Landon's voice cut through the air, and I froze, refusing to turn around.

"Everything I've done is to protect you," he went on. "That wasn't a lie."

I scoffed, spinning on my heel to glare at him. "You made damn sure we'd never be found after a fucking plane crash, and you call that *protection*?" I snapped. "What kind of delusional shit is that?"

His jaw clenched, but he didn't back down, his gaze hard and unflinching. "I know how bad it looks. But I did it to keep you safe."

"How?" I spat, my voice cracking with fury. "And from who, exactly?"

He hesitated, just for a heartbeat, but it was enough to make my chest tighten with dread. When he finally spoke, his voice was low and bitter.

"Your father."

20

ARIA

"No." The word tore from my throat before I could stop it. "You're lying."

Landon didn't move. Just kept staring at me like he was willing me to understand. But I couldn't. I wouldn't. This was just another one of his twisted manipulations, meant to confuse me and mess everything up inside my head.

"I know it's a lot to take in," he said, his voice rough with exhaustion. "But I swear it's the truth. You've been in danger for a long time, and it's all because of him."

My heart thudded painfully, and nausea coiled low in my stomach.

"No." I shook my head again, harder this time, like it might rattle the lie out of my ears. "I don't need to be protected from my own father. He would never hurt me!"

Landon didn't argue. Just watched me with that steady, unrelenting stare. Blood was still seeping from his abdomen, dripping down to stain the waistband of his jeans.

"Can we go back to the fire?" he finally asked, his voice quieter. "I need to take care of this before it gets worse. Then we can talk more."

I hesitated, torn between wanting to demand answers and the instinct to keep some distance between us. My mind was racing, desperate to make sense of what he'd said. My father. Protecting me from my own father. It didn't fit, didn't make any sense.

But Landon's wound had really opened up from the exertion of what we'd just done in the cave, and as much as I hated to admit it, the sight of his blood made a mix of sympathy and unease twist through my stomach.

I swallowed hard and jerked my chin toward the fire. "Fine. I'll help," I muttered, refusing to look at him. "But you're explaining everything afterwards."

A muscle in his jaw twitched, but he didn't respond. Instead, he just started walking back, his movements slower than usual. I followed a few steps behind, my mind spinning with too many thoughts. None of them were good.

When we reached the fire, Landon lowered himself to the ground with a sharp intake of breath. He peeled the fabric of his shirt away with a grimace, exposing the gash that had split open again.

"Can you find the antiseptic, some cloth, and a fresh plaster?" he asked, nodding toward his backpack.

I dropped down to rummage through his makeshift medical supplies. Once I'd found them, my jaw clenched as I watched him clean the wound, his hands methodical despite the obvious pain. He didn't ask for any more help—just kept working, his face set in grim concentration.

My mind refused to settle. I wanted to scream at him, to tell him he was full of shit, but a cold dread was seeping into my bones, gnawing at the edges of my certainty.

Finally, after what felt like ages, Landon pressed on another large plaster and leaned back, breathing hard. He looked at me, eyes shadowed in the flickering firelight.

"Okay, that's done." He dragged a hand through his hair, smearing a streak of blood across his forehead. "I'll tell you everything now. But like I said before... it's not that simple. It's going to take a while."

"Okay."

"I guess we'll need to start with the Dominion Club," he said, sitting up a little straighter. "You already know quite a lot about us, don't you?"

I nodded and reiterated what Professor Cosgrove had told me about the secret society—they used surveillance and strategic infiltration to gather intelligence and secrets in order to defend a particular set of ideals in the American government. If a political leader behaved in a way the society deemed harmful to American citizens, they'd use the information they had to force them out.

"He told me President Breeland got rid of the society back in the 80s," I finished. "But that's clearly not true."

Landon shook his head. "Breeland tried, but he failed to realize just how many members the Dominion Club had at the time. They went further underground after the purge, but they continued to exist, and still do to this day."

"And you're a member," I said flatly.

"Have been for two years now. I was recruited in my sophomore year," he said. "Anyway, several years ago, the society became aware of something regarding your mother's accident. Her death actually benefited your father in a—"

I cut him off. "Wait," I said hotly, lifting a palm. "Are you trying to suggest my father *arranged* that accident?"

"No, not at all. It was a real accident. I know because I saw it," Landon replied. He paused for a beat, giving me a hard look. "I saw *everything* that day, including what happened afterwards."

I averted my eyes, squirming slightly in my spot. "Right," I muttered.

"Anyway, as you very well know, the accident happened just three months before the election," he went on. "Before it happened, your father was deeply unpopular in almost every demographic."

"Was he?" I asked, frowning. "I know things weren't the best, but I don't recall it being *that* bad."

Landon lifted a palm. "Well, he was clearly popular enough to be selected by the party as their nominee," he said. "But he was only popular in one demographic, which just so happened to be the one in control of nominations— wealthy donors. Across most other demographics, he was pretty unpopular because of his anti-union and pro-corporate views, which he made clear while he was Governor of Maryland. Even his Secret Service code name reflected the average working-class person's sentiments toward him."

"What do you mean by that?" I asked, tilting my head.

"When the agents were suggesting code names for your family, they went with words that were associated with your favorite movie, right? Or at least tangentially associated."

I nodded. "Yes."

"Well, they suggested Baron for him. They knew he'd lap it up because of the royal connotations. But half of them secretly call him the Robber Baron behind his back. So it was actually an inside joke for them."

I swallowed thickly. "I didn't know that," I murmured.

"Neither did he, apparently." Landon frowned and went on. "Anyway, as I was saying, he was quite unpopular back in the day. When he was running against my mother, he was tipped to lose by a substantial margin."

"Elections are never predictable, though."

"Of course not. I'm just saying, that's what every pollster at the time suggested—that he'd lose the 2020 election by a landslide," he said. "But something happened after your mother's death."

I nodded slowly as understanding dawned on me. "A sympathy boost."

"Yup. Very well-known phenomenon in politics. A beloved family member dies, and suddenly a candidate gains twenty points in approval ratings due to the outpouring of sympathy and support from the public," Landon said. "Because your mother's death occurred so close to the election, the ensuing boost your father received secured the presidency for him."

My nostrils flared. "That's such—"

"A cold, harsh thing to say?" Landon interrupted. "I know. And I'm sorry. But when you remove all emotion from it... it's just what happened."

Tears stung my eyes at the reminder of my mother's passing, but I swallowed the lump in my throat and nodded. "I guess so," I murmured.

I hated to even consider it, but Landon was right. I remembered the memorial service that was broadcast nationwide, and the way my father's popularity shot up during our mourning period. Media sites and newspapers went from questioning whether he had what it took to win the presidency to hailing him as a steadfast, grieving family man, which boosted his favorability and almost certainly helped him on Election Day.

"Now, let's skip forward four years." Landon scratched his jaw and went on. "Your father's presidency hasn't gone as he hoped it would, and his approval ratings have been dropping by the day. That's why my mother decided to run against him again, because this time, her party was absolutely certain she could win."

"Okay," I said, brows furrowing. "What does all that have to do with the plane crash?"

Landon was silent for a moment. "A source approached us with some information a few months ago," he finally said. "He was in the wrong place at the right time on a certain day, and he overheard a conversation between your father and some of his loyalists."

"Who was this source?" I asked, eyes narrowing with suspicion. "And how do you know he could be trusted with information about my father?"

Landon scrubbed a hand over his face and sighed. "It was Gerald Foster," he said softly.

My heart lurched. "Agent Foster?"

"Yes. He fed information to the Dominion Club for years, for various reasons. But one of those reasons was *you*," Landon replied. "Believe me when I tell you that man cared about you like you were his own daughter. All he wanted was for you to be safe. He had no reason to make anything up."

A hard lump was forming in my throat. "So what did he overhear my father and his loyalists talking about?" I asked.

"It seems your father knew he was going to lose the election this time," Landon replied. His gaze lifted to meet mine again, dark and unwavering. "His team needed to do something drastic to turn things around."

My heart thudded as puzzle pieces started clicking into place.

"Go on," I said. I already sensed what Landon was about to claim, but I needed to hear him say it out loud.

"Foster overheard your father and his loyalists discussing a plot to harm you. Not to kill you. But at least hurt or maim you to the extent where he'd get another sympathy boost," he said. "A car accident that would leave you severely injured, for instance."

I blinked rapidly, as if that might somehow undo the words he'd just spoken. But they didn't fade. Just clung to the air like poison gas.

"No," I whispered, my voice hoarse. "That's not—no. You're lying."

But the strangely sympathetic look in Landon's eyes told me everything. He was telling the truth. Or, at the very least, the version of the truth he thought he knew.

My vision suddenly blurred, and I wrapped my arms around myself, trying to hold in the cry of shock and despair clawing its way up my throat. It felt like the ground was falling out from under me.

I just couldn't believe it. My own father, willing to hurt me just to secure another four years of power? That was beyond insane. It simply couldn't be real.

"No," I finally whispered again. "You're wrong. Foster must've misheard something."

"I'm not wrong, Aria. And neither was Foster."

I turned my gaze away, staring into space as my mind whirled.

Landon *had* to be wrong.

My father would never do something so terrible. He had his issues, that was for sure, but still... the man who kissed my forehead before every campaign speech couldn't possibly be the same man willing to maim his own daughter for political clout. It was just too cold and sinister. Too *evil*.

Landon rubbed his forehead and slid a little closer to me. "Once we realized you were in danger, we knew we had to protect you somehow. Do our best to stop your father and oust him from power."

"*Protect* me?" My brows shot up as a sudden hot twist of anger curled inside me. "Landon, you *stalked* me! You threatened me! And you—"

"Please just listen," he said, cutting me off. "You're right. I did all that. But there was a reason behind it."

"What reason?" I asked, voice almost cracking with a mix of fear and disbelief.

He exhaled deeply, rubbing his left temple. "We knew nothing about when and where your father's loyalists were planning to carry out their attack—or attacks—against you. So our best bet to protect you was to force him to drop out of the race. To do that, we had to get creative, so the original plan was to terrify you and gaslight you to the point where you'd have some sort of mental breakdown."

"*What?*" I snapped, eyes narrowing. "Why?"

"If you were hospitalized for a mental health crisis, it would become public knowledge pretty quickly, thanks to the media, and then your father would *have* to drop out, because it would look bad for him to keep going despite having a child who desperately needed his support," Landon said. He slowly shook his head. "I'm not proud of the fact that I was trying to drive you into a nervous breakdown. One that could seriously affect your life. But we all figured it was better than the alternative, which was you being paralyzed in a car accident."

"I see," I muttered, hands shaking as shock and fury collided in my stomach.

Landon's jaw clenched, his eyes flickering with regret. "I'm serious, Aria. I hated every second of it," he said. "Seeing you so scared, and watching you start to fall apart because of me... I wouldn't blame you if you never forgave me."

"Mm-hm," I murmured, not quite knowing what to say. I was still reeling from his revelation about my father. Still didn't know if I could believe it.

"Anyway, it didn't work, obviously," he went on. "But we managed to thwart the first attempt to hurt you, at least."

"The car bomb that was planted during the gala?" I asked in a tremulous voice.

"Yes." He dipped his chin in a curt nod. "That's why I was there that night. Foster was pretty sure something would happen then, and he was right."

I forced myself to swallow the tight lump in my throat. "And the Dominion Club card that was left on my bag that night? Was that supposed to be some sort of warning for me?"

"Not exactly," Landon replied, his fingers brushing over his jaw. "I left it there because I knew you'd figure out what it was and start asking questions about it. And, considering how most people dismiss the Dominion Club as nothing more than a paranoid conspiracy theory, bringing it up would probably make you look... crazy."

"So it was all part of the plan," I murmured, my shoulders sagging. "To make me look and feel insane."

"Yes. I had no idea that you'd actually track us down at one of our meetings," he said. "I have to admit, that was incredibly ballsy of you. Smart, too. But definitely unexpected."

"And the things I overheard that night..." I trailed off, eyes narrowing.

"We were talking about the car bomb. How we'd looked into it and determined that Foster's information was correct—that it was intended to harm you, but not kill you," Landon said. "We weren't responsible for the bomb. But I can see how you came to that conclusion without all the prior information."

I frowned. "You threatened me afterwards. Told me I'd regret it if I didn't stay away from the society," I said, folding my arms. "If you're supposed to be the good guys, and you don't want me hurt or dead, then why the hell would you do that?"

"Because the society guards a lot of high-level secrets, including the identities of every member," Landon said, giving me another hard look. "Just because we were working to protect you doesn't mean you're welcome to crash our meetings. So I was concerned about what might happen if everyone realized it was you who sneaked in that night, and I warned you to stay away so it wouldn't happen again."

"I guess that makes sense," I muttered, though truthfully, nothing was making sense to me right now. My head was spinning so hard that this entire conversation felt surreal, like I was trapped in some twisted nightmare.

Landon turned his gaze to the fire, his expression tense. "Anyway... we knew another attempt to harm you was coming eventually, and once we learned about your trip to Alaska, we figured something was probably going to happen there. Another car bomb, or something like that. That's why Knox, Sebastian, Theo, and Cole came along for the trip. They were going to help me thwart any attempts made to hurt you."

"Right."

My stomach suddenly twisted with nausea, because I knew exactly what Landon was going to claim next.

"We never thought your father would be ruthless enough to change tactics and try to kill you instead," he said softly, a trace of regret threading through his tone. "But... we were wrong. I realized that when things on the plane started going haywire. The crash was planned."

As his words sank in, the world seemed to tilt on its axis. I felt like I was falling again; plummeting through an endless void where reality made no sense and every tether to safety had been violently severed.

"I-it could've been a real accident caused by a bird strike," I said hurriedly, desperately clinging to the possibility that there was some other explanation. "We still don't know—"

Landon lifted a hand to cut me off. "The crash was definitely arranged," he said bluntly. "Tony and I talked again after we finished stripping the plane on that first day, and after all the extra time thinking about it, he was absolutely certain the plane was hacked and brought down on purpose. Nothing else made sense."

Suddenly I couldn't move. Couldn't breathe. The world still felt like it was spinning, but I was frozen in place as Landon's words twisted in my head, over and over, mocking me with their undeniable logic.

A part of me wanted to scream, but I couldn't find my voice. I wasn't even sure if I was still here. Was this really my life? This nightmare that kept unfolding in ways I couldn't even imagine?

"And you know what else?" Landon added, staring right at me.

"What?" I whispered, my heart pounding like a war drum.

"The one thing your father and his minions couldn't predict was the weather that day," he said. "Do you remember what the pilot told us before we left?"

"Our flight path changed," I said, voice still barely audible.

"Yes. That flight would usually go right across the Gulf of Alaska. It was only changed at the last minute because of the bad weather," he said. "If the plane had crashed on water, like they intended, everyone would've died, because it's almost impossible to survive a water crash. So whoever brought that plane down one hundred percent intended for everyone on board to die... including you."

A violent shiver of horror swept up my spine, and bile burned the back of my throat as the crushing weight of betrayal settled over me.

All my life, I'd loved my father despite our differences. Despite the way he so often made me feel so small. I'd convinced myself that no matter what happened, he was still my dad at the end of the day—the man who'd tucked me in at night when I was a child, promising to protect me from monsters.

But he was the real monster, wasn't he?

Ruthless. Calculating. Willing to sacrifice his own flesh and blood for the sake of his ambitions. Willing to sacrifice at least two hundred other innocent souls as well.

The harrowing realization was cracking me open from the inside out, leaving jagged fragments of trust and love shattered at my feet. How did I miss all of this for so long? How the hell could I have been so blind to my own father's true nature?

A cold shiver rippled through me as a memory suddenly hit. Back when I was stumbling through the haze of those berries, I'd hallucinated my mother, her face clear as day. *You're not safe, darling,* she'd said to me. *Not with him.*

At the time, I thought she was talking about Landon. I was sure of it. But now the truth slammed into me like a tidal wave. She wasn't warning me about him. She was warning me about my father.

But it wasn't really my mother talking to me that night. It was *me*. My own high, half-delirious brain.

That meant some subconscious, instinctive part of me must've suspected something was off about my father all along. I was just too blinded by love and loyalty to see it, so I'd buried it deep down, unable to truly face it.

A fresh wave of horror and disbelief suddenly washed over me, as if my mind were struggling to catch up with the reality of it all. I wanted to scream my head off, to fight against this new version of my father that had been hidden from me all along... but all that was left was an overwhelming emptiness where my trust and naivety once lived.

I knew it was the truth now. Felt it in my bones. He had really tried to kill me.

Now, I was left questioning everything, and the emptiness inside me was vast, terrifying. What else had he done? What else was I blind to?

"Why did you cut the ELT cable?" I finally asked Landon in a low, strained voice. "You still haven't explained that."

"I was getting to it," he said softly, rubbing his jaw. "Figured you needed a minute or two to process."

I took a deep breath, blinking back the tears stinging my eyes. "I'm ready to hear it now."

"All right." Landon nodded slowly. "I was conscious throughout the crash. Others passed out or hit their heads... but not me. I knew exactly what was happening and why. And that meant I also knew exactly what I had to do if we survived. I had to make sure no one would find us. Not for a very long time."

"Why?"

"I knew if the rescuers got to us quickly, your father and his minions would almost certainly find another way to make sure you didn't survive. You'd probably be smothered in your hospital bed or overdosed on meds, and then they'd pay off—or threaten—the medical team to claim you died from internal injuries sustained in the crash," he said. "Then the public outpouring of sympathy would begin, and he'd ride that boost all the way to a second-term victory."

I swallowed hard, my chest tight with conflicting emotions. "So that's why you cut the cable," I said in a hollow voice. "To keep me away from my father and his cronies."

"Exactly. I knew if I kept you out here until after the election, you'd be safe from him in the long-run."

"How?"

"Well, right now, you're considered missing and most likely dead, so he's probably enjoying another sympathy boost," Landon explained. "He'll defeat my mother in the election again and snag the presidency. But he won't be able to run for a third term. That means he'll have no reason to try to kill you again once we're back in civilization."

"But he'll still be the president for the next four years!" I said, throwing my hands up. "Are you okay with that? Given what you know about him?"

"Obviously we're going to tell the public the truth about him once we're finally found," he said. "He won't be the president for long after that, but for now... it's better that you stay out here. That was the decision I made at the time, and I stand by it."

"But leaving us stranded in the wild is insane," I said, eyes widening. "Totally fucking insane."

Landon steeled his jaw. "I know. But I had to do whatever it took to protect you, Aria. And that was what it took."

I shook my head, fury and frustration simmering beneath my skin. "Why didn't you just go to the damn FBI or DOJ when Foster first approached the Dominion Club with his concerns? Or even the media?" I demanded. "Wouldn't that be easier than... than all *this*?"

He shook his head, his jaw still tight. "There was no proof. Foster just happened to overhear a conversation about your father wanting to hurt you, and it was pure luck that he did," he said. "There was no recording or written evidence. Nothing that would hold up. So even if he tried to come forward with the accusation, it would just be his word against your father and his entire administration. Who do you think would win that fight?"

I swallowed hard, my hands falling back to my sides. "Point taken," I muttered.

"He did give us a name, at least," Landon continued. "He recognized the voice of one of the loyalists."

"Who?"

"Special Agent Marcus Randall."

My brows shot up. "He's the one I saw at the Dominion Club meeting when I sneaked in."

Landon nodded grimly. "Yeah. We tortured him for information that night, trying to get anything we could on the plan to hurt you. But the bastard didn't give up a damn thing," he said. "I wanted to kill him. I really did. But the death of a high-ranking Secret Service agent would attract way too much attention. So we had to let him go with a warning—that we'd come back for more if he ever breathed a word to your father about the fact we were onto him. That worked, at least. He didn't say anything about us. But he still kept working on a plan to harm you, obviously. A much worse plan, as it turned out."

My mind started spinning again, and I slowly shook my head. "Why did you go to such lengths to protect me, Landon?" I asked, my voice barely above a whisper. "Does the Dominion Club usually go to bat this hard for people threatened by politicians?"

He hesitated, his gaze dropping to the ground. "When I pitched the plan to keep you safe, I framed it like it was about taking down a corrupt president. That's no small feat, and it made sense to everyone at the time."

"Oh. Right."

His eyes lifted to mine, piercing and unflinching. "But that wasn't the truth," he said, his voice softer now.

"What's the truth, then?"

He took a breath, his expression shifting to something almost vulnerable. "I did it all for you, Aria."

My heart skipped a beat, caught between shock and disbelief. "Why?"

"Because I love you," he said, his voice low and raw with emotion. "I'm in love with you."

21

ARIA

"No."

The word slipped out before I could stop it, barely more than a breath.

Landon's brow furrowed, confusion flickering across his face. "No?"

I stared at him, heart thundering so loud I could hardly hear anything else. Then a bitter laugh bubbled up in my throat. "You don't *love* me," I said, fervently shaking my head. "You hate me! You've *always* hated me."

That was true... wasn't it?

I'd spent years convincing myself that Landon despised me. That I was just a thorn in his side. The enemy's daughter. Never in a million years did I think he could feel anything else. Certainly not love.

But the way he was looking at me right now... I couldn't make sense of it. And I didn't know how to process the way my heart twisted at the sight of him like this.

"I never hated you, Aria," Landon finally said, looking down at the fire. "*You* hated *me*."

"No," I said, more forcefully this time. "You've tormented me for years. This is just another one of your sick games."

His gaze lifted back to mine, stormy and intense. "I know I had to be cruel to you these last few months to make you think you were going crazy, but it was—"

I cut him off. "No, I mean *before* that."

His brows dipped in a frown for a few seconds. Then he raised his palms, nodding slowly. "I get it. I was a total asshole to you when we were kids," he said. "The way I treated you back then was really messed up. But if it makes you feel any better, I was having a rough time too. I was a really fucked-up kid."

"I'm not talking about childhood bullying, Landon!" I said hotly, jumping to my feet. "I mean what came after that!"

His forehead wrinkled. "What?"

I bit down on the surge of emotion threatening to choke me. "You know my secret. You're the only one who does," I said in a small voice. "And you've held it over my head for so long now. I've literally lived in fear for the last four years, always wondering how and when you'll finally decide to expose me and ruin my life."

Landon's confusion deepened, and he stood too, watching me like I was a puzzle he couldn't quite piece together. "What are you talking about?"

I swallowed hard, forcing the words out even though they felt like jagged glass tearing up my throat. "At my mom's funeral," I said. "You mouthed something to me, over and over. '*I saw you.*' Don't act like that didn't happen, because we both know it did."

Understanding dawned in his eyes, and he gave a slow nod. "You're right. I did say that."

My pulse thundered in my ears, and I struggled to breathe past the suffocating knot in my chest. "You said it because you know what I did after my mother's accident, right?" I said. "You even admitted it earlier. You told me you saw everything that day."

Silence stretched between us, thick and oppressive.

"Yes," Landon finally said. "I saw all of it."

A violent tremor ran through me, but I couldn't tell if it was from fear or shame. "I've spent years terrified that you'd use it against me," I said, tears brimming in my eyes. "That one day, you'd finally tell everyone and destroy me. Just to get your mother elected, or whatever the hell your game plan was."

His face softened, and something like regret flashed in his eyes. "Aria... I was never holding anything over your head. I never planned to tell anyone what you did."

I shook my head, disbelief and anger colliding inside me. "Then why did you come to the funeral and say that shit to me? Why would you torture me like that?"

He hesitated for a moment, then looked me square in the eye. "I only said '*I saw you*' the first two times."

"What?"

He took a step closer, his fingers brushing the side of my face with a tenderness that made my breath catch. "The third time, I didn't say '*I saw you*.' I said, '*I'll save you*.'"

I stared at him, stunned. "W-what?"

"I wasn't trying to threaten or scare you," he said. "Although now that you've told me all of this, I can see how it must've looked and felt on your end."

"So... what did you mean, then?" I asked, voice barely above a whisper.

"I just wanted you to know that I saw what you did, and that I'd save you if anyone ever tried to come forward and claim they knew something about that day," he said. "If some nosy journalist looked into it, for example. I would've covered for you. Made sure nothing bad ever happened to you. Because I saw myself in you that day."

"You did?"

"Yeah." His gaze burned into mine, fierce and unyielding. "You were desperate to make sense of the pain. Willing to do anything to take back control. And I loved you for it."

My mind reeled, struggling to process what he was saying. "You loved me for *that*? The worst thing I've ever done?"

Landon nodded. "Yes. I was proud of you, too. And I knew I'd do anything to protect you, no matter what."

My heart pounded so hard it hurt, and I didn't know whether to cry or scream. All this time, I'd been convinced he was holding my dark secret over me, waiting for the right moment to ruin me. But that was never true. In fact, the exact opposite was true.

"How come you never said anything else about it?" I asked, slowly shaking my head as confusion roiled in my guts. "Why didn't you ever have a real conversation with me about it, instead of mouthing stuff to me from five feet away at a funeral?"

Landon took another step forward. "Because I knew that was probably the only chance I'd get to talk to you for a long time," he said. "You and your father moved away right after your mum died, and with all the election bullshit going on, you were constantly surrounded by security. And there was no way they'd let me, the son of your father's biggest political rival, just come over and talk to you. At least not alone."

"But you could've said it to me in a—"

He cut me off. "I didn't want to risk putting what I had to say over text, phone, or email. Because if someone somehow got their hands on a copy of that, your life would be over."

I blinked, mind still whirling. "So all this time," I whispered. "You really didn't hate me? You weren't planning to expose what I did?"

His hand slid down to take mine, his thumb stroking softly over my knuckles. "No. Never."

I shook my head, still confused. "But you've always acted like you can't stand me."

"No, *you've* always acted like you can't stand *me*, Aria. I just kept my distance to respect that. And yeah, I was a little cold whenever we ran into each other, because you so clearly despised me, and I was trying to move on. Trying to forget my feelings," he said. "I figured I'd get over it eventually. But I never did. Not after all this time. And now you know it."

A choked sob escaped me, and I covered my mouth with my hand, shaking my head as the truth sank in. Landon reached for me again, his hand brushing my arm, and the warmth of his touch shattered the last of my defenses.

For the first time in years, I didn't feel hunted. Didn't feel like I was constantly looking over my shoulder, bracing for the blow that would end me. Instead, I felt safe. Like I'd finally found solid ground after years of drifting in open water.

"I... I wish I knew all of this before now," I said, eyes brimming again.

"There were a hundred times I wanted to talk to you about it and see how you were coping with what happened that day," Landon said, his voice rough with regret. "But you always looked at me like I was the Devil, so I figured bringing up your mom's death would just make it worse."

"And you didn't wonder *why* I looked at you like that?"

He shook his head. "I just figured you hated me because of what an asshole I was when we were kids. And I didn't blame you for that. I was a real piece of shit back then," he said. "Also, our parents were—and still are—direct political rivals. So I thought there might be some animosity because of that too."

"Oh. Right." My vision suddenly blurred as the weight of it all crashed over me, my chest tightening with the force of too many emotions at once. I sucked in the deepest breath I could manage, but it still felt like I wasn't getting enough air.

"Let's sit down again," Landon said softly, stroking my arm. "You need to try and relax."

I sank down next to the fire, my mind racing in a blur of disbelief. All these years... gone, wasted. All the mistakes I couldn't take back. All the lies I'd told myself to fill in the gaps.

The weight of four years of fear finally cracked open, and suddenly I couldn't hold back the sobs that tore free. Landon pulled me against his chest, his arms wrapping around me as I crumpled against him.

With each shuddering breath, he tightened his grip around me, one hand cradling the back of my head as if he could hold me together while I fell apart. His touch was solid and warm, grounding me while my mind spiraled through a storm of memories.

I squeezed my eyes shut, but it didn't stop the flashback from hitting me like a tidal wave.

That day, four and a half years ago, my mother and I were driving along a winding road through the mountains, just beyond our neighborhood—close enough to home to feel familiar, but isolated enough that the forest loomed on either side, dark and dense. Mom had the windows down, letting the crisp air swirl through the car.

It was one of the only times I felt free back then. At home and also at my school, the Secret Service were always hovering nearby, vigilant and watchful, seeing as my father had just secured the party's nomination. Mom and I were still allowed to go out together without any agents if it was away from the city, though. The security detail would only get ramped up to constant surveillance and suffocating control if Dad actually won the election.

"You know," Mom said, glancing over at me with a soft smile. "This might be a good place for you to practice your driving, now that you've mastered empty parking lots and quiet back streets."

I wrinkled my nose. "I don't know. It seems kind of scary with all these twists and turns."

She laughed. "It's not as bad as it looks. And it's less scary to practice here than on a busy city street, right?" she said. "Besides, getting comfortable with mountain roads will make you a much better driver in the long run. You've got to be prepared for anything out here."

I glanced out the window, taking in the rugged, tree-lined path winding up into the hills. "That's true."

"It's a really nice hiking spot too," she added. "Thomas Ashford used to bring Landon out here all the time."

My chest tightened a little at the mention of Landon's name. "Oh."

"I think Landon still hikes out here quite often. So maybe you two can go together some time, if those Secret Service agents will allow it," she said. "It would be nice to get away from the media hounding you, wouldn't it? And I'm sure Landon would appreciate the company now that his dad is no longer with us."

"I don't think so," I muttered. "We aren't really friends anymore."

Mom's smile faltered, and she glanced at me with a hint of sadness in her eyes. "Is it because of the election stuff?" she said. "Because you two can still be friends, you know. Just because your dad is running against his mother doesn't mean you have to dislike each other."

"I know. But we're still not friends."

"That's a shame. You two used to get along so well when you were little."

I sighed. "We didn't really. I just pretended to like him in front of you, because you were such good friends with Celeste, and I didn't want to make either of you feel bad."

Mom gave me a sideways look. "Really?"

"Yeah. And Landon didn't like me either," I said, raising a brow. "So I doubt that 'friendship' will ever be resurrected."

"Well, that's his loss," she said, squeezing my hand on the console. "If he can't see how amazing my daugh—"

Her words cut off in a strangled gasp as an SUV appeared from nowhere around a curve, right in our lane. Metal crunched and twisted as the impact hurled us sideways. The car spun, glass shattering, and the world turned into a blur of noise and chaos.

I didn't even feel the pain at first. Just a shockwave of terror and confusion. Then I saw my mother slumped over the steering wheel, blood pouring from her temple. The other vehicle was crumpled against ours, steam hissing from under the hood.

Reality snapped back into focus, and I scrambled to undo my seatbelt, hands trembling. "Mom?" I whispered, reaching out to touch her shoulder. "Mom!"

Her head lolled, and her eyes stared vacantly at nothing.

I grabbed her shoulder, shaking her, willing her to move, but she stayed limp, her eyes still unseeing.

Horrified disbelief crashed over me, stealing the air from my lungs. I pressed my forehead to her shoulder, sobs wracking my body as I whimpered, "Please, Mom. Wake up. *Please.*"

But she didn't move. She was gone.

A keening sob rose in my throat, and my fingers dug into her sweater, desperate to hold onto her warmth before it faded. Then I crumpled forward, pressing my forehead to her shoulder, choking on sobs that burned like acid.

The metallic taste of blood filled my mouth from biting my lip too hard, but I didn't care. I didn't care about the glass digging into my palms or the throbbing pain radiating through my skull either. I just wanted my mom back. I wanted her to open her eyes, to tell me everything was going to be okay, to hug me and make the nightmare go away.

"H-help."

At the sound of the pitiful voice carrying through the air, I looked up, squinting to see through the cracked windshield. The driver of the other car was slumped over in the front seat too.

"Help," he repeated. "P-please..."

Wincing, I pushed open my door and stumbled out of the car. As I stepped toward the SUV, I fumbled for my phone, trying to remember how to make my fingers work.

When I reached the shattered driver's side window, the man looked at me, blinking dazedly. "Please," he croaked, pressing one hand to his bleeding neck. "C-call... for help..."

"I will," I said, finally reaching my phone. "I'm just—"

My words dried up in my throat as I registered the smell emanating from the SUV. *Whiskey.* My eyes skated down to the man's lap, where a half-empty bottle was wedged between his thighs.

The driver wheezed, struggling to free himself from his seatbelt, but his limbs moved sluggishly, like he couldn't quite get them to work.

"You were drinking?" I said sharply.

"Just... just a bit," he muttered.

I'd initially assumed that his voice was slurred because of the pain. Now I knew better.

I looked over at my motionless mom again, and my throat started to burn as my vision blurred with tears.

The man in the SUV had done this. He'd taken my mother from me.

He kept struggling, his breaths coming faster now. "Please," he rasped. "You... you need to call. Call... 911."

But I didn't move. Didn't even breathe.

Fifteen minutes crawled by. I stared at him the whole time, watching the life drain from his eyes as his movements slowed, his breaths growing shallow and uneven.

It wasn't until he stopped moving entirely that I finally grabbed my phone and dialed 911, my hands shaking so badly I almost dropped it.

I didn't remember what I told the operator—something about how the other car just appeared out of nowhere. I was numb, hollowed out, and when the paramedics finally arrived, I couldn't look at them.

I heard what they said, though.

"It's a shame," one of them muttered as the man's body was loaded onto a gurney and covered with a sheet. "If we got here just five minutes earlier, we could've saved him."

I could've saved him. I could've called 911 when I said I would.

But I let him die instead, because all I saw in those moments was a red mist of rage clouding my vision, and all I felt was a searing hatred, coursing through my veins like fire.

The memory faded, and I snapped back to the present. I was still cradled against Landon's chest, his arms wrapped around me like a lifeline.

"It's okay," he whispered, his breath warm against my hair. "I've got you."

My fingers tightened against his shirt, clinging to him. He wasn't condemning me. Wasn't recoiling in disgust. He knew my darkest secret and didn't hate me for it. Instead, he understood it.

Somehow, that made everything hurt just a little bit less.

I blinked away a fresh set of tears and looked up at him. "How did you see what happened?" I asked in a tremulous voice. "I never saw you there."

"I was hiking out there. I went every Saturday, just to clear my head. It was the only time my mother's security detail would ever let me go out alone while all the election shit was going on," he said. He paused for a beat, exhaling deeply before he went on. "I heard the crash happen, and I ran down to the road to see if I could do anything. The first person I saw was your mom."

"There was nothing anyone could do for her," I murmured. "The coroner said she died instantly."

"Yeah. I could see that," Landon said softly. "Then I saw *you*, standing there, staring at the other driver. I figured you were just in shock, so I was about to come over and help. But then I heard what you said. That he'd been drinking."

"He had a half-empty bottle of whiskey on his lap," I said. I swallowed the lump in my throat and went on. "His car absolutely reeked of alcohol. And when they tested him afterwards, they said his blood alcohol content was 0.15. He was wasted."

Landon nodded. "That's what I figured when I heard you," he said, his voice steady and calm. "Then I realized you weren't calling for help. You were just standing there, staring at him. And I knew right then that you weren't going to save him."

A shiver ran through me, and I squeezed my eyes shut, guilt and shame swirling through me like a hurricane. "You really didn't think I was a monster?" I whispered.

He tightened his grip on me, cupping my cheek to make me look at him. "Of course I didn't," he said fiercely. "Not for a second. I just... I understood. That man was a careless, selfish bastard who thought he was above the rules, and he killed your mom because he didn't give a shit about anyone but himself. I would've done the exact same thing as you. I know because I've thought about it a thousand times."

"I've never felt that sort of anger and hatred for anyone before," I murmured. "It felt like my whole body was on fire."

"I get it." Landon's eyes flickered with understanding. "I've felt that before. And you know, it wasn't just *you* that day."

"What do you mean?"

"I mean, I could've done something too. I could've called 911. But instead, I tucked myself behind a tree and watched, just to make sure you were okay," he said. "I stayed until you finally made the call and waited until the ambulance and cops arrived. Once I knew you were going to be fine, and no one suspected anything of you, I quietly left." He paused and slowly shook his head. "But if anyone had ever come along and questioned the case..." He trailed off for another second, rubbing his jaw. "Well, I took care of that, for the most part."

"How?"

"After I left the woods, I went to the cops. I told them I'd been hiking up on Mt. Bankwell that day, and I heard a crash on the road below. I said there was no safe way to reach the road from where I was, but I was able to look through my binoculars to see the aftermath," he said. "I told them you were unconscious for about fifteen minutes before you finally woke up, and then you finally got out of the car, approached the other car to check on the driver, and got your phone out to make a call. I also told them I was trying to call 911 the whole time, but I had no reception in the spot I was in, so the calls kept failing."

"I never heard about that statement," I said, slowly shaking my head.

"Yeah, I figured you wouldn't, because the cops wouldn't have needed to follow up with you on anything. It was an open-and-shut case. Drunk driver veered onto the wrong side of the road and collided with another car," he said. He paused, rubbing his temple. "I always worried some nosy journalist might look into it all anyway, just to stir up drama around your family because of the election, but that never happened. But if it *did*... I was always going to be on your side. I was always going to save you."

Another lump formed in my throat. "So... you weren't just going to cover for me if anyone questioned the case afterwards," I whispered. "You already covered for me right after it happened."

Landon's fingers threaded through my hair, tugging me closer until our foreheads touched. "Just as a pre-emptive measure," he said. "Like I said, I was never going to let anything happen to you."

I took a shaky breath, trying to comprehend the gravity of what he'd done that day. He'd seen the ugliest, darkest part of me, and he'd chosen to protect me without a second thought.

He was never a threat.

In truth, I'd been the one keeping myself shackled to the fear all these years, replaying that terrible day over and over, convinced that Landon wanted to use it to destroy me because I was so wrapped up in my own guilt that it made me assume the worst. But he hadn't been my judge or executioner. He'd been my savior, even when I couldn't see it.

"I really wish I knew," I said, voice cracking with emotion.

"Well, you do now. Better late than never," he murmured.

I sniffed and wiped my face, pulling away slightly. "I don't deserve you," I murmured, shaking my head. "I was a total bitch to you for years because I had the wrong idea. And all along, you were protecting me in a million different ways."

"You weren't that bad," he said, squeezing my hand. "You were kind of rude to me sometimes, but I wasn't exactly an angel toward you either. So I'd say we're about even."

"Landon... I *stabbed* you today."

He smiled faintly. "It's fine. It looks worse than it actually is, because of all the blood."

"It's not fine. You were trying to save me from a bear, and I repaid you by shoving a pair of scissors into you," I said, the guilt still heavy in my chest. "How can you be so nice and understanding after how horrible and ungrateful I've been to you?"

"I already told you why, Aria," Landon said, tilting my chin up with two fingers. "It's because I love you."

Before I could respond, he leaned down and crushed his lips on mine.

22

ARIA

Landon and I stayed by the fire for a while, his arms wrapped around me as I leaned into his warmth. His kiss still tingled on my lips, sending little jolts through my core.

I craved more kisses, more passion, but I also wanted to keep talking, because now that I knew the truth, I wanted to hear everything he had to say. I wanted to soak up every word and hold onto this moment before reality set back in.

Eventually, the fire burned down to glowing embers, and the air turned colder, shadows stretching long across the riverbank. I couldn't stop shivering, my sweater and jeans doing nothing to block the chill seeping into my bones.

Landon glanced over, his gaze catching mine for just a moment before he nodded toward the cave behind us. "It's getting colder," he said, his voice low and calm. "We should go inside to sleep. We can figure out our next moves when it's light again."

I followed him into the tiny space, grateful to be out of the wind as he dug through his backpack. He pulled out a few articles of clothing, spreading them out on the ground to form a makeshift bed.

"Lie down," he said, jerking his chin toward the pile. "It's not exactly a five-star hotel bed, but it's better than the ground."

I opened my mouth to protest, feeling bad that there was only enough space for me on the makeshift bed, but the exhaustion dragging at my limbs won out, and I sank onto the surprisingly soft layers. Landon reached into another pocket on his bag and dug out a small bundle wrapped in cloth.

He tossed it to me, and I caught it awkwardly, unwrapping the fabric to reveal strips of dried meat and a handful of mixed nuts.

"Venison jerky," he said. "We made it back at the hunter's cabin."

"Thanks. Are you having some too?"

He nodded. "We'll eat half now, and then the other half in the morning. We'll need the energy."

I tore off a piece of the jerky, the smoky, slightly gamey flavor bursting on my tongue. My stomach growled, and I almost laughed at how good it tasted. "This is amazing. I think it's the first non-fish meat I've had in two weeks," I said between bites. Then a thought struck me, and I cocked my head. "Speaking of weeks... do you have any idea what the date is? I lost track ages ago."

Landon chewed on a bit of jerky, his brow creasing as he thought. "We've been out here for five weeks and four days. That makes it the 18th of November."

"So the election is in two days."

"Yup."

I took another bite, mind whirling with a mix of dread and hatred as the memory of my father's betrayal flooded back in. When I swallowed, I looked back at Landon. "I just thought of something," I said. "You think my father will win because of the sympathy boost, right?"

"Yeah. Definitely."

"But he's running against your mom, and you were on the

same plane as me. So you're also missing and presumed dead. Won't she get a sympathy boost too?"

Landon nodded. "Yeah, but I don't think it'll have the same impact as it will for your dad. He's the sitting president. So his team will spin it as, 'He has the most stressful job in the world, and now, on top of everything, he's dealing with the sudden loss of his daughter. But despite all that stress and grief, he's not dropping out, and he's still doing his best for the American people—because *that's* how much he cares.' People will start seeing him like a martyr. A superhero."

"Ah. Good point," I said, shoulders slumping. "He'll totally win with that strategy."

"Unfortunately, yeah."

I sighed and looked toward the cave entrance, my chest tight. "How long do you think we'll end up being stuck out here in the end?"

Landon slowly shook his head. "There's no way to know for sure. By now, we're all presumed dead, so it's no longer a rescue mission. It's a recovery mission," he said. "That means there'll be fewer people and resources assigned to it. We could get really lucky and be found tomorrow. Or we could be out here for another six months."

My stomach twisted. "I'm really scared we're going to run out of food," I said softly. "It's so close to winter, and things are already getting harder to find."

"Don't worry. Everything's going to be fine," Landon said, his voice steady and reassuring. "The guys and I have been hunting as much as we can and stockpiling whatever else we find—nuts, fruit, anything. And Knox hurt his foot a while back, so he's been staying behind at the cabin most days to preserve as much of the meat as possible by turning it into jerky. He's also been dehydrating fruit so it lasts. So we've got plenty to share."

"You guys would really do that?"

"Of course."

"But... why? After what our group did?"

"It's okay. We understand why you guys kicked us out," Landon replied. "You didn't want a murderer around, especially with Hannah there, and you didn't know which one of us did it. So we had to go. And honestly, it's good that we did, because we found that cabin much sooner than we might have if we'd stayed at the lakeside camp."

My heart lifted a little, hope flickering to life. "So you really think we're going to make it through the winter?"

His jaw tightened. "I'll make damn sure of it," he said, his voice thick with conviction.

"Thank you," I murmured.

"I've been keeping an eye on you this whole time, Aria," he added softly. "I was never going to let anything happen to you."

Emotion surged up my throat, a mix of guilt and unexpected relief. I hadn't realized just how much I'd been carrying until his words sliced through the weight, but now, all those restless nights and lingering fears suddenly felt a little bit lighter.

A shaky laugh slipped out. "I kept feeling like someone was watching me," I said, my lips curving despite the knot still lodged in my chest. "It was you secretly visiting our camp, wasn't it?"

He nodded. "Yeah. Just to check on you, and also your food supply. If it started dropping to dangerous levels, the guys and I would've started leaving meat and other stuff for you. We really don't want anyone starving."

"Thank you," I repeated, squeezing his hand. "I can't even tell you what a relief that is to hear."

"It's no problem."

"I guess that means all we really have to worry about now is the cannibal settlement. That's probably our biggest problem. Oh, and also figuring out a way off this damn riverbank tomo—"

Landon lifted a palm, his expression sharpening. "Did you just say *cannibal* settlement?"

"Oh, shit." My eyes widened. "I thought I mentioned it earlier, but I didn't, did I?"

I recounted what Leigh, Trent, Ryan, and I had discovered during our long scouting expedition a week ago. As I spoke, Landon's expression darkened, and he finally moved closer, pulling me into his arms again.

"I'm glad you got the hell out of there before they spotted you," he said, his voice low and fierce. "That was definitely the right choice."

"Yeah, I think so too. Leigh said they could just be... endo-cannibals, I think she called it? Eating their own dead as a ritual after they die naturally. But we didn't want to stick around and find out. Just in case."

"Yeah, they could be the peaceful type, but they could also be dangerous," Landon said. He cocked his head and frowned. "How far away did you say their village is from your camp? A four hour walk?"

"Four and a half."

He frowned. "That's far enough that they haven't noticed any of us yet, but I worry about what'll happen when the animals move out for winter. They might start hunting farther out, and that could lead them straight to the camp."

"That's what I'm worried about too," I said, goosebumps prickling along my arms. "We've got two people on night watch duty now, and we've got those guns too. But it's still really scary."

"Once we get off this damn bank, we should talk about reuniting the groups," Landon said grimly. "You'll be much safer with the six of us back. Especially with all the hunting rifles and gear we found in the cabin."

I nodded. "Yeah. We'll have to figure something out. But first... we really need to figure out how to get off this bank. There's no way I can climb that cliff, even with your help."

"I was thinking about it earlier." He jerked a thumb toward the left side of the cave entrance. "I noticed at that end of the bank, there aren't as many rocks in the river. And the river has to go somewhere."

"You're thinking we should try to swim for it?" I said, eyes widening.

"Not exactly. The current is too rapid for that, so there's too much risk of getting separated. Not to mention the drowning risk," he replied. "But even though the current's strong, it's not completely out of control. So if we can get something buoyant enough to stabilize us, we might be able to ride it out to a spot where the bank levels off."

I frowned, considering it. "What about downstream? We don't know what's ahead. There could be rapids or waterfalls."

He gave a grim nod. "Yeah, that's why we'll keep to the edge as much as possible," he said. "Anyway, I've got some ropes in my pack, so I was thinking we could grab a whole bunch of big sticks from those trees out there. Then we can tie them together to make a sort of flotation device."

"Like a kickboard?" I asked, trying to picture it.

"Yeah. Something we can hold on to while we're in the water. It'll help to keep us afloat and also keep us from getting swept too far apart," he said. "Also, we can tie ourselves together, so if one of us slips or loses grip on the raft, the other can pull them back. It's not perfect, but it's better than just diving in and hoping for the best."

I chewed my lip, considering it. "It'll be cold in there... but I guess it's the only real option we've got. We can't just stay on this bank forever."

"Exactly," Landon said, his gaze steady and determined. "We'll try to let the current carry us downstream to somewhere more manageable. Somewhere we can actually get out without breaking our necks. Then we can find our way back to the camp."

I glanced out at the river, my pulse quickening. "Let's do it. First thing tomorrow."

Landon nodded, giving my hand another reassuring squeeze.

"We'll make it work," he said. "But for now, we should rest. We've both had a really long day."

He tugged me closer, his arm wrapping around my shoulders as we lay together on the ground. The adrenaline that had been keeping me on edge for hours was finally starting to wear off, leaving me bone-tired and aching. I wanted to stay alert—wanted to keep planning and preparing—but exhaustion was already dragging me under.

Landon brushed a stray hair from my face, his touch gentle despite the calluses on his fingers. Then his hand moved down, tracing slow, soothing circles along my arm, and I felt his lips press lightly to the top of my head. "I've got you," he whispered. "Just rest."

I didn't mean to let go so quickly, but sleep rushed in like a tidal wave, sweeping me away before I could even try to resist. The rhythmic sound of the river outside the cave lulled me deeper, and Landon's steady breathing kept me anchored.

Safe. For now.

My last thought before sleep claimed me was that somehow, as impossible as it seemed, I actually believed him. We would make it out of here, survive the winter, and get back to civilization to make my father pay for his crimes.

With him by my side... I felt like I could do anything.

SUNLIGHT FILTERED THROUGH THE NARROW OPENING AT THE mouth of the cave, and I stirred, stretching lazily before cracking my eyes open. The soft warmth of morning touched my face, and I yawned, half-buried against the rough fabric of Landon's jacket.

I reached out, patting the empty space beside me, and my stomach clenched when I realized he was gone.

I sat bolt upright, heart pounding, only for my shoulders to sag with relief when I spotted him stepping through the cave entrance. His sleeves were rolled up, and his hair was slightly damp.

"You're finally awake," he said, smiling faintly as he drew closer. "How'd you sleep?"

"Like a log, thanks. But I almost had a heart attack when I woke up and realized you weren't in here," I said, laying a hand over my still-racing heart. "I thought something terrible must've happened to you."

His smile softened, and he crossed the cave to sit down beside me, leaning against the wall. "It's sweet that you're worrying so much about me, but you don't need to. Nothing's going to happen to me," he said, his eyes glinting with familiar determination. "I was just outside working on our kickboard. Or stickboard, I should say."

My brows rose in surprise. "You've already done it? I was going to help."

He gave me a quick, almost sheepish grin. "I woke up really early, and you looked so peaceful sleeping. I didn't want to wake you."

"Oh." I stretched my arms above my head and yawned. "In that case, I guess we should eat breakfast and head down to the river."

"We can eat, yeah. But we shouldn't leave for another three hours or so," Landon replied. "The water is absolutely freezing right now, but the sun is out for once, so that'll warm it up a bit. By the afternoon, it should be okay for us to go in for a while."

"That makes sense."

He reached for his bag and tossed me another big piece of jerky. My stomach rumbled at the thought of the salty, gamey taste, and I took a big bite, savoring it as the flavor spread over my tongue. "How did Knox get so good at making this?" I asked between bites. "It's seriously amazing."

"I showed him," Landon said with a casual shrug. "It helped that the cabin owner had a few bags of salt lying around in his supplies. There's a woodfired oven, too. That's what we use to dry out the meat."

"In that case, how did *you* get so good at it?" I asked, tilting my head. "And hunting in general. You said something about doing it with your dad, right?"

His lips pressed into a thin line, and he nodded. "Yeah. He was a big survivalist. Used to make me go out with him every weekend to practice shooting and prepping game."

"I never would've pegged him as that type of guy," I said, shaking my head. "Whenever I saw him, he was always in a suit and tie."

Landon's gaze dropped to the cave floor. "He was good at that," he muttered. "Showing different people different versions of himself."

My stomach twisted. "I'm sorry for bringing him up," I said softly, shaking my head. "I know how hard it is to talk about a parent who's gone, no matter how long it's been."

Landon's eyes met mine again, dark and conflicted. "No, *I'm* sorry. I didn't mean to make you feel bad," he said. "It's just... well, I know you're not supposed to say this stuff about a dead person. Especially a dead parent. But if I'm being honest, I don't miss my father."

My eyes widened. "You don't?"

"Nope. I guess we have something in common. We both have —or had—really shitty dads," he said, rubbing his jaw.

"I'm sorry. I had no idea." I scooted a little closer. "Do you want to talk about it?"

"With anyone else? No. But with you?" Landon reached for my hand. "Yeah, I want to. And I think I owe it to you, anyway."

"You don't owe me anything," I said, my voice soft but firm. "Especially if it makes you uncomfortable."

He shook his head. "No, I owe you the truth about me. The *whole* truth," he said. "Especially seeing as I know all your secrets. It's only fair you know mine."

I nodded slowly. "You can tell me anything you want. Your secrets are safe with me. Just like mine have been with you."

Landon stared at the opposite cave wall for a long moment, his jaw tense, eyes distant. Finally, he looked back at me, his expression unreadable.

"No one ever knew this, because he was so good at hiding it, but that man made my life hell at every opportunity he got," he said. "He was an abusive asshole. If I even stepped a toe out of line, he'd beat the shit out of me. And it wasn't just about my behavior. It was any kind of mistake. Like when we went out hunting, if I accidentally stepped on a crunchy twig and scared the game off—backhand to the face. Or if I missed a shot—gut punch. It was his way of teaching me."

The morning sun's warmth brushed over my shoulders as it crept into the cave, but I couldn't shake the chill racing down my spine. "Oh my god," I whispered, my stomach churning as I stared at Landon. "I had no idea."

"No one ever did, including my mom. Like I said, he was good at hiding it, and I was his only target," he said. "He never laid a hand on Mom. Treated her like a queen. But I think he resented me because while her career was taking off—which meant she had to spend a ton of time working in DC and staying in their apartment there—he had to take a step back from his own job and be there to take care of me at our main house."

"That's no excuse to abuse a child," I said, anger simmering beneath my skin. "And your mom was still there sometimes. How did she not notice the bruises on you?"

"He always beat me to the punch with excuses," Landon said, his mouth twisting in a bitter smile. "He'd call her ahead of time and say I fell off my bike or got into a fight at school. Anything to explain away the marks. At the same time, he painted me as a compulsive liar. Made sure everyone thought I was just a kid who made up stories for attention, so if I ever tried to tell the truth, no one would believe me."

"What a fucking asshole," I muttered.

A muscle jumped in Landon's jaw. "Yeah. The worst thing he did was when I was about ten or eleven. He went to my mom and told her that I'd claimed *she* was abusing me." He let out a humorless laugh. "Obviously, she wasn't doing that, so she was shocked and furious. Stormed into my room, screaming about how I could ruin her career if rumors like that got out to the media. Then she grounded me for a month."

My hands clenched into fists. "So he made sure you could never tell her what he was doing to you," I said, my voice low.

"Exactly," Landon replied. "She already believed I was the kind of kid who made up stories about parental abuse, so if I'd ever tried to say he was hurting me, she'd just assume I was lying again. Even though I never said a damn word about her. It was all bullshit he made up."

My hands were practically shaking with fury, my heart aching for him. I reached out, threading my fingers through his, and squeezed gently. "You didn't deserve that," I whispered. "None of it."

"I know that now. But back then, when I was still so young... part of me felt like I *must* deserve it. Because he didn't do it to anyone else."

"That must've really messed with your head," I said, voice turning thick with emotion.

He nodded slowly. "I think that's actually why I was such an asshole to you and other kids when I was young. It made me feel like I had a bit of power for once, being on the opposite side of the violence," he said. He paused for a beat and lifted a hand. "Not saying it excuses the way I bullied you or anyone else. It's just why I did it."

"I understand." I squeezed his hand again. "Honestly."

"I realized how shitty it was by the time I was thirteen or fourteen, and I thought about coming over and saying sorry to you," he muttered. "But I never could."

"Why?" I asked, brows knitting.

"I was ashamed. Firstly, because of all the shit I did to you. I figured I probably traumatized you or something. And secondly, because I was ashamed to even admit what he'd been doing to me."

My heart twisted. "How come? Did you think I wouldn't believe you?" I asked. "Because of the way he made sure your mom would never believe you?"

Landon shook his head. "It wasn't that. It's just that when you're a boy growing up in our society, you get slammed with all these messages every day, telling you what it is to be a man. Gotta be big and strong. Can't show weakness. So for a thirteen-year-old boy, it's humiliating to admit that you're getting the shit kicked out of you on a weekly basis. Makes you feel like you're failing. Like you'll never be a real man."

Tears stung my eyes, and I swallowed down the lump in my throat. "I'm sorry," I said softly. "I wish things weren't like that. I wish you felt safe enough to tell someone."

"It's all in the past now," he muttered.

"When did he stop?" I asked.

"When I was fifteen."

My stomach twisted. "So he didn't stop until he died," I said, shaking my head with disbelief.

"That's right."

I let out a heavy sigh, rubbing my forehead. "God, that must've been so confusing for you when it happened," I said softly. "Because you hated him so much, but at the same time, he was still your father. So it would've come as a huge shock."

"Not really," Landon said, meeting my eyes again. "That's the other part of the story."

I frowned. "What do you mean?"

He pressed his lips into a thin line and reached for my hand, his fingers tightening around mine. For a moment, his gaze was distant, like he was reliving his past all over again.

When he finally spoke, his voice was low and raw. "My father didn't die accidentally," he said. "I made it happen."

I blinked slowly as my brain scrambled to process what he'd just said. "Sorry... what?"

"My father's death wasn't an accident."

I drew in a long breath, slowly nodding. Then I tightened my grip on his hand, anchoring us both. "Do you want to tell me what happened?"

"Yeah." His jaw tensed, and he looked away for a moment before continuing. "By the time I was fifteen, I was almost as big as him. Almost as strong, too. So one day, when Mom wasn't around, he charged at me in the hall, furious about something as usual. But that time, when he hit me, I hit him back. Clocked him right in the jaw and sent him reeling." He paused, his eyes distant. "I thought that would be it. Thought the shock of me finally fighting back would make him stop for good."

"But it didn't, did it?" I murmured.

"No," he said, his face darkening. "His expression just... changed. Went blank. Like a shark with those dead eyes. You know what I mean?"

"Yes," I whispered.

"He went into his study, opened his safe, and pulled out one of his guns. Then he came back and found me. I was about to head downstairs, because I wanted to get away from him," he said, rubbing his head as if the memory physically ached. "But he blocked me from going down. He was waving the gun around, shouting all kinds of shit about what he was going to do to me, and then..."

Landon trailed off, his gaze fixed on the cave wall. When he finally looked back at me, his eyes were haunted. "You remember that feeling you had when you realized that guy on the road was drunk? Like you were on fire and about to explode?"

"Yes. I felt like I was going to split into a million pieces."

He nodded slowly. "That's how I felt right then. I just knew...

it was never going to end. No matter how strong I got, no matter how much I fought back—he was just going to get worse. Hurt me even more. So I snapped. I shoved him backward, and he fell down the stairs."

My heart pounded in my ears. "The police never suspected that it wasn't an accident?"

"No. But they probably would have, if it wasn't for Knox."

My brows furrowed. "What did he do?"

Landon let out a shaky breath. "After I pushed my father, I just... froze. I stared at his body for what felt like forever. I guess I was too shocked to properly process it. Then the doorbell rang, and it snapped me out of it. I thought it was the cops. Figured someone must've heard the argument. So I was ready to open the door and confess. Because I did it."

"But it was Knox at the door instead?"

Landon nodded. "Yeah. With all the shit going on, I'd totally forgotten that I invited him over to play the new Diablo game that day," he said. "He took one look at me and then at my dad lying at the bottom of the stairs. I told him I did it. Told him to call the cops and turn me in."

"But he didn't," I said softly.

"No. He told me he already knew what my father had been doing to me all those years. Even though I never said a word, he just... knew. But he never brought it up because he could tell I didn't want to talk about it," Landon said. His voice wavered, but he kept going. "He told me I didn't deserve to spend years locked up because of what that bastard did to me. So he cleared the scene. Put the gun back in the safe. Then he called the cops and told them his version of the story—that we were upstairs gaming when we heard a crash. Came out to find my dad at the bottom of the stairs. An accidental fall."

I took a shaky breath, my heart pounding with the weight of his confession. "And they believed it because he was your alibi."

"Yeah. And the way I was acting—still in shock from everything—made it look believable. Because what innocent kid wouldn't be freaked out after seeing their dad dead at the bottom of the stairs?"

"What about the mark on his jaw from where you hit him? Did they think it was one of the fall injuries?"

"Yeah. Luckily."

Silence settled between us, heavy and thick, as Landon's story echoed in my mind. My heart ached for him. For the boy who had endured so much and fought back the only way he could.

It was no wonder he instantly understood what I did that day after the car accident. He'd felt the same explosion of rage and helplessness that I did. Felt the need to reclaim some semblance of power, even if it meant crossing a line he could never come back from.

He spoke up again, looking me right in the eye. "Are you judging me now?" he asked, eyes flickering with vulnerability. "Now that you know I killed my own father?"

"Not even remotely," I said, shaking my head. "You did what you had to do to survive."

His shoulders sagged slightly with relief, and he leaned back against the wall.

I gave his hand another squeeze. "Thank you for telling me," I murmured. "You didn't have to, but I'm glad you did."

Landon offered a faint smile. "It's like I said before. I felt like I owed it to you," he said. "It's not fair for me to know everything about you without you knowing the same about me."

I nodded and leaned closer, losing myself in the warmth of his embrace. We settled into a comfortable silence, the kind that only came when you were with someone who understood you completely.

A shaft of sunlight eventually streamed through the mouth of the cave, painting golden patterns on the rocky floor. I squinted against the brightness, realizing how long we'd been sitting here, lost in the past.

"Maybe we should get moving," I said, glancing toward the cave mouth. "It might be warm enough in the river by now."

Landon nodded, the tension in his shoulders easing a little. "You're right. Let's go."

We stood up and quietly worked at repacking his bag. Then we stepped out of the cave, and as we headed toward the makeshift flotation board he'd constructed, I stole another look at his face. It was guarded but resolute. He was still carrying so much pain, but at least I understood it better now. That would make it easier for me to help him.

We walked down to the far-left end of the riverbank. Landon was right—there were less rocks in the water down here, so it was the best spot to get in. The current ran in this direction, anyway, so getting in farther upstream would only mean enduring the cold longer for no reason.

He put his backpack on and then picked up his last piece of rope to wind it around my right wrist and his left wrist, joining us together. Then he stooped to grab the board, motioning for me to grab it too.

"Ready?" he asked, eyes flickering with concern.

I gave him a brave smile. "Yeah. Ready."

23

ARIA

The water hit me like an electric shock, freezing me to the bone. I couldn't even imagine how much colder it would've been if we hadn't waited for the few hours of sun.

I clutched the stick raft, fingers numb against the rough bark. Landon's grip was like iron next to mine. The current yanked us forward, dragging us through the water faster than I expected, and I barely had time to suck in a breath before a swell crashed over my head.

I went under, cold slicing through me like a thousand knives, and panic seized my chest. I kicked wildly, lungs burning, but my head stayed submerged. A sharp yank on my wrist hauled me up, and I broke the surface gasping and coughing up water as I clung to the raft.

"I've got you," Landon said, voice steady despite the chaos around us. He didn't even look rattled, just kept his left hand wrapped tight around mine while I forced air back into my lungs.

The river evened out after that, the water still fast but smoother. I glanced at Landon, and he nodded once, as if telling me it was okay to breathe now. We were still being dragged along, and I couldn't feel my legs from the cold, but at least I wasn't drowning.

Ahead, the canyon wall started to fall away on the left, the sheer rock giving way to rugged ground dotted with brush and twisted trees. Relief surged through me.

"That's our way out!" I shouted. "Over there!"

"Yup." Landon grinned. "It's not even that far away."

Relief flooded my veins, but then I heard a low, rumbling roar that sent my stomach plummeting. My eyes widened as I looked ahead, and Landon's face hardened.

"Rapids," he said. That single word sliced through me like a blade.

"What do we do?" I gasped, already feeling the current picking up speed.

"We kick left," he said calmly, like we were just talking about the weather. "Fight the current as much as you can. Do you see that branch on the left? Sticking out just above the bank?"

I squinted. "Yes."

"We need to grab that and drag ourselves out once we get there. For now... kick left as hard as you can."

I nodded, not trusting my voice, and started kicking, using every ounce of strength left in my legs. Landon kicked too, angling our bodies toward the left, but the water fought back hard, pulling us faster toward that deadly roar.

We were almost there—just a few more feet—when something slammed into the stick-board from underneath. A sharp crack splintered the air, and the sticks broke apart, the rope snapping loose. I clutched Landon's hand, our wrists still tied together, but the board was gone.

"Keep kicking!" he shouted, and I did, fighting the surge that was trying to drag us downstream. My foot caught a rock and pain flared up my leg, but I ignored it, zeroing in on the branch just a few feet away.

With a desperate lunge, I managed to hook my arm around it,

fingers digging into the wood. I yanked Landon closer. The rope between our wrists strained, threads snapping one by one as he gripped my hand.

"Hold on," he gritted out, muscles straining as he pulled himself higher.

I squeezed his hand so hard I felt bones grinding together, terrified of losing him. Then the last strand of rope snapped.

"Landon!" I screamed, trying to keep hold of him. The current was too powerful for our grips, and it tore him away, dragging him into the open river. He didn't even have time to fight it before he was swept out of reach, water crashing over him as he vanished downstream.

I stared after him, my heart pounding so loud it drowned out the rush of water.

My grip on the branch was slipping, but I forced myself to dig my nails in deeper, dragging my body up through the freezing water. Every muscle screamed in protest, and my legs were so numb they barely moved when I kicked, but I refused to let go.

With a final, desperate pull, I hauled myself out, collapsing onto the muddy bank. I was drenched, shivering so hard I couldn't catch my breath, and my lungs ached from the exertion. My clothes were soaked through, clinging to my skin as the merciless wind bit at me.

For a second, I just lay there, chest heaving as I gasped for air. My pulse thundered in my ears, but I finally forced myself to sit up, wiping the water from my face.

Then it hit me. *Landon's gone.*

I scrambled to my feet, stumbling as my legs nearly gave out beneath me. My eyes scanned the river, wild and desperate, and I started running down the bank.

"Landon!" I screamed, the name tearing from my throat. "Landon!"

The current was brutal, churning faster and faster, and the sound of the rushing water got louder the farther I went. Panic flooded through me, and I tripped over a jagged rock, barely catching myself before I faceplanted into the mud.

My hands were shaking, and when I glanced down, something glinted through the fingers of my right hand. I opened my fingers and stared, heart pounding in disbelief.

I was holding the silver ring Landon always wore. The band dug into my skin, pressed so hard into my palm that it left an indent.

Somehow, when the rope snapped and he was pulled away, I must have clung so tightly to his hand that I pulled it off without even realizing. It didn't seem possible that I hadn't lost it in the river, and yet... here it was.

My chest tightened, and I choked on a sob, my fingers curling around the ring like it was the only thing keeping me from falling apart.

I pushed forward, running along the muddy bank as fast as I could, screaming Landon's name until my voice cracked. My throat burned, but I couldn't stop.

The roaring sound grew louder, and I realized what it was—a waterfall. My stomach dropped as I broke through a tangle of low-hanging branches and reached the edge, staring down the stretch of river just before it plummeted over a cliff.

I searched frantically, desperate for any sign of him, praying he made it out somewhere along the bank farther down. But he wasn't there.

My hands were trembling so hard that the ring slipped in my palm. I clutched it tighter, refusing to let go.

"Landon!" I screamed one more time, my voice splintering with fear and grief.

The only answer was the relentless rush of the water as it crashed over the falls, drowning out every other sound.

I forced myself to keep moving, even though my legs felt like they were made of lead and my chest was burning from sucking in so much frigid air.

THE WILD

As I ran, my mind raced with silent prayers. *Just let me find him. Please, please, please.* I didn't care if I had to jump back in the river, pull him out, and do CPR until he started breathing again. He'd saved me so many times. It was my turn to save him.

The trees along the bank thickened around me, branches scratching at my arms and snagging my wet clothes. I pushed through them, barely noticing the pain, my focus only on the river and the possibility of seeing Landon somewhere up ahead. The ground was muddy and uneven, but I kept running, glancing between the churning water and the dense woods.

A crackle of leaves somewhere to my left made me freeze. My heart pounded in my throat, and I strained to listen, terrified it was another bear.

Another crackle sounded.

I held my breath, gripping Landon's ring so tight it dug into my palm as I stared at the dense woods. A shadow blurred through the trees, too quick for me to get a good look. It didn't seem like the right size or shape for a bear, though.

My pulse stuttered, hope flaring like a match.

"Landon?" I whispered, my voice trembling. "Did you make it out?"

A figure stepped out from behind a massive tree, and my stomach dropped.

It was a man... but it wasn't Landon.

He was tall and muscular, his hands covered in smeared dirt and what looked like dried blood. His face was painted in a grotesque mask of white and black, streaked like a skull, and his eyes were dark, empty pits in the shadow of his face. He tilted his head, studying me with an eerie curiosity.

My blood turned to ice, and I took a slow step back. Every instinct screamed at me to run, but the petrifying sight of the man triggered something else entirely.

The fear that had been knotting my stomach for days unraveled all at once, spilling through me in a wave of numbness that left me hollow and exhausted. It was like all the previous stress and terror of the day—and the last few weeks—was finally catching up with me at once. Like my body was giving up because it was all too much to handle. This latest terror was the final straw.

So I didn't run. I didn't scream. I just stood there, staring at the man with his painted face and dead, empty eyes.

Suddenly a strange, detached calm washed over me, like my mind had also decided it was all too much to process. My knees buckled, and I felt the cold, wet ground rush up to meet me as the world tilted sideways.

Somewhere in the back of my mind, I knew I should fight. I should scream or run or do something—*anything*—but I just couldn't. My body simply wouldn't cooperate anymore. It was too tired, too battered, too broken.

The last thing I saw before darkness claimed me was the man's crooked smile and the glint of something sharp in his hand. Then everything went black.

24

LANDON

I HIT THE WATER BELOW THE FALLS HARD, THE FORCE SLAMMING into me like a freight train as I plunged beneath the surface. The world spun in a chaotic blur, and for a moment, I couldn't tell which way was up or down.

My lungs burned, desperate for air, but I fought the instinct to inhale, pushing myself toward the light shimmering above. When I finally broke through, I sucked in a breath, coughing up river water as I dragged myself toward the nearest bank. The current wasn't as strong here, so I was able to wade out without too much trouble.

I stumbled onto the muddy shore, adrenaline still coursing through my veins, and took a few seconds to catch my breath. Somehow, my backpack was still secured to my shoulders. If we'd lost our supplies... well, fuck, I didn't even want to think about that.

I checked the bag quickly, making sure nothing had come loose, and then turned my gaze back to the waterfall I'd just been hurled over. The cliffs were high and steep, but they sloped upward to the right, forming a jagged path that I could climb.

Aria.

The thought of her struck me like a physical blow, making my chest ache. I had to find her. Couldn't lose her now. Not after everything we'd been through.

We'd fought so damn hard to make it this far. She'd fought harder than anyone I knew—mostly against me, because she didn't know any better—even when she was terrified. The way she kept pushing forward, refusing to give up... I loved that about her, and I'd do anything to protect her.

I just needed to make it back to that branch she'd been clinging to. Hopefully, she'd gotten herself onto the bank and was sitting there waiting for me.

As I started up the incline, I kept my mind on her. On her stubborn determination, and that fire in her eyes when she was pissed at me.

It still felt surreal, having her by my side after everything that had happened. For so long, I thought she hated me. Thought I'd ruined any chance we had because of all the shit that went down between us over the years. I'd learned to live with it; forced myself to accept that she'd never see me the way I saw her.

Maybe I deserved it after everything I put her through... but it didn't change how I felt. Didn't change how much I wanted to protect her, even if it meant being the villain in her story.

She'd never known any of it until yesterday. Never realized that every move I made was to keep her safe, even when it looked like the total opposite. I'd never stopped caring for her, even when she utterly loathed me. Never stopped looking out for her.

And now... now that she was finally mine—now that she knew the truth and still wanted me despite all of it—I couldn't lose her. Not when I'd just gotten a taste of what it was like to really have her. To have her trust and her fire and the way she looked at me when she wasn't glaring daggers. I probably didn't deserve any of it, given all the heinous shit I'd done in my time, but I wasn't going to let go of it either.

We'd spent so long caught in this mess, in the lies and the

danger and the fear. But we were together now, finally, and I wasn't going to let that go. I'd fight the river, the woods, bears, her fucking bastard of a father—anything or anyone that tried to take her from me. Because no matter how confusing and twisted our past had been, one thing had never changed: I'd do anything for Aria.

Anything to keep her safe.

I finally made it up the slope and started moving along the bank, tracking the river's path and scanning every inch of the shore. The thought of Aria out here alone in this wilderness always made my stomach twist. I wasn't going to stop until I found her, no matter what.

I finally spotted the right branch, half-submerged in the water and trembling from the force of the current. My eyes darted over the muddy bank, desperate for any sign of Aria. Relief crashed through me when I saw prints leading away from the water—small, delicate shoeprints. Hers.

She'd made it out.

Raking my hand through my wet hair, I took a shaky breath, trying to gather my thoughts. There were drag marks on the mud, too, where Aria must've pulled herself up, and the footprints kept going, leading away from the riverbank, back the way I'd just come.

Of course. She'd headed downstream to search for me.

It hadn't even occurred to me to check for tracks on my way up here. I was too focused on getting to that damn branch and praying she was there.

My chest tightened, and I couldn't help the way my heart swelled with something fierce and warm. She'd gone after me. Looked for me, just as desperate to find me as I was to find her.

I turned back around, eyes fixed on the prints as I retraced her steps. It wasn't easy—some spots were too rocky, others too muddy for anything to stick—but I kept going, kept pushing forward.

As the woods thickened on my left, I hit a spot where the tracks just... stopped. Nothing in the mud to the right, and nothing in the dirt or leaves on my left. I scanned the whole area, trying to make sense of it.

A glint of silver on a pile of leaves caught my eye, and I bent down to pick it up. My brows rose as I realized it was my ring. The one I always wore on my right hand. Aria must've accidentally ripped it off me when we were separated in the river.

I frowned and turned the ring over in my fingers, heart pounding as I wondered why it was here when Aria wasn't. Had she dropped it by accident? Or did something happen to make her lose it?

I straightened, my pulse speeding up as I searched the ground around me.

That was when I saw it. A smear of red on the leaves nearby. *Blood.* And next to it... much larger shoeprints.

My stomach dropped like a stone. Someone had taken her.

A low, vicious curse slipped from my lips as a mix of panic and anger threatened to swallow me whole. *No.* No way in hell was I letting Aria be taken from me. Not after all the shit we'd fought through.

Not *ever*.

I jammed the ring into my pocket, forcing myself to think. I needed to find those prints again, needed to track whoever had grabbed her before they got too far.

Whoever they were, they'd just made the worst mistake of their life. Because I was going to find them.. and then I was going to make them pay.

25

ARIA

When I woke up, everything was blurry and slow, like I was trying to swim through thick honey just to open my eyes. My head throbbed, and it took a minute for reality to catch up to me.

I was lying on something soft—a bed, I realized. The blankets were old and faded, but surprisingly warm and gentle against my skin. They smelled faintly of earth and woodsmoke, and I could feel their worn edges against my fingertips.

I blinked up at the low, wooden ceiling, the beams above me rough-hewn and sturdy. Slowly, I pushed myself up onto my elbows, wincing as the motion made the ache in my head worse.

I was in a cabin.

A soft rustle caught my attention, and my gaze snapped to the corner. A man was there, standing near a crude wooden table. He was tall and muscular, his broad shoulders stretching the fabric of his thick flannel shirt—a red-and-black checkered pattern that looked like it had seen better days. Sturdy boots and dark pants completed his outfit, practical and rugged.

He must've noticed my stare because he turned to look at me, his expression calm but wary. His face was mostly clean, but there were a few small streaks of charcoal and clay smeared on his skin.

He dipped his chin, speaking in a low, steady voice. "Ah, you've come back," he said. "Steady now. No quick movements. Just sit up slowly."

With my heart pounding, I slowly started to sit up, pressing my hands into the thin mattress.

The man lifted his hands, palms up, like he was trying to soothe a spooked animal. "I'm sorry. My appearance must've seemed alarming to you earlier, but I didn't mean to frighten you," he said. "The face paint... it's just tradition. Something from long before I was around. And I obviously didn't expect to find you while I was out hunting."

My pulse was still racing, and I struggled to piece together what he was saying. "What happened to me?" I finally rasped.

He raised his brows. "You don't remember?"

"I remember being in the river," I said, wincing at the memory of the freezing current dragging us along.

Us.

Suddenly it all came back to me in a rush. Landon hadn't made it out of the river. My heart lurched, and I sat bolt upright. What happened to him after he went over the falls? Was he okay and searching for me? Or had he...

No. I couldn't bear to think of it. I had to believe he was all right.

"Easy now," the man said, lifting his palms. "You really shouldn't move too fast."

"Yeah, that was a bad idea," I muttered, wincing again as my head began to throb even harder.

"Anyway... to answer your question about what happened, I was out hunting and saw you skulking around on my land," the man said, rubbing his jaw. "You were soaking wet and covered in scrapes and bruises. Then you passed out right in front of me and banged your head on a rock. Hard enough to bleed. So I brought you back here to recover."

"Oh," I said, voice barely above a whisper. "T-thanks."

THE WILD

I glanced around the cabin, noticing more details now that my mind was a little less fuzzy. It was bigger than I'd first realized.

A large wooden table sat near the center, surrounded by mismatched chairs. A worn leather armchair was tucked beside a stone fireplace, the embers still glowing faintly. Shelves lined one of the walls, cluttered with jars, tools, and bundles of dried herbs hanging from hooks.

There were a couple of doors leading off from the main room —one partially open to reveal a few scattered belongings, while the other remained firmly shut. The cabin had a rustic, lived-in feel, like it had been a sanctuary for a very long time.

My mind raced as I took it all in, trying to piece together some sense of safety.

I had no way of knowing exactly where I was or who this man really was. For all I knew, this cabin could be part of the cannibal settlement. Maybe this man was one of them. Or maybe he was just some hermit living off the land, completely unaware of the horrors happening in this wilderness.

Or maybe he didn't live here at all. Maybe he just came through every now and then, using it as a place to crash when he wanted to get away from the real world for a while and do a bit of hunting and fishing.

Until I saw what was outside—whether it was the familiar rambling structures of the cannibal settlement or just forest stretching on forever—I couldn't be sure. And that meant I had to be very careful. I couldn't reveal anything about the other crash survivors, because if this man was one of the cannibals, telling him about the others would put them in even more danger.

He didn't *look* like a cannibal upon first glance... but then again, how would I know exactly what a cannibal looked like? They were just people, the same way I was. It wasn't like they wore glowing neon signs on their chests proclaiming their dietary habits.

Also, I couldn't just come out and ask him if he was a cannibal. It would be beyond rude if he wasn't, especially considering how he'd helped me after I passed out and smacked my head on a rock. And if he *was* one of them, accusing him could make him angry. Maybe even dangerous. So I had to be careful with every word that left my mouth, feel out the situation without giving too much away.

"You might notice some crusty patches on your hands, arms, and face," the man said, taking a step closer. "It's a mix of clay and pearwood leaves that I smeared on the cuts. It helps prevent infection."

I looked down at my hands to see a greenish-gray mixture smeared over some of the newer cuts I'd received after bouncing through all those cliffside trees yesterday. "Thank you," I murmured.

He jerked his head toward a small table beside the bed. "Cup of water there for you," he said. "I'm sorry I can't offer you anything to eat just yet. I wasn't sure how long you'd be asleep, so I didn't get anything started."

"That's okay. Thanks anyway," I said, forcing my lips into a small, grateful smile.

My heart pounded as I fought the urge to ask him a thousand questions. I wanted to *so* badly, but I needed to stay smart. Stay cautious. Until I knew for sure who he was and what his intentions were, I couldn't trust him, no matter how calm and gentle he seemed right now.

"My name's Josiah, by the way," he said, as if sensing my need for more information. "But everyone calls me Joe. What's your name?"

I briefly considered giving him a fake name, but then I realized there was no point in doing that. If he'd lived in the outside world at any point in the last few years, then there was a high chance that he'd already recognized me and was simply being polite in asking for my name.

"I'm Aria," I said.

Joe let out a short grunt of acknowledgement, but no flash of recognition appeared in his eyes. "Pretty name," he said. "Can't say I've ever heard one like that before."

For a second, confusion clouded my thoughts.

I'd gotten used to people knowing who I was before I even opened my mouth, because being the president's daughter came with that burden—every smile, every word, every photo scrutinized and analyzed by strangers who thought they knew me. But this man really didn't seem to have a clue.

My initial instinct was to assume the worst. That he was one of *them*, living in that brutal settlement where news and politics didn't exist. But then I mentally kicked myself for being so self-important.

Not everyone followed politics, even back home in the States, and even those who did might not care about the president's family. So plenty of people wouldn't have a clue who I was. Besides, why would a man living off the land in the Canadian wilderness know—or even give a damn—about the American president's daughter?

Just because he didn't recognize me didn't mean he was one of the cannibals. It didn't mean anything. I needed to stop jumping to conclusions and think clearly.

"So, Aria," he said, sinking into a chair by the table. "How'd you find yourself all the way out here on my land? And how on Earth did you end up in that river?"

Shit.

I couldn't tell him about the plane crash. Then he'd know there were others, and I still had no idea if he was a safe person to confide in.

"I, er—"

He lifted a palm. "Wait, no... let me guess. You're another one of those scientists, eh?"

"No," I replied, brows rising. "Why would you think that?"

"Last two people that got lost all the way out here said they were scientists. Doin' research on climate change." Joe paused and sniffed derisively. "As if anyone needs to study that. I've been all around this land for decades, so I can tell you firsthand how much things have changed around here."

My pulse sped up. "Where'd the scientists come from? A nearby town or city?"

"Nah. They told me they got dropped off in, er…" He trailed off and threw his hands up, eyes flicking toward the ceiling. "Well, shit, my mind's suddenly gone blank."

"A plane? Or a helicopter?"

Joe grinned and nodded. "That's it. Helicopter dropped 'em off somewhere by a lake. Then they camped in various places. Took samples of things like water and soil."

"And they got lost?"

"Yup. Happens easily in a place like this. They stumbled up here—" Joe paused again, brows dipping in a contemplative frown as he rubbed his jaw. "Must've been at least a year ago by now. Anyway, they found me out hunting. Asked me for directions and spare water or food."

"And, um… what happened then?"

He waved a casual hand. "I took care of them. Helped them along. Same as I'm doing for you."

Relief loosened my chest. That sounded promising.

"Do people get lost out here quite frequently?" I asked, trying to tease out a possible location for the cabin without being too obvious about it. If people found themselves lost here a lot, that could mean we were relatively close to a tourist town or mountain lodge popular with hikers and campers.

Joe shrugged. "Wouldn't say it's *frequent*. But it happens from time to time. Maybe once a year or so."

"How does it happen?" I said lightly. "Just campers? Or do you get lots of climate scientists out here?"

He shook his head. "Nah, those last two were the only scientists I ever met. The others are usually hikers who like to go on long journeys through the wilderness. But they aren't experienced like me, and they get turned around. End up walking in the wrong direction for days."

My heart sank. That made it sound like the nearest population center could be a three or four-day hike away. Maybe even longer.

"So where's the closest town?" I asked, cocking my head.

Joe scratched his jaw. "Closest would probably be Grande Cache. But it sure as hell ain't *close*."

"Is it a difficult hike to get there? Or just a long one?"

He shrugged. "Wouldn't know. I've never been there. My father told me about it when I was a boy," he said. "He went there once when *he* was a boy. My grandfather took him there. It was a rough few winters and they needed help, so they took some of their moonshine and exchanged it for some grains."

I gulped. "So... you grew up here?"

"Sure did. Right here in the community."

My stomach flipped. He'd just confirmed that his cabin wasn't a standalone one. That meant the chances of him living in the cannibal settlement had just skyrocketed.

Then again, there could be more than one settlement of people in the wilderness. And Joe had helped the lost scientists get home, which suggested that he and his people had no desire for human flesh. Or at least not the flesh of strangers.

"Which community would that be?" I asked, still trying to keep my voice light. "Would I have heard of it?"

Joe shook his head. "We've never needed to name it. But back in the day, it was the Cold Mountain mining camp," he said. "My people worked up there in the mountain, and we never left. We've got almost everything we need out here. River close by with fresh water. Food. Clean air. No need to deal with the outside world."

My heart pounded harder. A town with no name... people who

never contacted the outside world unless they absolutely had to... it was all beginning to sound a little too unsettling.

"I just realized something," Joe said, frowning. "You didn't answer my question. How'd you end up out here?"

Shit. I still hadn't come up with an excuse.

"Oh. I, er... I was on a hiking trip."

"With friends? Did you get separated?" he asked, cocking his head.

"No. It was just me."

"You were hiking *alone*?" he said, brows drawing together in a skeptical expression. "This far out in the wild?"

"Yes. I just needed to get away from the outside world for a while. Clear my head, you know?"

He nodded slowly. "Ah, I see. I can understand that," he said. "A lot of the hikers that've come through here actually said the exact same thing. Getting away from the rat race, one of 'em called it."

"That's exactly it. Anyway, I started out in... Denham," I said, inventing a made-up town name on the spot.

If I'd said a real town or city name, that could make Joe suspicious, because the place could turn out to be a thousand miles away from this cabin, and that would cast doubt on my hiking story.

"Denham, eh?" Joe frowned. "Not sure I've heard of that."

"Oh, really?" I said, feigning innocence. "I guess it's a pretty new-ish town. They built it after they discovered coal in the mountains in the 80s."

He nodded. "I see."

"Anyway, I started out there and headed west, and then..." I trailed off, slowly shaking my head. "I'm not sure what happened. It's all such a blur."

"You hit your head pretty dang hard on that rock. I'm surprised you recall anything at all, to be honest."

"Yeah, that must be why I don't remember much," I said,

nodding fervently. "But I definitely remember falling in a river at some point, and then... well, I guess that's when I met you."

"Well, don't worry." Joe smiled faintly. "I'll take good care of you. You might even enjoy your time here in the community. None of that outside world frustration, eh?"

I swallowed hard again, heart still hammering in my chest. Before I could truly relax, I needed to know if I was in that damn cannibal settlement or not.

I glanced toward the window on my left, followed by the one on the right. If I could just get closer to one of them, I could find the answer to my burning question.

"Sorry, is there a bathroom I can use?" I asked.

Joe jerked his head toward the left side of the room, where two rusty buckets sat. "No toilets here, I'm afraid," he said. "But you can use the bucket on the right. Don't worry, it's clean. Gets washed out in the river twice a day."

"Oh. Okay. And what can I use to—" I paused, miming a wiping gesture.

"There's cloths on the windowsill. Grab one of them and dump it in the other bucket once you're finished. It'll all get cleaned up later," he said, rising to his feet. "And don't worry. I'll turn around while you do your business."

"Okay. Thanks," I murmured.

I slipped out from under the blankets, only to feel something cold on my foot. I looked down, and my heart instantly sank.

A length of chain was around my ankle, secured to the end of the old bed. It looked long enough to let me move through most of the cabin... but still, finding myself chained to a bed wasn't exactly reassuring.

Joe saw the look on my face and lifted a palm. "Don't scream," he said. "There are sleeping babies next door. They don't need to be woken."

My heart thundered in my chest. "Why the hell am I chained to the bed?"

"For everyone's safety, including your own," he said. "As I told you earlier, you bumped that head of yours pretty damn hard. I was worried you were concussed. If I happened to be away when you woke up, you might've been confused and gone outside to figure out where you were. Then you could've accidentally hurt someone in your confused state, or you could've run right back out into the wild. And then where would you be, eh?"

A flicker of suspicion coiled in my gut. His story made sense, but... why was I *still* confined? He could see I was no longer confused, and I certainly wasn't flying into any sort of violent tantrum that could endanger other members of his community.

He caught the disbelieving expression on my face and sighed. "It'll come off when I can be sure you ain't gonna do anything stupid," he said. He motioned toward my forehead. "When I can be sure that head of yours is screwed on properly."

"Right," I muttered, stomach still twisting with unease.

My instincts were screaming at me to stay on guard. I didn't trust Joe, or the calm way he watched me like he already knew my next move, and alarm bells were ringing loudly in my head, warning me that one wrong step could cost me a lot more than just my pride.

He turned around, palms raised high. "Go on, then. I told you I won't watch you."

While he wasn't looking, I took the opportunity to move toward one of the shelves on the other side of the room. Something orange caught my eye, and I crept closer, squinting to check it out. It was a small waterproof bag with black words printed on it. ***University of Alberta.***

Heart in my mouth, I took another small step closer. There was a camera only inches away from the bag, and it looked very modern. Expensive, too. There was no way a scientist or hiker would leave it behind on purpose. Not unless...

Oh, no.

A cavernous dark pit opened up inside me, threatening to swallow me whole.

"What are you doing?"

I jumped at the sound of Joe's voice and snapped my gaze to him. He must've realized that I wasn't actually using the bucket, because I wasn't making the expected sounds.

"I... I was just looking at your things," I said in a small voice, taking a step backward. "And I noticed one of the scientists left their stuff behind."

"Well, he didn't need it anymore, did he?" he said, stepping toward me. "Not where he ended up."

I looked down at the chain secured to my ankle, heart hammering so hard it ached. "This isn't really for my safety, is it?" I asked in a low voice.

"Of course it is. As I told you, we can't have you running back outside. Could get eaten by a bear or something. And then what use would you be to us?"

"What *use*?" I said, jerking my head back up. "Tell me the truth, Joe. Am I free to go or not?"

He smiled faintly. "No."

"But you... you said you helped the others leave!" I spluttered.

"*Did* I say that?" he asked, cocking a brow. "Because I don't believe those were my exact words."

I narrowed my eyes. "You said you took care of them."

"And I did. Never said I helped 'em get home, though, did I?"

"Yes, you did! You said you helped—"

"Helped them along," he said, cutting me off.

"What's the difference between that and helping them get home?"

"I just meant... I helped them along. Made sure they didn't suffer too much."

A chill raced down my spine.

Those scientists hadn't made it out of here. They never even had a chance. And it was probably the same case for all the hikers who'd inadvertently found themselves lost in this part of the Rockies.

God, how had I missed it? How had I second-guessed myself into believing that this man might actually be harmless? Just because he didn't seem monstrous at first glance didn't mean he wasn't.

I should've known better. Should've listened to my instincts when they were screaming at me to run away from him in the woods earlier.

"You're one of *them*, aren't you?" I said woodenly. "You eat people."

"From time to time, yes," Joe said, nodding slowly. "Might seem strange to an outsider, but for my people, it's the most natural thing in the world. Meat is meat."

"No." I vehemently shook my head. "There's a difference between eating a fish or deer and eating a *person*!"

"Not to us," he replied. "Times get tough out here on occasion."

"Surely they can't be *that* tough," I said, stomach roiling with disgust.

"They can be. Especially these last few years," he said, forehead creasing. "It's like what I told you before, with the climate and all. Things have been different over the last decade or so. There's fewer animals around. Shorter growing seasons. A lot of the soil's gone hard and unforgiving. So when a stranger wanders in from time to time, we know it's our Watcher bestowing a gift upon us."

"A *gift*?" I said incredulously.

"That's what you are too. A gift for us."

"So you're going to eat me," I said, eyes stinging with brimming tears.

After everything that had happened—everything I'd suffered over the last couple of months—this was how I'd finally go.

Killed, dismembered, cooked, and eaten by a bunch of society-shunning savages.

Joe shook his head. "You're a different kind of gift, Aria."

I blinked, confusion cutting through my terror. "What?"

His slow smile spread wider, eyes glinting with something that made my skin crawl. "We've got other plans for you," he said softly. "So don't worry. You're going to be just fine…"

26

LANDON

My heart pounded as I pushed through the trees, following the trail—or what I thought was a trail—through the dense undergrowth. The signs disappeared almost instantly. No broken branches, no shoeprints. Just untouched forest stretching out like a damn labyrinth around me.

Whoever took Aria knew exactly what they were doing. It was someone who knew this land better than I did. Someone who always covered their tracks.

I gritted my teeth, fighting the frustration and fear burning under my skin. I should've been faster. Should've stopped her from running off that cliff. Should've protected her like I'd sworn to do.

I stopped, dragging in a breath to steady my thoughts, and a memory clicked into place. Aria had told me something about other people out here. A group that had lived off the grid for god knows how long, feeding off anyone unlucky enough to cross their path. If they had her...

No.

I couldn't let myself think that way. Not yet. Not until I was sure.

The problem was, I had no idea where those people lived. I knew nothing about them except what Aria said—that she came across their settlement with Leigh, Trent, and Ryan.

That meant my only option was to go back to the lakeside camp and speak to the others. But first, I had to make it back to the hunter's cabin and let the other guys know what was going on, because while I was desperate and determined, I wasn't a total fucking idiot. If I was going to take on a whole village of cannibals, I'd damn well need help.

I glanced up at the sky, trying to get my bearings. The river was on my left, winding back toward the cliffs. From there, it was just a matter of finding a way back up to the elevated part of the forest where we started.

The trek along the riverbank was slow, the terrain uneven and slick with moss. Every step felt like it was dragging me farther from Aria, but I forced myself to keep moving.

An hour in, my mind was spinning with all the ways this could go wrong. What if I was too late? What if...

No. I couldn't think like that. Aria was smart. Strong, too. She would fight.

After another half-hour of moving upstream, I finally spotted the cliff up ahead, jagged rock cutting into the sky. I followed the base to the right until I found a slope that wasn't as steep—somewhere I could climb without breaking my fucking neck. It was rough going, hands scraping on sharp stone, but I made it up.

Once I was back on higher ground, I spent another hour pushing through brush and weaving around the thicker trees before the hunter's cabin finally came into view. Relief crashed through me, but it was hollow. Aria wasn't here. She was out *there*, and every second I wasted felt like a death sentence.

I burst through the door, catching the others off guard. Knox was on his feet in an instant, eyes sharp with worry. "Where the fuck have you been?" he asked. "We thought something happened to you!"

"I was with Aria," I said, my voice rough and raw. "Someone took her."

I ran through the last thirty-six hours, laying out everything from our run-in with the bear to the blood and massive shoeprint I found at the edge of the woods.

"Cannibals," Theo muttered, shaking his head. "As if we needed any more shit thrown at us this year."

"You're sure they've got Aria?" Knox asked.

I nodded. "Pretty sure. I don't know who else it could be."

"And she said their settlement was about four or five hours away from the lake camp, right?"

"Yup."

He rubbed his chin, frustration etched into his features. "That could be fucking anywhere."

"Yeah. So we need to talk to Leigh and the others. Get them to show us where it is."

Sebastian rose to his feet. "They won't be happy to see us. Especially when Aria's gone missing. They might think we've kidnapped her or something."

"We'll take a peace offering," Cole said. "Giant bag of venison jerky. They won't say no to extra food."

I looked at the guys, one by one. "So you'll all help with this?"

Knox nodded firmly. "Of course, man."

I turned my gaze to Matthew. I'd always felt a little bad for him getting dragged into the exile mess I'd created after killing Mark. The other four guys had been my friends for years, and we were always willing to go to war for each other, but Matthew... he'd been lumped in with us from the start based on nothing but his height.

He dipped his chin in a curt nod, smiling faintly. "You're gonna need all the help you can get. We have no idea how many of these so-called cannibals are out there."

By the time we reached the lakeside camp, dusk had settled in, painting the sky in bruised shades of purple and gray. The fire crackled in the center, its glow flickering over the drawn, exhausted faces of the group. They were huddled close together, roasting a few measly fish, but none of them were talking. Even from a distance, the worry and tension in the air was palpable.

Leigh especially seemed affected. She was hunched forward, hands clenched between her knees, like she was trying to hold herself together.

The realization hit me like a punch to the gut: Aria had been missing for about five hours, which was already bad enough, but for this group, it'd been over a day and a half since she disappeared. They must've been petrified.

I lifted my hand and waved as we approach, calling out, "It's us! Don't shoot!"

Heads snapped up, tension coiling instantly. Leigh scrambled to her feet, eyes widening. Relief flickered over her face when she realized we weren't cannibal invaders, but it was still quick to sour when she realized it was us. The others followed suit, and I braced for the barrage of questions about to hit.

"What the hell are you doing here?" Carrie asked, crossing her arms. "Our deal was separate existences as long as we're stuck out here."

"I know. But look." Knox tossed the huge bag of jerky toward her. "We brought you some food."

"Why would you do that?" she asked as Tony skeptically opened the bag.

"Because you need it, and we need your help," I said, taking a step closer. "I was with Aria earlier, and—"

"I knew it!" Leigh shrieked, cutting me off. She shook a finger at me. "I *knew* someone took her! I knew she didn't just get lost!"

I lifted my hands in a placating gesture. "Someone *did* take her. But it wasn't me. Wasn't *us*," I said, motioning to the guys around me. "I think it was those cannibals."

Silence fell over the lakeshore, thick and heavy.

"No. You're lying," Leigh finally gritted out. "You did something to her, and now you're spinning some bullshit story to cover your ass."

"Why the hell would we do that, Leigh?"

"Because you're a fucking murderer!" she snapped. "Or at least *one* of you is. And we still have no idea which one it is, because none of you are willing to be honest. So why the hell should we trust any of you?"

"It was me," I said calmly.

Leigh's eyes widened. "*What?*"

"I did it. I killed Mark. I'm ready to be honest about it, if that's what it takes for you to start listening to us."

Knox stepped forward. "You're gonna want to hear him out before you start freaking out."

I laid it all out for them—Mark's heinous plan, along with my desperation to protect everyone that first night. As I spoke, the group's expressions ranged from shock to distrust to grim acceptance.

"I was worried I was going to wake up the next morning and see little Hannah dead. Or you, Leigh. Or Clint. Any number of you," I said. "I did what I thought I had to do to keep everyone safe."

"That all sounds very noble in a twisted kind of way, but how do we know if any of it is actually true?" Leigh snapped. "You could've killed Mark for some other reason, and now he's very conveniently no longer able to tell his side of the story. So maybe Aria figured out the real reason, and *that's* why she's gone missing!"

Knox spoke up again. "I've known Landon since we were toddlers. He can be an asshole sometimes, but he's not a psychopath. He would never hurt or kill someone unless he had a good fucking reason to do so. And as for Aria... well, he's loved that girl since he was a teenager. All he wants to do is keep her safe. That's why we're here."

Leigh scoffed. "Oh, okay, so his best friend of twenty years said he's a nice guy who only kills bad people. I guess we should instantly trust him now," she said. "Because friends can never be wrong or lie to protect each other, can they?"

Carrie lifted a palm. "Leigh, calm down. We should at least hear him out," she said, eyes fixed on me. "What happened to Aria?"

"I ran into her in the woods yesterday. She was alone," I said, eyes flickering back to Leigh. Her gaze instantly dropped to the ground, face stricken. "A bear was stalking her. She ended up running right off a cliff. It was pretty much a blind drop, so she didn't see it."

"A *cliff?*"

I nodded. "I climbed down to get her. She was okay, because a tree broke her fall. Just a few cuts and bruises. We camped out together, and then we got separated by a river this afternoon." I pulled the silver ring off my finger. "I found this when I went looking for her. She had it with her, but she must've dropped it. And in that same spot, there was some blood and a few massive shoeprints. So whoever grabbed her must be a pretty big guy."

Mutters rippled through the group.

"You're sure it was one of the cannibals?" Tony said, voice tense.

"I don't see who else it could be," Knox replied, face set in a grim expression. "In all these weeks we've been stuck in this place, we haven't seen evidence of anyone else living out here. We didn't even know about the cannibals until Landon filled us in on what Aria told him. But apparently they're really out here, so it follows that they're the ones who took her, doesn't it?"

"Yeah, I suppose so."

Leigh lifted a hand, eyes narrowed. "Can I please just say one more thing?"

I nodded curtly. "Go ahead."

"Knox just told us that you've been in love with Aria for years, and you've also made it sound like your only goal in life is to protect her, with that nice little cliff rescue story of yours. But here's what's confusing me," she said, folding her arms. "I remember the way Aria used to look at you and talk about you when we first arrived here, and she *definitely* didn't think of you as a lover or even a friend. She described you as an acquaintance at best. An old neighbor who happened to be in the same social circles. And she looked at you like she'd rather eat cockroaches than be anywhere near you."

"Yeah, that's true," I replied. "My feelings weren't reciprocated for a long time."

"So then you can see why I'm having trouble believing your story," she said, eyes still glimmering with a mix of anger and distrust. "How do we know you didn't take Aria and hurt her as some sort of revenge thing for her not wanting you back? How do we know this whole story about the cannibals isn't just a cover story?"

I gave her a hard look. "Aria and I spent hours talking last night, and she wouldn't have told me half the things she did if she didn't trust me," I said. "Like the name your group gave us, for instance. The Lost Boys. Or how she was so worried about you, Leigh."

She looked taken aback. "About *me*?"

I nodded. "She said you were in pain yesterday, and she suggested you go back to the camp to rest. That's why she was alone in the woods. After what happened to her, she was worried you'd feel guilty. Like it was your fault for leaving her behind. But she didn't want you to feel that way," I said. "She also told me about the berry thing. She said you were scared no one would trust you ever again after that. That they might vote to throw you out. And she knew you'd worry about that even more after she got separated from the rest of you, because you'd probably feel like everyone blamed you for it. But, again, she didn't want you to feel that way. Because it wasn't your fault."

Leigh's face went slack, her throat tightening as if all the air had been sucked from her lungs. "Oh," she whispered, the word sounding hollow. A single tear slipped free, followed by another, and then they came faster, streaming down her cheeks.

"She really doesn't want you to feel bad, Leigh. She cares about you," I said. "She cares about all of you. And right now, she really needs your help."

"So what can we do?" Trent asked, forehead creasing.

"We need you to show us where the cannibal settlement is."

Trent hesitated, anxiety creasing his brow. "Listen, I really do want to help, but if those people see us and come after us, we're all totally fucked."

"That won't happen," I said, lifting a palm. "You don't even need to get close. You only need to show us how to get there, and then you can hang back once we get to a point where we can find the rest of the way ourselves. And we know how to be careful. We know how to avoid detection. So no one will find their way back here and hurt anyone."

Trent still looked uncomfortable. Frightened. Ryan looked the same.

"Look, guys," Knox said, raising his voice. "We have enough food in our cabin to feed all thirty-three of us through the winter. But if you show us where this village is, we'll give you all of it."

Silence reigned on the lakeshore for another moment. Then Leigh spoke up again. "You don't need to do that," she said in a husky voice, wiping her cheeks with the back of one hand. "Sharing would be nice, but you need to eat too. So I think we should work together."

"Does that mean—"

"Yes." She sucked in a deep breath and lifted her chin. "I'll show you where the village is. I'm pretty sure I remember most of the way."

Trent sighed, raking a hand through his hair. "You've only been there once, Leigh, and it's going to be dark soon. I know the way better. So I'll come too."

Ryan nodded, his face drawn but resolute. "Same here. I won't lie, I'm scared shitless of those people, but... we can't just leave Aria there."

Knox clapped Ryan on the shoulder. "We'll all watch each other's backs. No one's going to end up as some freak's dinner."

Theo piped up. "We should move now. The longer we wait, the worse things could get."

Leigh wiped her eyes again, steeling herself. "You'll need a lot of weapons," she said. "Those guys could be armed. Maybe even have traps set up around the place."

"We've got rifles," Theo replied. "A couple of shotguns too. We found a whole cache of them at the cabin we've been staying in."

"We've got extra food in our bags to share too," I added. "We'll need the energy for the hike."

"Hold on." Tony lifted his palms. "You're risking a hell of a lot on this. If you're wrong, and she's not there..."

I clenched my fists, shoving my dread down into a cold, focused place. "She's there," I said through gritted teeth. "I know it."

Knox eyed me and nodded slowly, his gaze unwavering. "Let's go get her."

27

ARIA

I jerked awake at the sound of footsteps crunching outside the cabin. My ankle throbbed where the chain had bitten into my skin after hours of yanking on it to no avail, and my head was still sore too. I swallowed down the rising tide of panic threatening to choke me. It was dark now—night had settled in while I drifted in and out of restless sleep.

The door creaked open, and Joe stepped inside, silhouetted by the faint glow of firelight from outside. He didn't say anything at first. Just stood there, his gaze heavy and unreadable. Then he moved closer, kneeling beside the bed, his hands brushing over the chain binding my ankle.

"When you finally realize it," he said, his voice low and calm, "when you've accepted that there's no way out of this wilderness —no way back to the life you used to know—you won't have to sleep chained up anymore." He glanced at me, almost like he expected me to agree with him. "Until then, you'll either be chained to this bed or free but attended. Either by me or the others."

He loosened the chain, and blood rushed back to my foot,

prickling painfully through my toes. Joe pointed to my shoes on the floor, signaling for me to put them on.

"Come on," he finally said, nodding toward the door. "It's time for you to meet the community."

My stomach twisted, but I forced myself to follow him through the door, my legs shaky and unsteady. I didn't know what to expect, but the sound of crackling flames and low, murmured voices greeted me as soon as we stepped outside.

A bonfire roared at the center of a clearing, its light shadowing the faces gathered around it. I counted them quickly—twenty-two men and thirteen women, their ages ranging from teenagers to gray-haired elders. Fourteen children wove in and out of the crowd, some small enough to be carried, while others gathered in a group, whispering and pointing at me.

Joe gripped my arm just hard enough to keep me at his side, his presence solid and unmoving. When he spoke, his voice was loud enough to cut through the hum of conversation.

"The Watcher has delivered a gift to me," he announced, his tone reverent and proud. "A new wife."

The words hit me like a punch to the gut, and I forced myself not to flinch. Everyone's eyes were on me, either curious or suspicious.

A young woman toward the front of the fire squinted at me. Then her eyes widened. "Holy shit, you're—"

She clapped a hand over her mouth to cut herself off, but I already knew what she was going to say. She recognized me. And that meant she wasn't from here originally.

Even the way she spoke gave her away. 'Holy shit' didn't sound like a phrase common to a group of wilderness dwellers who'd been isolated from the world for over two hundred years.

"What?" the man next to her snapped. "What were you going to say?"

The woman's face paled. "I... I just wanted to say that she looks very pretty. That's all."

Joe grinned beside me. "You're right, Helly. Aria is a real beauty. She'll look even better once all these cuts and bruises heal."

The man next to Helly suddenly backhanded her across the face. "What have I told you about speaking out of turn, eh?"

As she cried out, I swallowed the scream lodged in my throat, knowing that nothing good would come from showing fear or resistance. Not when I was so outnumbered.

Joe squeezed my arm, his grip a silent warning. "I see she's still learning, Riordan," he said stiffly. "Aria will learn her place here too. Just give her time."

I stared at the fire, not wanting to meet anyone's eyes. All I could think was that I needed to survive the night—then the next —and somehow find a way out of this nightmare.

One of the other men stood. "Welcome, Aria," he said, voice booming through the clearing. "Everyone, let's drink to this wonderful news. This wonderful gift."

Most of the men, and some of the women, lifted cups to their mouths and drank deeply.

Joe clapped a hand on my shoulder, his grin still plastered on his face. "Now that introductions are over... let's eat!" He leaned closer to me, murmuring in my ear. "Don't worry, Aria. Tonight is just caribou. I think you'll like it."

A few of the women trudged around handing out plates of roasted meat and root vegetables. I gingerly took a bite of the meat as Joe stared at me expectantly. It wasn't too bad. No salt, but they'd flavored it with some sort of herb, and it was cooked well.

When the meal was over, a few women rose to gather the plates and cups. Joe nudged me. "Go with them," he commanded. "You should start learning your duties right away."

Relief washed through me. I'd much rather be around other women than anywhere near him. I picked up our plates and fell into step beside Helly, who gave me a weak half-smile. One of the teenage boys followed us as we made our way to a worn-looking shack with a tin roof, presumably tasked with ensuring we didn't try to run away.

"This is the washing room," Helly explained, dipping her chin toward one of five rusty sinks. "We don't have detergent, but there's hot water, at least. From the fire."

"No sponges or scrubbing brushes either, I assume?" I muttered.

She shook her head. "There's some rags. They do the job well enough, as old as they are," she said, raising a brow. "I'll start on these plates. You can dry."

I moved to her right and picked up a cloth. She turned her head over her shoulder, presumably to make sure no one else was trying to listen in, and then she leaned closer to me and spoke in a hushed voice. "You're Aria Hagan, aren't you?"

"Yes."

"How the hell did you end up here?" she asked, eyes wide with disbelief.

"It's a long story," I replied, not wanting to confide in her about the plane crash. At least not yet. She clearly wasn't one of these villagers originally, but I had no idea how much she'd been brainwashed by them at this point. So if I told her there were other crash survivors, she could very well pass it on to the men. "How long have you been here?"

"Two years," she said flatly. "I went on a hiking trip with my friend in a national park. We got lost, and we had no phone service. Then it turned out our compass wasn't working properly. We thought we were heading south, but we were actually heading north all along. For three days straight."

"Then these people found you?"

"Riordan did, yeah." Her mouth twisted in disgust. "That's my husband, as you saw out there," she went on, spitting out the word 'husband' in a sarcastic tone. "He found me, so he got to claim me. Same as Joe did with you."

"What happened to your friend? Is she here too?"

Her jaw tightened. "My friend was a man, and they had no use for him. So they..." She trailed off, voice thickening. "I don't even know how to tell you this," she finally went on. "The things they do here are so fucked up."

"I think I already know what happened to him based on what I've been told so far," I murmured. "I'm so sorry."

"They didn't make me take part in it, at least," she said, slowly shaking her head. "But still, when I see a plate of meat now—any kind of meat—I feel sick to my stomach. It reminds me of that night."

My stomach lurched. "I'm so sorry," I repeated. "I can't even imagine what you've gone through in your time here."

She flashed me a grim look. "You'll find out soon enough."

I cast my gaze over my shoulder to check if anyone was listening again. When I was satisfied that no one was paying attention to us, I turned back to Helly. "We won't be here much longer. I'm sure of it."

She looked at me again, a glimmer of hope surfacing in her eyes. "I guess people will be searching for you like crazy, right?" she said. "Seeing as you're the president's daughter and all."

"Yeah, something like that," I said softly.

I wasn't thinking of my father, though. I was thinking of Landon. I had to believe he'd made it out of that river, and I knew he'd be doing everything in his power to rescue me from this horrible place.

Helly suddenly frowned. "Wait... is your father still the president? Or has there been another election? It's so hard to keep track of time out here."

"The election is actually tomorrow, believe it or not," I said, raising a brow.

"Well, I hope to god your father wins again and sends the entire goddamn US military out here to find you," she said. A hopeful note had entered her voice. "This wilderness is big. But nothing's so big that the president's kid can be lost forever, right?"

I gave her a faint smile. "Right."

"It's so weird how no one else here has *any* idea who you are in the real world," she went on, slowly shaking her head. "When I saw Joe bring you out to the fire, I honestly thought I was seeing things."

"So they have no idea what's going on in the outside world at all?"

Helly shrugged. "Not really. They know it exists, obviously, and they know about certain things like planes and cars, because they've either seen them or heard of them before, from the few members who've visited outsider towns. Or the female hikers they've kidnapped over the years. But they have no interest in taking part in it. To them, this is their home, and they want to live here and be left alone. Forever."

"Are you the only other outsider here right now?" I asked.

"No, there are four other captive women here. But they were all taken between ten and fifteen years ago. That's why none of them recognized you."

"Ah." I nodded slowly. "Do you know much about Joe?"

"I know he hasn't had a woman in a long time. Not since his first wife died eight years ago," she said. "But sometimes Riordan shares me with him, as a kindness."

My stomach twisted. "That doesn't seem very kind to *you*."

She shrugged. "They don't care. Women are just holes to them. Holes who can also cook and clean," she said. "It's such a contradiction. They talk about us women like we're super-rare royalty because there's so few of us compared to them, and they love what we can do. But then they treat us like fucking slaves at the same time."

"When you say they love what we can do, do you mean—"

"Babies," she said bluntly. "They need women around to birth their kids for them. Keep the place going. But there's no such thing as doctors or hospitals around here, so a lot of them don't survive it."

"That's why there are more men than women here, right?"

"Yup," she said, pressing her lips in a thin line.

"Have you had any babies here?"

She shook her head and lowered her voice to a whisper. "I had a contraceptive implant put in my arm a few years ago. They have no idea what it is, so they think I'm just not getting pregnant because of sheer bad luck."

"I have one too," I said. "How much longer is left on yours?"

"They're usually effective for about three years, so it'll stop working soon." A shiver ran through her. "I've been dreading the day it finally happens. But I guess once I'm pregnant, Riordan will stop jumping on me every night. So that's the silver lining."

"I hope it doesn't come to that," I said, stomach lurching at the thought of carrying a stranger's baby.

"It will, if no one ends up coming for us," she said bitterly. "And it'll happen to you too, once your implant wears off."

A shudder went through me. "Have you ever tried to escape?"

"No point. The nearest town takes several days to hike to, and I wouldn't even know which direction it's in. So even if I stole enough food and water to last a week, I wouldn't make it."

"Oh. Right."

"Once you've accepted that, Joe will let you roam freely," she said. "It took Riordan a whole month to let me do it. But Joe's nice."

"Nice isn't really the word I'd use for any of these guys," I muttered.

Helly let out a sardonic laugh. "*Nicer*, I should've said. Compared to some of the others," she said. "Except when he's in a bad mood. You really don't want to be around him on those days. My husband shared me with him on a bad day once, and... *oof*. I couldn't sit right for a week."

My stomach was churning now. "When will he start wanting sex from me?"

"Right away, probably."

"Is there any way I can hold him off? Could I say I'm on my period?"

She scoffed. "The men here don't care about that. If anything, they *like* women getting their periods because it reminds them of their fertility," she said. She hesitated for a moment, brows dipping in a frown as she wiped a plate under the water. "Actually, there's one thing you could try."

"Yeah?"

"The people here are shit-scared of outsider diseases," she explained. "They've all heard horror stories from the old ones. They lived through some pretty heavy stuff."

"Like what?"

"Riordan told me that sixty years ago, some of them ventured to the closest town to trade some stuff. Out of the six who went, only two survived. The others caught what sounded like a flu, or maybe even just a cold. Once the two survivors made it back, they infected the rest of the community, and another twenty-seven people died."

"Holy shit." My eyes widened. "Their immune systems must be different to ours because they've been isolated for so long."

"Exactly," she said. "That flu wiped out half their population in a week, and they still haven't recovered. That's why they're so nuts about having as many kids as possible."

"Makes sense, I guess."

"Anyway... you could try that tonight with Joe. Fake some sniffles and say your throat hurts," Helly went on. "He'll probably give you a wide berth for a few days. But once he realizes you're healthy... well, then you're out of time."

"Thanks for the tip," I murmured. "I'll definitely try it."

Once the dishes were done, Helly led me out of the washing room and wished me good luck. The teenage boy who'd followed us in earlier put a hand on my shoulder and pushed me toward Joe's cabin, which stood on the far end of the settlement.

Once we arrived, Joe thanked the boy and stepped aside to let me in. He'd taken off his boots and jacket, and the top buttons on his shirt were unfastened. A lecherous glint flickered in his eyes as he watched me take my sneakers off. Then he stepped over to fasten the chain around my ankle again.

"You can take the rest off too," he said, motioning to my clothing. "Usually, people wait for the ceremony, but I don't see much point in that."

I gulped at the thought of his foul hands and mouth on me. "There's a ceremony?" I said. "Like... a wedding?"

He scoffed, like I'd asked a stupid question. "Of course. We aren't total savages."

Sure.

I suppressed the urge to roll my eyes and faked a huge sniff as I slowly peeled off my sweater. Then I inhaled sharply and covered my nose and mouth with my hand, pretending to sneeze.

Joe froze. "What was that?"

"Oh, it's just a cold," I said, waving a casual hand. "I've been sneezing a lot, and my throat really hurts."

"You're *sick*?" His eyes had gone saucer wide. "Why didn't you say anything earlier?"

"I didn't notice at first, because my head was aching so much from when I fell down," I said. "But I think I must've caught a bug just before I left on my trip. And that must be why I got so lost and confused. Sickness can make you delirious sometimes."

He took a step backward. "I'll sleep in the other room tonight," he muttered. "Probably best to wait until after the wedding before we consummate things."

I breathed a quiet sigh of relief. *Thank you, Helly.*

Once he was gone, I climbed under the blankets with a heavy sigh, stomach still churning. I was terrified about what might happen tomorrow, but I couldn't let this place break me. Couldn't let them snuff out that last fragile thread of hope. Because Landon was still out there. He had to be. And he'd never stop searching for me.

I squeezed the blanket so hard my knuckles hurt, the ache in my chest almost too much to bear as I silently pleaded in my head.

Please hurry, Landon. Please find me.

28

LANDON

I CROUCHED LOW BEHIND A THICKET THAT LAY JUST BEYOND the fence, watching the firelight flicker through the trees. Most of the cannibal men were still gathered around the central fire, loud and careless, completely unaware of my presence mere feet away.

Knox and the other guys were scattered along the perimeter too, staking out the rest of the village. We'd agreed to meet up after two hours to report our findings and come up with a plan.

I'd seen Aria by the fire earlier, alive and unharmed. It seemed quite obvious that the people didn't want to eat her, as we initially suspected. They were keeping her instead, and it didn't take a genius to figure out why.

After they'd fed her—something I hoped to God was animal meat—she went off with some other women to a large shed on the far left of the settlement, laden with plates. Presumably, the women were tasked with most of the domestic work here, including dishes.

After the women were done in the shed, I saw a scrawny teenage boy escort Aria to a cabin on the far side of the settlement. He delivered her right to the big, burly man who'd paraded her around the bonfire earlier.

It took everything in me not to rush in and snap the bastard's neck as I watched from the shadows behind the fence. I forced myself to move quietly instead, following their movements in the cabin through the windows, every muscle tight and ready to strike if necessary.

Thankfully, the man didn't try anything with her. He simply chained her foot to a bedpost, disappeared into a smaller side room, and shut the door behind him.

I kept low and crept around to another window, where I spotted the glow of a candle. When I squinted, I realized he was reading an old, battered book. Probably something that had been passed around for decades.

I returned to the first window and scanned the cabin again, making sure there were no other threats. Aria was lying on the bed with her eyes squeezed shut, but she didn't look hurt. Whatever that man wanted from her, it wasn't happening tonight.

Still, I couldn't just slip in and grab her. Not with her captor still awake and alert only feet away. I needed a proper plan, because if I rushed in blind and something went wrong, Aria could end up dead.

I tightened my grip on my knife, determination solidifying like steel in my veins.

"Hold on just a little longer, baby," I whispered to the darkness, wishing Aria could somehow hear me. "I'm coming for you."

I pulled away from the window and slipped back into the woods, heading toward the meeting point. My steps were silent, my breathing even, but my mind was racing.

When I arrived at the spot, around two hundred yards away from the village, Leigh lifted a hand in greeting. "I think you're the last one back," she said. "Did you see Aria?"

I nodded and scanned the small group. "She's okay for now. Where's Knox?"

Leigh glanced around. "I don't know. I must've missed him. Do you think he's okay?"

I nodded again. "He can take care of himself."

"And you know what he's like," Cole added with a shrug. "Always late. And he's been walking slower ever since he hurt his foot."

"Well, let's just start without him," Leigh said, anxiety lacing her voice. "We can catch him up when he gets here, whenever that is."

"Fine." I filled the group in on what I'd seen, and the others took turns doing the same. Leigh, Trent, and Ryan listened intently, faces tight with concern.

"So there's twenty-two men altogether?" Leigh asked.

I nodded. "By my count, yes. And thirteen women, not counting Aria."

"Plus the teenage girl I spotted in one of the cabins," Theo added. "She was babysitting two sleeping newborns."

"I couldn't count all the kids around the bonfire," I said, scratching my jaw. "They were running around too much. But I'd say at least ten. Probably closer to fifteen."

"So there's probably around fifty people altogether, including kids and babies," Trent said. "That's more than I expected. Might make things difficult."

Leigh raised a hand. "Before we jump into the game plan to get Aria out... there's something the anthropologist in me simply has to say."

"Oh, for fuck's sake," Cole muttered, rolling his eyes upward. "You really think *this* is the time for that shit?"

"Please just listen." Leigh kept her palm lifted in a placating gesture. "Because we know these people are dangerous—or at least *can* be—your instinct might be to rush in, guns blazing, and kill them all. Or at least kill the men. But I'd like for you to consider other ways."

My eyes narrowed. "Why?" I spat out. "They're fucking cannibals! And they've kidnapped Aria!"

"I know, and if it ends up being a life-or-death situation, then obviously you might have to do something violent to save her. That's understandable," Leigh replied. "But here's the thing. This settlement has clearly existed for a long time. The inhabitants have been raised from birth to believe in certain things, and as messed up as those things are, it's not their fault. So it's not up to us to be judge, jury, and executioner just because we find their way of life to be morally reprehensible."

"But—"

"Hold on. There's more," Leigh said. "Think about it this way. If you kill all the men, that still leaves thirty-odd women and children here. We'll then be responsible for all of them, because we can't just leave them here to starve, can we?"

"That's actually a good point," Theo muttered, rubbing his jaw.

Trent nodded slowly. "We have no idea when we're getting rescued, and it's already hard enough to feed *our* group. Adding an extra thirty people could really fuck things up," he said. "Especially when those people might be hostile to us, as they likely would be after seeing all their men massacred."

"Exactly." Leigh nodded fervently. "So if it's possible to get Aria out of there with little to no violence, I think that's the best course of action. Once we're rescued, we can tell the authorities what we saw out here, and they can deal with it."

I gritted my teeth, forcing down the anger roiling in my gut. I wanted nothing more than to pummel the asshole who'd captured Aria until his head was nothing more than a bloody mess, but I had to admit, Leigh had made a very good point.

Still, the idea of leaving Aria's captor unharmed made my blood fucking *boil*.

I took a deep breath, trying to calm myself as my mind raced. Then I looked at Cole. "Do you still have that cigarette lighter we found in the hunter's cabin?"

He nodded. "Yup. What are you thinking?"

"I can go back to the cabin where that motherfucker is

keeping Aria," I said, staring back at the distant settlement. "Once I'm there, you guys can set fire to the fence in multiple locations. Maybe even that empty shed the women were in earlier. The men will rush over to see what's going on and start putting the fires out. That guy with Aria will probably rush out too. Then I can kick down one of the closest fence posts, sneak into the cabin, and grab Aria while they're all distracted."

"That's a good idea," Leigh said, relaxing a little. "That way no one has to die."

"Are you all happy with that plan?" I asked, looking around at the others.

Before anyone could respond, a rustle sounded in the bushes. Knox slipped out of the darkness like a shadow, his eyes scanning the group before he spoke. "Sorry I'm late. Thought I was being tailed, so I had to lie low for a while." He huffed. "Turned out to be a fucking owl."

We filled him in on everything he'd missed, and as I laid out the plan, he frowned and shook his head. "We can't do that."

"Why not?"

"That shed Aria went to after the bonfire—I was very close to it. So I saw her clearly when she approached, along with the woman she was walking with. And I recognized that woman."

My brows rose. "You did?"

"Her name's Helena Logan. She went missing in the Rockies while she was on a hiking trip with a friend two years ago."

"How the hell do you know that?" Trent asked, frowning.

"They made a whole-ass documentary about her and her friend," Knox replied. "One of those true crime sorta things. I know because my sister is obsessed with all that shit, and she made me watch a few episodes with her a while back."

"If Helena is a kidnapping victim like Aria, then there could be others too," Leigh said, eyes wide. "For all we know, half the women in this town could be captives."

"Shit," I muttered, slowly shaking my head. "That means we can't just grab Aria and leave."

"Exactly. We can't leave Helena behind," Knox said. "Along with any other captives they might have in there."

"But we have no way of knowing which women to rescue," Cole said. "And we can't just take them all, because some of them might be from here originally, so they probably wouldn't appreciate us swooping in and kidnapping them."

"Fuck it," I muttered, jaw clenched. "Sorry, Leigh, but your non-violence plan just went up in smoke."

Her brows shot up. "Landon, you—"

I cut her off. "I'm not saying we need to kill anyone. We just need to incapacitate them long enough to get Aria and all the other captive women out," I said. I cleared my throat and raised my voice. "Here's the new plan. We set all the fires like I said before. At least six of them. But when the men come to stop them, you guys need to knock them out, shoot them in the legs, tie them up... whatever the hell it takes."

"Are you sure you guys can handle that?" Trent asked, raising a brow. "It'll be twenty-two of them versus six of you. Or five, seeing as you'll be off getting Aria, Landon. I don't really like those odds."

"They'll split up into smaller groups to check out all the fires, and some of them will probably run away to grab water at first," Theo pointed out. "So we'll only have to fight one or two at a time."

Knox nodded. "We can handle that. Easily."

"Well, if things start to look like they're going badly, Ryan and I can try to jump in to help out," Trent said, scratching his head. "But we're not exactly trained fighters, so please don't expect too much."

"What happens *after* you guys have got half the village knocked out or tied up?" Leigh piped up, eyes narrowing. "Do we just leave like nothing happened and hope they don't come after us seeking revenge somewhere down the track?"

"We'll figure that out later," I said brusquely. "Right now, I just want to get Aria out before it's too late."

Knox gave a grim nod. "Let's do it. We'll split up, set the fires, and hit anyone who shows up to put them out."

My pulse thudded, tension simmering like a live wire. This plan was messy as hell, but it was our best shot. And I wasn't leaving without Aria.

I moved swiftly through the trees, heading back toward the far end of the settlement. My knife was gripped tight in my hand, ready to strike if anyone spotted me.

When I reached the spot I'd chosen earlier, I dropped low behind the thick bushes that lined the fence, keeping my body perfectly still as I stared at the cabin. Through the grimy window, I could see Aria lying on the bed, her foot still chained to the post. Judging by the candlelight flickering through the other window, her captor hadn't moved from his spot in the smaller room.

I clenched my jaw, every muscle primed to move the second I saw the first signs of smoke or flames.

We'd agreed on six fires. The first would be the shed, since it was mostly empty and isolated enough not to set anything else alight. Then the guys would light up five separate spots along the fence.

Time crawled, and I forced myself to stay calm, inhaling and exhaling slowly through my nose. Then, finally—

A muffled whoosh and a sudden glow in the distance.

The shed was on fire. Flames were licking up the side, catching on the brittle wood and spreading rapidly. The men around the bonfire noticed immediately, springing to their feet and yelling to each other. I kept my gaze fixed on Aria's cabin, my grip tightening on the knife.

It took less than two minutes for the other fires to ignite, the fence posts catching like dry tinder. More men ran from the bonfire, shouting orders to each other, scrambling to grab water from the barrel near the central fire. The place was rapidly descending into chaos.

Finally, the man in Aria's cabin appeared at the doorway, squinting toward the distant shed with his face twisted in confusion. He glanced back inside, as if debating whether to leave Aria alone.

Another shout came from the direction of the fence fires, and he made his decision, charging out into the open with the rest of the men. He moved to the left, barking orders at two younger guys to grab more buckets.

Now.

I sprang up and rushed to the fence, planting my foot against the thick log at the base. I kicked as hard as I could, twice, until it cracked loose and toppled inward. Ducking through the gap, I sprinted to the cabin and rushed inside.

Aria shot up, her eyes wide and disbelieving. "Landon!"

"Yeah, it's me," I murmured, striding to her side. I cupped her face briefly, brushing my thumb over her cheek. "You're okay, baby. I'm right here."

She bit her bottom lip, eyes watering. "I knew you'd come," she whispered. "But the chain—"

I glanced down. The thick metal was bolted to the bedpost, padlock glinting in the candlelight. I gritted my teeth and yanked it hard, but it barely budged.

"Bastard must have the key on him," I muttered. "Stay here. I'll look for something."

I raced to the small room where the man had been reading earlier, and I quickly searched through his belongings—a pile of clothes on the floor, some half-empty bottles, and a makeshift shelf cluttered with random junk. No sign of a key.

"Dammit," I hissed, glancing around. My gaze landed on an ax propped in the corner, its blade stained with old rust.

I grabbed it and rushed back to Aria. "Hold still, baby," I said, positioning the blade over the chain. "I'm gonna break it off."

She winced and pressed herself back against the headboard, eyes squeezed shut. I raised the ax and brought it down with all my strength, the clang of metal on metal reverberating through the room.

It barely dented the chain. I gritted my teeth and raised the ax again, striking even harder this time. Another blow, another clang, and finally, a weak snap. The links buckled enough that I could force the chain through the padlock, slipping it off her ankle.

"Got it," I said through gritted teeth. "Come on."

Aria threw herself at me, arms wrapped tight around my neck. I held her close for a brief second, then pulled back, keeping my hands on her shoulders.

"We need to move," I said. "Stay right behind me."

She nodded, and I took her hand and led her to the door, peeking through the gap to make sure the coast was clear. The fires were still roaring, flames licking up the sides of the shed and multiple logs along the fence. Most of the men had rushed toward different spots, split up by the many infernos, and they'd been met by Knox, Cole, Theo, Sebastian, and Matthew.

"Let's go," I muttered, guiding Aria out of the cabin and ducking low.

I caught glimpses of the guys fighting for us as we slipped past the broken fence and moved through the surrounding woods. Knox was currently moving like a shadow between two men, slamming the butt of his rifle into one's face while sweeping the legs out from under the other. He stomped on the second man's wrist to keep him from reaching for his knife, then bound his hands with a length of cord.

Cole was farther down, brutal and efficient as he disarmed one of the men with a sharp twist of his arm, sending his knife clattering to the ground. He grabbed the man by the back of the neck and slammed him face-first into a fence post, knocking him out cold. Another guy lunged at him from behind, but Cole ducked low and jammed his elbow into his gut before using the man's own belt to tie his wrists together.

Theo was at another fire, wielding an ax he'd found somewhere. He swung it low to take out a man's legs before delivering a swift blow to his shoulder to keep him down. One of the other cannibals tried to tackle him from the side, but Theo sidestepped and brought the flat side of the ax down on his head, sending him sprawling to the ground. He made quick work of tying their hands behind their backs, his movements ruthless but controlled.

Sebastian and Matthew had taken up position at the far end of the fence, cutting off any escape routes. Sebastian fired his gun at anyone who got too close, aiming for their legs to bring them down without killing. One of the bastards tried to sneak up behind him with a club, but Matthew intercepted him, jamming the butt of his shotgun into the guy's gut before delivering a swift kick to his ribs. Once the man was doubled over and gasping for breath, Matthew yanked his hands behind his back and secured them with a length of rope.

Grunts, shouts, and gunshots filled the night, the heat from the fires making sweat drip down my neck. I glanced at Aria, who was wide-eyed and pale, but she didn't falter.

A deep voice suddenly called out from behind us. "You're not taking my woman, outsider."

I turned around to see Aria's captor standing on the path. He must've doubled back to his cabin to grab something to fight with after seeing all the chaos erupting by the fence. Then he must've spotted the broken fence and followed our trail from there.

I stepped in front of Aria, keeping her behind me as I tightened my grip on the ax.

"*Your* woman?" I shot back, my voice low and dangerous. "She doesn't belong to you."

The man sneered, eyes flicking between us, and then he

moved closer, rolling his shoulders like he was getting ready for a fight. "She does. The Watcher granted her to me, fair and square."

"That's not true, and you're gonna regret putting your fucking hands on her," I snarled.

The man lunged forward, aiming a punch at my face. I ducked, swinging the ax handle up to block his next move, but he caught my arm and shoved me backward, trying to rip the ax from my grip. I twisted hard, driving my knee up into his gut. He grunted, doubling over just enough for me to shove him back.

He recovered quickly, launching himself at me again, and I dodged, feeling the rush of air as his fist skimmed past my jaw. I swung the ax up, aiming for his shoulder, but he grabbed the handle, and we wrestled for control. He headbutted me, making stars explode behind my eyes, but I didn't let go. Instead, I rammed the ax handle into his throat, forcing him back.

He choked and stumbled, and I seized the opportunity to drive my fist into his jaw, once, twice, until his nose bled and his lip split open. He staggered but didn't go down, roaring as he lunged again. This time, I caught his wrist, twisting it sharply and forcing him down to his knees.

I slammed the ax handle down on the back of his head, and he groaned and slumped forward, still conscious but dazed.

I grabbed him by the collar and smashed his face into the ground, grinding his cheek against the dirt. He made a weak attempt to push me off, but I slammed his head down again, and finally, he went still.

I turned to Aria, my breathing rough and unsteady. "Run back to his cabin and grab that broken chain," I said. "We'll use it to tie his wrists and ankles."

She hesitated, glancing nervously at the man's unmoving form, but I gave her a reassuring nod. "He's out cold. Just hurry."

She nodded and rushed away, back the way we came.

I dragged her captor onto his stomach, yanking his arms behind his back. Blood was pooling under his face, soaking into the dirt, and I resisted the urge to beat him senseless again just for touching Aria.

She returned a moment later, chain in hand. I took it from her and looped it around his wrists, using the broken links to secure them together. Then I wrapped the remaining length around his ankles, making sure he couldn't kick or crawl his way free.

When I was satisfied he wasn't going anywhere, I straightened and wiped the sweat from my forehead. Aria hovered nearby, her hands shaking. I reached out, cupping her face and brushing my thumb over her cheek.

"You're safe now," I murmured. "I've got you."

She sagged into me, relief flooding her features, and I pulled her close, holding her tight.

She was safe, but the night wasn't over yet. The fires were still blazing, and shouts were echoing from every direction. We needed to get to the others. Help them take down any remaining men so we could rescue the other captive women.

I took Aria's hand, guiding her through the shadows as we made our way toward the front of the village. The fire on the shed had spread to the neighboring building, and the whole structure was now engulfed in flames, shooting high into the sky.

Most of the twenty-two men from the village were already down—either unconscious, restrained, or nursing wounds that made it impossible for them to move. Knox and Cole were fighting the last couple of stragglers, subduing them while the other guys kept watch.

Leigh, Trent, and Ryan had also shown up to help, moving from man to man to make sure they were securely tied.

The villagers who weren't part of the fighting had started gathering at the edges of the clearing—mostly women and children, their eyes wide and fearful. None of them moved to defend the men. They just stood there in stunned silence, whispering to each other.

One of the women spotted Aria and rushed forward. I

stepped in front of Aria, eyes narrowed, but she lifted a hand to signal that it was all right.

"You were right!" the woman said in a tight voice, throwing her arms around Aria. "It's over!"

It dawned on me that the woman was probably Helena Logan—the missing hiker Knox had mentioned earlier. Aria must've reassured her that help was on the way, because she'd never stopped believing in me for a second. The thought of that made my chest swell with pride.

Leigh watched the two women embrace, presumably waiting for her own turn to hug Aria. "What the hell are we going to do now?" she asked, turning her attention back to the gathered villagers. "All these people..."

"I don't think we need to worry about it," Theo said, lips quirked in a strange smile.

"Yes, we do. It's not fair to—"

"Seriously." Theo cut her off, jabbing a finger toward the night sky. "We don't need to worry about it. Look!"

I followed his gaze upward. Everyone else did the same.

"Holy shit," Aria said as she returned to my side. "Is that...?"

"Yup." I stared upward, eyes wide. "It sure is."

A small cargo plane was slowly passing overhead, and it looked like it was flying much lower than it usually would.

"It's probably on its way to one of the mining towns out here," Theo said, stepping up beside me. "Someone on board must've spotted the fire and realized it was too big to be a campfire, so they dipped lower to check it out."

"So... we're getting rescued?" Aria whispered, her voice trembling with disbelief. She glanced up at me, her eyes wide and bright with hope. "We're going home?"

I cupped her face in my hands, brushing my thumbs over her cheeks as a grin turned up my lips. "Yeah, baby. We're going home."

Her breath hitched, and before I could say anything else, she surged forward and kissed me, her hands tangling in my hair as she pulled me closer. I wrapped my arms around her waist, holding her tight, pouring every ounce of relief and love and pure fucking gratitude into the kiss.

When we finally broke apart, I kept my forehead pressed to hers, loving the way her lips curved into a shaky smile. Around us, the others were talking excitedly, shouting to make sure the plane didn't lose sight of the settlement.

"It's signaling with its lights!" Cole said, waving his arms in the air. "They definitely spotted us!"

Aria looked up at me, her eyes welling with tears. "I can't believe it," she whispered. "We're really getting out of here."

I kissed her forehead and pulled her against my chest, holding her close as the plane continued to circle above. Relief washed over me like a tidal wave, and for the first time in what felt like forever, I allowed myself to believe it was really over.

I knew there'd be a whole pile of shit to deal with once we got back to civilization, but for now, we didn't have to think about any of that.

Right now, all that mattered was that we were alive. We were safe.

And we were going home.

29

ARIA

ONE DAY LATER

"IN WHAT'S BEING HAILED AS THE 'ELECTION DAY MIRACLE,' President Hagan's daughter, Aria Hagan, and thirty-two other TA589 survivors were found alive in the early morning hours of November 20, nearly six weeks after their plane vanished over Canada. Their dramatic rescue came mere hours before Americans headed to the polls, and while President Hagan was already projected to win by a substantial margin after a recent uptick in support, the news of his daughter's survival only solidified his overwhelming victory. Crowds across the country erupted into cheers as—"

I shut the TV off before I did something stupid, like hurling the remote across the room to crack the screen. My jaw was clenched so tight my teeth ached.

I took a slow, steady breath, forcing my muscles to relax. Losing my temper wouldn't help. At least not yet. Landon and I didn't have solid proof of what my father had done—of how far he was willing to go to protect his power—so until we did, I had to be careful. Had to play the dutiful daughter, so very grateful to be alive and supported by my *amazing* father.

For now.

The knock at the door was soft, almost hesitant, and I knew who it was before it even swung open.

President Hagan didn't enter like a man who'd recently tried to have his daughter killed. He walked in like a father overwhelmed with relief.

"Aria." His voice cracked as he said my name, and then he was crossing the room in long, urgent strides. Before I could brace myself, his arms wrapped around me, pulling me into a firm, practiced embrace. "God, it's so good to see you."

It took all the inner strength I had to force myself to hug him back. My muscles locked into place as his familiar cologne wrapped around me, but he didn't seem to register my stiffness.

He pulled away just enough to cup my face, searching my expression with an intensity that might've passed for fatherly concern. "They told me you've been resting, but I wanted to see you the second you woke up."

I made myself meet his eyes, trying to push down the revulsion twisting in my gut. "Yeah, I've been a little busy," I said, forcing my lips into a faint smile. "Checkups. Tests. Making sure I'm not dying of anything."

His lips pressed together, an imitation of sympathy. "I can't even imagine what you've been through." He exhaled heavily, sinking into the chair beside my bed, and wiped a non-existent tear from below his right eye. "I really thought I'd lost you."

You tried to lose me!

I swallowed the words, pressing my fingers into the hospital blanket to center myself. I still couldn't let him see the storm raging beneath my skin.

His gaze drifted around the sterile hospital room before settling on the pale blue curtain dividing the space. His mouth twitched in disapproval. "You know, you don't have to stay in a shared room." He leaned forward, his tone gentle, coaxing. "You're still the president's daughter, remember? If you want privacy, I can arrange it immediately."

"No," I said, a little too quickly. I cleared my throat, forcing my voice to steady. "I wanted to share a room with Leigh. She's one of the other survivors. And my Secret Service detail said it was okay."

His brows lifted slightly, but he nodded. "Leigh Merz, right? I saw that name on the list of survivors," he said.

I nodded, and he rose to his feet, stepping toward the curtain. "I'd love to meet her," he went on. "Your fellow survivors must feel like family to you now, after what you all went through together. And that makes them family to me too."

Panic surged up my throat as his fingers reached for the edge of the fabric. "Not right now, Dad. She's fast asleep," I said. "I told her I'd let her meet you once we're out of here, so she can dress up a bit."

The lies left my lips smoothly, calmly.

My father turned and gave me a small, understanding smile. "Of course. I'll let her rest," he said, returning to his seat. "But I'd love to meet her soon."

I forced myself to exhale, loosening my grip on the sheets.

He leaned forward again, wrapping me in another hug. "I still can't believe you're really here," he said. His voice had turned gruff, like he was on the verge of tears, but I could tell it was forced.

God, how had I never noticed how fake he was before now?

"I can't believe it either," I murmured. "When the plane crashed, I thought that was *it*. I thought I'd never wake up again."

My father drew back to tuck a stray strand of hair behind my ear in a show of tenderness. I had to bite my tongue to remind him there weren't any journalists here to observe his behavior and report on his caring façade.

"You're a true survivor, darling," he said. "And I'm not just talking about the crash. You went through so much out there. I even heard there was some awful business with a group of cannibals."

"That's right. The Canadian authorities are dealing with it."

He patted my hand. "I'm so proud of you for getting through all of it."

I smiled sweetly. "Thanks, Dad," I replied. The words felt like acid on my tongue. "Can I ask you something?"

"Of course, darling. Anything."

I cocked my head. "You know that agent on your detail? Marcus Randall?"

"Yes. Why?"

"Do you think he's a trustworthy guy?"

"Of course. I trust all my Secret Service detail members with my life."

I let out a heavy sigh. "Well, I guess you haven't seen the news in the last thirty minutes, then," I said. "Because Randall just put out a statement about you."

Something flickered in my father's gaze. *Fear.* It was only there for a flash, but then it disappeared, and he composed himself. "What did he say?"

"That you paid him to arrange for hackers to bring down my plane so you could win the election from the sympathy boost."

Shock flared in his eyes this time—too raw, too fast to be faked. His throat bobbed as he swallowed. "What? That... that's preposterous!" he spluttered, voice cracking on the last word.

"It really is. I can't believe *anyone* would try to kill their own child just to secure an election," I said, keeping my voice level. "But that's what Randall is claiming."

It wasn't true, of course. Randall was a loyalist to the end when it came to my father, as the Dominion Club had discovered all those weeks ago. But my father had no reason to think I was lying right now, so he didn't know any better.

"He's lying," he snapped. "God, what a snake in the grass. You can't trust anyone these days."

I cocked my head. "You said you trusted him with your life. Why would he suddenly turn on you?"

"I have no idea." My father rubbed his collar, head slowly shaking. "He's been a little off ever since that snake bit him back in September. Perhaps the venom addled his brain."

"Yeah. Maybe."

"I really can't believe he's spouting this absolute garbage." His face was slowly turning red. "And I can't believe no one on my team told me."

"They probably want to let you savor the election win for a while," I said, raising a brow. "Or maybe no one's heard yet. I only saw it on the news a few minutes before you came in."

"Well, it goes without saying that there's no truth to Agent Randall's claims," he said, leaning forward to hug me again. "I would never, *ever* hurt you. You know that, don't you?"

I didn't answer the question. "Can I ask you something else, Dad?"

"Yes. Of course."

"Did you at least hesitate? Even for a second? Or was it an easy decision?"

He pulled back, frowning. "I'm sorry, darling, I don't know what you're talking about."

"Let me put it another way. If I was born a boy, would you still have decided to kill me? Or would that have been too hard?"

"*What?*" Naked shock twisted his face again. "Aria, you don't actually *believe* Agent Randall's ridiculous claims, do you?"

"You always said you wanted a boy to carry on your legacy. I was just the consolation prize you ended up with," I said. "So I'll ask you again. Would that plane have come down if I was born male? Or would you have found some other twisted way to steer the election in your favor?"

"Aria. *Stop.*" My father lifted a palm, eyes narrowing. "I know you're still in shock after the hell you endured out in that wilderness, so I understand why these wild claims have gotten under your skin so easily. But none of it is true. Marcus Randall is just crazy. That's all."

"Hm. It's funny you say that, because he named the hacking group in his statement, and they've taken full credit for it now that they know the story is out there. It's an anonymous group of people based in another country that doesn't extradite here, so they aren't worried about legal action," I said. "Also, two of your other Secret Service agents came forward and admitted their involvement in the scheme after Randall's statement went public. I guess they realized it was only a matter of time before their names came out, so they wanted to get ahead of it all."

The practiced lies slipped easily off my tongue. Perhaps I *did* take after my father in one regard.

He slowly shook his head, his eyes wide. "Those people are—"

"All lying? All crazy? Or... let me guess. It's all a massive conspiracy theory designed by an opponent to make you look bad, right?"

He rose to his feet, face turning stony. "I really cannot believe you would speak to me this way, or believe such heinous lies about me. My own daughter, betraying me—"

"Oh my god, you're such a fucking hypocrite!" I snapped, cutting him off. "You tried to kill me, and you have the audacity to say that *I* betrayed *you*?"

"I did nothing of the sort!"

"Oh, come on, Dad," I said, shaking my head. "It's just you and me in this conversation, and we both know the truth. We really don't need to pretend anymore."

"I'm not pretending. That plane crash was caused by a bird strike."

"Oh, really?" I tilted my head. "Did you happen to hear about a survivor named Tony Delmonico?"

"Yes, I told you I saw the list," he muttered, eyes narrowing. "What about him?"

"He was one of the pilots. They almost *never* survive crashes, because of where they're positioned in the plane. But he survived. And he told us all along that the plane was hacked. He knows because he was literally flying it," I said. "So... the evidence really seems to be stacking up against you, doesn't it?"

My father tugged at his collar again as a bead of sweat slipped down his temple. "It doesn't matter how many people claim what. There's no proof," he said. "And even if they *do* find proof that the plane was hacked, there's absolutely nothing tying me to any of it."

"I figured you'd say that," I said breezily.

"I said it because it's the truth, and you know it," he replied. His tone had turned ice cold, and a self-assured glint had appeared in his eyes. "No one will ever be able to prove anything. And even if you, Randall, and the others continue to make these ludicrous claims against me... who do you think people will believe? The agents who are clearly being paid off by the Russians? The girl who recently suffered multiple head injuries along with terrible mental trauma after surviving a plane crash and six weeks in the wilderness? Or *me*, the goddamned President of the United States?"

I nodded slowly. "You're right, Dad. As the president, you certainly have a lot of sway. But you only became popular recently because of *me*. Because of the sympathy boost you got from everyone thinking I was dead after my plane vanished," I said, slowly sitting up straighter. "Before that, you were pretty damn unpopular. So I think quite a lot of people out there will want to listen to what I have to say about you. And I'll keep saying it, over and over again, until more and more of them listen. Until the whole damn country listens."

"You won't do that," he seethed, shaking his head. "You would never."

"Oh, I *would*, and I fully intend to," I said. "So I guess that means the only way you can stop me is to finish the job right now, with your own hands. Because if you don't, I'm making a call to the Washington Post as soon as we're done here. I'll also contact some TV networks too. I'm sure all of them will be frothing at the mouth to secure an interview with me, given how my name is currently on everyone's lips."

My father's face was almost purple by now. "You'll do no such thing."

"I will, and like I said, there's only one way to stop me. And for once, you'll have to do the dirty work yourself," I said in a goading tone. "But you're too much of a coward to kill me with your own hands, aren't you, Dad? You'd never have the guts to—"

My words were cut off as he snatched up a pillow and pressed it down on my face, cutting off my air. I'd finally pushed him far enough.

I thrashed, but my body was still weak from weeks of hunger and injury, and his hands, strong and unrelenting, were pinning the pillow down with all the force of a man who had everything to lose. The muted sound of his voice filtered through the suffocating fabric, eerily calm.

"I really wish it didn't have to be this way, Aria." His voice was almost tender, like he was tucking me in for the night rather than murdering me in my hospital bed. "I do love you, in my own way. But you've really left me no choice here."

I tried to scream at him, but the sound was muffled into nothing. Then—movement. A rush of air. The weight on my face vanished.

I gasped in a ragged breath as my father was ripped away from me, my vision clearing just in time to see Landon slam him against the wall with enough force to make the framed hospital evacuation plan tremble.

He choked on a breath, his face stunned, as Landon's arm pressed against his throat, pinning him in place.

"You really are a stupid son of a bitch, aren't you?" Landon growled, his voice thick with disgust. "Did you honestly think you'd get away with that?"

My father struggled, his hands grappling at Landon's forearm, but Landon didn't let up. His lips curled into a smirk as he leaned in closer, lowering his voice. "Smile, Mr. President," he murmured. "You're on camera."

I turned my head slightly, wincing as I pushed myself up on trembling arms. The cell phone I'd propped up against the tissue box on the bedside table was still recording.

My father's eyes darted toward it, fear flashing across his face.

Landon's grip didn't waver. "You really shouldn't have let your guard down in here," he said. "But I'm not surprised you did. In fact, I was counting on it, because you've *always* underestimated your daughter. You've never thought for even a second that she might be smarter than you."

"Exactly." I let out a weak, breathless laugh, my throat raw from the lack of air. "I'm just a girl, right? I'm not capable of subterfuge. Only surface-level things."

"I...I..." That was the only sound my father could get out right now, his mouth opening and closing like a fish out of water.

"What do you think will happen when the American people see this video, huh?" Landon mused. "Their president trying to smother his own daughter in her hospital bed?"

My father's lips parted, but no words came out. His face was still an ugly shade of red, beads of sweat rolling down his temple.

"You were right about one thing, Dad," I said. "No one would ever be able to tie you to the plane crash. But what you just did? It's undeniable."

Landon finally eased his arm back, just enough for my father to suck in a ragged breath. He immediately tried to compose himself, smoothing down the front of his suit, but there was no coming back from this.

"By the way," I went on, lips spreading in a cold smile. "I lied about Randall and your other agents making those public statements. They're all totally loyal to you, so no one ever would've suspected you of anything before now. But they will once they see that video."

His eyes bulged, and he shot one arm out to grab the phone. He hurled it to the floor before stomping on it, shattering the screen. Landon and I watched him calmly, not making any moves to stop him.

"That video was live-streaming to my friend, who was recording it," I said. "So it really doesn't matter if that phone is broken beyond repair."

"I'll say it was a deep fake," Dad said in a low voice, nostrils flaring. "Those things are everywhere now."

Landon smirked. "We thought you'd say that, so we came up with a backup plan," he said. "Aria's friend Sabrina is a very talented hacker. She's not quite advanced enough to bring down a whole plane, but she's certainly good enough to hack a hospital security network. So she's got copies of all their surveillance footage."

I pointed to the camera in the corner of the room. "I guess you thought you could pay someone to make that footage mysteriously disappear once I was dead," I said. "But unfortunately, like Landon just explained, that's not going to be an option."

My father's mouth had returned to the fish-out-of-water act, rendering him speechless.

Landon took a step closer to him. "You *really* thought you'd get away with all of it, didn't you?" he said, slowly shaking his head. "It's incredible, really. The hubris is genuinely mind-blowing."

"Isn't there some old legend about hubris?" I asked, scratching my chin. "Some guy flying too close to the sun and crashing back down to Earth? I've gone blank on his name."

"Icarus," my father mumbled, finally finding his tongue.

"That's right. Icarus. You're just like him." I smiled sweetly.

"But don't worry, Dad. Speaking as someone who's literally fallen out of the sky and crashed back to Earth... there's a tiny, *tiny* chance you'll survive. But it's going to hurt like hell."

My father exhaled sharply, his nostrils flaring. For the first time in his life, he had no words. No excuses. No carefully spun lies to manipulate his way out of this situation.

Then, slowly, he turned toward the door.

Landon and I didn't stop him. We didn't need to. He was walking out of here a dead man, and he knew it. At least figuratively dead.

By the time he reached the door, his hand hovering over the handle, Landon's voice cut through the tense silence. "One more thing, Mr. President."

My father hesitated, his fingers curling slightly before he turned around. The moment he did, Landon's fist shot out, cracking against his face with a sickening crunch.

Blood spurted from his nose as he staggered back, his hand flying up to his face. A strangled noise—half gasp, half curse—escaped him as he doubled over.

Landon shook out his hand, flexing his fingers. "That was for Aria."

I crossed my arms, watching as my father slowly straightened, his eyes watering from the pain. He looked at me, something unreadable flickering across his face, but I didn't give him the satisfaction of a reaction.

"You can get out now," I said coldly.

For once, he listened to me.

As the door clicked shut behind him, the tension that had been holding me upright finally snapped. My body sagged, the weight of everything landing on me all at once. Six weeks of running, fighting, surviving. Every moment building to this. And now... it was over.

Landon turned to me, his knuckles still bloodied from the punch, his chest rising and falling with steady breaths. For a second, we just stared at each other, as if making sure this was real. That we'd actually won. Then, with a quiet exhale, he stepped over to the bed and pulled me into his arms.

I melted against him, pressing my face into his chest to inhale his scent. His arms tightened around me, one hand threading into my hair as he pressed a kiss to the top of my head.

I tilted my face up, and before I could say anything, he kissed me, slow and deep. When we finally broke apart, I let out a shaky breath and leaned my forehead against his.

"It almost doesn't feel real," I murmured. "Everything we've done... surviving a plane crash, living in the wild, taking down a fucking cannibal village. And then, on top of all that, we came back here and took down a corrupt president."

Landon nodded slowly. "It's a hell of a lot, isn't it?"

"Yup." I let out a dry laugh, shaking my head. "So... what are we going to do next?"

He grinned, his thumb brushing over my cheek. "Whatever the hell we want, baby."

EPILOGUE
ARIA

18 MONTHS LATER

The party was beautiful—soft golden lights spilling from the chandeliers, glasses clinking in quiet toasts, the hum of conversation weaving through the grand halls of the Vice President's home.

But even with all the warmth and elegance, I needed a moment to breathe.

I slipped out onto the terrace, letting the crisp night air cool my skin. The garden stretched beyond me, dark and quiet, a contrast to the lively event inside, which was filled with politicians, lobbyists, donors, and other DC power players.

It was the sort of event I'd attended a hundred times before. And yet, so much had changed in the last year and a half.

After Landon, Sabrina, and I revealed the truth about my father's crimes, the country had turned against him, the truth unraveling everything he'd built. Protests filled the streets as people demanded to take back their votes, and when the Electoral College met to cast their votes in mid-December, they flipped their choice—at least in the states where that was legal. By the time the count was official, the presidency no longer belonged to my father, and his party lay in ruins. Celeste Ashford had been sworn in instead.

I was supposed to be collateral damage in my father's rise to power, a sacrifice made in pursuit of something greater. But I had survived.

We had survived.

I leaned against the terrace railing, my thoughts drifting to Landon. To everything we'd been through together.

We had defied death. Defied nature. Defied everything and everyone working against us, even when one of those people was me and my stubborn, know-it-all attitude.

A part of me still couldn't believe I had Landon. That after everything, we'd carved out a life together. It wasn't perfect—the media hounding was still at an unbelievably high level—but it was ours, and sometimes, when I looked at him, when I felt his hands on my skin, I couldn't quite find the words to tell him what he meant to me. How he'd given me back something I never thought I'd have again. Safety, love, a future.

I wished I could reach through time, back to the girl I'd been before the plane crash, and tell her to hold on. To tell her that no matter how dark things became, one day she'd find someone who'd burn the world down to keep her safe... and that person might be the most unexpected one of all.

A breeze whispered through the garden, rustling through the hedges beyond the terrace. My gaze drifted toward them, a flicker of mischief sparking to life in my chest.

The Vice President's estate had a hedge maze, installed decades ago by one of his predecessors. It was massive, sprawling. A quiet, secluded space that no one would dare wander into at this hour. The perfect place to steal a moment for myself.

I'd been inside it once before, when I was sixteen or seventeen, sneaking off between dull conversations about policy and re-election campaigns. It hadn't been too hard to figure out. If I kept my hand on the hedge to my right and followed it all the way to the center, I'd never get lost.

I glanced back at the two Secret Service agents assigned to my detail. Even though my father was no longer the president—and was currently rotting in a maximum-security prison—I would still have security for at least another two years. Possibly longer, if Celeste decided to extend it.

"I'm going to take a walk in the maze," I said. "Is that okay?"

The agent on the left nodded. "Of course, Ms. Hagan," he said. "We'll follow you, just to make sure you don't get lost."

I smiled. "Thanks."

I turned and walked toward the maze, my heels clicking softly against the stone path. As soon as I stepped inside, the sounds of the party faded. The hedges rose high on either side of me, their dense, leafy walls swallowing most of the glow from the estate.

I hummed softly as I moved deeper inside, trailing my fingers along the hedge. Then I stopped dead in my tracks.

A figure stood ahead of me, blocking the path. Tall, hulking. Dressed in black. A gas mask obscured his face, its dark lenses swallowing the dim light. In one hand, a glinting knife dangled loosely, almost carelessly, like he had all the time in the world.

The shadows made it impossible to see his eyes, but I could *feel* them boring into me. Watching. Waiting.

A sharp spike of adrenaline shot through me, and my pulse hammered in my throat. My body knew what this meant. *Danger.* But my mind... that whispered something else entirely as a slow, creeping heat curled through me, twisting the initial spike of fear into something darker.

The masked man didn't lunge toward me. Didn't speak. He simply stood there.

"Who are you?" I called out, voice almost cracking.

No answer. Just a tilt of his head, slow and deliberate.

I sucked in a deep breath and spoke up again, summoning as

much courage as I possibly could. "I don't know what sort of game this is, but you're playing it with the wrong girl," I said. "I've survived *much* worse than running into a strange man in a maze. And in case you hadn't noticed, I also have a security detail right behind me."

The masked man spread his hands in a silent, mocking question. A sliver of unease crept into my spine, and I glanced over my shoulder. My agents—my supposed protection—were nowhere in sight. I was alone and unguarded after all.

When I looked back at the mysterious man, his hands were back at his side, and somehow, I just *knew* he was smirking behind that mask.

My breath came faster as my pulse thrummed, and I took a single step backward. He took one forward.

"Please," I said, breath hitching. "What do you want?"

He didn't answer. Just tilted his head again, like a predator considering its prey.

"What do you want?" I repeated.

Slowly, he lifted the knife and jabbed it in my direction. The meaning of the gesture was unmistakable.

You.

A shiver ran down my spine, and without another word, I turned and ran.

There was a rustle behind me, followed by heavy footfalls pounding against the dirt path. The chase was on.

My breath hitched, a mix of adrenaline and fear coursing through my veins. My dress—something silky and far too delicate for this—snagged against the hedges as I tore through the maze, my heels abandoned somewhere behind me.

I didn't care.

The rhythmic thud of the man's boots grew louder, closer. Every step I took, he matched with ease. He clearly knew he was faster than me, but he was a predator biding his time, just for the delicious thrill of the chase.

Fear curled through me again, cold and unrelenting, but beneath it, laced within every frantic footfall and desperate gasp, was something else entirely.

Excitement.

Despite everything I'd been through—despite the real terror and fight for survival that had nearly broken me in the past—this part of me had never changed. The part that craved the chase. The part that ached for the hunt. For *this; t*he knowledge that I was being pursued by a brutal man, that he was right behind me, relentless and inevitable.

A thrill shot through me, mingling with the adrenaline already surging in my veins. My body didn't know the difference between fear and desire. It only knew the sharp edge of danger, the intoxicating rush of it, and the way my pulse pounded in anticipation.

I was supposed to be running for my life, and yet, I wanted to be caught. Wanted to feel the man's strong hands wrap around my wrists, pin me down, and remind me that no matter how fast I was, I could never truly escape him.

The pounding of his footsteps was getting louder. Closer. The maze twisted and turned, the towering walls of green swallowing me whole. Left. Right. Another left. I had no plan, no strategy. I was already lost.

My heart pounded wildly as I turned another sharp corner, only to find an unbroken hedge blocking my path. A dead end.

Shit.

Before I could react, something slammed into me from behind.

A gasp ripped from my throat as my body was shoved against the hedge, the rough branches pressing into my bare skin. A strong, gloved hand wrapped around my throat. Not squeezing; just holding me there, keeping me still.

My chest rose and fell in rapid, shallow breaths as I stared into the black void of my captor's gas mask. The sound of our breathing filled the tight space between us—his calm and controlled, mine ragged and uneven.

Fear and excitement coiled together in my stomach, my body thrumming like a live wire. The man's other hand came up, the cold edge of the knife tracing the line of my jaw. Not enough to hurt. Just enough to remind me of its presence.

"You ran fast," he murmured, his voice dripping with dark amusement. "Almost like you thought you could get away."

I shivered, my body still vibrating from the chase.

The masked man leaned in, his lips brushing the shell of my ear. "But we both know you didn't want to."

No, I hadn't. Because no matter how many times I played this game, the ending was always the same.

I didn't run to escape. I ran so this man could catch me.

He reached up and pulled the mask from his face, and the breath I'd been holding escaped in a soft, shaky exhale. "You got me."

Landon smirked. "You always were easy to catch, baby."

The knife in his hand flipped, the blade disappearing as he slipped it into his jacket pocket. Then both hands were on me, one gripping my jaw, the other pinning my hip against the hedge. He groaned low in his throat, his grip tightening as he yanked me closer, molding my body against his. Then his lips parted against mine, his kiss instantly turning sharp, desperate, a clash of teeth and hunger.

The hedge behind me scratched at my back, but all I could focus on was him—his heat, his strength, the way he kissed me like he owned me. Like he would chase me through every darkened maze, through every nightmare and dream, and still find me in the end.

He pulled back, eyes glinting in the dim light. "Take your panties off and get on your knees," he commanded.

I did as he said while he undressed himself from the waist down, letting his cock spring free. He didn't move, beckoning me to crawl closer with one hand instead. Once I was there, staring up at him through my lashes, his fingers stroked across my lips before pressing my mouth open.

"You're going to take every inch of me in here first," he said, thumb caressing my bottom lip. "I want my cock to hit the back of your throat. Understood?"

I nodded, mouth already watering at the thought. "Yes."

I reached between us and wrapped my hand around the thick base of his cock, applying the exact amount of pressure he liked. At the same time, I slowly licked the shaft, worshiping every vein and ridge.

Once every inch of him was wet with saliva, I opened my mouth wider. He let out a low groan, hips jerking forward. "That's it, baby," he muttered. "You can take all of me."

I obeyed, letting him fill my mouth with every inch of him. He hit the back of my throat, making my eyes water a little, but I took deep breaths through my nose and kept going, letting him thrust faster and harder.

"Fuck, yes," he muttered, one hand yanking on my hair as the other reached down to cup my chin. "Don't stop. Don't you dare fucking stop."

I kept going,

I moaned loudly as he thrust forward again, burying himself to the hilt. The vibrations from the sound drew another low groan from him, and his thrusts started to slow down as he tried to restrain himself.

He let go of my hair and slid out of my mouth, chest rising and falling with harsh breaths. "You're so fucking good at this, baby," he murmured. "But I don't want to come just yet."

I wiped the saliva dripping from my chin and rose to my feet. Landon watched me, eyes glinting with unbridled need.

"Turn around and put your hands against that," he said, motioning to the thick wall of hedge behind me. "Then arch your back."

I turned, bracing my hands against the hedge. Landon hitched up my dress, fingers tracing a path over my exposed ass cheeks before gripping my hips.

"Anyone at that party could decide to take a walk in this maze soon," he murmured, one hand moving between my legs. "They could see us like this. But you like feeling exposed, don't you?"

"Y-yes," I whimpered, desperate to feel him inside me.

His cock pressed against my entrance, the thick head slick with precum and saliva, and I gasped, arching even more as he inched into me. Finally, he was buried to the hilt, fingers digging into my hip.

"So wet but still so tight," he said, his voice husky as he withdrew before slamming back in. "So. Fucking. *Good*."

I let out a moan, unable to form words. My whole body felt like it was on fire.

Landon reached up with one hand, fisting my hair and yanking my head back to bare my neck to him. He leaned down to press his mouth into the sensitive spot just below my ear, biting it just enough to make me cry out as a delicious mix of pain and pleasure swirled in me.

"Harder," I managed to choke out as my pussy clenched around his cock, desperate to pull him even deeper. "Fuck me harder."

Landon's thrusts became relentless, pounding into me faster and harder. I gasped and whimpered with each one, my voice half-choked with desperation.

"Let's see how much more you can take," he muttered against my ear.

He slid out of me, confusing me for a split-second, but then I heard a rustle as he retrieved the knife from his jacket pocket. There was a click as the blade sprang free from the handle, and then he leaned in, holding it out in front of me with the thick black rubber handle facing my mouth.

"Spit on it," he ordered.

I obeyed, getting it nice and wet for him. Once I was done, I threw a sideways look over my shoulder, wondering what he was going to do with it.

"Arch your back again," he said. His free hand traced over my lower back before trailing between my ass cheeks. I moaned as his fingers settled against my asshole, pressing just slightly inside.

"Relax," he murmured. "Let me in."

He withdrew his fingers and spat on them. Then he moved them back to my ass, circling and teasing, pushing just slightly inside before withdrawing. I whimpered, my body trembling as I pushed back against his hand, seeking more of the thrilling pressure inside me.

"Greedy thing, aren't you?" he said, voice dripping with amusement. "Stay still now."

I did as he said, staying as motionless as possible even though every inch of me was pulsing with need. Landon's fingers slid away from my ass, and seconds later, the thick knife handle slowly pressed inside me instead.

He waited for me to get used to the feeling before sliding it a little deeper. I gasped at the burning sensation as it stretched my ass, and another flood of arousal dripped from my pussy.

"You take it so well," Landon muttered, sliding the handle in and out, slowly building up momentum. "How does it feel?"

"I... I feel so full," I gasped.

"And?"

"I-I'm scared too," I admitted, voice barely audible. "It's a knife. I... I could—"

I couldn't get any more words out. I was too turned on, my breathing too ragged. The mixture of fear and arousal was utterly intoxicating, just like it'd always been for me.

"You could get hurt," Landon murmured, finishing my sentence for me as the handle slowly twisted in my ass. "But I'm not gonna let that happen. Am I?"

"No," I choked out. "Never."

"Think you're ready to take my cock here now?"

"Yes!" I whimpered. "Please!"

He slowly pulled the knife out and put it away. Then his fingers dug into my ass cheeks, spreading them as he adjusted his hips to line himself up with my asshole. He spat between us, letting the saliva drip down onto the head of his cock, and then he slowly began to push himself into me.

"Oh my god," I breathed, eyes scrunching half-closed as he stretched me. "That feels... so fucking *good*."

He was more than halfway in now. One of his hands reached around to rub at my clit, and I let out a whimper, every nerve ending suddenly ablaze.

"No matter how much I fuck you here, you're always so tight for me," he muttered, sliding all the way to the hilt. "And you always look so pretty getting fucked."

Another loud moan slipped out of my mouth.

"That's it, baby. I hear you," Landon muttered. "I love those moans. Get as loud as you want."

He pulled himself almost all the way out before slamming back in, making me scream. His fingers kept rubbing at my clit as his hips jerked behind me, thrusting faster and faster.

"Oh, fuck," I whimpered. An uncontrollable pressure was building up in me.

"You love this, don't you?" he growled, fucking my ass harder. "You love me owning every inch of you. Every tight little hole."

Yes.

I loved how he always took control, making me feel completely lost in him.

"You're such a good girl. You want to finish for me, don't you?" he muttered, rubbing another rough circle on my clit. "Do it. Come on my cock. *Now*."

That command was all it took to push me over the edge.

My orgasm hit me like a flood, and I screamed, hands digging into the hedge in front of me as my entire body quaked. My vision blurred, my senses overwhelmed, until there was nothing left but the feeling of Landon inside me, brutally claiming me.

Five more thrusts was enough to bring his own release, and he let out a low, slow groan as he came inside my ass, fingertips digging into my skin as he gripped me.

He finally pulled out, breathing raggedly. I was still panting too, and I couldn't stop trembling.

Landon slid his arms around me, pulling me close. "I love you," he murmured, lips ghosting over my ear. "So fucking much."

"I love you too," I said breathlessly. Suddenly a giggle exploded out of me. "Can you imagine if someone had actually walked in on all of that?"

Landon laughed softly, ruffling my hair. "The president's son fucking the ex-president's daughter in the Vice President's garden. There's some word salad for you."

"We'd never live it down," I said, lips still quirked with amusement. I drew back and glanced around. "Any idea where my underwear wound up? Or my shoes?"

"Your shoes are back there," he replied, jerking his thumb over his shoulder. "As for your panties, I have no idea, but they've got to be around here somewhere."

"Yeah, they couldn't have gone *that* far," I said, still scanning the dark ground to no avail. "But I don't see them."

"I guess you'll have to go back to the party commando," Landon said, flashing me a teasing smile as he zipped his pants back up. "But don't worry. No one's gonna look under your dress."

I let out a groan. "I just realized that everyone's going to see all the snags on this," I said, brushing my hands over the silky fabric of my dress. "Imagine all the weird looks I'll get."

"We can just say you got caught on a hedge in the garden, which is technically true," Landon said with a roguish grin. "But people always stare at you anyway, because you're so goddamn beautiful."

I smiled, cheeks flushing warm from the compliment.

"Thanks. But honestly, I think they're actually staring at me all the time because I'm Jonathan Hagan's daughter. They're probably worried that I'm going to turn out like him one day."

He shook his head. "Nah, they look at you because you're stunning. And if they're thinking of your father at all, it's only because they're wondering how such a miserable bastard produced such a strong, smart daughter."

"Maybe some of them think that," I said, lips still quirked in a grateful smile. "But I've definitely gotten a few nasty side-eyes from certain people over the last year."

"Some people are just assholes. But don't worry. You're nothing like your dad, and you never will be," Landon replied. "But hey... if you really want to lose some of the association with him, you could always change your name."

"Seriously?" I let out another soft laugh as I resumed the search for my underwear, eyes skating over the ground. "You think I should change my *name?*"

"Just the last one."

I whipped my head back around to look at him, and my breath instantly caught in my throat.

Landon was kneeling on the ground, his dark eyes locked onto mine, intense and unwavering. In his hand, glinting under the moonlight, was a ring.

My pulse skittered wildly. "Landon..."

"I've been carrying this around for weeks," he said, his voice rough. "Waiting for the right time in the perfect location. I know this isn't that, not by a long shot. But I don't want to wait anymore." He exhaled sharply, like he was trying to steady himself. "I want to spend the rest of my life knowing you're mine in every single fucking way."

Emotion swelled in my chest, making it hard to breathe.

"You're it for me, Aria. You always have been," he continued, his grip tightening around the ring. "Marry me?"

I stared at him, heart hammering, hands trembling. And then

I did the only thing that made sense. I dropped to my knees in front of him and grabbed his face, crushing my lips to his.

Landon groaned against my mouth, his arms locking around me like he'd never let go. And he wouldn't. I knew that with every beat of my heart.

Our love wasn't fragile or fleeting. It was wild and unyielding, forged in fire and sharpened by survival. The kind of love that endured.

I pulled back just enough to meet his gaze, breathless and trembling. "In case the kiss didn't make it clear... I'm saying yes," I whispered, my lips brushing his. "A thousand times yes."

A slow, wicked smile spread across his face. "Good," he murmured, slipping the ring onto my finger. "Because you're mine, Aria. Now and forever."

I smiled, my fingers curling into the fabric of his suit jacket. "And you're mine."

Landon was the same man I'd once fled from, desperate and terrified, but now I knew the truth. He wasn't my ruin. He was my match in every way that mattered. My home.

With him, I was exactly where I was meant to be, and I'd never run from him again.

Unless, of course, it was for one of our games...

THE END

Printed in Dunstable, United Kingdom